**The old Escort was accelerating
like a rocket launcher—*right at me*.**

I froze so long I could see Max's eyes narrowed in fury and his fingers clenched white-knuckled on the steering wheel.

My boyfriend was trying to kill me!

Shocked into action, I dived for the protection of the concrete bus stop bench. With as much anguish as fear, I screamed, "Damn you, Max!"

The heat of the engine was almost upon me as I fell to the sidewalk behind the bench on already bruised knees.

At the pain, I automatically cried out, *"Damn you to hell!"*

The rusted Escort slammed into the light pole where I'd just been standing. I shivered and huddled in the protection of the bench. In horror, I watched as the pole cracked and the car kept on going, careening into the bank's brick wall. Metal and mortar flew.

I felt the impact like a small earthquake. Scrambling backward, I could only stare in alarm as the cracked light pole split in two, teetered ominously, and then tilted. Snapping under the tension, live wires crackled and sparked—igniting the gas from the shattered car in a ball of fire that engulfed the Escort.

With Max inside it.

I screamed. And screamed some more.

JAMIE QUAID

BOYFRIEND
FROM
HELL

THE SATURN'S DAUGHTER SERIES

Pocket Books

New York   London   Toronto   Sydney   New Delhi

Pocket Books
A Division of Simon & Schuster, Inc.
1230 Avenue of the Americas
New York, NY 10020

This book is a work of fiction. Names, characters, places, and incidents either are products of the author's imagination or are used fictitiously. Any resemblance to actual events or locales or persons, living or dead, is entirely coincidental.

Copyright © 2012 by Patricia Rice

All rights reserved, including the right to reproduce this book or portions thereof in any form whatsoever. For information address Pocket Books Subsidiary Rights Department,
1230 Avenue of the Americas, New York, NY 10020

First Pocket Books paperback edition October 2012

POCKET and colophon are registered trademarks of Simon & Schuster, Inc.

For information about special discounts for bulk purchases, please contact Simon & Schuster Special Sales at 1-866-506-1949 or business@simonandschuster.com.

The Simon & Schuster Speakers Bureau can bring authors to your live event. For more information or to book an event contact the Simon & Schuster Speakers Bureau at 1-866-248-3049 or visit our website at www.simonspeakers.com.

Interior design by Davina Mock-Maniscalco

Manufactured in the United States of America

10   9   8   7   6   5   4   3   2   1

ISBN 978-1-4516-5635-0
ISBN 978-1-4516-5636-7 (ebook)

BOYFRIEND
FROM
HELL

1

Over the door, the tin scales of Lady Justice dipped ominously to the wrong side as Andre Legrande strolled into Bill's Biker Bar and Grill. The boss had been up to no good again, and our miniature Lady disapproved.

Personally, I thought the dipping scale meant the little statue knew Andre was a fraud, but I was keeping my head down and my mouth shut these days. Rather than feed my boss's arrogance by admiring his assets, I propped my corrective boots on the stool rung and leaned over my tally sheet, pushing my cheap, black-framed reading glasses up my nose and letting my overlong bangs hide my face.

The weird anomalies—like moving statues—that had begun appearing in the Zone after the first chemical spill ten years ago now seemed an everyday part of my life. I'd taken a job in this South Baltimore neighborhood two years back when no respectable place would hire me. That's pretty much the story of everyone in the Zone.

Society's flotsam and jetsam gathered in what would be the world's largest Superfund site if the authorities had the guts or the funds to rope off more than just ground zero. But all they did was fence off a strip along the harbor around the contaminated Acme plant where they used to make nerve gas. After a series of spills and that final flash fire, the harbor was shut down for half a mile on either side of the plant. Fishermen really didn't appreciate glowing attack fish.

The EPA ignored the homes and businesses farther inland, because, let's face it, we're a slum. As long as no one reported rising cancer rates in the area surrounding the original spill, the government considered their work done. Officialdom had moved on.

The contamination, or whatever in hell was left behind, was moving as well—unless you wanted to believe inanimate objects developed weird lives of their own. If anyone noticed that sometimes the gargoyles took days off from their perches on buildings, they shrugged it off as a gimmick meant to attract more lowlifes to the bars littering the area.

Observing the statue's dip from the reflection in the mirror behind the bar, Andre smirked. Or maybe gazing at his own handsome image produced that smug smile. *Legrande*, after all, means "the large one," and I'd figured long ago that he'd made up the name to match his ego, if not his size. Not particularly tall but elegantly lean, he wore fitted silk shirts that emphasized his sleek muscles. Except silk belonged onstage with the Chippendale dancing boys, not in this industrial blue-collar backwater.

Andre had a reputation for toughness, though I'd never really seen it in action. Still, he'd lived here all his life, and the weak don't survive long in the Zone. Harmless yuppies seldom found their way into an area marked with DANGER: ENVIRONMENTAL HAZARD signs.

I have a weakness for old cowboy movies where the bullies always get what they deserve. I thought of Andre in the part Jim Garner plays in *Support Your Local Sheriff*. He'd just stand there and eat his beans while the fistfight flowed around him—until a punch came his way, and then I suspected Andre might turn lethal. I didn't want to be around to find out.

"Got my reports yet, Miss Clancy?" Andre asked, making himself at home behind the bar and pouring tonic over ice. He disliked being ignored, even by a nonentity like I tried to be. He was deliberately irritating me by not calling me Tina as everyone else did. It could have been worse. He could have called me Tiny, and I'd have had to take him down.

Running late, I was in no mood for old jokes. He

always asked for, but never looked at, my reports, and we both knew it. "They're in your office, growing mushrooms," I replied, bundling up the cash I was counting from the till. Modern cash registers, like most electronics, rarely worked well in the Zone. When they did work, they weren't to be trusted for anything like accurate accounting. So this one was an enormous brass-encrusted mechanical model that looked as if it belonged in a western.

"Having a bad day?" Andre taunted. "Doesn't your best—and only—boss deserve at the very least a cheery greeting?"

"I'm having a bad life, and cheery gets you killed around here."

At the end of the day, my hip muscles protested my uneven stance, but I hurried through the count as best as I could, still hoping to make the five o'clock bus. I filled out the deposit ticket, added the numbers to my tally sheet, and shoved my glasses in my messenger bag. I was about to escape when the front door rattled unexpectedly.

Customers were a rarity before five, when the industrial plants up the road changed shifts and their workers streamed down the street, hunting for the aforementioned bars. I carried out my accounting tasks after my morning law classes, before night fell and happy hour packed the Zone like it was Mardi Gras. Normally, I had the bar to myself. Even Bill the bartender was hunkered in back, doing liquor inventory.

I glanced up just as Lady Justice's scales dipped seriously to the right. Either the newcomer was a saint, or the jury was still out on Andre. But watching her enter, I cynically concluded that I hadn't seen many saints with plastic boobs. I might have been a bit jealous of women with breasts bigger than mine, but these were simply ostentatious on a woman thin to the point of emaciation. Her long, dirty-blond hair scraped a bare collarbone that stuck out like a skeleton's. Her hollowed cheek wore a fading bruise, and I did a quick check for needle tracks. None.

"Do you need any help?" she asked self-consciously. "I'm looking for work."

"Sure," Andre answered without hesitation. "Clancy here needs an assistant, don't you?"

I needed an assistant like he needed more teeth in that lying white smile. But accounting jobs for women with arrest records were hard to come by, so I didn't dare rock the boat. I just responded with cheery obedience. "Why not? Want her to run the deposits to the bank?"

As if he'd trust his cash to a stranger. There might not have been much brain needed for my job, but honesty was a major factor, with street smarts a distant second. I had a proven track record. The newcomer hadn't been tested for either.

"Nah, I'll take her back to my office to learn the books while you're finishing up. We'll see if she fits into your routine on Monday," he said smoothly, leaning against the bar, drink in hand. In that masculine bad-boy manner that made most women drool, he eyed the goods the newcomer was displaying with her cleavage-revealing tank top.

This was where the spunky female protagonist in the western would sock him in the gut for being a sexist pig, but his abs were rock hard, and I needed my fingers to work.

The woman looked uncertain and even more nervous than when she'd entered. Smarter than I'd originally thought, I concluded, if she recognized that Legrande's slick dark looks hid a dangerously amoral character.

"He owns Chesty's," I warned her. "If you're into pole dancing, you're hired. Don't let him talk you into his office."

She looked to be my age, but too frightened and vulnerable to be on this street. Were I a true heroine, I would have steered her in a safer direction. But not having a lot of time if I wanted to catch the bus, or any places to tell her to go, I figured I'd done the best I could.

I picked up the locked deposit bag with the cash from all of Andre's businesses, shackled it to my wrist with the handcuffs I carried for this purpose, and limped for the door. I'd chosen boots that looked like knee-high biker boots, but I ruined the attitude with a skirt long enough to cover the scars that ran from my hips to my knees. Above me, Lady Justice peeked from beneath her blindfold and winked.

"Clancy, you're no fun at all!" Andre shouted. "I can always replace you."

He was right. I was immensely overqualified for

this two-bit job and easily replaceable. Until I figured out how to expunge my arrest record, I was spinning wheels even bothering to take law classes. That didn't mean he had to rub it in.

Without turning around, I wiggled my middle finger at him and hit the street. I'd lost control of my life so long ago that obscene gestures were the only weapons I had left in my arsenal.

The bar was the last stop on my tour of Andre's enterprises. From there, I would drop the deposits at the bank a few blocks farther inland, a neighborhood where computers actually worked—outside of the contaminated Zone—and head for home, and, with any luck, my Friday night date with Max. I had no desire to linger in this neutron-infested industrial stinkhole where the buildings lit up after dark— literally. After the last flash fire of chemical waste, the streets and bricks of the remaining edifices glowed neon blue without the benefit of electricity.

The winking statue of Lady Justice was just one tiny aberration among much greater weirdnesses haunting these few blocks along Baltimore's industrial harbor. My theory was that seepage from underground tanks had spread over the years. Or the new Acme plant was burning loco weed. I didn't know precisely how far the affected area stretched, since the blue didn't show up in daylight, and I was never down here at night.

As best as I'd been able to gather, the infamous flash fire had started at the now-abandoned brick chemical plant three blocks north. The fire spread down Edgewater Street, where I worked, and spilled across the docks and tanks into the harbor. The fire probably stopped at the stone pier and burned-out warehouses half a mile south near the bay. I didn't know everything, just enough to know better than to live down here.

I hit speed dial on my cell phone to tell Max I was running late and might miss the bus. Seeing Officer Leibowitz on the far side of the nearly empty street, I slipped into the shade of an overhang. Thanks to the Middle Eastern part of my heritage, I'm small, dark, and blend well with shadows. I had no hope of running from danger with my uneven stride, but I'd devised any number of alternatives. Hiding in plain sight was a good one.

Leibowitz was tall, heavy, wore a walrus mustache, and sported a permanent sunburn from patrolling on foot. Even if thieves would have let cars keep their wheels in this neighborhood, the rubber was likely to melt to the blacktop if they cruised the chemical-laden street too often. The city rightfully refused to pay for equipment to be operated in the Zone. Given his size, Leibowitz could have afforded to lose a few dozen pounds walking his beat.

I've had a grudge against the law ever since I was unfairly arrested for starting a riot on campus. Admittedly, I started the riot. But if I hadn't, no one would have listened to our protests about the corruption in the university provost's office. The Pennsylvania school held a grudge as well as I did, which was why I was attending classes in Baltimore and avoiding officers of the law these days.

My call actually reached Max's voice mail. In the Zone, that wasn't always possible. Other days, I'd used the same number and gotten a pizza joint in Brooklyn and a McDonald's in Juneau, Alaska. Apparently the Zone got hungry. Limping quickly down the street, I left a message for him to pick me up at the bank.

The buses only ran once an hour after five. If I didn't catch the five, I'd be here as the steel plants emptied and the bars lit up. Max had my car, since I refused to park my only reliable means of transportation in the Zone. I didn't ask what he did with the Escort all afternoon as long as he kept the tank filled. My boss might have had a sophisticated bad-boy look happening, but Max had him topped by three inches, twenty pounds, and a cosmic blue-collar attitude. Andre didn't dare hit on me if he wanted to live, not that he'd ever noticed me beyond recognizing I was female, and therefore flirtworthy.

Nervously, I was aware that Leibowitz had crossed the street and followed a block behind me. To save wear and tear on my damaged leg muscles, I usually took shortcuts. Rather than jaywalk with a cop nearby, I waited for the light at the intersection like a good citizen, even though the light was currently pink, and I'd have to guess blue meant go if it was having one of those days.

The bank was on the edge of a lower-middle-class

neighborhood several blocks from the harbor. Despite the cash I carried, I felt reasonably safe walking the deposit to the teller. Before my leg got trashed by cops, in channeling my frustrations against the bullies of the world I'd taken lessons in every form of martial arts known to mankind. And even now, when my uneven gait messed with my balance, I could still whack boards with my hand.

Still, I wasn't naïve enough to believe I had a chance against a bullet. I kept a wary eye on my surroundings. The light turned purple, and I crossed the street, leaving the Zone.

The five o'clock bus rumbled to a stop in front of the bank. I swore under my breath. Even if I could run to catch it, I still had to make the deposit. I'd be stuck here for another hour if Max didn't pick up my call, and I really needed to sit down on something softer than concrete.

Max had become more and more unreliable lately. I was irritated that he couldn't be bothered to pick me up regularly when he had free use of my car in return. We'd only been together about six months, but we used to go out on his bike and have a good time in the evenings. Lately, he was too tired and didn't come over at all, or he just wanted me to fix him a free meal and help him get his rocks off. I didn't object to the sex. He was good in bed, and a girl like me couldn't be too choosy.

Okay, despite that errant thought, and my current policy of keeping my mouth shut, I didn't actually have self-esteem issues. Like the spunky movie heroines, I knew that I deserved better than a man who took me for granted, one who could at least be listening for my call on a Friday night.

Still aware of Leibowitz trailing me, I didn't cross diagonally to the bank like I usually did. Since I had to wait for another light change—a normal one this time—before reaching the bank, I watched the passengers unloading from the bus. The usual gang of teenagers returning home from ball practice or glee club climbed off, jostling one another and throwing insults as they spread out in different directions.

As the light turned to let the kids cross, a long sleek black car peeled out of the bank drive-up lane with a loud screech, fishtailing on the curb of the narrow side street. Hopping backward in case the driver lost control, I bumped into a newspaper box. Someone stepping out of an air-conditioned doorway roughly shoved my shoulder. Already off-balance, I stumbled forward on my bad leg, hitting the sidewalk with my knees. The limo completed the turn without bouncing off me and sped toward the bus corner.

I screamed a warning when I realized he meant to run the red while the kids were crossing. *Too late*.

I watched in horror as backpacks, laptops, and kids went flying.

The limo didn't even stop.

Shouting obscenities, I lurched to my feet and started hobbling for the corner, only to realize my bank deposit bag was no longer attached to the shackle on my wrist. I swung around, but it was nowhere to be seen. Neither was whoever had knocked me from behind.

Leibowitz was jogging, belly bouncing, in the direction of the corner where kids were now shouting, crying, retrieving their crushed belongings, and helping each other up. He had his phone out, calling in the mishap. If he'd seen whoever had robbed me, he wasn't giving any indication.

Cursing, torn between retrieving my money and helping those terrified kids, I opened the glass door that had been at my back and glanced into an enormous empty lobby. No security guard, nothing but open elevator doors on the far wall.

Unfastening the handcuff so I didn't look like an escaped convict, I went back outside and checked for an alley where the thief could have hidden, but unless he was in a Dumpster spilling over with boxes and trash bags, he was gone. And so was Andre's deposit. I was so screwed.

I couldn't panic and trash an alley in search of filthy lucre while kids were crying and hurt. Abandoning my fruitless hunt, I tucked the handcuffs into my bag and hurried up the street to prevent Leibowitz from forcing a girl with a crumpled leg to her feet.

"Her leg could be broken, numbnuts! Block off the intersection until the ambulance gets here." Ignoring the twinge of pain, I kneeled down and cradled her head on my lap while her friends gathered around, cursing and sobbing.

"You." I looked pointedly at the guys in their team

shirts. "Get out there and help the officer stop traffic. Did anyone get a look at the license plate? Write it down while you can still remember it."

"That was Dara's new computer," the injured girl whispered. "She babysat monsters for two years to buy that."

A once-shiny laptop now bearing a tire track lay crumpled beside a weeping girl holding the hand of the limo's victim. Knowing how hard it was for anyone in this neighborhood to raise that kind of cash, how proud she must have been to have her own computer, I felt her pain. Even I couldn't afford a nice setup like that one had been, and I had ten years on these kids.

"We'll get the bastards," I muttered, more to myself than to them. I'd seen enough of the license plate to know where to start. The Zone was an hour's drive and a gargantuan psychological distance from D.C., but those were government plates I'd glimpsed while on my knees.

I saw disbelief in the kids' eyes, but they politely refrained from arguing—rightfully so. They knew no one cared what happened to people who lived in a blighted area so poor that the inhabitants couldn't escape their unmarketable homes. And I looked more like a bronzed garden gnome with limp hair than a champion of justice.

I could hear the ambulance siren wailing in the distance. I prayed the buzzing in my pocket was Max texting me that he was on his way. "Leibowitz, did you catch the license plate number?" I shouted.

Standing in the intersection, directing traffic around

him, he shot me a disgruntled look. "You want me to lose my job reporting a *senator*? You really think I'm that stupid?"

Yeah, I did. "That's what you get paid to do! They're not above the law!" I yelled back, but maybe I was the one who was stupid, expecting justice in the face of all evidence otherwise. "Did you see who ripped off my deposit bag?"

This time, he stared in disbelief. "Did the bus hit you in the head? Don't go blaming me for theft if Legrande accuses you of stealing. There wasn't nobody back there but us."

Visions of unemployment and homelessness danced in my head. Andre would be furious. I'd had a lot of bad days in my twenty-six years, but this one was promising to rank right up there with the day I got arrested and had my leg crushed.

2

The ambulance arrived. Leibowitz took names. I took the partial license plate one of the kids had written down.

Seething with repressed rage at failing in my responsibility to Andre, frustrated at my inability to help innocent kids, and exhausted from overexerting my bad leg, I checked my cell phone for Max's message. There was none. The buzz had been a wrong number.

The very bad awful day threatened to escalate.

My knees ached from where I'd scraped them on

the sidewalk. That's what I got for trying to look professional by wearing a skirt when jeans would do.

I also did it to annoy Andre, who'd learned his lesson about believing anything in a skirt was available. That didn't make my scraped knees feel better or reduce my guilt over losing the deposit. If Andre docked my next month's pay for his lost cash, I couldn't pay rent or buy groceries. I'd have to drop out of school within weeks of finals. Or study in the streets.

With medics and cops to care for the kids, I sat dejectedly on the bus stop bench and tried Max's number, again. No answer.

What in hell had I ever seen in him in the first place? Yeah, he was a sexy bad boy who made my heart go pitter-pat when he grinned, but grins and hot sex didn't make a relationship.

Facing my uncertain future, I finally understood that I couldn't afford his chronic irresponsibility. I'd never really had someone I could count on, but repeating the mistakes of the past was not a sign of intelligence. I'd been a sex-starved idiot. Six months of neglect was more than enough to prove that he would never change—especially now that he wasn't taking my calls. I knew I wasn't any prize and that Max could have any woman he wanted. I could either get mad or get depressed. I chose the former.

Buoyed by self-righteous rage, I tried to reach him one more time. This time, when all I got was his cheery "Enjoying life. Later!" I shouted, "We're finished! Done! Kaput! Bring me my car and get the hell out of my life, Maxim MacNeill!"

I wasn't so good at laying it on the line in person.

I don't know why I'd put up with Max and his bad habits for this long. Because my mother would hate him, was my best guess. But my mother was in Bolivia with the Peace Corps and hadn't been home in years. Dee Clancy had barely been able to wait for me to leave for college before taking off. Motherly, she was not.

Which was no explanation but an excuse.

I was still sitting on the bench long after the ambulances and police cars had departed, furious to the point of tears. I was making up lists of all the things I would say to Max should I ever speak to him again, when a weak, prolonged blare of horn rattled my already overstimulated nerves. I sought the source, but the semi pulling into the intersection blocked the view of the hill behind.

Cursing the limp hair falling in my face, I brushed it out of my eyes and stood up to see around the semi as its trailer cleared the intersection. Behind it, coming down the hill, I recognized the rusting hood of my old red Escort.

From the way he was hitting the gas, Max must have received my message. Fine. Let him be mad. He couldn't be any angrier than I was. And I had far more reason.

Wishing I had enough hair to pin the limp strands out of my face so I didn't look so pathetic, I stepped up to the curb. I blinked in astonishment when the Escort didn't slow down.

He wasn't stopping.

The Escort was accelerating like a rocket launcher—
right at me.

I froze so long that I could see Max's eyes narrowed
in fury and his fingers clenched white-knuckled on the
steering wheel.

My boyfriend was trying to kill me!

Shocked into action, I dived for the protection of
the concrete bus stop bench. With as much anguish as
fear, I screamed, "Damn you, Max!"

The heat of the engine was almost upon me as I fell
to the sidewalk behind the bench on already bruised
knees.

At the pain, I automatically cried out, *"Damn you
to hell!"*

The rusted Escort slammed into the light pole
where I'd just been standing. I shivered and huddled
in the protection of the bench. In horror, I watched as
the pole cracked and the car kept on going, careening
into the bank's brick wall. Metal and mortar flew.

I felt the impact like a small earthquake. Scrambling
backward, I could only stare in alarm as the cracked
light pole split in two, teetered ominously, and then
tilted. Snapping under the tension, live wires crackled
and sparked—igniting the gas from the shattered car in
a ball of fire that engulfed the Escort.

With Max inside it.

I screamed. And screamed some more.

The paramedics insisted on taking me to the hospital.
I had no insurance and no desire to spend one more
minute of my life in a hellhole of sanitary captivity.

I insisted on walking out after they'd taken my vital signs and established I still lived.

I was too numb to process more than mobility. Not until I was outside in the humid Baltimore heat did I realize I had no way home.

I preferred being numb to believing Max had tried to kill me or reliving that giant ball of flame. I didn't want to know where he might be or what he might be suffering right now. I should have asked, but my head was still filled with horror. Thinking made my aching head worse, so I closed the door in my mind for now. My survival instincts were strong and my internal GPS was set on Go Home.

I was standing in the diesel fumes outside the emergency room, trying to figure out how I would get there, when Andre's electric blue Mercedes sport coupe screeched to a halt at the curb.

He got out and stared, looking as white-faced as I felt. "What the devil did you do back there?"

That wasn't precisely the way I wanted to look at events. Without being asked, I settled into his comfy leather passenger seat and leaned it as far back as it would go. Sitting down relieved the inequality of my legs, giving my hip muscles a chance to relax and unknot.

He climbed in and glared when I gave him my address as if he were a taxi driver. Rudeness held back my tears. I was almost out of defenses, and I despised being weak.

"Did you at least make my deposit before you blew up the bank and your boyfriend?" he asked, but his voice lacked the venom the words ought to have conveyed. For Andre to avoid his usual sting indicated a high level of concern, probably for his cash and not for me.

"Nah, I spent it at a spa and boutique on the other side of the harbor," I said, trying to recall events in the order in which they happened, still seeing only a white-hot burst of electricity and orange flames. "Can't you tell from my designer shirt?" My hand-dyed silk top was torn and had blood on it, although whose, I couldn't say.

"You fly as well as fry?" he asked sarcastically, knowing how long it would take to reach the ritzy port in rush hour, even if I could afford the toll road.

A TV news van raced into the hospital parking lot. Man, that was all I needed—the media, which could easily draw attention to my imperfect past. I sank deeper into my seat as if I had guilt written on my face for everyone to see.

"I'm not thinking too straight right now, Legrande. Fire me and get it over with. But give me the courtesy of dumping my carcass somewhere close to home." I was aware of aches and scrapes and my smoke-seared lungs, but they didn't register well inside my buzzing head.

"If the money is gone, it's gone," he said with surprising pragmatism. "If some nurse is opening a new back account with it, I won't begrudge her the lagniappe. Since your spectacular debacle of flames will be all over the news, I can report the deposit to the bank's insurance company as lost in the fire, and no one will know the difference. You kept a tally, didn't you?"

Grateful for this one small candle in the darkness, I grunted acquiescence and remained silent the rest of the way to my place. The memory of what had happened to the deposit lurked behind a door in my head that I didn't want to open.

When we finally pulled up to it, at least Legrande didn't comment on the run-down tenement housing I called home. He knew how much he didn't pay me. I doubt if he knew I was probably the only student in the universe actually attempting to pay back my loans while still attending classes.

"Thanks for the ride." I opened the door myself.

From beneath a dip of dark hair, Andre drew down his eyebrows and cast me a dubious look. "I ought to walk you up. You don't look so hot."

"Leave these fancy wheels for two minutes and you won't have any. I can make it to the elevator." I didn't mention that the elevator wasn't working. "Thanks again."

I climbed out and limped off without looking back. Getting friendly with Andre wasn't happening. I liked keeping my work and private lives separate. Besides, Andre wasn't trustworthy. I understood why Lady Justice was ambivalent about him. Even though he was thoughtful enough to take me home and let me off the hook for the missing deposit, he'd just worked out a scheme to cheat the bank's insurance company. I liked my men obvious, and Legrande was far too murky for my simple needs.

Although Max's reason for trying to murder me was none too clear.

I dragged my aching knees and burning lungs up the three flights of stairs to my apartment without anyone noticing or caring what state I was in. I wanted oblivion. Maybe the nightmare would go away if I got some sleep.

I kept my keys and coins in a rawhide pocket pinned inside my waistband where pickpockets and purse snatchers couldn't grab them. I was always cautious. I couldn't believe I'd left the manacle unlocked on the bank deposit bag.

I was obsessing about my error in duty rather than thinking about the empty apartment I entered.

Max's leather jacket lay across my sagging sofa. *Crap.*

I dropped onto the hideous gold upholstery, hugged the jacket, and cried, rocking back and forth as if I were quieting a wailing baby. I didn't know if I mourned Max or my lost innocence. I could be a bitch, but no one had ever tried to kill me before.

I must have fallen asleep on the couch. I woke to the gray light of a cloudy morning and tried to orient myself. I added "aching back" to my list of woes as I listened to the silence. Or almost silence. Garbage trucks crushed trash in the distance, and the interstate traffic was a persistent dull roar in the background.

I still held Max's jacket. I felt strangely empty. My face was sticky with tears.

Preferring to hang on to my current state of

numbness, I struggled to remember what day it was and decided it was Saturday. I didn't have class. Good thing. I didn't have a car to get there.

I contemplated just lying there for the rest of the day, but even though my body liked that notion, my head couldn't tolerate inaction. Images of fireballs were already springing to life.

I needed something to do, something to keep me occupied, something to keep thoughts of Max at bay.

I had a senator's car to track down and the mystery of a missing deposit bag to solve. That should get me started. Anything except think about Max.

I stumbled into the shower and fought to shampoo my hair with the cheap stuff I'd bought at the dollar store. The water pressure was down again, and I could scarcely rinse out the meager suds. I was used to living like this. I'd spent the first years of my life living in an RV while my tree-hugging mother traversed the country looking for who knows what. Vagabonds R Us.

Maybe she had the right idea and I should join the Peace Corps. My noble notion of becoming a lawyer and standing up for the little guy wasn't working out so well. Almost being murdered by my boyfriend had finally warped my idealism—two weeks short of completing my law degree.

Eventually getting rid of the suds, I wrapped a towel around myself and stood in front of the steamy medicine cabinet mirror to dry my oddly electrified hair. Mousy brown and limp, my hair wasn't worth expending much energy on. Pins and barrettes merely slipped out of it. Today, just to annoy me, it possessed abnormal springiness.

As I glared at the tangled mess, a black scrawl on the mirror caught my eye.

I blinked, trying to decipher the scribble. The *backward* scribble:

ytsuJ

Pain struck me right between the ribs and twisted. My full name is Mary Justine Clancy. Everyone called me Tina—except Max. He had insisted on calling me Justy.

Why would Max have written my nickname backward on my mirror?

I tried to erase the letters, assuming they'd been written sometime in steam. But the letters didn't come off.

They'd been etched from *inside* the glass.

3

How had Max etched my name *behind* the glass? And why? Had he popped acid or gone insane before he tried to kill me?

My doorbell sounded, and I considered not answering. But, totally creeped out, I didn't want to be left alone with that weird mirror message or the anguish it caused. I shoved a clip in my damp hair, dragged on capris and a tank top, and hurried to answer the persistent ringing.

Crossing the bare linoleum squares of the living

room, I missed the noisy blare of the radio that Max left on every minute of his waking day . . . and sometimes longer. On weekends, he was usually outside, tinkering with his bike and revving the engine instead of helping me with chores. I tried to summon annoyance and be glad he wasn't around anymore. It was nuts to miss a man who wanted me dead.

My aching head couldn't believe yesterday was real. Until I knew for certain, I was hanging on the thin edge of a crumbling cliff of sanity.

I peered out the peephole but didn't recognize the narrow-eyed, square-jawed Clint Eastwood type in the corridor. Keeping the chain lock fastened, I cautiously cracked open the door.

"Miss Justine Clancy?" the man asked, flashing what appeared to be a badge. "I'm Detective Leo Schwartz. May I come in?"

A policeman. The hated specter of my past. The last one I'd had a close encounter with had crippled me for life. Did I really want to hear what the Man had to say?

Considering the alternative of sitting here, trying not to think—maybe. That said something very unhealthy about my state of mind.

I cautiously opened the door. "Come in, Detective. You look hot." Okay, stupid thing to say to a man, even if he was a hunk. Policemen make me nervous. "May I get you something to drink?"

"Water would be fine. Doesn't this place have air-conditioning?" He dabbed at his high brow with a real cotton handkerchief, drawing my gaze to his blond buzz cut and Slavic cheekbones. The detective had some interesting ancestry.

"Not that anyone wants to pay to fix," I replied. I poured two glasses of ice water, added slices of lemon, and would have carried them to the front room, except the detective had followed me back to the kitchenette. He took a seat on a counter stool and sipped gratefully at the drink.

It was early May, but the humidity was high, and he'd apparently abandoned his jacket in the warmth. Broad shoulders and muscular biceps looked good in his neatly pressed blue short-sleeved shirt. I supposed cops had to wear some kind of regulation dress, but if it included neckties, he'd lost his. I don't do cops, so I resisted any escapist fantasies and focused on his disapproving demeanor.

"How may I help you, Detective Schwartz?"

"I need to complete the accident report," he said, removing pencil and paper from his pocket.

A flashback to the limo crashing into a corner of children had me taking the other stool. I hadn't reported it. Had Leibowitz given my name as a witness? I really didn't want to revisit yesterday. "Do they usually send detectives for accident reports?"

I slid my finger through the condensation on the glass and felt my newly heavy hair fall out of the meager clip. I shoved the clip in a pocket and raked my hand through more hair than I knew I possessed.

"When a car loses control and runs off the street, narrowly missing a pedestrian, it's usually an accident," he said without expression. "It's not quite as clear-cut when a car accelerates and narrowly misses the car's owner. And the car's driver is in a relationship with said owner."

Put like that, my moment of terror almost sounded like a TV movie. I'd rather have talked about the kids, but I'd learned authority had a one-track mind. "You make it sound like a domestic dispute. I'd called Max to pick me up. I don't know what else to tell you."

"Did you two have an argument?"

He sounded professional and disinterested, but he was watching me as if I'd driven Max to road rage. Maybe I had.

"He never answered his phone that afternoon, and I wanted him to give me a ride," I said, trying to avoid the flaming angry place in my mind. "I left messages. I got mad and yelled at him." I could do this, open the door to yesterday, if I took one small step at a time. I'd been really angry. Apparently, so had Max. "I think I told him it was over between us. I'd had a pretty rotten day."

The detective nodded curtly. "I'm sorry for your loss, Miss Clancy. I know what it's like to lose a partner, even if you're mad at them at the time."

My loss. Max really was dead.

Schwartz shattered my self-defensive illusion that he might still be alive.

Laughing, taunting, cynical Max—*dead*.

I wanted to weep, but I'd shed all my tears last night.

Still, I couldn't wrap my head around the fact that I'd never see him again. Maybe the message in the mirror was throwing me off. Coming back to haunt me after he was dead would be the kind of annoying antic Max would pull.

"I don't even know where they took his body," I murmured, willing to be distracted by an attractive cop who thought I was guilty of enraging my boyfriend. Even talk of funerals was preferable to revisiting that ball of flame.

"They're performing an autopsy to see if there were drugs or alcohol in his system. He was traveling pretty fast for a city street. Are you sure he hadn't said anything to you? You didn't even have a brief exchange?" he demanded, pushing me with his tone.

I rubbed my brow, hoping that would clear away the red haze that kept me from recognizing this man as a potential enemy. "I talked to Max in the morning, and we'd discussed where we were going last night. That was the last time I heard his voice, except on voice mail."

"He didn't live here?" He jotted a note.

"He had his own place." My hand shook too badly to pick up the glass as I dared the question I had to have answered. "Did he really try to kill me?"

"Other than your voice message, we can't find any motivation," he said stoically. "Our experience says, though, that in domestic violence situations, when a man's authority is defied, he can sometimes lose control. Did the two of you ever become physically abusive?"

Startled, I glanced up and met the detective's neutral expression. There was a question I could answer with clarity. "Do I look like an idiot? He was a foot taller and a hundred pounds heavier. I'd be *dead* by now."

Except Max was the one who was dead. I could see his point. Maybe he was thinking I did something to the car, but everyone knew Max was the one who worked on it. I wanted to remember Max on his bike, his hair flying in the wind, carefree and happy, not the face of rage I'd last seen.

Schwartz glanced skeptically at my damaged leg, and I bristled. "Max didn't do that, the cops did."

The good detective knew better than to follow that lead, and backed off by jotting a note.

"I'd like to see him, if I can," I requested.

"I wouldn't advise it. Burn victims look like hell," he said bluntly.

The room spun, and I gripped the counter to keep from falling. Or upchucking.

I'd told Max to go to hell.

And he'd gone—in a spectacular ball of flame.

"May I call someone?" the detective's voice asked from somewhere far above me.

I held a hand to my whirling head and realized I was sitting on my couch. Had he carried me there? I couldn't remember. I shook my head at his questions. I had no life, no one to call. Until now, I'd liked it that way.

"I'll be fine. I think the doctors gave me something to make me spacey."

"Some drugs can be too strong if you're not used

to taking them," the detective agreed, handing me my glass of water. "I don't think you should be alone."

It was on the tip of my sharp tongue to ask if he meant to spend the day with me, when the doorbell rang. I glanced up, and Schwartz took that as a signal that he could answer it. *Alpha males,* I thought blearily. They liked taking charge.

"Good seeing you again, Miss Isabel," he said, opening the door. "Isabel is your last name, isn't it?" I could almost see Schwartz checking his notebook, but I didn't want to turn my head to see.

"Cora? What are you doing here?"

To my memory, Cora had never visited. She worked at a detective agency Andre owned. I hadn't even known she knew where I lived, but I guess detectives knew that kind of stuff—witness Schwartz knowing her.

"Pretty Boy is concerned, and what concerns Legrande, concerns me." With a long-legged sway, Cora crossed to the couch and gracefully wiggled to the seat beside me.

I thought the detective's eyes might pop out. Cora had an hourglass figure that she liked to flaunt in skintight leopard spots. Tall, toned, and possessing the photogenic coloring of an African goddess, Cora was all that I was not, physically, at least. She wore her tight curls cut close to her head to emphasize her exquisite bone structure. I wore my mousy brown hair in bangs and shoulder-length hanks that hid my sallow, narrow face and unprepossessing features.

"You're here because Andre sent you?" I asked. That seemed hard to believe.

"I'm here to see how you're doing. You scared our butts off. Besides, my shithead boss was worried his receipts went up in flames. We had a big check come in yesterday."

I almost smiled as Schwartz lost his glazed look of lust and jotted notes. Cora's elegance was only skin-deep. She had a smutty mind and a potty mouth and looked at the world through black lenses. She was actually holding back for the detective's sake.

"Miss Clancy might have a concussion," Schwartz said. "She almost passed out just now. Can you stay with her for a while?"

"Yeah, sure. I'm going to start hunting attorneys in case that car accelerating was Ford's fault. Want to send me your report when it's ready?"

Schwartz looked uncomfortable, then nodded curtly. "I'll see what I can do." He jotted something on one of his note pages and handed her a business card.

Cora took the paper, tucked it into her cleavage, and winked. "Thanks, Lieutenant."

I almost smiled as the detective cleared his throat at the promotion she'd just given him. The entertainment value of watching these two was almost worth my aching head.

"Detective," he corrected.

"Lieutenant shortly," Cora said with assurance. "My mama was a voodoo queen. I know these things."

I did laugh then, then caught my head to keep it from falling off.

"Sorry, Detective, I wish I could have been more

helpful," I said when he turned all that tempting masculine concern in my direction. He really was good-looking in a Nordic god sort of way, but I was carrying enough guilt without his suspicion carving out my guts.

"I'll leave my card on the table in case you think of anything else. Take some aspirin, at least," he said. "And try to stay awake for a while."

"Just let me know about Max," I whispered, tears welling. Even if Max was a bastard, he'd been *my* bastard. We'd had some good times together. I didn't let too many people into my life. His loss was a gaping hole.

"Yes, ma'am." Schwartz tipped an invisible hat and let himself out.

"I like that man," Cora announced when he was gone. "You could do worse. You *did* do worse."

"How do you know Schwartz?" I asked, ignoring her painful comment.

"Works for Andre, of course. If you hung around the Zone more, you'd know that. Now let's get you up and functioning again. What are you going to do now?"

"Go to bed," I said firmly.

"Uh-uh, hon. If you have a concussion, you're staying awake. Let's call lawyers for fun."

She pulled the latest shiny piece of technology out of her designer purse and began pushing buttons.

I just leaned into the worn sofa and stared at a cobweb near the ceiling.

My boyfriend had tried to kill me.

Did I really want to know why?

Was I a candidate for aluminum-foil-wrapped colanders to stop the voices whispering *guilty* in my head?

It didn't take long for the media to find me and jar me back to the concrete jungle.

Thinking of Max, I stupidly answered the first phone call out of habit. When a reporter from a local TV station began identifying himself, I left the cell open on the table and walked away.

Cora correctly gauged the incident, stood up, and began stuffing her collection of phones and computers into her oversize, rhinestone-encrusted purse. "Let's get you out of here, get that hair of yours did, and take your mind off things."

I hadn't had the energy to check any more mirrors. I crunched my now silky-dry hair between my fingers and didn't recognize it. It felt like hair in a shampoo ad, the kind where the model tosses her long tresses and they fall in sleek, sexy waves to her shoulders, not one flyaway strand out of place. Sexy was so not me. I'd probably get long hair caught in a meat grinder.

"I need a car, not a cut," I said, surprising even myself. I'd been mourning a killer and going paranoid over mirror writing, when I should have been worrying over my loss of wheels. I needed to set my muddled head straight. "I can't get uptown to classes from here without a car."

"Go put on your hottest dress. I'll take you to Sam's

Salon. And then we'll go car shopping. You want the best price, you gotta make nicey with the slime."

"The bank won't loan me money," I protested.

"We don't do *bank* loans in our part of town," she said scornfully, as if I were a naïve farm girl. "You just pretty yourself up and we'll find something."

Did I really want to know what kind of loans the Zone preferred? Probably not.

"Why are you bothering with me?" I asked, still resisting. "Andre isn't interested in whether or not I get to class."

"Let's just say there are a lot of people invested in what happens to you. You're one of us now, girl, and we take care of our own."

When I didn't move, she marched back to my tiny bedroom, pulled back the curtains that served as my closet door, and began rummaging for appropriate attire.

"I'm not one of *anybody*," I argued insensibly, following her and taking a baby-doll nightie out of her hand to shove it back in the closet. Max had given me that. "I've only worked for Andre for two years. I didn't even live in this state before that. I don't invite people over, and they return the favor. So tell me what's really going on."

She pointed at the mirror over my crummy dresser. "You go look, hon, and tell me what you see."

I didn't want to. I had a horrible premonition that I'd grown horns and a tail.

She found a shimmery bronze sundress I'd bought

for two bucks at the consignment store but hadn't dared to wear because it revealed too much of my scars. She shoved me in front of the dresser mirror and held the dress up so I could see how I looked.

My usually lank, mousy brown hair hung in rich mink-brown waves to my shoulders. Even the bangs I'd cut with fingernail scissors fell in come-hither lengths to one side of my face.

My sharp nose, crooked teeth, short eyelashes, and blah brown eyes remained unchanged, but who would notice if I tossed that glossy mane?

In disbelief, I reached out a hand to my reflection.

The instant my fingers touched the glass, the mirror darkened, and a smoky image of Max appeared superimposed over mine.

4

Pulling my hand back, I choked on a scream, swayed, and the blur disappeared.

I was hallucinating.

Noticing nothing wrong, Cora picked up a brush to stroke my hair into obedience, not that it needed much. Just like in the model ads, with a few strokes it fell in perfect waves to my shoulders. There was so much of it now, somehow.

"What's wrong with me?" I whispered, thinking she would say that we grow hair that eats our brains and then we go mad, which was why she was being so nice to me, out of pity.

"It happens to all of us working in the Zone, sooner or later, but this hair effect is a real winner," she said without a shred of sympathy. She apparently did not see vengeful hallucinations in mirrors. "Wish I could get me some of that. Now put on the dress and let's give Sam a thrill."

"*What* happens to all of us?" I grabbed the brush and the dress and headed for the bathroom, not daring to look in my dresser mirror again.

"We light up at night like the buildings," she called after me. "That's a metaphor!" she added, not so reassuringly.

"I have radiation poisoning?" I asked as I peeled off the tank top and looked for a radioactive glow in the bathroom mirror. For a moment, I'd stupidly forgotten the backward writing. It was still there. No neon glow, though. I turned my back on my reflection for fear Max would show up again. Hallucinations brought on by guilt, I unprofessionally diagnosed, without bothering to explore why I should feel guilty.

"No one's died of blue glow yet," Cora replied, leaning against the hall wall. "The Zone isn't radioactive. We've just been inundated by chemicals. Maybe you got into a shampoo goo spill. The Acme plant makes chemicals for beauty products, among other things."

Shampoo goo. Right. More likely I'd accidentally dropped Max's acid and my life was just one giant delusion. I would try to refrain from leaping off tall buildings in any attempt to fly.

I wiggled into the shimmery spandex dress Cora had chosen and didn't care if I looked like a ho or if my scars were ugly. I wasn't checking the mirror to find out.

"Short Stuff, you got what it takes!" Cora crowed in triumph as I hobbled out in bare feet. "You got any heels?"

"I limp, remember?" I showed her the hanging shoe rack behind my bedroom door. "The only way I can wear heels is if one is higher than the other. Otherwise, I break my neck." At five-two, I used to wear heels all the time. No longer.

"These ugly things match." Cora held up a pair of cork-soled, wedge-heeled sandals with a fat bronze flower over the toes.

My espadrilles, the reason it had been so easy to knock me down the stairs in the fall that had broken my leg in three places. I'd been so damned proud of those consignment store treasures that day. Rioting in sandals had probably been pretty stupid. Trusting an angry police officer, even stupider. Just looking at them now returned that painful memory of iron bars, concrete stairs, and fat arms shoving.

"They're Clarks and made for walking." Annoyed at myself for letting a memory stop me from wearing pretty shoes, I slipped them on. "Tell me how this will get me a car."

"It's magic, baby." She whistled the tune of the old song and headed for the door.

Grabbing my cell and keys and adding them to the metal-reinforced purse I slung across my chest, I stomped after Cora. It's pretty hard to sway sexily when one leg is longer than the other.

Radiation magic, maybe, to go with the hallucinations. Fine, I wasn't comfortable in my own home anymore anyway. Obviously, I was ready to do anything to ensure I finished my classes. I'd be accepting e-mail prizes from Nigeria next.

I was disappointed when Sam lopped off inches of my newly glorious hair. I'd rather liked the feel of all that heavy weight falling on my neck and swinging coquettishly. But I had to admit, the curly look suited my skinny face, and the highlights set off my naturally bronze coloring.

Thick, shiny brown curls softened my square jaw, making it almost look as if I had cheekbones. If hair like this was what shampoo goo got me, I wasn't complaining. Better yet, the mirrors in the salon reflected only me, with no Max in sight.

I couldn't afford Sam's prices, but he assured me the first cut was free, that he'd make it up when I had to come back every two weeks. I knew I couldn't afford to come back, but once I had wheels, I wouldn't need to put on a show, so I didn't worry about it.

While Cora drove us to the used-car lot, I got my head in a little better working order. "Can you track government license plates?" I finally had the sense to ask.

"Sure, those are easy if you've got someone on the inside, and we do. What you need?"

"I want the guy who almost killed a couple of kids yesterday, crushed all their books and computers, then drove off." I could think about kids and justice far more easily than I could think about balls of flame.

"I heard about that. Be interesting to know which big dog is slumming in this part of town and why, but you know you can't do nothing about it, don't you?"

She was probably right, but I needed action to take my mind off my hallucinations. "One step at a time," I answered. "Let's just see who it is, if we can figure it out from a partial."

Tina Clancy, girl detective. Worked for me.

"Give me the make and model of the car and we can narrow it down."

"Big, black, shiny," I replied, biting back a smile. For just a second, it almost felt normal to be bantering with a friend.

She punched my arm and veered her beat-up Mini Cooper into a used-car lot.

I wasn't much for putting myself on display. I preferred my mousy camouflage so I could stay focused and get my work done. But Cora seemed to think I'd get a better deal if I strutted, so I did my shrimpy best. With only my rent money in my checking account and no collision insurance on the Escort, I couldn't imagine affording more than a bicycle. Maybe I could sue Max's estate and get his Harley.

Where did that ugly, spiteful thought come from?

"Hey, Joe, Andre says my girl here is good for a

thousand. What've you got for us?" Cora asked the portly, balding gentleman waddling from the glass-walled office.

Andre said I was good for a thousand? Was he planning on docking my pay? I'd have to quit buying groceries, if so. Maybe I should give up school and find a real job. It wasn't as if I would even be allowed to take the bar exam with my record. Would Schwartz look up my riot-inciting arrest and conclude I was violent enough to drive Max to murder? Even I was beginning to suspect me, and I didn't have a suspicious mind.

"Ain't nothing here for that kind of money," Joe protested. "Tell Andre not to be such a tightwad."

Oh, well, anything was better than thinking. "Ah, hon," I purred, using the ubiquitous Baltimore endearment and tapping Joe's arm as I passed by, "I bet you say that to all the girls."

Not wanting to owe my wicked boss any more than necessary, I sucked in my gut and stepped carefully, doing my best to swing my hips as I approached a shiny red Miata convertible. Miatas are made of plastic. To be on a car lot on the slummy side of town, this pretty toy was probably held together with duct tape and baling wire. Up close, I could see that the vinyl seats *and* the windshield had cracks. I wiggled behind the steering wheel, flashing a lot of leg. "Let me see what it does, hon." I flashed him a sparkly smile, and he perked right up.

As Joe hurried back for the key, Cora climbed in

the other side. "You're evil, girl, you know that, don't you?"

Yeah, I was starting to get that impression.

I waved good-bye to Cora and drove away in the red Miata, feeling a grand poorer and a whole lot of stupider. I didn't have Max to repair the rolling junk heap. I'd probably be up to my neck in repair bills and end up with a car on blocks while owing Legrande forever.

But I needed to do something to swing my head back on straight, and it looked like being stupid was it. I breathed deeply for the first time since the "accident" and enjoyed the wind blowing my newly cut hair as I cruised home. Even the kids in my tenement wouldn't be dumb enough to steal a plastic Miata, so I figured it was safe.

The clouds were rolling in thicker. I tied a tarp to the mirrors—the convertible top didn't work—and shimmied back to my apartment. Shimmy was about all I could do in spandex. I needed to change into something a little more practical.

I'd been ignoring the buzzing of my cell phone all morning, figuring it was more TV news goons wanting to know how it felt to have a boyfriend go up in flames before my eyes. How did they think it felt? I refused to do tears for public entertainment.

I hadn't noticed any van in the parking lot, but a cameraman was standing in the corridor when I stepped out of the stairwell. We startled each other.

I slammed back to the stairs, removed my sandals, jerked my skirt up my thighs, and performed my best uneven dash upward to hide on the roof. Yeah, yeah, I know, only stupid movie females run to the roof in times of danger, but there was a method to my madness. I had the keys to the roof door, and I figured the TV guy would think I'd gone down instead of up.

If I was really lucky, he hadn't even recognized me. I hardly recognized myself. I was definitely not liking being the center of attention again. I'd learned a lot of hard lessons in Pennsylvania. Being locked in jail with my face plastered across the front page under the headline STUDENT MENACE hadn't enhanced my impression of journalists. The provost got less press when he "resigned" a year later. I didn't see any articles about a STUDENT HERO who saved the university's rear end. But I was busy picking up the pieces of my life by then. Maybe I missed the story. I'd have laughed hysterically at my humor if I wasn't trying to be quiet.

I locked the door behind me and walked barefoot on hot asphalt to the edge of the roof to see how I'd missed the van. He'd parked on a side street past the parking lot entrance, the rat fink.

Pity I couldn't send TV vans to hell.

A tickle at the back of mind said it might be better if I didn't think like that.

Camera Guy emerged from the front exit, looked around, then went back inside. I sauntered over to the rear of the building and watched him exit there. Poor baby. He'd just experienced the Incredible Disappearing Woman.

Just thinking about disappearing gave me the shudders after everything that had happened. Had Cora really meant it that the chemical waste pollution of the Zone had done something to the people who worked there? I should have asked what it had done to her. She'd been there longer than I had. Did it give her those skin-slashing cheekbones?

The thought was so patently ridiculous that I figured I should punch Andre for making Cora tell stories to get his way.

Except for that fact that Lady Justice was a piece of tin with personality. And buildings glowed without electricity. The magnifying glass in the sign advertising Cora's detective agency often disappeared for days at a time and sometimes returned with photos of people inside it. The list of objects was long and strange—but I'd never noticed *people* being weirder than usual.

I tried not to think too hard. It made my head hurt. Maybe all those new hair follicles really were hacking my brain.

TV guy apparently got fed up. I watched him wander back to the van, talk to someone on his phone, and climb in. When he rolled off, I returned downstairs, grateful to Max for lifting that roof key and giving me a copy. I didn't want to know what he normally did with roof keys, but I liked going up there to escape my life.

As I reached my floor, a tall, slump-shouldered man with wild gray hair was unlocking the door across from mine. I knew the student who lived there, but I didn't know this stranger.

"Are you looking for Lily?" I asked, hiding the suspicion in my voice. I was learning to be wary.

He turned and studied me in a way that gave me creeps.

"*Stay away from his family,*" he said ominously, before entering the apartment and shutting me out.

I blinked in shock. There was something about his dark eyes that seemed a little too familiar. . . . I hurriedly unlocked my door. Hallucinations and paranoia are a really bad mix. *Stay away from his family? Whose* family? Why? Not going there.

Once I was safely inside my apartment, I broke down and scrolled through the list of messages on my cell. Numbers without names. Newspapers. Who the devil gave these people my private number? Max's friends, of course. Dimwits. Did they hate me, too? I was almost afraid to check Facebook. I might have to delete myself.

But Facebook was about the only way I stayed in communication with my roving mother and my fellow college friends in crime. For now, I let it alone. I had more important goals in mind.

I slapped tomato and cheese on some bread and called it lunch. I ate while changing into jeans and a tank top. I was just starting to feel almost normal, so I avoided looking in the mirror. I really didn't want to go all *Exorcist* again.

I had no idea what the news was saying about me or Max. I didn't want to know. With any luck, I was a twenty-four-hour wonder and by now a semi of rabid chickens had overturned and shut down the Bay

Bridge and they'd leave me alone. I had better things to do, and so should they.

I slipped on a pair of wraparound shades, checked the windows for TV crews, and hoped for the best as I aimed for the bus stop. Moist, heavy air was turning into droplets.

With my head clearing, I had a more distinct memory of what had happened to my deposit bag. I hadn't lost it in a ball of flame or had it lifted by hospital personnel, as Andre had assumed. It had been stolen, probably by the jerk who had jostled me. I'd examined the shackle I'd dumped in my bag; it had definitely been cut. Unless someone was walking around with powerful metal cutters for fun, I was wagering they'd been waiting for me. I wanted another look at the Dumpster. Thieves always flung purses into the garbage after they'd grabbed the cash. Maybe I could save Cora's boss his big check.

The bus ran only once an hour on Saturdays, and even then, it wasn't crowded. The Zone was a workingman's hangout, and most of the industrial plants were weekdays only. People partied on Saturdays, but the lights didn't go on until after dark.

Which made me wonder if the radiation or whatever was in those buildings affected visitors as well as people who worked there, and if it got into the beer they drank or the water they sipped. Or if the chemical aroma hanging in a miasma over the area was infectious. Or if the whole thing was a fairy tale.

I'd seen plenty of evidence that the Zone affected *things*, say the naked-lady statue at Chesty's that blew bubbles and did the hula. It had been years since the last big chemical spill, before my time. But if the chemical stew was slowly seeping into the water and affecting people, shouldn't government officials have been all over it?

Well, if it just meant good hair and cheekbones, probably not. Maybe if *people* instead of buildings started glowing, they'd have to do something. I hoped.

I got off in front of the boarded-up bank. A sign said it would reopen on Monday. Scorch marks stained its bricks and the sidewalk by the bus stop, and shattered glass still littered the ground. I tried not to notice or I'd hurl. I choked back nausea and crossed the street to where I'd been standing when the limo had hit the kids. I wanted to do something decent to ease my guilt, but instead, I was wondering if there was any way of hacking the bank's computers to see who had made a transaction just before five, when the diplomatic vehicle had pulled out.

I was almost a lawyer. I knew better. Hacking was illegal, not decent, but still.

I checked the bank for security cameras, noting one over the drive-through window.

I returned my attention to the building the presumed thief had emerged from. It was a multiple-office building, closed and locked on Saturdays. I could run a cross-check on the number and get a list of names for this address, but there could easily be a dozen offices inside. And a hundred employees or more, not to mention customers.

As I examined the door, I had the uncomfortable

feeling of being watched, as if I had a target painted in the middle of my back.

I glanced around, but there was no one in sight.

Shrugging off my apprehension, I turned down the alley behind the building. A pretty orange tabby kitten looked up at me expectantly, and I leaned over to scratch its head, grateful for a little normality. "You're a tailless wonder," I murmured, admiring his wiry form. "Does that make you a Manx or one of us weirdos?"

He bumped my hand with his head, and I mentally promised him any fish I found inside the Dumpster. Luckily, the bin hadn't been emptied since yesterday. I swung inside, encountering mostly boxes and papers that people were too lazy to recycle. A few fast-food wrappers didn't offer anything promising for the kitten.

My deposit bag was a bright blue denim on the outside, not the brown vinyl the bank handed out. The color ought to stand out in this mountain of white and tan. I continued searching. The denim concealed a metal mesh liner supposed to deter the sharpest knife. The zipper had a lock that only I could open. As I said, I'd learned caution with age. If nothing else, I wanted the bag back. I quite liked it.

After flinging a mountain of boxes and trash to the alley, and half a hamburger for the kitten, I spotted blue fabric sliding down a paper avalanche at the back. Snatching a corner before it vanished, I retrieved the bag and examined it for knife slashes—but it was the lock that had been broken.

Swearing, I climbed out of the bin and sat on the curb to examine the zipper. Still feeling as if I was being watched, I shuddered as unease crawled up my spine. Not liking creepy men or Leibowitz staring at me was one thing, but being fearful of nothing was not a good sign of mental stability.

I glanced around to be certain I was still alone and tried to shake off the silliness. Max really had done a number on me if I started feeling afraid all the time.

The kitten rubbed my ankle and purred, but my mind was otherwise occupied while I studied my portable fortress. Except for the lock, the bag looked intact.

Not expecting to find anything, I checked the contents. *Only the cash was gone.* The large check from the detective agency and all the smaller ones were still there. So it was still an amateur thief, if he couldn't cash the checks. Good to know.

Succumbing to another uneasy feeling, I glanced around again.

Was that a shadow on the other end of the alley? Still too jumpy after yesterday, I fled for Bill's Biker Bar and Grill, deposit bag in my hot hand.

5

Bill was big and burly, with an unruly haystack of fading ginger hair and usually a three-day beard. I'm not sure how guys manage to always have stubble, and I wasn't going to ask. I was jittery and needed security, and Bill was it. I'd seen him heave a two-hundred-pound trucker through a plate-glass window, just like John Wayne in the movies. He was strong.

He was polishing the bar and looked up in surprise when I burst in, since he never saw me down here on weekends.

My fear must have been obvious, because he strode out from behind the bar and checked down the street as I landed on one of his stools, gasping for breath and from the pain in my hip. The sidewalk down the block had suddenly taken a notion to turn to green mud, and I'd nearly broken my neck sliding through it. Usually the Zone was kinder to me. I was ridiculously grateful to have Bill at my back.

"No one out there," he reported, ambling back to the bar and pulling out a diet Sprite, my drink of choice.

"There was no one there when this got stolen, either." I slapped the bag down on the bar and gratefully accepted the icy soda. I wasn't particularly coherent, but Bill frowned and nodded as if he understood.

"It's been happening here and about," he agreed. "I lost all my hundreds one night when there was no one here but me, so I keep the cash drawer locked now. Andre gets antsy when things like that happen."

I stared. "You're saying ghosts are stealing cash?"

He shrugged and began hanging beer mugs in the overhead rack. "I'm just saying you have to watch your back down here. Don't knock invisible just because you can't see it."

I pulled the contents of the bag out and slapped the checks on the bar. "Then I want a bodyguard from now on when I go to the bank. And tell Andre if he files the insurance claim for Friday's entire tally sheet and he wants to commit theft by depositing these later, he'd better figure out how to do it, because I won't."

He nodded sagely. "You gotta be honest in your business. He gets that. Sorry to hear about your fella. Let us know when the funeral is."

Anguish ripped another hole in my heart. I needed to check with the good detective to see what happened with bodies after autopsies. Even if I ought to hate the bastard, I didn't want Max going unclaimed. And I *really* didn't want to think about Max as a corpse. Maybe that was why I thought I'd seen his face earlier. I wanted him to come back. To not be gone. My rattled mind had simply conjured his image.

I was afraid to go out on the street again, which meant I had to leave immediately and get over myself. Finishing my drink, waiting until it was almost time for the next bus, I waved at Bill and sauntered out as if I hadn't just run from shadows like a jackrabbit.

The tailless kitten was waiting right outside the door. Big yellow eyes and a pleading *mew* broke my already broken heart. "My bodyguard," I told him, picking him up and tucking him into my messenger bag. He promptly burrowed down and went to sleep, and I was glad to be able to give someone, something, the feeling of safety that I had just gained from Bill.

I wasn't much used to people looking out for me. With my track record, I decided I probably shouldn't get too comfortable with it, either.

I made it home without further incident. Even the green mud had disappeared, replaced by new gray cement with a footprint in it that could have been mine.

Once I reached the tenements, I walked around the block, checking all the alleys for news vans first. I didn't like the looks of the leather-clad stranger lurking near the front step, so I eluded him by going in the back, by the garbage cans. Reporters ought to be made to wear PRESS signs on their hats like in the old cartoons. And if that was one of Max's biker buddies, I didn't want to know about it. They might kill me if they blamed me for his death.

I paid one of the kids playing in the lobby to go up and see if there was anyone near my door. Once assured the coast was clear, I fell into my apartment with a sense of relief, locking up behind me. I'd had enough of the world today. Life was easier when I slipped past everyone's radar.

My new furry pal tumbled out and began exploring. I didn't know why I thought I could keep a kitten. I was woefully unprepared. I apparently needed to be needed. Or wanted company so I didn't have to think too deeply.

I had a hundred and one errands to run, plus new-kitty duty—like acquiring cat food and litter box—not to mention finals to study for.

Instead of attending to any of that, I picked up Schwartz's business card and dialed his number. I left a message asking when Max's body would be released. I tried to sound very professional and business-like. I broke down and cried when I hung up. Kitty leaped onto my lap, arched his back, and stroked under my chin.

I knew I had to be stronger than this, but knowing

and doing were two different things. I'd been pushed to my limits these last twenty-four hours, and the strain was showing.

I couldn't face the world with tear streaks down my cheeks. I scratched the kitten behind its ears. "You need a name, fella. You don't look much like a Kitty."

He purred approvingly and kneaded the sofa cushion, then swatted a pillow to the floor. That was a pretty strong stroke for a bitty kitty.

"Pillow?" I suggested. "Billow?" I think he snarled at me. I didn't blame him. "Milo?"

His head bobbed before he curled into a ball and settled down to the business of sleeping. Milo he was.

Determined to keep moving forward, I dragged out the little netbook I'd bought refurbished for next to nothing on Craigslist. If my mother had taught me nothing else in our years of wandering, it was how to live cheaply and how to avoid personal contact through use of the Internet.

Putting on my reading glasses, I checked e-mail and found a few electronic sympathy cards from several of the offices I worked with. I'd only lived here two years and had been with Max for only six months, so we didn't have a lot of mutual friends. I'd met his biker pals, but I didn't know how to get in touch with them short of driving to their hangout. With me going to school and working, Max and I had barely had time for ourselves.

With no small degree of trepidation, I opened my Facebook page.

Some jackass had posted video of the fiery crash.

Who in hell had been there to film the fireball and thought it cool to show me? My invisible thief? That gave me cold shudders. I couldn't watch it. I left a message saying I was home and coping and deleted the video.

Before I signed out, an instant message arrived from Themis Astrology and Tarot. Weird. I hate letting people know when I'm online, so I always had my IM turned off. Probably some kind of computer burp. I scanned the odd message. Could IMs be sent in cerulean blue with birds twittering in the corner? It wasn't as if I was any expert. . . .

> Your Saturn transit is almost complete and the asteroids are in position. Conga-rats, newest daughter. Use your talent more wisely next time.

My talent? Was this some sick reference to Max's death? Appalled at the thought, I deleted the message and ran a search-and-destroy mission on "Themis" in my address book, but nothing called anything similar was there. Maybe the message wasn't even meant for me. I really didn't need to add paranoia to my growing list of neuroses, but I was beginning to feel hunted. I slammed the machine shut.

The possibility of a grocery and Laundromat run popped into my head, but my energy wasn't there. Saving it for the next day, I went into the bedroom for my law books—forgetting I'd left them on the dresser.

The instant I brushed against the mirror to pick up

the books, a flare of fire appeared that I could have sworn looked like a scared and furious Max.

The room spun. I clung to the peeling veneer of the dresser, refusing to pass out, forcing myself to look. Shadowed eyes resembled deep dark pits of despair, without their usual laughing cynicism.

In my hallucination, I could have sworn I heard him shouting, "*I didn't do it, Justy!*"

6

Needless to say, I didn't get much done all weekend. I freaked out and took the Miata and Milo to a pet store and spent my paycheck on cat supplies. I contemplated moving out of my newly haunted apartment.

I don't know a whole lot about love, so I couldn't say if I'd loved Max while he was alive, but I certainly didn't love the idea of his ghost throwing accusations at me from my mirrors. But moving would have cost more money and time than I could conjure up and might not solve the problem if it was in my head.

On Sunday evening, Detective Schwartz finally returned my call to let me know that no drugs or alcohol had been found in what remained of Max. Max liked his beer and a joint at a party, but he wasn't into heavy stuff, so that told me nothing new.

"What do I do now?" I asked, sitting in a park and watching Milo pounce on a cricket while we talked. "I don't think he had life insurance for a funeral."

"His next of kin have already been notified. The funeral home will take care of everything for the family," he said reassuringly.

I wasn't reassured. *His family?* What family? The one he'd told me he didn't have? He'd said he was estranged from his parents, like me. I'd thought we were alone together.

Max had lied. My big bad biker boy had lied. Big surprise.

Maybe I should go back and confront the bastard in my mirror. Since I obviously knew nothing about him, maybe Max was actually a serial killer, and I'd fouled up his plans by not dying.

Did this have something to do with the old guy warning me away from "his" family? *Max's* family?

Too much gloom and doom. I took down the name of the funeral home and hung up. I was getting mad at Max all over again. Was I too shabby for him to introduce to his parents? Did they even know I existed?

I called the funeral home and secured the time and date. I wondered if his *family* would even want me there. Did they all blame me for Max's death? Or was that just my guilt talking?

Milo attacked my ankle, and I gave up my morose thoughts.

Picking up the kitty, I went home and pounded on Lily's door to see if I could find out about the creepy gray-haired guy. No one answered. Still outraged and confused, I returned to my place, fired up Facebook, posted the funeral arrangements, and let the world take care of itself.

Before I went to bed, I stopped in front of my dresser mirror and dared Max to put in an appearance so I could yell at him. True to form, he didn't show when I wanted him.

I flung a blanket over the mirror and went to bed with Milo.

On Monday, I left Milo in his new kitty bed and drove my sassy new hair and semi-sassy Miata over to the university, where everyone had their noses buried in books and didn't notice my existence, thank the Universe. I sank into the security of normal, where I could study the wonderful logic of torts and contracts until after two.

After two, I parked the Miata at the apartment, limped up to grab a sandwich and tuck Milo into my bag, and nearly broke my neck dashing for the three o'clock bus. Monday deposits were usually my biggest. I knew I had little chance of making the five o'clock bus back on Mondays, so I didn't bother rushing once I reached the Zone.

I stopped for the deposit at Discreet Detection first to check in with Cora. The magnifying glass on their sign had an image of me in it today. I wondered if Frank, the real detective running the place, had a hidden camera and a setup posting those photos. I didn't want to know badly enough to ask, though. Up until now, noninvolvement in Zone business had seemed best. Still, I was starting to doubt that policy, since I wouldn't have made it past Friday without the help of Andre, Cora, and Schwartz.

"Hey, look at you," Cora crowed as I entered. "Enjoying that convertible?" Spotting Milo, she left her desk to tickle his tufted ears. "Where did your new fella come from?"

"The alley up by the bank. If you know anyone missing a ginger tabby Manx, let me know." I would have a hard time parting with Milo if anyone claimed him, but I figured the chances of anyone reporting a missing cat were small, so I opted for honesty. "Did you find anything on those license plates?"

Cora leaned her hip against her desk and reached backward to grab a file folder. "Four with those first numbers on black, limo-size vehicles. Leaves a lot of room for error, kiddo, starting with the boy remembering the numbers right."

"Yeah, I know. What I need is someone who can hack the bank's drive-through teller for transactions just before five or get into their security cameras. I should have taken computers instead of accounting and law. They'd be more useful."

"Not down here." Cora flipped through her old-fashioned Rolodex and produced a business card. "Tell this guy it's Andre's business. Boris doesn't live in the Zone but he knows Andre."

I whistled in appreciation and tucked the unassuming card into my shirt pocket. "Do I need to be making anonymous deposits to your account for all your help?"

"Karmic deposits, hon. Buy me a beer at the bar in the meantime. I hear you retrieved the boss's big check over the weekend. He's plenty happy, so I'm happy."

"If Andre makes the bank cover it, then deposits it again, he should be doubly happy. So maybe karma works."

"Not today," she admitted. "Andre was just in here snarling because the bank's been giving him grief about our deposits. One too many checks shifted numbers and a few too many laughing Georges in the tally. They're talking about canceling Zone accounts."

We'd had several dollar bills with Washington's usually solemn figure sporting a big grin. The banks didn't approve. I grimaced. The banks had a point, but we were treading a slippery slope. The Zone inhabitants had earned that money. Could they help it if the government hadn't fixed their chemical waste zone? "Got anything in the till today?"

"Not even a George. Go forth and make an honest man of Legrande." She waved me off.

Both the machine shop and the florist had had a good weekend. I had to wonder how Andre had accumulated so many businesses in the Zone—and why—but he was employing a lot of people in a poor neighborhood, so I continued keeping my big mouth shut.

I ran into the new girl at Chesty's sweeping floors. For the first time, I noticed she had a tattoo on her shoulder blade, sort of like Lady Justice's balance scales. "Hey, glad to see Andre found you a place. I'm Tina Clancy."

Still a little wary, the big-breasted blonde turned to look more at Milo than me. "I'm Sarah. Pleased to meet you, Tina."

She sounded as if she were repeating rote phrases learned in a foreign language class: *Mucho gusto, señor. ¿Cómo está usted?* has been permanently emblazoned on my brain since high school Spanish. But this was the Zone. If I could have mink-brown model hair, she could have big breasts and language problems. After watching Max die and haunt my mirror, I wasn't having any difficulty with minor weirdnesses.

"Is it okay if I let Milo loose? It will take me a while to count the cash."

"Why isn't it tallied electronically?" she asked hesitantly, reaching for Milo with a more open smile.

"Something about the Zone and computers and Andre's paranoia equals keeping me employed. So I don't complain."

I'd occasionally had reason to wonder if Andre didn't just create jobs for people in need, but then he'd do something particularly obnoxious—like buying another business and firing all the employees—so I didn't give him bonus points. I had concluded he just liked people to owe him.

"Lookin' good, Tina," Ernest Modesto—Ernesto to most of us—said, surprisingly. Ernesto ran Chesty's. He was a rotund, bald man not much taller than me. Think Danny DeVito without the charm. He liked his employees to be towering Barbies, so he usually didn't notice my existence, and I was fine with that. "Done something different with your hair?"

Ewwww. Leave it to Ernesto to notice. "Singed it," I said wickedly. "Guess that makes me too hot to handle, huh?"

He backed off at that reminder of what had happened to my last boyfriend and unlocked the safe without further comment. I don't know if he really believed I was responsible for Max's fiery demise, but I was okay with him considering it. Ernesto had happy hands and I didn't want them on me.

I could have sworn Milo growled when Ernesto tried to give my ass an absentminded pat of farewell an hour later. I dodged his grimy fingers and tucked Milo into my bag without further ado.

"You're not a pit bull, Milo," I warned him. "Cute is your key to prosperity."

He gave a kitty snort and hung out of the bag to see whom I'd bring for him to play with next. That would be Bill.

Lady Justice dipped left when I entered. So maybe she just tilted with the wind and not to any scale of justice. Unless, of course, she believed I'd killed Max. I was obviously off my rocker if I was starting to worry about how tin statues thought of me.

"Is Andre here?" I asked as I entered and saw only

Bill behind the bar. I needed to make arrangements to pay back the car loan, and the closest thing Andre had to an office was here. This was where I left my reports and collected my paychecks.

"He said to tell you the car is a finder's fee for the deposit you recovered. Which means he's cheating somebody else, so you might as well take it."

Keeping my mouth shut, I didn't comment on Andre's Robin Hood complex but dropped my messenger bag on the bar Bill was wiping down.

He warily examined my cat. "Health department frowns on animals in food establishments."

Bill served burgers and fries at most, but he was one of the good guys, and I respected his rules. "When was the last time the health inspector set foot in the Zone?" I asked, proceeding to the till but keeping Milo in my purse.

He conceded the point with a nod. "I like to keep high standards. It's too easy to let things slide down here."

"I appreciate that. I'll keep Milo off the floor. Will that be okay?" Sliding my glasses on, I began listing receipts and counting cash.

"He looks like a good mouser." He tickled the tabby under his chin. "I used to live on a farm and had a cat this color."

This conversation constituted more words than I'd ever heard Bill string together at once. I hid my surprise.

"Do we have mice in the Zone?"

"Got one the size of my shoe living in the alley.

Bigger than Milo here. Some of the roaches are mouse size. Maybe he could catch them. I could let him loose in the storeroom. That shouldn't be against rules."

Who was I to come between a six-foot-seven hulk and his mouser? Milo eagerly crawled out of the bag and into Bill's hands and the pair ambled off together. Wow, I never knew pets had such an effect on people! I'd picked up stray kitties and once even a hamster in my peripatetic childhood. Since I hated keeping creatures caged, they'd seldom earned anything but kicks and shouts from my mother's friends.

Maybe it was time to start making friends of my own, ones who liked cats.

The lights flickered slightly, and I had the uneasy feeling of being watched again. But Bill was within shouting distance, so I kept a close eye on the cash and continued counting, easing my aching muscles by sitting on a stool.

I didn't like the idea of an invisible being snatching cash and my bag. If I believed in invisibility or ghosts, I would have to believe Max might live in a mirror. Wasn't going there.

But a little superstitious trash talk wouldn't hurt. "I dare you to touch this cash," I snarled aloud. "I can break boards with my hand." I might have managed to crack a few bones, although probably not on a ghost.

Regretfully, no one gave me an opportunity to express my pent-up rage. When I shouted at Bill that I was done, he returned, rubbing Milo's head and carrying a sack that smelled like fish. I raised a questioning eyebrow.

"It's been in the freezer," he said with a shrug. "If you can get it back to your place quick enough, it shouldn't defrost. Cats need real food sometimes, not that cardboard garbage they sell in stores."

I'd just spent my grocery money on that "garbage," but I nodded in agreement and returned a very satisfied Milo to my messenger bag. Obviously, Andre had not provided the requested bodyguard, but I hadn't really expected him to. Surely a thief wouldn't strike the same person two times in a row.

But just in case, I'd bought a new lock and handcuff for my deposit bag. Of course, if the thief could break the old ones, he could break the new ones. I didn't have a better solution for super thieves except for more caution. After slinging the messenger bag strap over my head, I tucked the shackled deposit bag under my armpit and gripped it for extra measure.

Outside, Leibowitz was berating a skinny teenager with tats and nose ring. I slid into the shadows under the awnings and hoped the cop didn't notice me. He'd been no help whatsoever when my bag was stolen the first time, so I preferred my normal avoidance of authority.

Andre was just coming out of the office building across from the bank as I passed by. I didn't know if that was coincidence or him keeping an eye on his assets.

"If you think I need a babysitter, you might as well take the deposit on your own," I told him ungratefully.

"I just thought the bank ought to be more aware of

my presence," he replied, striding across the middle of the street without regard for jaywalking laws.

I knew how Andre normally operated—under the radar. So making his presence known had another purpose, and given the size of the missing deposit and his argument with the bank, I could surmise what.

"The Monday deposit is pretty hefty," I acknowledged. "You're hoping to impress them with your importance when you file an insurance claim on your lost money."

He flashed a wicked white grin. "Yeah, and that, too."

Damn, even though I knew he was a lying cheat, he rattled my hormones when he smiled like that. I had always been a sucker for a bad-boy smile. And we all know how well that had worked out.

Max had been fun, but Andre was just plain toxic.

7

I'd had such a normal day that I'd forgotten about reporters. Since they'd left me alone all day Sunday, I had just assumed I was no longer a person of interest. *Wrong.* Milo's growl woke me from my stupidity the moment I emerged from the stairwell into the hall to my apartment.

The slumped figure leaning against my door did not inspire fear. Wearing frayed khakis, a blue button-down shirt that needed ironing, and a long brown ponytail, she didn't look much older than the kids I went to school with. She didn't even glance up until she heard me walking down the tiled corridor.

Warily, she crawled her back up the wall until she was standing. She was taller than me, naturally, but not by much. I'm fairly toned and she wasn't. And she didn't have a camera. Bonus points for her.

"Miss Clancy?" she asked. "I'm Jane Claremont from the *Baltimore Edition*. Could I ask you a few questions?"

The *Baltimore Edition* was an online newspaper run by unemployed journalism graduates and older reporters who had been laid off from all the major rags in the area. I never read it. I didn't think anyone else did, either. That made them underdogs, and I was a sucker for underdogs.

"You can ask. I may not answer," I said, unlocking my door.

"First, I'm sorry about your loss," she said hastily, as if she'd been practicing the line all day. "Even if he did try to kill you."

I wasn't as comfortable with that spin as I had once been. Hallucination or not, Max's panicked cry in the mirror had twisted my thinking. Of course, just the possibility that I was seeing Max in the mirror was enough to warp my brain, but now that the shock of *that* was passing, so was my anger. I simply couldn't believe Max wanted me dead. He had been perfectly capable of saying "'Bye, babe," and walking out. Besides, he'd never been a violent person.

Anger had been a lovely shield to hide behind. If I started remembering the real Max, I'd be a basket case in no time flat, so I was performing some kind of emotional balancing act by letting the reporter in.

At my nonresponse, she continued nervously, "I ran into the old guy across the hall. He told me his family hates reporters and to keep out. What's his story?"

"Have to ask Lily. She lives there. I've only met him once." I probably ought to have checked on Lily again, but I was a bit preoccupied these days. I set Milo loose and proceeded into the kitchen. I deposited the fish in the freezer, opened the refrigerator, and indicated the assortment of cans and bottles left from Max's last shopping expedition. "Drink?"

"Cold caffeine of any kind," she said gratefully, settling at my counter and removing a palm-size recorder from her overflowing knapsack. "You're kind of hard to reach. I've been calling for days."

"You and a thousand other nosy hounds. I may develop my neighbor's hatred of reporters." I popped a can, handed her a glass of ice, and helped myself to a bottle of water. Environment be damned. I wasn't drinking tap water from anywhere near the Zone.

"Yeah, I kind of figured that. Sorry. It's a tough business out there. People want sensationalism, and you offered it in 3-D Technicolor. And now you're frustrating the heck out of everyone."

"The heck?" I asked in amusement. "Is that what they teach you in journalism school these days? Non-abrasive cursing?"

"No, that's what I learned while trying to raise a two-year-old who repeats anything I say." She produced pen and notebook to go with her recorder. "I'm crazy to get into this business these days. It's hard with all our paper outlets disappearing. But without the media, there will be no one to report government corruption or uncover stories that would otherwise be swept under the rug. So I'm an idealistic idiot."

With a two-year-old. That had to be hard. I lifted my bottle in salute. "I'm going for a law degree for the same reason. To idiots."

She clanked her can against my plastic bottle and we drank to idiots everywhere.

"No one has heard your side of the story," she continued, shifting to a professional tone. "We've all heard the bare facts of the police report—your boyfriend, Maxim MacNeill, drove your car at high speed into the bank near where you were standing. He narrowly missed you, hit a pole, the electric wires sparked in spilled gas, and fire ensued. Is that correct?"

"I don't know any more than that," I warned. "Max was not a violent person. He did not drink to excess or do drugs. He had reason to be mad at me at the time but not sufficient reason to kill me."

Those were conclusions I'd reached during my sleepless nights. I had inadequate information beyond that. And to avoid insanity, I hadn't attempted to think further. There was a time for grief . . . and whatever.

"So you conclude that the car's brakes were tampered with?" she asked with wide-eyed innocence.

"That's a neat leap." I took a frozen dinner from the freezer and slid it into the microwave. "Since the car was mine, are you saying someone wanted to kill me or Max?"

"That's kind of what I wanted to know. Do you know of anyone who wanted either of you dead?"

I wasn't about to explain my neurosis about damning Max to hell, so I contemplated her version of events. "I don't know enough about Max to know if anyone wanted him dead. If they had, it would have been simpler if they'd monkeyed with his bike instead of my car, though."

"His family says he was a mechanic who worked for some pretty important people. Do you know their names?"

I wasn't about to admit I hadn't even known his family existed. I was still bitter about that lie. "Hardly. He worked on cars and bikes for anyone who paid him. If he kept any books, they're in his apartment, but I'm betting he only took cash and kept no records. Max called himself a citizen of the world. He didn't believe in paying taxes for wars, so he spent a percentage of his income helping the people the government doesn't."

Jane snorted. "Another idealist, but creative. Wish I'd met him."

"Max preferred helping his biker buddies buy beer," I pointed out, taking an edge off her pretty picture. "Child care might be more important than unemployed bikers, but vets were more important to him than kids. That's why government is a more democratic method of distributing the wealth. Theoretically."

She frowned and made notes. "Maybe his biker buddies didn't like your opinions?"

"Most of them don't have the foresight to look

beyond the next ride. Don't go looking for them in some conspiracy." The idea bulb struck, and I diverted the topic. "If you really want a story, you ought to look into the diplomatic limo that ran over a bunch of inner-city kids just before Max performed his flameout. One kid had her leg broken. Another lost a computer she'd worked for years to buy. Hard to tell what other damage the driver did. I got a partial license number from a government car pool but don't have the resources to track it." That last was a lie but she didn't have to know I was on the case.

She looked mildly interested. "Not as sensational as a fireball, unless you have video."

"It's sensational if we can nail a corrupt congressman. Ask yourself why someone that powerful would be in South Baltimore, much less near the Zone. Why would they be in a hurry to leave the bank? What kind of slime would leave kids injured in the street? You want him running our government?"

And was there any chance the limo had anything to do with Max's death less than half an hour later? But that was stretching credulity a little thin.

She frowned in thought. "Interesting, but I don't have many resources, either. Fireballs catch the public eye, but people already expect slime from our public officials. 'Dog Bites Man' equals boring."

"So much for idealism if sensation is more important than corruption." I wrote down the partial plate from memory and shoved the paper at her. "Poke at it and let me know what you find. He was in the drive-through lane at the bank. I have no experience in investigating. Pretend he might have something to do with Max's death."

She tucked the paper into her notebook. "Timing was wrong. He was long gone before your boyfriend crashed. I do my research. Maybe whoever he was will do something spectacularly noticeable someday. One never knows. So you don't think Max would be a target for murder?"

I liked the way she thought, but I couldn't help her. "I think the whole episode was a horrible accident. Or the Zone effect is spreading and causing mechanical weirdnesses. Maybe the congressman's brakes didn't work that day, either."

"I like that!" she said with more interest. "I can work with that. Kind of like an area-oriented Mercury retrograde. Machines and communication break down in the Zone. Maybe it comes and goes. I can track other accidents down there, see if I can develop a pattern."

I rolled my eyes and popped my dinner out of the oven. "Glad I can be of help," I said dryly. "Now, if you don't mind, I have studying to do."

She packed up and politely offered her hand. "Thank you, Miss Clancy. It was a pleasure to meet you. And I really will look into the diplomatic incident if I have time."

I didn't hold out high hopes, but I shook her hand and saw her out. If nothing else, I'd learned something new. I could take tools of the media and use them for my own purposes. Sort of. Live and learn.

I ate my dinner at the table with my books spread

out in front of me. Milo fell asleep in his food bowl. This was probably the first time in his short life that he'd ever had enough to eat. Judging by the size of his paws, he would grow into a good-size cat. I was fine with that. I'd encourage him to growl at all strangers.

By the time I'd staggered off to the shower, my brain was fried, and I wasn't thinking about Max and mirrors. So I was pretty sure it wasn't my paranoid imagination that conjured the words scrawled on the bathroom mirror.

rethgad s'nataS was painstakingly inscribed across the glass beneath the backward *Justy*.

Max never could spell worth a damn.

Satan's daughter? Me? Literally or figuratively? Was Max cursing me as I had him, or warning me? Either way, I freaked. Forgetting the shower, I dived under the covers rather than face any more mirrors. Even Milo couldn't comfort me.

After another night of tossing and turning, insanely wondering if Satan—who I was pretty sure I didn't believe in—had marked me as his, I remembered the weird message from Themis Astrology. I got up, found my glasses, and opened my netbook before I braved the shower, but I didn't know how to retrieve a deleted instant message impossibly sent from someone who didn't exist. Maybe the Zone had moved into my apartment. Maybe I'd carried shampoo chemicals and other pathogens home. Or maybe I was cuckoo and should check into a nest.

But my legal mind wanted logic and explanations. I recalled the message had said something along the line of: *Your Saturn transit is almost complete.* And *congarats, newest daughter.*

Daughter. *Saturn? Satan?* Coincidence that the words were almost identical to those in the mirror phrase? Could Max read my computer from wherever he was? Of course, that was assuming Max was behind the glass, which was pretty far out even for the Zone. Cuckoo territory.

Exhausted from too little sleep, under too much pressure from looming finals, I was on the very edge of freaking out all over again. As far as I was concerned, the devil was a figment of Bible Belt imaginations. How could anyone be a daughter of Satan?

Maybe my mother never spoke about my father, but given her free-spirited tendencies, I figured that was because she didn't know who he was. Still, I kind of thought I'd have had some clue that he was the devil by now. My mother had a few skanky friends, but on the whole, they were pot smokers and slackers, not outright evildoers. I didn't remember any of them being short and dark like me. I have my mother's coloring, except she looks like Cleopatra and I don't.

I was definitely going to find someone who could replace that medicine cabinet. Right now, I had classes and work and couldn't afford a day in bed.

I was so stressed, I didn't even care that a photographer caught me driving out of the parking lot in my rattle-heap Miata when I left. If they wanted a real story, they'd have to see my bathroom mirror. Maybe I should take a hammer to it. Vandalism wasn't my usual modus operandi, but I figured I was justified.

I was now undecided about going to the viewing at the funeral home tonight. The Max I'd known deserved my last respects, only I was too unnerved to pay them in front of a roomful of staring strangers and a passel of reporters and a family who didn't know me. But I couldn't skip class to attend the church services scheduled for tomorrow morning. Besides, I wasn't even certain I'd be allowed inside a church without a bolt of lightning striking me—that's how far my nightmares had taken me.

I argued with myself all day as I went through the routine of school and counting cash without incident. The viewing was that evening. I probably should have watched the news so I could get some idea of how the reports were being spun, but I couldn't stomach reliving that crash over and over again.

Walking from the bus stop to the tenement, I ran into the gray-haired stranger, who was looking more disheveled and wild-eyed than before.

"Hide," he muttered without stopping. "Don't let them find you."

No way was I confronting a crazy man. I hurried home to debate the funeral.

In the end, my respect for Max won out. I might not have known him well, but we'd had a good few months. We'd fought and argued like any couple, but we'd never gone to bed mad. He might have been a little too full of himself, but he'd been a decent, fun-loving guy. Unless some demon had taken him over, I couldn't believe he'd really tried to kill me. I might have been willing to buy any theory, no matter how unlikely, but that he was a demon wasn't one of them. I'd had a bad day. Maybe I'd just imagined his fury.

So I donned my best little black dress and tucked a compact and lipstick into my messenger bag to repair myself after I arrived. I wore Max's jacket, pinned my old college skull-and-crossbones earring in one ear, and drove north, past downtown, to the funeral home.

His family had chosen a place in an upper-middle-class neighborhood of traditional brick houses and tree-lined streets, nowhere near the Zone or anyplace Max might have hung out. I hoped his buddies would be there, because I couldn't relate to anyone who lived this kind of lifestyle. I couldn't imagine burly Max growing up here. I'd thought he was my kind of educated trailer trash. What else had I been wrong about?

Once inside the funeral home, I didn't have any problem locating the viewing room where they'd set up his coffin. His biker friends were hanging around outside, their stringy long hair and leathers looking as out of place in this quiet, proper sanctum as I felt.

I limped up to them warily, but they were simple guys. They didn't read motives into anything. The big lugs hugged me and fought tears and passed me around as if I were a beer can. I was good with that. I was more than good. I let the tears ruin my mascara and accepted their big shoulders as pillows to cry on.

The experience was the catharsis I'd needed to relieve some of the lump of molten lead in my chest.

"If you ever need anything, kid," said Lance, Max's closest friend, "we're here for ya. And we've got someone working on getting that car out of impound."

"Yeah." Gonzo, Max's mechanical partner pounded me on the back so hard that I almost fell over. "We're taking that Escort apart. Ain't no way Max would have crashed that baby."

"You'll let me know if you find anything?" Stupid, but it cheered me to know someone wasn't writing off the fireball as the result of a domestic dispute. Nothing could bring Max back, but knowing someone was at least looking into his death made me feel less helpless. And maybe a shade less guilty.

"You'll be the first to know," Lance assured me. He hugged me and led me into the viewing room as the organ music began.

All the proper citizens were already in place. The family was sitting to one side, what there was of them. I studied a regal, gray-haired woman wearing a hat with a veil straight out of the sixties and wondered if that was his grandmother. She didn't look up when we entered.

A distinguished gentleman sat at her side, holding her gloved hand. He wore a light gray suit that set off his head of silver hair to perfection. I wondered if he had hair implants. No man of his age should have had that much hair. He looked up with a slight frown as we scraped chairs at the back of the room.

A woman in her thirties, probably a few years older than Max, openly scowled at us. Really, I couldn't blame her. We represented the side of Max's life that had taken him away. If this was his family, he should have been up there in a tailored suit and neat haircut, wiping away his sister's tears, assuming that's who she was. He shouldn't have been driving my ancient Escort and cruising too near the edge of nowhere that was the Zone.

Maybe I should have been looking into Max's background instead of hunting for a diplomatic limo. Why the devil had someone from that family been hanging out with bikers instead of working in a white-collar office?

I couldn't ask Lance or the other guys, not in here. They might not know any more than I did. I tried to let the organ music drown out thought, but then they let a preacher get up there to bleed over the audience, and his unctuous tones and ambiguous moral prosing made me want to hurl.

I got up and walked out, thinking I could go back in when the preaching stopped. I thought I caught a glimpse of Lily's weirdo slipping out the front, and I followed, out of stupid curiosity. What would my wacko neighbor be doing at Max's funeral? And why had I only noticed him after Max died? My paranoia was starting to show, and I decided I'd feel better if I confronted the problem instead of hiding.

The moment I limped down the front steps, my vision disappeared in a blinding flash of cameras.

I was teetering on the brink of exhaustion, frayed

and distraught, with a mascara-streaked face. I'd had enough surprises for a lifetime. I could have reacted very badly. Instead, I swung to beat a hasty retreat to the pillared porch.

Cutting off my escape by trespassing on the funeral home steps, a talking head from the TV station got in my face with his microphone.

"How did the MacNeills react when you showed up this evening, Miss Clancy? Do they blame you for the loss of their son and heir?"

Son and *heir*?

Unnerved and off guard, I did not behave with decorum. Lacking a gun and a fast draw, I yanked the microphone out of his hand and snapped it into wires. A cameraman raced to film the incident. From my position on the steps, I kicked his knee to unbalance him, grabbed his video camera, and flung it against a brick wall, shattering it.

The crowd closed in, suffocating me. Some other jerkwad yelled and swung his mic too near my nose. I grabbed his wrist and may have broken it, from the pained sound of his cry. I was weeping too hard to care. I'd spent two years avoiding confrontation, for this?

The shouts and altercation brought Max's buddies running.

I was nearly crushed in the abrupt melee of flying fists and boots. Before I could catch my breath, Lance had the pretty-boy newsman on the ground and was unprettifying his face. Horrified, I didn't want the boys arrested for my sake, and I certainly didn't need any more black marks on my record. I wanted a do-over, but fleeing was about the best I could arrange—if I could miraculously limp through the battleground without being noticed.

In a fair world, a tornado would have blown the scrimmage across the lawn like autumn leaves.

Even as I thought about it, an unnatural wind whistled through the stately elms, gusting through the pillared porch and shoving me forward. Huge trees dipped and bowed their heads. Leaves blew sideways and men toppled. With the fearful wind at my back, I fled down a path that amazingly cleared across the lawn. Maybe I was crying so hard, I wasn't seeing straight. I just ran, head down, tears falling.

Despite shouts of surprise and fright, I reached the Miata, gunned the engine, and got the hell out of there, too terrified to look back.

8

In bed, I cried my eyes out. Even Milo's purrs and licks couldn't comfort me. I think it was as much pity party as grief. I didn't know what was happening to me, and I was terrified.

I needed to know *I* was directing my life. For all my growing-up years, I'd had a flighty Fate in the form of my mother uprooting me from one home after another. Once on my own, I didn't want anyone tugging my strings. I needed to make my own decisions. But suddenly, I was being buffeted and redirected by strange winds. *Literally*.

Mini-tornados did not drop out of the sky to aid my escape in any world that I knew. Maybe I'd just imagined my abrupt departure from the funeral home. Or maybe I could go completely around the bend and believe the weird guy I'd been following was a Harry Potter magician. I could take that idiocy further and believe that what had happened to Max had been unnatural, but that wasn't easing the pain.

And neither incident had happened in the Zone. They'd happened around *me*—unless I was a candidate for that aluminum colander hat, which was a very strong possibility. Maybe stress had fried my brain cells. I didn't have time—or patience or money—for counseling.

In the morning, after tossing and turning until dawn, I decided I had to confront myself as well as the world. I had to take back my control. I got up, tore the blanket off the mirror, and, pounding the glass, shouted, "Wake up, Max, you bastard! Where are you?"

I nearly had a heart attack when he actually appeared.

Biting my lip to keep it from trembling, I reached out to trace the familiar face blurrily superimposed upon mine. The image looked grouchy and uncertain as I touched nothing but glass. I'd once told Max he looked like Burt Lancaster with black curls. He hadn't appreciated the sentiment.

So how did one confront insanity? By accepting it?

"Where are you?" I asked mournfully, wishing he was real. My hallucination only provided his face, so I couldn't tell if he shrugged in reply.

"*I didn't do it, Justy,*" the voice inside my head said again. "*Help me.*"

Schizophrenia? I'd rather have believed in Max than in insanity.

"How? I don't even know where you are. Or what you are." I was surely losing it. Guilt, I self-diagnosed. But I was ready to believe almost anything at this point. "You didn't tell me you had a family!" I remembered to throw at him.

"*Sorry.*" And then he faded.

In frustration, I whacked my wooden hairbrush against the glass, hard. It cracked.

Well, that was helpful.

Having faced my worst fear and accomplished nothing, I showered and got dressed and had time to check my netbook. Nothing new from Themis Astrology. I ran a Google search and a phone/address search on the company and found nothing. Maybe its proprietor existed on an astrological plane. Wikipedia told me Themis was a Greek goddess, the embodiment of divine order, law, and custom, so I assumed I was dealing with a female with a high opinion of herself.

I sent an e-mail to Boris, the hacker genius named on the card Cora had given me, asking if it would be okay if I dropped by around six. I had hopes of finishing early, since Wednesdays were usually slow.

In the spirit of taking control, I decided that if I

meant to confront my new life, I couldn't continue hiding from the real world. I Googled a local news station on the Internet.

That was almost worse than confronting Max. A video showing the melee at the funeral home was abruptly cut off, apparently when the reporter's camera was torn from his hand by a high wind. The camera filmed tossing branches and screams before the screen went dark.

The headlines beside the video shouted FREAK STORM DISRUPTS BIKER BATTLE OUTSIDE FUNERAL HOME. In smaller letters, it went on to speculate about the ghost of a biker lost in a fiery accident joining his friends in attacking guests at the funeral home.

Since I knew at least half that story was lie—those weren't guests but reporters—I snorted and shut it down. So much for the media. If they couldn't admit the error of their own ways, they'd make up something. Ghosts!

That was no ghost. That had been me.

Wearing Max's jacket.

With no better idea of how to research the impossible and ridiculous, I went to where idiocy lurked and Googled *Saturn transit* and *Satan's daughter*. The first site gave me pages and pages of gobbledygook about Saturn causing negative and positive changes depending on what house the transit occurs in or some illogic like that. I snorted in disbelief, although I did note that a complete transit happens roughly every twenty-eight years. I had my twenty-seventh birthday coming up, which was a little close for comfort. I couldn't believe I was that old already and had accomplished so little.

The second search gave me even worse crap about Satan having no daughters because he can't reproduce, plus a lot of websites for people with unhealthy perversions. Googling *Saturn's daughters* opened a site that claimed they were ruled by the planet of justice— shades of Themis! But when the blog went on about the daughters not living long because they were either punished for vigilantism or sent to hell for misuse of power, I bookmarked it for further examination and shut it down. One of these days, maybe I'd figure out how to investigate Internet scam artists and fear-mongers.

Deciding I just had to get back into my routine, I drove downtown to school. This was Wednesday. Thursday of next week was my last final. Providing I passed, I was less than two weeks from being a law school graduate. I had no intention of piling up those loans and not finishing. After watching the news, though, I was tense, anticipating trouble.

But my classes were so huge, and I was so totally anonymous behind my black-framed glasses and limp that no one seemed to connect me with the ugly stories. Or maybe they didn't read newspapers, either. My kind of people. We kept our noses to our books. For a few hours, I reveled in the straightforwardness of rules and regulations, the normalcy of books and teachers.

Once the last class was done, I heaved my backpack into my plastic car, left the real world, and cruised home. Maybe the rationality of law classes would end my episodes of insanity.

Milo was growling when I entered my apartment, so I had to assume someone had been prowling in the hall, but they were gone now. I glanced around to see if anything had been disturbed—but who could tell? A carton of old clothes I'd meant to take to Goodwill looked as if it had been moved, but Milo could have been jumping on it. I was nervous over nothing. I'd lived here for two years and no one had bothered breaking in to steal my netbook.

I cuddled the kitty, called him my guard cat, and fed him an extra fishy treat until he was purring happily again. Forget boyfriends. Cats were easier.

To keep up my new proactive attitude, after I grabbed a sandwich, I ran into the bedroom to glare at my cracked mirror. My newly thick hair still startled me, but I was learning to get past it. "Why Satan's daughter?" I yelled at the glass, hitting it with my fist until shards fell out. "*You* almost killed *me*! I didn't do anything to you."

Damn if I didn't see Max's image instantly wavering over mine. I could almost swear he was glaring.

"*Did not!*" he shouted in my head.

Okay, definitely guilt talking. I was arguing with myself. "Then tell that to Detective Schwartz. He thinks you did," I reassured myself.

"*You,*" he tried to say, but he was fading fast. "*Saturn, not Satan.*"

"Saturn is a damned planet!" I shouted, but the image was gone. I wanted him back. Other people just told their boyfriends to go to hell and could take back the words later and make up. Me, I had to actually send mine there.

I wasn't ready to believe I was actually seeing Max and not experiencing hallucination-by-guilt, but where had the Satan/Saturn nonsense come from? Maybe that weird Themis message had sunk into my psyche and my hallucination had reproduced it. In mirror writing? I'd have to ask someone else if they could see it, but I didn't want confirmation of my mental state.

Thinking uneasily of the website about Saturn's daughters dying young, I figured my mind was simply feeding on my fears, like nightmares do.

Not entirely certain proactive insanity was working for me, I tucked Milo into my messenger bag and headed downstairs with catching the bus in mind.

Andre was waiting for me in the parking lot. He threw open the passenger door and gestured for me to climb in.

I had half a mind to walk on by, but he was my boss. My lunacy has its limits. I slid in and lifted my eyebrows questioningly.

"We have to talk." His pretty-boy visage looked grim as he shifted into gear and peeled onto the street.

My stomach knotted. If he meant to fire me, I'd never find another job as convenient as this one. Sure, the pay sucked, but at what part-time job didn't it? There probably ought to be combat pay included for working in the Zone, but nasty jobs like mine went to beggars who didn't have the resources to fight for their rights.

"There are reporters crawling all over Edgewater Street," he finally said when I refused to encourage him. "They're looking for you, but they're asking questions we don't want asked."

I hid my surprise. Had Jane really sicced her fellows on the story I'd fed her? Or was this a different vendetta, created by the little episode last night?

"Personally, I think it's time people started asking questions," I said, before I could bite my tongue. So much for keeping my head down and my mouth shut.

"You want to ask questions, ask me. But the media is only out for sensationalism and page views, and that's not going to help us. Next thing we know, they'll have a congressional committee down there wanting to turn the area into a landfill. Then where will we go?"

With his serious face on, Andre looked manly and intriguing instead of sly and irritating. I still didn't trust him. "You'll just take all the money they give you for your property and find another impoverished slum to infect. Do you really care what happens to the rest of us?"

"The Miss Snide act is going nowhere," he informed me curtly. "You know nothing about the Zone. You don't live there. You come and go without getting to know any of us. And that's not lasting much longer. I've set up an office for you at Chesty's. Everyone will carry their cash receipts to you there so you don't have to be on the street until the reporters clear off."

"Wow, my very own office," I chirruped, clearly out of my mind. Was I looking to get fired? "Does it come with my very own porn on the walls?"

"I'm covering your ass, which isn't half as good as the ones on Ernesto's walls, so shut up until you know what you're talking about. Your fancy college degrees haven't taught you anything about real life."

Andre looked pretty hot when he was mad. Not John Wayne studly, but better in a slick *Maverick* sort of way.

"I think I've seen plenty of real life," I reminded him. "It sucks. And it's getting suckier by the minute."

"That's the kind of argument they teach you in law school these days?" he asked with almost a laugh. Maybe a snort of derision. "I think I like you better when you don't say anything, but you have to keep your eyes and ears open if you want to stay alive."

"Will you quit being so damned mysterious and just spill it?" I demanded as he swung into Chesty's parking lot. "I've had a crappy week, and I'm starting to really, really hate changes in my routine."

"We'll talk tonight. I'll have Cora make the bank deposit. I'll buy you dinner at Chesty's." He stopped the car and waited for me to climb out.

"I have plans for later this afternoon," I informed him, aiming for aloof and not pathetic, and not exiting at his command. "What time do you want me back for dinner?"

"I don't want you on the street at all!" he shouted.

Nice. I'd finally crawled under his skin. I kind of liked that, since he'd already gotten under mine. "Well, isn't that just ducky dandy. You want to tell Geek Boy to come visit me at Chesty's so I don't have to go to him?" That was the unoriginal company name on the business card Cora had given me. Since she said the owner knew Andre, I assumed he knew Boris.

Andre clenched the steering wheel in much the same way Max had that last time I'd seen him alive. I took the emotional punch to the gut without flinching. Much. Milo poked his head out of my bag to see what was happening. I scratched the spot between his ears and hoped it would unknot my insides.

"What the devil do you want with my geek?" he asked, narrowing his eyes and releasing his grip on the wheel.

"You don't own me, Andre," I warned. "You don't have to know everything about me. Don't even try or I'm outta here." I gathered my courage and asked, "Or is that what this is all about? Do you want me gone? If you do, say so. I'll go."

I tried not to hold my breath. I was just starting to think I had friends down here. If he fired me, I'd probably never see them again. I desperately needed a few friends right now.

"You are the most obtuse female who ever walked the planet!" He grabbed the back of my head, dragged me half across the console, and planted a hot one on my mouth.

Before I could even respond to the electric shock spiraling from my lips down to lower parts, he jerked away. "I'll send the geek to your office. Get inside before that flake over there recognizes you."

My head was reeling so badly that I could barely glance out the window to the blue-jeaned kid studying Andre's slick Mercedes. I pushed open the door and slid out without comment. I was so not ever opening my mouth again.

Andre kept the car between me and the door until I slipped inside. He'd probably only been hiding me from reporters, and I'd been imagining the passion but . . . wow. Just wow. Four-eyed gimps simply didn't get kissed by sex machines. Ever.

Still trying to wrap my head around that spit exchange, I checked the darkened interior of the club. Sarah was sweeping the floor on the far end by the stage. She glanced up at my entrance.

I'd have to open my mouth to talk. I couldn't walk around in a daze like a high school nitwit who'd just locked braces. I didn't want to be fired, but I didn't want Andre taking advantage of me, either. My head said, *Back off.* The rest of me wasn't so sure about that. The man kissed like dynamite.

He kissed like dynamite because he had experience, my head corrected. *And he's dangerous.* The man had had more women than I'd had years, months, and probably weeks. I didn't want to be anyone's special of the day.

"Andre says I have an office," I said to Sarah, passing the bare tables with chairs slung over them. For some reason, half the tables had turned a bilious green—the Zone's opinion of last night's act or the food? "Tell me it isn't the broom closet."

Sarah smiled tentatively and laid the broom against a table. "Andre had them partition off Ernesto's office. I'll show you."

"Did you hear any of the discussion?" I asked,

feeling safe talking to someone who practically dis-appeared into the woodwork, except for the hooters, of course. Maybe Sarah's diffidence was a result of the stares she attracted. "Why did they decide I needed to be hidden?"

"I try not to listen," she said apologetically. "It's not any of my business."

"I'm beginning to suspect that in the Zone, every-thing is everyone's business. Keep your ears open, if only for your own good." I was regurgitating Andre's earlier speech, I realized. I hated to admit it, but he had a point.

A strand of her frizzy hair fell across her face as she stared at her feet and nodded. She was starting to remind me too much of me, and I wasn't liking the picture.

Ernesto had a fancy mahogany paneled door with an engraved brass name plaque. I entertained evil ideas of insisting on a plaque of my own as Sarah turned the knob and showed me what they'd done.

The front right-hand corner had been partitioned off into a cubicle so my desk was the first anyone saw as the door opened. Ernesto would be livid. I wasn't much happier, since my cubicle had no door and no way of shutting out his wandering hands. I contemplated fastening a paintball machine gun to the battered metal desk they'd found for me. The ugly fluorescent overheads cast a bad light across both spaces. Ernesto's desk was black and shiny and littered with expensive chrome accessories. Mine was empty.

Still, it was a desk, when I'd had none before. I just couldn't figure out what I'd do with it.

A male voice suddenly erupted from the barroom. "Anyone here?"

In an instant, Sarah had vanished. In her place, a chimpanzee wearing baggy jeans clung to the top of the partition.

And just like that, with Milo leaping from my bag to examine the chimp's feet, I knew I could no longer blame these Zone phenomena on hallucinations.

9

"Okay, I didn't see that coming," I muttered, wondering if I ought to reach up and haul the chimpanzee down before she collapsed the partition of my brand-new office.

The Zone could turn us into chimps? Should I run like hell or admire the entertainment?

"Who is it?" I yelled back instead, afraid to leave Milo alone with a chimp. Or Sarah. Or whatever in hell had happened here. Those sure looked like Sarah's shoes discarded on the floor, and that was Sarah's tank top clinging to monkey shoulders. The baggy jeans had slid off but the top covered her.

"Andre said someone named Clancy needs a geek?" called a voice from the lounge.

"Okay, be right there." I studied the chimp. "Sarah? Will you be all right if I go out there and close the door?"

The chimp glanced at the drop to the floor, and I caught on. I dashed back to the lounge, waved at the short guy nervously peering at obscene murals, grabbed a chair, and zipped back into my office. I set it beneath the chimp's feet, and she nodded, reaching for the chair back with her toes.

This was just too weird. "Milo, don't go any-where," I warned, insensibly. Heck, if chimps could understand me, why not cats?

I shut Ernesto's—*our*—door and returned to greet the Geek, who probably thought I was nuts by now. But if he knew Andre, he was used to it, probably more so than me. I'd learned to tolerate weird behavior in objects—but shape-shifting chimps, not so much.

If things like this happened frequently down here, Andre was right: I'd been clueless. I kinda thought I'd like to remain that way.

The cavernous dark lounge smelled of cheap beer, not precisely an office environment but probably suitable for this transaction.

"Hi, I'm Tina Clancy." Preferring to maintain my professional persona, I stuck out my hand to the mus-cularly deficient, middle-aged nerd not more than a few inches taller than I. I felt safe calling him a nerd, because he so obviously wanted to be one, from the thick eyeglasses to the pocket protector—in a T-shirt pocket. I mean, who has pockets in their T-shirts? The eyeglasses, those I understood. No one notices us bespectacled types.

"Boris the Geek," he said, taking my hand. "Best not to know more about me than that. Andre says you wanted to see me?"

I would have liked to use my new office about now, but no way was I taking him back there if Sarah was morphing into a human video game. "I have a question that probably can't be answered without doing something illegal," I said cautiously. "If you have a problem with that, then thanks for stopping by, but I don't want you involved."

His dark bushy eyebrows rose above his steel glasses frames. "Just a question answered? I wouldn't have to do anything actively illegal? Other than hacking," he amended.

I could swear one of the wall mural nudes was leaning closer to listen.

I lifted a chair from one of the bilious green tables in the middle of the room, away from the walls, and offered it to him, taking another for myself so we could talk privately. "Are there different levels of illegality in hacking?"

"Different levels of difficulty, but it's *all* illegal. Me? I just figure if the feds can do it without permission, then we all ought to have freedom of information."

"That's warped logic, but I won't argue with it. What about a bank?"

He glanced over my shoulder, and I turned around to see Sarah—in her normal big-breasted form—easing out of Ernesto's office. She threw a nervous look to us and hurried over to her broom.

"She's off-limits," I said, bringing his attention back to me.

"I just looked." He still appeared a little shame-faced. A man didn't go into a club called Chesty's and *not* look at the scenery. "Banks are pretty high on the difficulty scale. It will cost you."

Of course it would. Dang. I sat there and thought about it, remembering those poor kids and that expensive car. I couldn't do anything about Max, so I really needed to do something about those kids.

"Maybe we can barter services," I suggested slowly, letting the idea develop. "Do you need any book-keeping?"

He looked wary. "I need cash more."

"Don't we all?" I frowned at the table. "Maybe I can come up with another part-time job. If I tell you what I need, can you quote me a price so I know how much I have to earn?"

"Can't you just ask Andre for the money? I can't believe he makes his girlfriend work!"

I scowled. "I am so *not* his girlfriend. I'm an independent contractor. He doesn't even pay my pay-roll taxes." Neither did I; Andre paid me in cash. It wasn't as if I expected to ever collect social security.

Andre must have put the rush on him to get him down here this quickly. Boris didn't look as if he believed me, but he apologized and we got down to business while Sarah swept the floor and put chairs back. By the time we were done, Cora and several of the others had arrived with their deposits. They all looked disappointed that I wasn't entertaining them in my new office.

I kind of liked using the lounge. It was less claustrophobic than a cubicle. After Boris left, I set a stool behind the counter as I'd always done and began counting the day's receipts and tallying them against the cash register tapes. I didn't see the point of the desk for counting cash.

During a lull, Sarah crouched down behind the bar to dust the shelves and bottles. "I'm sorry," she whispered. She was well hidden down there. Even I couldn't see her.

"For what?" I wrapped a band around a stack of twenties. Credit cards, obviously, did not respond well to the Zone's bugginess. "Because I'm a clueless idiot?"

That silenced her for a bit. I heard a few bottles clanging around. I couldn't admit that I was curious, not after she had looked so hangdog. Maybe Sarah was one of those things Andre would explain tonight.

"I can't help it," she whispered semi-defensively. "It just happens when I'm startled or scared. Men scare me."

I was gonna just have to go with the flow. "So you camouflage yourself by turning into one of them." I snickered at my own humor and started on the next deposit. "Shame you're not big enough to be an ape."

I thought I heard her snort in some semblance of

amusement. "I hadn't thought of it that way. . . . It's kind of embarrassing."

"Well, yeah, men scratch their bellies and speak gibberish and would still be swinging from trees if we lived in jungles. They probably wouldn't bathe and would still be picking nits, too, except the ones with small weenies learned they could make money to compete in the testosterone wars and civilization happened."

Sarah was just starting to laugh when a heavy hand fell on my shoulder and a masculine voice intruded on our private party.

"Clancy's theory of evolution?" Andre asked dryly. "Why aren't you back at your desk where you belong? Anyone could have sneaked up on you here. I did."

I didn't like how his hand disturbed me. That kiss earlier had opened prospects I'd never really considered. Andre was way out of my league in so many ways that he might as well be from another planet.

Playing it cool, I finished writing down a total, then swung on the stool to face him. His face was too refined to resemble Max's smashed-nose look, but the fire in his eyes reminded me a lot of him. I fought a stirring below my belly in response, especially when he stroked my newly modified hair with a knowing look I immediately detested. I shook him off.

"I'm not any safer in a dark cubicle than out here where I can see who's walking in. And I'm not real terrified of reporters. Want me to break your arm and show you why?"

"You have to learn quicker response times if you want to break arms. You need to learn street fighting instead of that wimpy martial arts crap. You too, Sarah. If you're living down here, you have to be tough."

Sarah popped up from behind the bar, stared with big blue eyes, then popped back down to finish her dusting.

"Right, and I have time for that," I said sarcastically. "You have something against me getting sleep?"

"How long have you been hiding in classrooms?" he asked with equal sarcasm. "Keep it up and you'll be the world's oldest student."

"Jealous, Andre?" I taunted. "You did finish school, didn't you? After all, I'm the one counting your cash, not you."

"Not fast enough," he countered. "Do you have the deposit ready for the bank yet?"

"I thought Cora was taking it. And no, it isn't ready."

Milo leaped to a chair and over to the bar, strutting down the polished counter to paw at my deposit bag. Andre started to lift him down, and Milo snarled, his back arching and his tail stub shooting up.

"What's with the cat?" Andre asked, backing off. "Where did it come from?"

"Courtesy of the invisible thief," I said recklessly, rather pleased that my kitty had told off the head honcho. And if I had to believe in monkey girls, I could have invisible crooks, too. "Now go suck someone else's blood and let me finish here. I'll deliver it to the bank."

"No, you damned well won't." He grabbed the collar of my halter-top sundress and hauled me off the stool, dragging my skirt up my scarred thighs in the process. "Just look outside and use your head, will you?" He shoved me across the room, toward the narrow window beside the front door.

I peered through the one sliver of daylight allowed in Ernesto's cave.

A black limo sat across the street. The blue-jeaned kid was leaning against a pole, talking into his phone. The gray-haired loony from Lily's shambled down the street. Cora's boss, Frank, was aiming a handheld camcorder at the kid, the car, the bar, and generally anything that moved. An unlabeled van had parked in the lot, and a pair of dudes in suits talked to each other on the corner.

Nothing overtly suspicious for any busy city street. Except this was the Zone. No one was ever out there at this hour except Leibowitz, who was oddly absent.

"I don't suppose the limo over there has diplomatic plates," I said casually, hiding my tension. They couldn't all really want *me*, could they? Why?

"Not this time," Andre said, revealing he'd heard about my side investigation. "Frank's catching them all on film so we can try to identify them. My guess is at least half of them are media."

He stopped without explaining. I wasn't into waiting patiently. The media didn't drive limos. I limped away from the window and returned to my work. "And the other half?"

"After that tornado incident, the other half mostly wants to know if you really might have been responsible for Max's death."

10

The world was not only a scary place, but it was growing creepier by the minute.

I am not a particularly courageous person. In my experience, every time I got noticed, I got hurt. I'd taken martial arts training to prevent being beat up at every new school I attended. I hunkered down over my books because I didn't want to have to deal with the inexplicable actions of the people around me.

However, neither method would work if those people out on the street really wanted *me*. After the college riot fiasco, I preferred a no-commitment/no-involvement policy. Hell, I even stayed out of Max's way and tolerated his absences for the same reason. I was *not* taking responsibility for media thugs and stupidity.

"I did not raise a tornado," I stated flatly. "If there's a God, he objected to fighting during a religious service. For all I know, Max's family are Satanists who called up demons. That's my theory, anyhow."

"I don't care if you're an angel in rags and his family walks on hooves. Those men wouldn't be out there if you weren't in here," Andre asserted cruelly. "Maybe it's a slow news week. Maybe Max's family has an ax to grind. Maybe the congressman hired goons to eliminate a witness to his carelessness. Whatever the excuse, *you* instigated it. I want them gone, and I want them gone now. They won't leave if they think they can get at you."

Despite the embroidered vest, Andre didn't look so much like an easygoing Jim Garner anymore. He looked prepared to bite my head off.

Was he insinuating the local mob was interested in me? I'd sooner fight demons than AK-47s. I swallowed the bile rising in my throat, fought my anxiety, and glared at him. "Fine, then I'll go out there, shake hands, say my how-d'ya-dos, and they'll all go away. Is that what you want?"

"Not until we know what you are!" he shouted, grabbing my shoulders and nearly shaking me until I shrugged him off. He cooled off quickly, frowned, and strode toward the bar to pour himself a tonic.

What I was?

This was taking a few weirdnesses too far. As far as I knew, no one knew about Max in my mirror or that I'd damned him to hell—figuratively I hoped, because I thought my curse and the fireball had to be a coincidence. He was speeding. He went boom. Gas ignites. Not too far out there. Not my fault, right?

Except now Max was talking in my head. Maybe I should start plugging in music and not listen to me.

Ernesto sauntered in from the back, apparently avoiding the spectators in his front parking lot by trespassing on the officially marked EPA ground zero behind the restaurant. An entire encampment of the homeless had moved into the no-man's-land along the burned-out harbor strip, and the original chain link blocking it off had been appropriated for other uses over the years, mostly as shells for makeshift shelters. Everyone used the contaminated alley these days.

Ernesto cast me an evil eye but, seeing Andre, bit his unholy tongue. Assessing Andre's scowl, he diverted his path, entered his office, and shut the door. The man was smarter than I'd thought.

People, instead of walls, were giving me claustrophobia. My stress level was such that I almost understood Sarah's need to turn into a chimp to escape.

I returned to my cash counting, wondering what I was, too. "I assume you will explain that comment over dinner?" I asked icily.

Even Sarah was looking at me warily now. Had I an ounce of backbone, I'd have slapped the back of

Andre's head to knock some sense into it, but, as I've said, I wasn't into active protest anymore.

"Yeah, yeah. Hurry up with the cash." Andre sipped his drink in obvious disgruntlement. So much for the insouciant image he usually projected.

He'd kissed me, and now he thought he was protecting me.

"I have no reason to hide," I taunted him.

He didn't respond, just gathered up my tallied cash and began stuffing it into the deposit bag.

"I need a second job," I told him. "I need some quick cash. Have you got anything?"

I kept counting, unwilling to register his disbelief or scorn. If I focused on my goals, I'd get past him eventually.

"Yeah, Ernesto always needs more help. Seems women don't like working with him," he said dryly. "Want me to put in a word for you?"

I tallied the last deposit, slapped it on top of the bag he was holding, and, without answering his taunt, marched over to Ernesto's office—I couldn't really call it *our* office, since I'd yet to use it. I didn't hesitate at the door but limped in.

The scumbucket glanced up, glowered, and waited. I think one of his chrome desk ornaments skittered away and hid in a drawer.

Undaunted, I stated my case. "I need to earn some extra cash. Andre says you might have an opening. I don't dance. I can waitress, hostess, tend bar, and handle cash. I have a résumé if you need one."

"I need a kitchen flunky. You don't look the part of our front-end personnel." He smirked.

"Fine. I'm having dinner with Andre tonight. I can start anytime after that. When do you need me?"

Like I had time for flunky. I'd hoped for a waitress job so I could earn enough tips to work this off quickly, but Ernesto had a point. I didn't have big hooters. And as the evening progressed, I would start limping like a three-legged dog—not what the customers wanted.

"Tomorrow," Ernesto responded, "starting when I say, until Cook says to go home. If you quit after the first night, you don't get paid."

Beggars couldn't be choosers. I walked out, closing the door after me. Andre had already left with the deposit bag.

I tasted the sourness of defeat but didn't show it when Sarah sent me a look of sympathy. My brains and efficiency were pretty much wasted in a kitchen. It was my choice not to look elsewhere. I glanced at my watch. The five o'clock bus had gone. I might as well hang around to see what Andre had to say.

My stomach twisted uneasily, and I wasn't in the least hungry. I'd almost rather have gone home and berated imaginary Max some more.

I rummaged in my bag to see if I'd left the compact there from the other night. Dinner was dinner, and I was female enough to powder my nose and put on lipstick before a date. It was nice not having to mess with the hair.

I flipped open the compact, glanced in the mirror, and nearly tossed it before I recovered my senses.

Max stared back at me, almost as startled as I was.

"Lookin' good, babe. Didn't think I could pull this one off. Your mirror connection is way *stronger here,"* he murmured inside my head before fading away.

I sat down on a stool and snapped the compact shut. *What was I?* increasingly seemed a more and more valid question under the circumstances—one I couldn't answer.

Customers began filing in just before six. Sarah had disappeared into the kitchen before the first customer entered. Ernesto's current mistress, Maria, in black miniskirt and plunging neckline, took her station at the door. The model-tall bartender with flowing blond hair began polishing glasses. I'd take Bill's bar any day, but then, I didn't possess the requisite equipment to appreciate this place.

I took a booth in a dark back corner, switched off the little table lantern that provided the only light, and, succumbing to my new obsession, watched everyone entering. The blue-jeaned kid sauntered in, trying to look cool. Maria zeroed in on him, and he forgot being cool or a reporter or whatever he was. With his gaze firmly on her nearly bare assets, he couldn't see me.

Fortunately, the wall nudes had stopped moving, but I could see Andre's point about keeping the looky-loos out of the Zone.

A few industrial workers marched in, obviously regular customers who didn't even notice the newly green tables. A scantily clad waitress sidled up to take their orders.

A big bloke already looking half loaded staggered up to the bar. He pinched the rear of one of the dancers on her way back to the dressing rooms. She hauled off and whacked him one, but he just laughed, as if they'd been flirting. I grimaced at the byplay.

I didn't have issues with sexual exploitation—it worked both ways, the way I saw it. But years of being tyrannized by thugs bigger than me had instilled an active dislike of bullies, and a childhood spent watching Clint Eastwood westerns had given me an over-inflated sense of justice. I took an instant dislike to the blowhard and wanted him gone. I wanted to be a bouncer, but the crippled leg had diminished my martial arts skills, and I didn't own a gun.

I wasn't sure what Andre meant for me to learn by hanging out down here, but once I got past the bully, I will admit I was amused when a couple of business suits entered, looking wary. I expected them to tug on their white shirt collars in discomfort. We didn't get suits in the Zone. The suits were the people Andre was really concerned about.

I know Zone inhabitants are often derisively referred to as trolls. If we were trolls, these guys were gold-digging gnomes. Or maybe treasure-hoarding dragons. Creeps with money.

The drunk at the bar scanned the room, looking for more trouble. I thought he nodded at the suits, but that could have been my paranoia. I disliked the look he cast in my direction.

"That's the chippie sent her boyfriend up in flames?" the drunk asked of no one in particular, glaring unsteadily through the gloom in my direction. "There's people who would give good money to hear how she did it."

Like a balloon, he started to rise, but a waitress distracted him with her cleavage, and he settled back down to salivate.

A nervous shudder wracked me. What people? And did they really believe I'd killed Max? That was ridiculous. That had to be alcohol and hot air talking.

A plate of spaghetti slid onto the table in front of me, and I looked up to see Andre slipping onto the bench across the table. He deposited another plate of pasta there. He did not look like a man who had just kissed the snot out of me and wanted to do it again. I couldn't decide if I was disappointed. I liked the kiss. Andre, I wasn't so hot about.

Had he heard the drunk? I refused to inquire.

"No salad?" I asked, picking up the napkin-wrapped utensils a waitress hurried to lay down, pretending the kiss had been an aberration like all the other aberrations around me.

"It's coming." He unrolled his napkin and spread it on his lap without acknowledging me, just as if this were a business dinner. "Nice table choice, but you should be sitting over here, where people can't see you."

I relaxed. I could do casual. "Old cowboy trick, back-to-the-wall defense. Besides, I'm enjoying the view. The suits are the ones who have you worried?"

The spaghetti was edible. I made better marinara, but not often. Cooking was merely a survival technique.

The brute at the bar shouted an obscenity. I glanced up to watch one of Ernesto's bouncers leaning on him. Ernesto's efficiency went up a notch in my estimation. I dragged my wandering mind back to Andre. He hadn't even noticed I'd wandered.

"It's that the suits are here at all that worries me," he said in reply to my question. "They're from the city. If they visit just the once, they'll dismiss the vanishing clock and talking manhole covers as special effects, not know your hair isn't natural, and everyone else will stay out of their way. They'll leave without understanding what we are. But if they keep coming and bring more eyes and ears with them, our days are numbered. The EPA will cordon off Edgewater as well as the harbor, and we'll all be out of luck."

He was biting off more than I could chew. I put my fork down, held up my hands in a time-out signal, and tried to formulate a thousand questions into one. "Beginning, please. I moved here two years ago, went looking for a job on the bus line, and you hired me. At the time, I was a tourist who thought the blue buildings were special effects. Are you telling me that most of the city is stupid enough to believe this?" I wasn't in my happy place, and he wasn't making things better.

"The rest of the city knows we're regularly hit by floods, engulfed in chemical stenches, and that industrial waste is dangerous. They stay away, and we don't advertise. Acme pays off the EPA, and the media forgot about us years ago. We don't have much in the way of families requiring government agencies coming around. The cops know what goes down, but I take care of them."

"Bribery?" I asked in disbelief. "Why?"

"Just think of it as protective coloration. We want outsiders to overlook us."

I had vaguely grasped that the Zone was weird, but I'd always considered it more like fun-house weird. Someplace one would go to be entertained by the oddities. Of course, up until Max died, I hadn't met invisible thieves or chimpanzee shifters, either. "And you want to keep out others, why?" I asked.

"You'll understand if you stay here long enough," Andre said, not even looking up from his pasta. "None of us is exactly what we seem, which is why we're keeping an eye on you. Blowing up boyfriends is not on our list of accepted activities. Blowing away reporters *might* be."

"I didn't do either of those," I protested indignantly, forgetting drunks and bouncers and bribery in my outrage that Andre could believe the reports. "Max crashed my car! I didn't ask him to do that. And his biker friends trashed the media. Anything else is pure imagination."

The salad was delivered, but I'd lost my appetite. What had I done by coming to work down here? Had I ruined my life even more than I had protesting crooked provosts?

"What are *you* if you're not what you seem?" I returned to his earlier statement, diverting the subject from myself. Besides, I was curious. Everything about Andre was out of place in this sleazy bar.

He forked his lettuce and chewed it thoughtfully, his gaze considering me. He had disgustingly thick lashes for a man, and eyes of a peculiar blue-green. "I'm not sure I ought to tell you."

"You *can't* tell me, because you're making all this up to scare me and haven't the imagination to pretend you're an illegal immigrant who smuggles drugs." I was getting even for his earlier cracks.

He snorted and nodded toward the bar. "I started out like him, except over at Acme."

I turned and watched Detective Schwartz, wearing a security guard uniform, take a glass of water from the bartender. He looked damned good in khaki. He didn't see me, and I pulled back into the booth. I hadn't known he worked for Ernesto. Apparently Andre was right: I didn't know a lot.

"You were a cop? You moonlighted as a security guard? And then what, you started blackmailing the Man, made enough to buy your first bar, and the rest is history?"

"You should write a book," he suggested wryly. "I was a boy from the hood who went to war, got messed up, came back and took a job as security, and got caught in the first chemical flood. And that's all you need to know until I figure out if you'll fry me for saying more."

"If I knew how to fry you, I'd have done it long since." I blew a strand of hair out of my face in frustration. I wanted to know more about getting *messed up,* but Andre's expression made it clear he was done talking about himself. "So you're nailing me as a freak simply because I got my hair fixed?"

He looked impatient. "You could have dyed, permed, and added extensions to your stringy mop and it wouldn't look like it does now. Down here, good looks come at a price."

Andre's calm acceptance of Zone peculiarities was chilling as well as eye-opening. I didn't want to believe anything he said, but either I believed I was morphing into weirdness or believed I was insane. I wasn't even sure which I'd prefer.

I snorted. "Good looks come at a price anywhere. Check out your former high school class. What do the beauty queens and athletes look like now? Unless they're paying for upkeep, they look like the suits over there." I indicated the paunchy, saggy-jawed specimens ogling the pole dancer who'd just emerged onstage. But he was right again, damn him. My hair wasn't real.

"Your glibness doesn't disguise the changes we can see with our own eyes. It's happened too often down here for you to hide from us. Sarah isn't our only shape-shifter. Until now, though, no outsider has paid attention to our oddities. If Max was an unfortunate accident, I'm sorry for all of us. We're a pretty reclusive lot, and we prefer our privacy. No one else has ever done anything quite so media-worthy as blowing up their boyfriend and a bank in the same blow. Do you even know who Max really was?"

I propped my elbows on the table and shoved both

hands into my hair, not meeting his eyes. "I thought he was my boyfriend. If you want to tell me more than that, go easy."

"Max's father was once a senator who decided he'd make more money as a lobbyist. Word is, he was persuaded to that decision because of a few bad political and personal calls, including influencing the zoning for the chemical plants, but for some odd reason, the media never followed up on the rumors. Max had a healthy trust fund. He left it to a half-dozen environmental agencies."

Oh, crap and filth.

I'd sent a rich do-gooder to hell.

11

Apparently sensitive to my distress, Milo leaped up to the bench beside me. He smelled of fish. I was beginning to think that feeding him fish from the Zone was not a good idea, except he'd probably been born down here. Were the defects genetic by this point?

I wanted to pull out my compact and yell at Max for not telling me he was a damned trust-fund baby, but I resisted that particular eccentricity. "Is it the air or the water or the food or what exactly are you claiming is hazardous to our health?" I asked.

"Probably all of the above. The nonprofits that Max left his money to are all out to shut us down as a toxic waste dump. I suppose they could have people out on the street now, trolling with the rest of the suits, but nonprofits are notoriously understaffed. I doubt they move that quickly. Max was different. He had connections to Acme, the plant that caused the spill."

Trust funds and matters of money made mighty good motives for killing an annoying insect, and much as I liked Max, he was more than annoying. He could be a worse tick under the skin than Andre.

So just who might Max have been biting before he died? And could they be after me now? And *why*? Suddenly, looking into the limo hit-and-run and Max's death wasn't guilt-relief but a matter of survival.

I glanced at the drunk now pawing another dancer. Was he a regular? Or one of the creeps out to spy on me? And did I really want to know? Because he was causing an ugly gnawing in my gut. Maybe I'd better go back to keeping my head down. Had *Max* been using me to spy? That would certainly have explained why a trust-fund hunk would take up with a pint-size gimp. I didn't have issues about my body but I'm a realist, and the possibility hurt, bad.

"And there's some reason *why* the Zone shouldn't be shut down?" I demanded, releasing my pain in obnoxiousness. "Just exactly how dangerous is it?"

"No one knows, but there's nowhere better to give misfits a second chance. Frank used to be a bum living under the bridge until he developed a nose for finding things. Bill has served time for beating up people for a living, but he graduated from bouncer to bartender after he settled a few fights with some weird Zen hum. I was an addict who could have gone postal at the drop of a pin until buying out people I hated became more important than attacking them. At the same time, we've had other inhabitants turn to murder or end up in the homeless camp or lunatic wards. Nothing about this place is predictable except knowing that if you stay, you'll change. Ernesto is new. We're holding out hope he'll improve."

"After I chop off his hands," I said cynically, dismissing Ernesto while trying to imagine Cora's boss as a homeless bum. Frank disappeared into shadows like a spook, but he had an uncanny way of finding things. *Uncanny.* I sighed. That explained a lot. It was harder to believe that gentle, cat-loving Bill had been a goon. "So you have some funny idea that the Zone makes some people better, and that's why it should exist?"

He shrugged. "I *know* it changes people. You'll see for yourself once you open your eyes. Because we're different doesn't mean we should be destroyed."

I'd seen Sarah turn into a chimp. I didn't know if I was ready to see more. And yeah, it didn't seem fair to throw her into a loony bin or to the media if she wasn't hurting anyone.

"But should you allow the innocent to be polluted?" *Innocents like me,* I wanted to shout in fury, but Milo bumped his head against my chin and I behaved myself. Or I was distracted by the drunk hurling obscenities as the bouncer frog-marched him out the door. No one seemed to find the altercation unusual, but I was relieved to see the back of him.

"At this point, the innocents who suffered the initial spills are gone, and mostly what we get are people coming down here looking for something," Andre continued with a shrug. "We get kids occasionally, slumming, but we're not Disney World. They get roughed up and go home. Adults who stray down don't generally hang around unless they're already lost. It's not as if there's anything down here for them."

Was that the drunk's excuse for being obnoxious? He was *lost*? Would the Zone save him from himself? Still not buying it.

"If you hadn't fit in here, you wouldn't have hung around, Clancy." Andre didn't look in the least apologetic for possibly ruining my life by hiring me.

"I think you're making this up as you go along." I tucked Milo into my bag and slid out of the booth. "I have studying to do. Are you going to tell me I can't go home?"

"You'd be better off staying down here now, but if you want to go home, I'll take you. I'll have someone clear the halls at your place before we get there, although the reporters have probably all left by now."

"But you think other interested parties might not have? Really, you have a bigger imagination than I do if you think anyone would bother with someone as insignificant as me. But—since I don't like taking the bus at this hour—your offer of a ride is accepted, thank you. Shall I sneak out the rear exit or make heads turn by marching out the front?"

He pinched the bridge of his nose and stood up with me. "Sneak, please. You're going to be a pain in the ass, aren't you?"

"I haven't decided yet," I said nonchalantly. If he meant to yank my chains, he'd learn I yanked back. "If I can't stay out of trouble by keeping my head down and working hard, then where's the point in keeping my mouth shut?"

Andre didn't even bother to sigh in exasperation but planted his taller breadth between me and the rest of the room as we walked behind the stage of gyrating dancers. I was more aware of him physically than was healthy; there's no explaining hormones.

The evening was young yet, and the girls were barely warming up. There were only two onstage, garbed in harem outfits and lackadaisically writhing around poles to some weird version of Egyptian music. The poles seemed to be writhing back. The guys at the front tables were more interested in their beers and burgers.

Behind the stage was an exit customers weren't allowed to use. The dancers and waitresses mixed in this hall between the club and the kitchen, going out back for a smoke or just taking gossip breaks. A couple of scantily clad waitresses looked up as we passed. I recognized one of them as the one the drunk had pawed, but Andre didn't bother speaking to them, so I followed his example.

Outside, the back lot was cloaked in darkness.

Ernesto was apparently too cheap to spring for bulbs in his security lamps, and ground zero to the harbor had no lighting except a few scattered campfires near the water. Schwartz was watching over Andre's Mercedes in the alley by the Dumpsters. The good detective raised his eyebrows at me, but we didn't exchange greetings. I was beginning to feel like a mafia moll with Andre leading me around and telling me what I could or could not do.

I was too disturbed to complain. I needed to process the overload of information. That there was more to learn, I understood. I just didn't want to know more until I digested what I'd been told. I didn't believe everything Andre said, but I'd seen enough evidence to worry some of it had to be true, no matter how weird.

As we drove away, I saw the fat drunk stagger around the corner. He stared at the Mercedes as we passed by, keeping my fear intact.

When we reached the tenements, I noticed a shiny Escalade had parked next to my Miata. The parking lot sometimes contained a battered gas-guzzler or two, but on the whole, this was a neighborhood of students who preferred to save their money for food, not gas, so we bought small and cheap. Escalades were neither.

I was now officially paranoid about strange cars. Who would be interested in *me,* the Queen of Non-entities? I couldn't tell them anything. I was so ignorant, I didn't know shampoo goo could grow hair. Shouldn't we have been bottling the stuff? Provided we could figure out how to make it, since I was pretty certain the only kind I'd used was from the dollar store, so I didn't know how Zone chemicals could have crept into it.

I still wasn't about to believe in magic, so goo it had to be if I wanted to explain my hair.

Rather than stop near the Escalade, Andre drove through the lot, down the alley, and up to the rear entrance by the garbage cans. He checked his phone, then looked over at me. "Clear now. I can't promise it will be in the morning. I have a vacancy closer to the Zone if you change your mind about the hassle. Any surveillance equipment these people might have won't be as reliable down there."

Surveillance equipment? Now that really was carrying paranoia a little far. It wasn't as if I was on the FBI's most-wanted list.

"I have classes," I responded, too wound up to trash his concerns. "I don't want to waste half my day commuting." Besides that, I was striving for normal. I didn't want to be a mutant. "Thanks for seeing me home, but I've been fine this long. The media leeches will find someone new to suck dry soon enough."

I was almost tempted to lean over and kiss Andre's frown, but I'd had enough shocks for one evening. I'd save my destructive impulses for a better cause.

I slid out, closed the door quietly, and used my key to enter through the back. I hurried up the stairs and checked to see if the corridor was clear. When I reached my door, I locked it behind me with a sigh of relief and let Milo loose to prowl.

Rather than contemplate all the other notions

Andre had planted in my head, I strode straight back to the bedroom and the familiar—Max. I'd left the blanket off the mirror, and the hallucination appeared the instant I knocked, although the cracks strained his image.

"*Stay away from Andre,*" he shouted inside my head. "*He's slime!*"

Well, that was definitely me talking to me.

"At least he's *alive* slime," I retorted, almost enjoying taking out my pent-up anger on a cracked mirror. "Who the devil were you, anyway? *Trust fund,* Max? Do you even know how to be honest?"

The image was actually clear enough for me to imagine an impatient grimace. "*Check Themis.*"

"Who the hell is Themis?" I shouted.

I thought he replied, "*Your grandmother,*" and then he was gone.

I didn't have any grandmothers. These conversations, such as they were, were increasingly frustrating. I flung the blanket back. I didn't want mirrors watching me undress anymore, not after what Andre had insinuated this evening.

The next morning, I wore jeans instead of a skirt, and a T-shirt under my button-down, not my usual law school attire. I flung all my textbooks into the Miata. I had to study every spare minute, and I wouldn't have time to come back home and change before mop duty. I didn't know how I would have time to check out the four names Cora had given me, either. Washing pots at Chesty's would ruin my study time.

I waved at the Escalade. If they wanted to follow me, it was their wasted day, not mine. Maybe I'd bore them into leaving me alone. With a full night's sleep, I was again leaning back toward believing Andre had lived in the Zone too long. So, yeah, I was hallucinating Max. That didn't make me any different than half the population fantasizing over big-screen movie stars.

So maybe shock had affected my hair. That was hardly anything to get crazy about. And this was Baltimore. We got wind and freak storms. Those reporters were just looking for excuses to lose the fight. And the accident was totally Max's fault. I was so not taking the blame for that one. My self-esteem was still quite healthy, thank you very much.

I aced my contract law test and was flying pretty high on ego when I drove the Miata to the Zone. Maybe Detective Schwartz would keep an eye on my car, too, if I parked next to Andre's Mercedes. If the tires melted, I'd sue Andre.

The gray-haired, slump-shouldered man from Lily's was just walking out of the kitchen with a carryout box. He looked at me, then the Miata. "That's one of those plastic cars, isn't it?"

"Tires are rubber. Engine is metal." I defended my hunk of junk.

He nodded. "Not safe," he said, as if agreeing with me. "Plastic wheels might do it. Plastic engine parts . . ." He shook his head and wandered off muttering.

There was one Zone inhabitant who hadn't improved with age. At least now I knew the guy was more curmudgeonly crazy and less threatening crazy. So maybe I was learning more about the Zone, as Andre had said I needed to do. Quite an education.

My cell phone beeped and I frowned. Very few people knew my number besides Max.

An impossibly lengthy text message scrolled across my screen: *Saturn is the planet of justice. It comes around every twenty-eight years to dispense karmic reward and punishment. This time, it comes in conjunction with the asteroids of change. The cycle is just beginning. Your time is almost here.*

Oh, crap. I almost flung the phone over the fence into the biohazard zone. But I couldn't afford a new phone, and after last night, I was almost regretting deleting the other Saturn message.

I checked the sender. *Max.*

My stomach seized in knots until reason began to win out. Max was never parted from his phone—it would have gone up in blue blazes like my car. The Universe, by way of the Zone, was messing with me. The Zone had managed to mix up the numbers. I glanced over my shoulder at the Superfund site over the fence and wondered if someone like the Geek lived back there, playing with electronic transmissions.

Besides, I was only twenty-six—and even if the message was meant for me, what in heck did planets and daughters have to do with each other anyway?

Leaving my books in the minuscule trunk, I slipped in through Chesty's back door, ignoring the dudes in suits leaning against a slightly askew security-lamp pole that seemed to be craning its neck to look at them. I could understand the lamp's curiosity. The dudes looked a whole lot out of place, but at least they weren't kidnapping me and throwing me under a microscope.

On the off chance that someone would feed me lunch, I peered into the kitchen. Sarah was putting together a sandwich under the supervision of a burly cook in a chef's hat and tomato-splattered apron. I was trusting the red was tomatoes.

She waved at me to enter. Not being shy, I helped myself to the loaf of bread on the counter and began building my own lunch out of fresh tomatoes, mozzarella, and basil.

"How long have you been living down here?" I asked Sarah while debating dirtying a frying pan I'd have to clean later. Grilled cheese was better than cold.

"Since I got married, right before the flood," she whispered, casting a glance over her shoulder to the cook who seemed to be in his own world.

Which would have made her something like sixteen when she married, if my guesstimate that she was around my age was anywhere close.

She was so nervous that I didn't want to sound like I was interrogating her, but I trusted anyone better than I did Andre, and it was time I started learning more about my new life.

"So, how long have you been a chimp?" I tried to sound casual.

She grimaced. "Since my husband called me one. I think maybe it's all in my head. Now that he's gone, maybe I can get back my self-respect."

"Gone? To the hereafter?" My suspicion antenna went on alert.

She nodded diffidently. "He beat me up one too many times. I think the chimp strangled him. I woke up with these"—she glanced down at her big breasts—"and Bert was gone. I had a bad dream while I was unconscious, about Bert and a Dumpster, so I checked the one out back. He was in it, looking kind of blue." She looked almost defiant as she finally raised her gaze to me. "He weighed over two hundred pounds. I'm not strong enough to lift that much weight. So I left him there and went looking for a job."

In shock, I absorbed the realization that Sarah had killed her husband and gotten great boobs in return.

12

Aside from learning that Sarah was homicidal and possibly delusional, the rest of my day ran reasonably smoothly. I stationed myself at the bar with the receipts, making myself comfortable with a bottle of water and a stool adjusted to my height. Heeding Andre's warning, I checked that the back door was locked and kept an eye on the front door. I had to leave it open so people could bring me their deposits. I preferred being outdoors in the sunlight to this cave of a place with shifty nudes peering over my shoulder, but I was willing to be cautious. For a while.

After Cora took the locked deposit bag to the bank, I had time to study in my cubicle. Not having to make the deposit or take the bus won me almost an hour of study. Helping myself to soup in the kitchen saved cooking time. Milo found a nest of dirty laundry to sleep in and no one objected to a cat in the kitchen. As Andre had suggested, Ernesto had a way to go before he became a good citizen. Or even civilized. Fortunately, he didn't come in early today.

The kitchen didn't get really busy until after seven, about the time Ernesto finally put in an appearance to tell me to start scrubbing. Carrying my books through the bar, I noticed the tall, drunken bully from yesterday had returned. He grabbed the neckline of one of the older waitresses, and she put his wrist in a grip that should have broken bones. Looked like things were under control. I might have wanted to stomp the laughing blowhard, but it wasn't my place, even though his buffalo head swung to regard me as I passed.

I went out the back and took in a few rays of spring sunshine while I threw my books into the car. I tossed my classic button-down in with them, then tied the laces on the ugly boots with the modified heel required for standing on my feet for hours. I returned inside to cover my jeans and T-shirt with a clean apron from a closet before grabbing a mop and bucket. Since I didn't see Sarah again, I assumed she only worked the day shift. I nodded to a couple of the waitresses, but mostly I kept my head down and my mouth shut.

A restaurant kitchen was its own corner of hell, I decided, mopping up a greasy spill. It was only May, but in here, the heat had already escalated to inferno proportions. Steam spilled from pots on half a dozen flaming burners. Cooks shouted, cursed, and waved knives big enough to chop off heads in a single blow. I didn't know why they weren't throwing bodies out the back door on a regular basis.

I mopped. I scrubbed burned pots. I loaded the dishwashers. I figured out where to find the rubber gloves after my hands turned red and raw. I even cleaned off tables when one of the busgirls quit.

The drunken molester stepped into my path while I was carrying a bin full of dirty dishes.

"You and me, we gotta talk," he said, crowding me with his big stomach. "I got a car outside. You could make some money."

That was so disgusting that I didn't bother answering. I trod on his toe with my heavy heel and skirted past him as he winced and stumbled back.

The midweek crowd died down after ten, and Ernesto told me to go home. He was not only uncivilized but cheap. It would take me months to earn Geek Boy's fee if I only worked three hours a night for a lousy minimum wage. I needed to find out who had been in that hit-and-run limo, if only for the sake of those kids. I couldn't make myself believe it had anything to do with Max's death, but now that I knew Max had enemies . . . I couldn't ignore the possibility.

Too wiped to debate whether this was a wise use of my time, I dumped my apron and gloves, gathered up Milo and my messenger bag, and headed out back to my Miata. I'd only seen Schwartz once during the evening, when he'd poked his head into the kitchen to grab a burger. I hoped he'd been patrolling the dark alley so I would still have wheels.

Maybe if I drove my car down here often enough, the engine would start talking to me. Or repair itself? Something truly helpful would be nice for once.

The stench of hot grease followed me into the foggy spring night, mixing with a strong odor of chemicals unable to dissipate in the humidity. Milo growled and my gut did a little gnawing. Ridiculous to think of a kitten as a guard cat, but cats had good instincts. Ernesto was apparently too cheap to repair or turn on the security lights, or maybe he didn't want to encourage smokers to linger. The blue glow of the buildings did little more than cast eerie shadows through the fog. This was the first time I'd been exposed to the full effect of the ultraviolet light, and despite the warm night, I shivered at the weirdness.

Andre's Mercedes was gone, replaced by what I assumed was the club owner's big honking Hummer. Small weenies compensate with big cars, right? My Miata was closest to the building, with the hulking SUV blocking most of the alley behind me. I could get out, just barely.

Still checking warily around me, I rolled back the tarp protecting the seats and set my purse and Milo on the nest the cover made on the floor. Before I could climb in, I heard a muffled shriek from somewhere past the Hummer, in the thick shadows behind the garbage. Already nervous, I jumped nearly a mile at the sound.

I should have climbed in the car and hit the gas. But I was constitutionally unable to ignore trouble, even though the Dumpster loomed like an ogre in my mind. After the invisible-thief incident and Sarah's story about finding her husband in one of those garbage heaps, I was beginning to look at the big green boxes as hungry vultures lurking to scoop up all evidence of dark deeds. I didn't want to face any more bizarre scenes, and now the giant bins had started shrieking. I would be imagining bulging eyeballs popping out of the rusted sides if I didn't leave soon.

But the rhythmic pounding noise I heard next was of this earth and not my imagination.

It sounded very much like a metal bed rocking against a wall during a moment of heated passion, but the frightened, angry cries accompanying the pounding were definitely not the utterances of consensual sex.

Red rage obliterated both my common sense and my head-down, mouth-closed attitude. I grabbed a tire iron from my trunk and eased down the trash-strewn alley to the far side of the garbage bin.

In the feeble blue light emanating from the building next door, I could make out two shadows: one big, bulky, and upright; the other slender and up against the stinking bin. The bulky shadow had one hand clamped against the smaller one's mouth, holding her pinned and muffling her shrieks. I really didn't need to see what the other hand was doing. The woman's bare legs and struggles told me more than I needed to know.

My hands tightened around the iron. I admit, I had an anger management problem. I'd worked on it. But at times like this . . . maybe the planet Saturn took over. That was as good an excuse as any. All the martial arts training in the world couldn't guarantee a gimpy shrimp might trounce an aroused creep three times her size, but I had no intention of running from this trouble.

I couldn't approach without being seen, but the bastard was too busy wrestling with his belt to stop because of a skinny shadow racing at him. Not until I screamed my fury and swung with all my strength, applying the tire iron to his spine, did he take notice—big-time.

He reared back and grabbed for my weapon. "Whadya hafta do that for?" he roared, grabbing the tire iron and jerking.

I barely had a second to recognize the drunken bully from the bar before reacting. He had weight on his side. I had leverage on mine. Gripping the iron as hard as I could, I applied a swift sideways kick with my boot to his kneecaps that unbalanced him more.

While the brute's attention was diverted, his victim crumpled to the ground, crying. She wasn't much help as I triumphantly wrenched the iron from a sweaty clasp. My kick was just enough to propel the hulk backward but not knock him over—giving me the opportunity to aim at his balls with my deadly heel.

I missed, catching him on the thigh with my heavy

boot instead. He roared in pain, but, recovering his balance, he succeeded in yanking the tire iron away this time. "You!" he roared. "I just wanted to talk to you." He swung at my head with my weapon.

"You call this *talking*?" I ducked. My aching leg crumpled, and I ended up face-first in the dirt, spitting gravel. I didn't have time to fear that my presence was the reason this monster was here hurting someone. Muttering epithets, I rolled as he came after me again.

"Freaking creeps give us all a bad name!" he shouted, bringing the iron down. "I could have made you a good deal on the boxes."

Boxes? Great, even the rapists down here were more nutso than usual.

I wasn't really listening while fighting for my life. I dodged and swung my foot to slam his shin with the built-up heel on my bad leg. Rubber bounced off the tire iron he was swinging, but I clipped his kneecap. He was so close, I could smell his sweat and beer breath.

An unearthly shriek, followed by a very human howl, had me scrambling backward, looking for banshees or wildcats. At this point, I was even prepared for demons.

In the blue light, I stared in astonishment at a streak of giant snarling fur landing on my attacker's back and ripping at his ear. Still howling, the brute reached over his shoulder, grabbed the animal, and slammed the creature against a wall, where it slid lifelessly down the glowing blue bricks. My fury escalated back to red rage.

"Damn you!" I shrieked, recovering from my shock. I leaped to my feet and grabbed the weapon he'd dropped. I wished my atrophied leg muscles were stronger so I could drop-kick the bastard into next week. "If that's my cat, you're going to hell!"

Not rational conversation, but blinding wrath filled my head, replacing my brains. I swung the iron straight at his midsection with my full hundred pounds behind it. I was weeping, cursing, and wanting to see if that had really been my brave Milo rushing to my rescue, but first I had to eliminate a worthless, drunken blob.

"Damn you to hell!" I shouted as I swung. Using my martial arts training, I visualized the iron as a giant broadsword to add strength to my blow.

The iron hit solid blubber and—*kept on going*. Unbalanced by a swing I hadn't expected to complete, I lurched forward, falling on my hands. Shaking my head to clear the ringing in my ears and my blurred vision, I scrambled to my knees to see from which direction I'd be assaulted next. And met silence.

Blubber Man's victim had stopped sobbing to stare past me. With trepidation, I followed the direction of her gaze. A very large, very still body lay in the gravel . . . in two pieces.

But it was dark and foggy. I could have been mistaken.

A kitty whimper turned my eyes away from the impossible.

I could swear, in the dim light, the animal that had leaped to my rescue was half as big as me, but that must have been the adrenaline talking. Over by the wall, poor little Milo struggled to his feet, then limped over to lick my hand. The ruff on his neck was standing straight up, and I petted it down, checking to see if he'd been injured.

A weak flashlight beam emerged from the darkness and a familiar baritone shouted, "What's going on out here?"

I looked up into the barrel of Detective Schwartz's gun. He towered over us, legs spread in proper defensive position, arms outstretched with his weapon aimed at my head. A gorgeous but useless hunk.

"Next time, move faster, Leo," I snarled, cuddling my kitty and scooting back to the waitress huddled against the Dumpster. I'd brought trouble here. Somehow, this was all my fault.

The waitress I'd saved was weeping, one of her false eyelashes falling down her mascara-streaked cheek. There hadn't been much to her costume to start with. What was left had been shredded. "Go get the biggest tablecloth you can find, Schwartz. The fun is all over."

"He's dead, isn't he?" she whispered hoarsely as the good detective quickly grasped the situation and obeyed orders.

"I don't think I want to look to find out," I whispered back. "Did you see what happened?"

She shook her head. "There was a horrible howl, and this giant beast leaped from the wall, and he went down. That's all I know. And I hope he's *dead*," she said fiercely.

If he was a goner, I had a nagging suspicion I was the beast that had killed him. Milo could barely kill a mouse. I was still too stunned and appalled to fully grasp what had happened, but I recognized opportunity when it knocked. The beast theory might let me off Schwartz's hook.

"A beast, like a wildcat or something? Or maybe something with a sword?" I suggested.

She nodded vigorously. "It had to be something awful. The bastard was bigger than both of us put together."

Yeah, I agreed with that. "Like a swamp monster with an ax. Whatever it was, saved our lives." I was going to hell for this, I knew it. But I was tired of people looking at me as if I'd killed Max and thrown reporters to the winds. I wasn't taking the blame for this one.

Even though I was pretty damned certain that this time, I really was guilty. I just didn't know how it was possible. I might have been able to break boards with my hands, but it took a lot more than a tire iron to sever spines and several hundreds pound of lard and muscle. And now I'd have to live with a man's blood on my hands, and the fear of whoever had sent him—because I was rapidly concluding he was one of the goons Andre was trying to protect me from.

What the devil had he meant about boxes? Now I'd never know.

Schwartz reappeared with a paramedic, a uniformed cop, and aprons and towels to cover both victim and rapist. Chesty's didn't do tablecloths.

I let Ernesto identify the perp as the customer his bouncer had thrown out for drunken lewdness.

Schwartz retrieved the corpse's wallet and identified him as some minor bureaucrat in a quasi-governmental organization. Why would he be looking for me? I was starting to shiver with shock and wasn't entirely certain I wanted to know.

It took two men to load the body parts onto a stretcher and haul the massive body away. The paramedics were trying to decide between ax wounds and machetes. They weren't buying swords. Nothing explained the lack of blood splatter. No logic applied. Maybe the Zone was thirsty and took the blood itself.

No one considered either of us large enough to have done the damage, particularly since there was no weapon beyond the Miata's feeble tire iron—which might have accounted for the corpse's bruises but not the slicing in two.

I learned that the waitress's name was Diane and that she'd gone outside for a smoke when she'd been attacked. She swore I'd saved her from certain death and that some avenging beast had leaped tall buildings to save us both.

Superstition and legend could easily grow out of the fires dancing along the dark harbor water beyond the pier. Schwartz scowled at the improbability of the swamp monster rumor Diane had repeated after my suggestion, but everyone cast wary glances over their shoulders at the shadows playing across chemical-laden ground zero nonetheless.

Ernesto tried to look down my shirt. The cop took notes, and the last paramedic eventually persuaded Diane into an ambulance.

I refused to do another emergency room. I'd spent nearly a year in hospitals with my splintered leg. Even if I'd had insurance, which I didn't, I wasn't entering one of those mausoleums again if I could prevent it. The ambulance attendants gave up arguing and painted my hands and knees with antibacterial ointments, clucking over my scars. And my tire iron got confiscated.

To top off the good time, Andre arrived just as Schwartz was grudgingly allowing me to go home. He spun his Mercedes into the alley, blocked my escape, and climbed out, still tucking his silk shirt into his creased trousers.

"I'm not going through it all again," I said defensively. I jerked my head toward Schwartz. "Ask him. Now move your vehicle and let me go home."

"That's our delicate rose," Andre said sardonically, glaring at me. "Have you patched up the thorn wounds yet, Schwartz?"

It was unfair. They were both wide-shouldered men, bigger than me, one dark, one light, both scowling as if I was no more than a fly in their soup. I was too tired to lash out at both of them. I probably had to face an angry Max in the mirror when I went home. Why didn't I deserve a man who offered reassuring words and comforting hugs after I was nearly killed trying to help somebody?

"She saved Diane's life tonight," Schwartz said unexpectedly. "You need to have more security back here. I can't be everywhere at once, and Ernesto keeps forgetting to fix the lights."

"We could post an army and that wouldn't keep Clancy out of trouble," Andre growled. "If you have any influence, persuade her to stay home."

"Me?" Schwartz asked in surprise. "What influence would I have?"

"I'm not a bone to pick over, you know," I said, climbing into my car and gunning the engine. "So if you don't get out of my way, I'll have to run over you."

So maybe I wasn't the kind who needed hugs and sweet words.

Andre reached over the door and confiscated my keys, tossing them to Schwartz. When I jumped out of the Miata, ranting, the good detective threw me over his shoulder. I whacked his back with my fists for good measure, but I didn't have much energy left.

Andre indicated the Mercedes and pulled a large bill out of his pocket, handing it to Schwartz in exchange for depositing me in the front seat of the expensive two-seater. I slumped down and sulked. "I want my cat," I insisted before Andre sat down.

Milo was already half out of the Miata. Schwartz scooped him up and dropped him into my lap. I cuddled purring fur against my chest all the way home, refusing to listen to Andre's ranting about getting help next time before I did anything foolish. My shirt had streaks of blood on it from Milo's paws when I finally let myself into my apartment.

I'd killed a man. I'd taken a life. And I was pretty sure I'd damned him to hell.

But more important, I needed to know: what *was* I?

13

Thunder cracked overhead, jarring me out of my nightmares. I glanced at the clock and winced. I'd forgotten to set the alarm last night, and I was late for my first class.

Anticipating the usual morning pain of rearranging damaged leg muscles, I eased out of bed. I stumbled awkwardly and almost tripped over Milo, who had made a nest out of clothes I'd abandoned on the floor. While I grabbed the dresser to stay upright, he stretched and gave me an evil eye. I'd left a window open, and the air coming in was cool. Summer hadn't quite reached Baltimore after all.

Grateful that my leg wasn't cranky from the cold, I rushed to dress for class, not bothering to shower, since I didn't need the steam to be functional this morning. I didn't even stop to see if Max had left more messages in the medicine cabinet mirror.

I yanked on a pair of khakis . . . and stared when the hems rose three inches above my ankles. I yanked them back off again, cursing cheap laundry machines . . . and blinked in gut-wrenching disbelief.

My bad leg was whole.

No scars twisted my thigh into misshapen flesh. My leg hadn't looked so good since before the cop had knocked me down the jail's mile-high concrete steps.

I stomped my foot, *hard*. No pain. Real muscles. I squeezed them to be certain. Real flesh, solid muscle. Not a wrinkle or scar to be seen—on a leg that had undergone thirteen surgeries and countless pins.

I threw the khakis on the floor and went back to bed. Maybe I needed to wake up again.

Except as soon as my head hit the pillow, the mindless rush of I'm-late panic morphed into shocking comprehension—*last night's nightmare hadn't been a figment of my overworked imagination.*

I'd *killed* a man. Somehow. And my leg was healed? Like Sarah had grown boobs.

My stomach lurched, and I pulled the covers over my head to make the world go away.

My cell phone began ringing before I could settle all the ugliness scuttling around inside my skull. I pulled the pillow over my ears and debated moving to Seattle. Maybe I could steal an RV and hit the road.

Someone began pounding on my door—loudly. The neighbors got ticked if anyone got too rowdy. I was almost looking forward to being run out of the tenement on a rail. But not this close to graduation.

"Go get 'em, Milo," I muttered, dragging myself from my cozy cave into the chilly air.

Milo strutted off, stubby tail up, just as if he'd understood.

I slept nude and didn't own a bathrobe. I got dressed, tugging on a tank top and broomstick skirt—which nearly met my kneecaps instead of hanging to my newly developed calves. I could wear high heels now. Max would have been thrilled.

I cast a snarly glance at the blanket-covered mirror and trudged to the front room.

I peered through the peephole and saw Jane, the reporter. With a sigh, I let her in and locked the door behind her. I headed for the kitchen without speaking. I needed caffeine before I could even begin to be coherent. Looked like I wouldn't be making class today.

"You were there last night," Jane said without preamble. "You must have seen the monster. I *need* this story. I get paid by the word and I *need* rent money. Tell me everything."

I yawned and filled the yard sale coffeemaker I'd bought for a quarter. "Truth or a long story to fill the pages?" I asked.

She actually hesitated. I glared blearily at her and got down two mugs. I could reach the shelf without standing on my toes. Even with a straight leg, how could I be three inches taller? I wanted to pound my head against the cabinet to see if my brains were still inside my skull, but I resisted.

Jane shrugged and pulled out her tiny tape recorder. "Give me your version of the truth, and I'll find the other witnesses and get theirs. That ought to make for lots of words."

"The only witnesses were me and the victim. And the dead guy," I amended. I wanted to be a lawyer, after all. I ought to be good at details. I didn't think I'd give her all of them—like the perp wanting to talk to me about boxes. *My fault* warred with *Why me?* in my uncaffeinated brain. "There isn't much to tell. Are your guys responsible for the suits hanging around the Zone these days?" I could at least attempt to make some sense of events.

"My guys?" she asked, startled. "I don't have guys. I told my editor there was something freaky happening in the Zone and that I wanted to do a story, but he's put me on human interest. Says I'm not tough enough to do investigative reporting. The only reason I'm here is because I'm the only one you'll let in."

"Well, tell him you're the only one we'll talk to in the Zone, and see how that flies. No one will talk to reporters down there, and we can spot them a mile off." Another lie. I was going straight to hell.

I debated adding Splenda—lifted from IHOP— or real sugar to my coffee, wondering which added more chemicals to my chemically enhanced body, and decided to heck with it and added sugar. I had no milk. I handed a mug to Jane and sipped from mine. It didn't improve my humor by much.

She poured two packets of Splenda into hers and stirred. "I could try that. We don't have much money for real investigations."

"Whatever. It's not as if anyone can explain what goes on in the Zone. Last night I hit a rapist with a tire iron. He knocked me down. A howling cat leaped out of the darkness. Or maybe it was a panther. Next thing we knew, the guy was dead in pieces in the alley. I'm pretty sure even a panther can't cause that kind of damage." I refrained from mentioning my second tire iron blow. Maybe I wasn't cut out to be a lawyer. Maybe I really was Satan's daughter, even if the poor devil couldn't have kids.

"And you didn't see a raging monster?" she asked in disappointment.

"I'd have shit my pants if I had—the guy was up, then he was down. It was pretty anticlimactic after thinking I was going to be dead in a few minutes. Maybe we have ghosts. Maybe he was a robot."

If I started enough rumors, the media would have something more fun to focus on than bothering someone as boring as me.

I didn't know if it would be safe to mention that there hadn't been as much blood as I'd expected. On film, there was blood spatter everywhere. This guy had been like a hot-air balloon, except for the blood on Milo's paws.

Hot-air balloon. I'd called him a blowhard. Maybe he was one of Andre's weirdnesses. I got thicker hair,

Sarah got to be a chimp, and this guy turned into hot air. That totally worked for me.

The legs and new height . . . I didn't know what to make of that just yet. Not after suffering painful treatments by teams of doctors over the years, all to no avail save for developing a resistance to most helpful drugs.

Jane nodded and took notes. "Can you introduce me to the waitress? And Detective Schwartz? Maybe more evidence has come to light."

"I usually don't head down there until after lunch." I glanced at the rain sheeting the dirty windows. I couldn't drive the Miata in rain without getting soaked. It would be a good study day. Or maybe I could start checking out those names Cora had given me.

I was trying very hard to pretend everything was normal, that I hadn't grown three inches overnight. I kept swinging my leg, waiting for it to lock up and hurt. I wanted to try knee bends. I wanted to run, like I used to do. I'd been on the track team at one high school I attended.

At the same time, I was totally terrified of what was happening to me. But I'd spent a lifetime presenting a fearless attitude to the world. Couldn't change now. In fact, I itched to stand up to Andre and verify I could almost look him in the eye.

Jane made a moue of dissatisfaction at my uselessness. "Would you happen to know Schwartz's phone number? Or the waitress's? I have to pick up my kid at day care at two, so now is the only time I can talk to them."

"Nope, and you're not going to find either of them at work in the mornings. You might find Schwartz at the precinct, but I'm betting he won't talk while on duty. I don't know Diane's schedule, or if she'll even come back to work. I wouldn't, if I were her."

"Dang, maybe I ought to just move down there. I'm supposed to be out of my apartment by Sunday unless I make my rent." Looking as if someone had just run over her dog, Jane tucked her notebook away and blew on her coffee.

"The Zone's not a good choice for a kid," I warned, trying not to sympathize. "Why don't you ask my landlord? This place is cheap, if you don't mind students barfing in the parking lot after ball games."

"I already checked. No vacancies. Student housing goes fast. It's the Zone or the streets. I'm only kidding myself to believe I can blow a near-rape story into enough words to make the rent, even if Schwartz claims he tracked a monster into the harbor and sailed the seven seas in pursuit."

"Andre's been wanting me to move closer to work," I told her, mentally rolling my eyes at myself.

Maybe instead of law, I should have taken astrology. Maybe then I'd have a better understanding of why I do what I do. The world was a lousy place, and I knew I couldn't change it. And yet time after time, I kept trying.

Maybe it was all about Andre and my new horniness. That would make some tiny bit of sense, at least.

"He says he knows a place. Maybe if I move down

there, you could sublet this place until my lease is up." Given my test schedule, I really had only a week left of school. I could commute for finals.

I wasn't entirely certain I wanted to leave my place behind, but I guess I just decided her kid having a roof over its head was more important than my neuroses.

She stared at me in astonishment. I understood the reaction. I was pretty astounded myself.

"You really mean that?" she asked. "You're not just saying that because you feel sorry for me or you want to get rid of me or because there are monsters under the bed or something?"

She didn't know how close she'd hit home. "Feel free to look under the bed. Check the mirrors, too," I advised, figuring I'd play it safe before uprooting my life. "I'll be taking the furniture if I can find a truck, but the dust bunnies are all yours."

She glanced around my tiny kitchen/living room combo. "It's bigger than my place," she whispered uncertainly. "I can't give you a deposit."

"Go look at the bedroom. There's only one," I warned. "You got me out of bed, so the place is a mess. It's not the Hilton."

I finished my coffee while she was taking my advice and checking the bathroom and bedroom. I didn't hear any shrieks at the mirrors. Milo sauntered out, looked at me cross-eyed, and checked his food bowl.

I had an uneasy feeling that I'd stopped keeping my head down and my mouth shut. Max's death had shaken something loose inside me.

Or maybe now that I had hair and legs, I wanted

to show off. Idly wondering how long I'd have to live in the Zone to add two or three sizes to my bust, I abruptly realized something terrible—I'd grown hair after Max died and legs after *killing a rapist*. Something similar had happened with Sarah, after she killed her abusive husband. . . .

That was just too creepy for words.

That Seattle idea was more attractive by the minute. Pity I had no money.

Moving to the Zone wasn't any smarter, really, but I wanted to do it, which might have been even weirder than growing legs overnight.

Andre's notion that only people who belonged in the Zone stayed in the Zone came back to bite me. After I'd found the job with Andre, I had never attempted to look for a better place to work. Even when I'd known working at Chesty's was way below my skill level, I hadn't asked elsewhere. I'd been in Baltimore for two years. I knew my way around now. I could find better. I just didn't want to, it seemed.

After spending a lifetime traveling the country, I had found a home in an industrial waste zone. I was seriously damaged. Which was Andre's point.

But now that the caffeine was kicking in, my mind was perking up. I checked out the front window. The Escalade was still out there.

Jane was looking considerably more chipper when she emerged from exploring my limited territory. Apparently Max hadn't decided to leer at *her*.

"Your bathroom mirror is damaged," she told me cheerfully. "But your plumbing is better than mine. If you're really sure you want to do this, I have a friend with a truck who can help you move," she said with the first excitement I'd seen her express. "Have you looked at the place you're considering?"

I didn't even know where Andre's vacancy was. I didn't know of any apartments along Edgewater Street, and he'd said it was just outside the Zone. I supposed being closer to work would save me time. And Andre's nagging.

Since it didn't look like I was making it to class, anyway, I dug my cell phone out of my messenger bag. I checked to see who had called earlier, but it was an anonymous number. I dialed Discreet Detection and Cora answered on the first ring.

"Girl, you gotta tell me what happened last night! Rumors are flying every which way."

"If I make up a really good story, will you find out if there are any vacant apartments down that way for me? Andre's been nagging, and I've found a good renter for mine."

Cora hooted. "That man's on the make. Watch out, girl. He owns a place just at the end of the street, one block up from the harbor, behind the storage depot. Nice place, too. Make him give you a good deal."

Curiosity, my besetting sin. A *nice* place?

Before I could decide if I really wanted to do this, the doorbell rang. Jane looked at me questioningly, and I shrugged. Hanging up on Cora, I sauntered over to the peephole and checked out the newcomer. *Crap, Schwartz.* Maybe my new abode would be the county jail.

I unfastened the door and let him in. "Just in time to be interviewed by the *Baltimore Edition*," I warned him. "Need caffeine?"

"No, thank you." He glanced at Jane, who was hastily gathering her notebook and pen, even though she probably didn't recognize her prey. He was wearing his tie today, and a long-sleeved blue shirt. Very official and quite yummy.

I was definitely horny. Authority figures are usually not my cuppa, and cops were on my shit list.

"Jane Claremont, Detective Schwartz. If you're taking me to jail, Jane would like to have my apartment." I checked my refrigerator for something Studly Doright might drink. "I've got tomato juice." I wouldn't try to guess how old. Max had liked an occasional Bloody Mary.

"Water is fine. Good to meet you, Miss Claremont." But Schwartz wasn't looking at Jane. His gaze had fastened on me. On my untethered breasts, to be precise.

Now that I was taller, he finally noticed I was female? Or had he been put off by my limp?

"I need to ask a few more questions to clarify my report," he said, dragging out his notebook.

"I don't think I'm any clearer on what happened this morning than I was last night," I informed him, presenting him with a bottle of water. I was getting more careful about stocking the pure stuff.

"Friend of yours?" He glanced at Jane with suspicion.

He was warning me, but I had nothing to hide and Jane needed the story.

"She's good," I assured him.

Miraculously, he took me at my word instead of snarling, the reaction I usually got from cops.

"Diane said the perp attacked her when she went out for a smoke," he continued. "She fought him, but he held his arm against her throat. Then you arrived and struck him, apparently with the tire iron." He looked up for me to confirm his statement.

"Sounds right to me, although he was covering her mouth by the time I arrived. She was trying to scream. I almost didn't go look. That's a scary alley back there." I didn't mention I'd grabbed the tire iron out of a fear the Dumpster was screaming.

He scowled. "You could have gone back inside for help."

"And he could have strangled Diane while I tried to get someone's attention." I glared back. I think my newly perfect hair had infected my brain. I shouldn't have been arguing with an officer of the law. I *knew* better.

Jane was discreetly scribbling, but Schwartz ignored her. Everything we said aloud was in the police report, available to the public. Jane couldn't read our scowls.

He returned to reading his notes. "So, he knocked you out, and the next thing you remember is waking up to find him sprawled in the alley, dead."

I hadn't said that. He raised his baby blues to pin me into silence. Ah, maybe he *did* realize there was a reporter in the room, and he was planting his own version of the story. So who was he protecting, me, the Zone, or himself from the laughter of his fellow cops?

"More or less," I agreed cautiously. "Does the guy have a family?"

"Not on record. He was just out on bond after a minor sex offense."

"A government official arrested for a sex offense, and he's still got a job?" I asked in disbelief. "Who did he pay off for that and what does it have to do with the Zone?" My suspicion-ometer cranked up. Maybe Andre was right to be paranoid.

Schwartz shook his head at me. He'd revealed as much as he'd intended.

"We don't know why he was down there." He tucked his notebook back in his shirt pocket.

The creep had been down there for me. Someone had sent a sex offender after *me*. Someone in government? Who wanted boxes? They didn't have enough boxes of their own?

Schwartz had come down here to feed me the story that would go into official reports, not to ask questions. How was I supposed to take that?

With relief, for now. I didn't need any more media haunting my hall. Which returned me to the task at hand. I gestured for the good detective to follow me to the front room. Jane tagged along. Still astounded that I was feeling no pain, I pointed out the Escalade in the parking lot. "One of yours?"

He looked at me in disbelief. "You're kidding, right? The budget's so tight even the chief is driving a Mustang. Cadillacs aren't in the picture." He took another look, frowned, and began prowling my living room, looking at light fixtures and electric outlets. "I changed my mind. Want to fix me a cup of joe before I head out?"

Jane and I looked at each other. I caught on first. He was looking for bugs! Shaken, I played along with his act. "Sure, take it black?"

He didn't answer, so I rattled around in the kitchen. I turned on my MP3 speakers and added background music. Those bastards in the SUV were *listening* to me?

They'd heard me talking about moving to the Zone. Crap.

Jane started to speak, but I waved her quiet. "Cora says the vacancy's been filled," I told her, shaking my head to indicate it hadn't. "Maybe you ought to move in here. I just need a place to sleep and the couch is comfortable. I can study down at the bar. With two of us paying rent, we'll be able to get ahead."

Her eyes widened but watching Schwartz crawling around behind my furniture, she played along. "Really? You wouldn't mind? That's fantastic! Thank you so much!"

She was kind of overdoing the enthusiasm but if anyone was listening, they wouldn't catch that. Schwartz straightened and pointed at a device hidden in the outlet behind my couch. He began examining the overhead lights and found another in the burned-out socket of the kitchen light.

"I have an old sleeper bed I can give you," he said, as if he were part of the conversation. "I'd feel a lot better if you both had company. The world isn't safe anymore."

It wouldn't be safe for those creeps in the Escalade if I took a tire iron to their heads. But Schwartz had taken my weapon. He glared at me as if he knew what I was thinking. Maybe I could wish for legs that didn't need shaving while I killed the eavesdropping creeps.

Oh, holy crappola. *I'd wished for stronger legs last night when I was beating off the swamp monster.*

So not helpful. I sighed and finished my coffee and tried not to remember what I had been thinking before Max combusted. "Gotta study, friends. I appreciate the support and all. Might take you up on that sleeper, Schwartz. If you have any more questions, give me a call."

He jotted a note and passed it over. *I'll check out the license plates. Don't touch the bugs yet.*

I signaled agreement with a salute. The instant he left, I grabbed Milo by the scruff and added him to my bag. We needed to get the heck out of Dodge. Jane and I were going exploring for a new place to crash.

14

I sent Jane out to make a show of driving away, then had her circle back behind the block. Pulling on a rain slicker with a hood to conceal my easily identifiable messenger bag, I carried out a bag of trash, heaved it in the garbage, and kept on going, as if I were any of a dozen tenants scurrying for the bus stop. Maybe my new height and lack of limp would add further camouflage.

She picked me up at the corner, and we wheeled away, hopefully without anyone following.

"What was all that about?" she demanded as soon as we were out of sight of the tenement.

"Absolutely no idea." I threw back the stifling hood and directed her to the donut shop, where I sprang for an assortment. Sugar was definitely required to feed the adrenaline rush. "I asked you about the men showing up in the Zone. If those aren't reporters stalking me, I have no clue who they are or who is bugging my apartment."

"Rich people," she said through a mouthful of jelly cream. "Not us."

Yeah, I was getting that impression. The only rich people I knew of were Max's family. Why would they be spying on me?

I didn't even bother questioning how they'd got into my place to bug it. The super had a key. They had money to stuff his pockets. Voilà. I'd never been concerned about lack of security because I never thought myself interesting enough to be a target of thieves, much less spies. The times, they were a'changing.

"That seals it," I said. "I'm finding a new place. When you move in, we'll make a show of having some guys over to childproof all the sockets. You can wonder about the strange little devices and yank them out."

She nodded warily. "Okay, but how will you move without anyone knowing where you're moving to?"

"I'll work on it." I tore viciously at an apple fritter. I really wanted answers, but I had a gut feeling that I was the one who had to supply them. *Me*, the bonehead who wished for legs and miraculously got them, but didn't know how. I just couldn't comprehend events not covered in books. My legal mind preferred orderly explanations.

Maybe Andre had a point about my permanent student status. A man who was occasionally right was pretty scary.

Driving to the south end of the Zone and up a hilly street in the direction Cora had given us, we spotted the row houses at the same time. I had never been this far down the harbor. Had no reason to go there. Below us and along the waterline was the foggy miasma that covered the official environmental hazard zone of burned-out storage tanks. On high-humidity days, the vapors from the chemical plants hung low.

Above the fog we could gaze at the fabulous view of fishing boats bobbing on white-capped water, and I vowed to explore the sights outside the Zone more often.

At the top of the hill were grand old brick Victorian row houses with big bay windows on the second floor overhanging the wide porches on the first. The trim on all of them had been painted in funky rainbow colors, making me think different people owned each house, but chances were good in this neighborhood that they each contained several apartments. I didn't see any vacancy signs.

"I'll have to track down Andre," I said in disappointment. My heart had gone pitter-patter at the sight of these substantial homes, and my territorial instincts were screaming *I want*. For a change, it wasn't Andre I wanted. I wanted a real home like these. One without electronic bugs and SUVs in the yard. But I was seriously resisting asking Andre for anything. I didn't want to give him any ideas.

"Maybe we could ask someone?" Jane said tentatively.

She probably had as much house hunger as I did. She had a kid to think about, after all, and she looked as if she was about to drool, so I nodded agreement.

She parked her rusting Kia across the street from the houses. This side of the street wasn't very promising, consisting mostly of abandoned shops and warehouses with boarded up windows. Andre probably owned them, too. He seemed to own everything down here. That might be convenient in keeping out government nosiness, but not so much if Andre became my privacy-invader.

Could he possibly own all the houses, too? Wondering which one might be his so I could avoid it, I perused my choices. I studied the windows, looking for ones without curtains.

"The blue and green one," I decided. "No window coverings on the second floor, and the flowers in the window boxes are dead."

Jane whistled admiringly. "You ought to be the reporter, not me."

"Yeah, well, let's not get our hopes up. The foundation shrubbery is pretty tattered, so the whole house may be abandoned. Let's knock and see if we can stir the spooks."

I think I meant that literally. Seeing these gorgeous homes sitting here amid the wreckage of an industrial slum was a little surreal, a little rainbow of optimism.

True, this street was on a hill above the Zone as I knew it, but this end of the harbor had never been a good place to live, even before the chemical flood. Who built expensive homes above storage depots?

Of course, if these really had been here since the late 1800s, then maybe the area hadn't been that bad then. Maybe ship captains had lived here. I really needed to learn my Baltimore history.

Milo peered out of my messenger bag as we crossed the street. The silence was awesome. It was too far from the interstate to hear the traffic, and the wrong end of the harbor to hear the equipment at the factories on the north side of the Zone. Still, I doubted my ability to afford the place, even if it was in a bad part of town.

Crossing the street, dodging raindrops, I felt as if we were being watched, but between Andre's tales and this morning's electronic-bug discovery, I had good reason for my paranoia. At least there weren't any news vans. I was already trying to figure out how I could move without anyone following me.

"If I do this, you have to promise you won't tell anyone where I've gone," I said as we stepped up onto a spacious front porch dotted with clay pots of dead plants.

"Yeah, I got that message," Jane said with a shrug. "The only media tracking you now are the rags. And me. I have no incentive to aid my competition. I can't help with the spies, though."

"Maybe I'll get a new phone, too." I was really liking the idea of being anonymous again. I looked for a doorbell and, not finding one, used the iron knocker and shivered a little. I refused to believe that it was from fear. It was just cool on the porch. I shouldn't have left the slicker in the car.

Jane was only wearing a tank top and didn't seem to feel the chill. Maybe I was just feeling a little like a trick-or-treater on Halloween. Except my new legs and swishy hair reminded me that I was more likely the ghoul than the little kid at the door.

Feeling sufficiently strange about not looking like myself, I nearly jumped out of my wedge-heeled sandals when the door finally creaked open a crack. One faded blue eye peered through the opening.

"What do you want?" a querulous old voice asked.

"I was told you might have a vacant apartment," I replied insouciantly. Lying seemed to be coming to me naturally lately. Of course, given my current circumstances, who wouldn't shade the truth a little?

"Who told you?" she demanded.

I could mention Andre and see if she slammed the door in my face or opened it wide. But I was tired of relying on my boss, and if invoking his name was the only way to get a place down here, I didn't want any part of it. I shrugged and started to turn away. "If I'm wrong, sorry to have bothered you."

"Wait." She fumbled at a chain lock. "You look like nice girls, but I don't have anything with two bedrooms."

Not daring to hope, I turned back to the door. "Jane is just helping me look. I'll be the only tenant."

The door opened to reveal a short stout granny

with a head full of graying curls and no front teeth. "No boyfriend?" she asked suspiciously.

Except in my mirror. "No, ma'am. Just me. I go to school and work, so you'll hardly ever see me." Until the week after finals, anyway.

She narrowed her eyes and studied both of us but moved out of the way to let us in. "I'm real careful about tenants," she warned. "I can't do the repairs, so you have to be able to do your own."

I scarcely heard the warning. The foyer paneling was gorgeous dark hardwood. So was the magnificent staircase. I'd never lived in a place with so much wood and had no idea what kind it might be. It needed dusting. And waxing. Apparently she didn't do maintenance, either. Cobwebs decorated the high ceiling and the ornate brass chandelier. Substantial six-paneled doors on either side of the foyer concealed the downstairs rooms. A hall beside the stairs led to the back of the house.

"Spooky," Jane murmured as the old lady limped toward the stairs.

Max in the mirror was spooky. Cobwebs weren't.

"I'm Tina Clancy." I introduced myself and held out my hand to the old lady. "Your home is lovely."

She straightened a little and shook my hand. "Pearl Bodine, dear. My lumbago won't let me go upstairs anymore. I don't know what you'll find up there. The last tenant disappeared before his rent was up. I still owe him his deposit."

That wasn't real promising, but the word *deposit* had me on edge. I didn't have one if Jane couldn't give me one. I still wanted to see what the place looked like. "Do I need a key?"

She produced one from a hidden panel beneath the stairs. "Top of the stairs, on the right. I hardly ever see the tenant on the left. He's so quiet, he won't bother you. And the third floor has a separate entrance, so you'll never see him, either."

An all-male boardinghouse, very interesting. No wonder the plants were all dead. We thanked her and hurried up the worn stairs. They really needed carpeting. The boards were cupped and precarious from use. And not once did I trip, falter, or feel the pull of weak muscles.

"This is the most excitement I've had in years," Jane whispered as we reached the landing, keeping me in the moment. "This is a fabulous house!"

"Yeah, but we haven't talked money yet. I don't have any." The key turned easily in the lock, and we let ourselves in.

The minute I entered, I was ready to sell my soul to live here. Gorgeous dark wood floors and real wood molding, a huge bay window overlooking the street letting in what feeble gray the day provided. On sunny days, the room would be flooded with light. High ceilings, electric sconces in antique brass on the cream-colored plaster walls—I didn't have a stick of furniture I could move into this place.

"Check the kitchen and bathrooms," Jane warned pragmatically. "These old houses have rotten plumbing."

"You want rotten plumbing, you should live in an

RV," I muttered, remembering all the campground outhouses from my youth. I worshipped good showers. Even the ones in the dorms had seemed like heaven to me.

We passed through the solid-panel swinging door into the back of the apartment. Modern remodeling had done some serious damage to the Victorian charm back here. What had once been a bedroom had been turned into a small kitchenette and dining area. The kitchen had more cabinets than my current one, but the appliances and countertop were just as old. I tested the gas burners and they worked. The refrigerator was running. I couldn't have asked for more.

I wondered what the landlady had done with the previous tenant's furniture if he'd disappeared without a trace. I opened a cabinet and found some chipped dishes and cheap glassware. Maybe they came with the place.

Leaving Jane to explore plumbing, I took the door to the next room. It led to a small hall with a bathroom to the right, behind the kitchen sink. Straight ahead, at the back of the house, was a reasonably spacious bedroom with a closet on the same wall as the bathroom. Whoever had divided this old house into apartments had made the best of every available inch.

The bedroom had a sliding glass door to a porch overlooking the backyard. Nearly speechless, I wandered out, testing the old wood for rottenness before putting my weight on it. More dead plants. The prior tenant must have had a green thumb, and these poor plants must have been missing him.

The backyard was a collection of old tires and dead appliances. From this height, the balcony overlooked the ugly white metal storage tanks lining the harbor. But if I looked past all that, I could see the water. There was a sailboat opening its canvas, heading out for sea.

I was in love. I *needed* this house. In sheer exuberance, needing to share, even if Max was in my imagination, I dug out my compact, flipped it open, and held it up to the view. With Jane still in the kitchen, I felt free to whisper. "Take a look at that, Max. A room with a view!"

"*The Zone,*" Max said so clearly in my head that I almost dropped the compact in shock. "*You can't live in the Zone. You have to get out of there. I mean it, Justy. They're going to warp you.*"

I turned and looked at the mirror in amazement. Max was just as visible as if he were looking into the glass instead of me. I either had to accept that I'd taken a buggy trip from reality, or that Max was truly talking to me. "Max? Is that really you?"

He didn't look too happy but his head made a nodding movement. "*Looks like it. I can really see you here. You look amazing, kid.*"

My eyes teared up as I stared at his familiar, wry smile. I loved that little half-moon scar on his cheek. I touched the mirror to stroke it. I could live with crazy. "I can talk to you here," I whispered. "You're stronger near the Zone."

"*Looks like it. I should have made you get out while I could. My bad . . .*" He faded away.

Oh, crap. I leaned against the rail and looked down to the moss-covered brick patio underneath the porch. If I'd needed further proof that I was really talking to Max, finding him here ought to have given it. Now if only I could figure out where he was . . .

With a sigh, I tucked the compact back in my bag and returned to watch Jane examine the plumbing beneath the sink.

"You should have taken plumbing classes," I told her. "More profitable than reporting."

"My dad's a plumber. No thanks. No leaks that I can see. The toilet flushes. The shower works. Now if she'll only take nothing down and nothing per month, I could take this place."

I snorted. "This is *my* find, and besides, *no way* are you raising a kid here, dimknob. I warned you that the Zone is a disaster waiting to happen, and it's just down the block. Let's see if we can perform a magic act."

"If the Zone is really dangerous, what are you doing down here?" Jane asked, wisely enough, as we headed back downstairs. I was still feeling no pain.

"Apparently, I'm already warped. I fit in. Don't do that to your kid."

I didn't want to believe Andre, but I didn't have much choice. I hadn't been precisely normal when I'd first moved to Baltimore. I'd been emotionally bruised by my wandering childhood, physically and, while I hated to admit it, probably psychologically damaged by the fall, and overall jaded by what I'd seen of ivy-covered towers. After the riot and my arrest, I'd been hammered by cops and school officials and my cynical mind. No wonder I'd felt at home here.

A kid needed a clean slate, not nomadic statuary and big-breasted chimpanzees.

Mrs. Bodine sat on the old boot bench in the foyer, waiting patiently. "Did the movers leave it neat? I had them take the last tenant's furniture down to Goodwill, but I haven't bothered hiring someone to clean."

"No scrapes on the floors and no holes in the walls," I assured her. "It will be convenient to my work, but I'm afraid my budget is limited while I'm paying on student loans. How much are you asking?"

To my ultimate shock, she actually named a price lower than my current rate; behind me, Jane choked and coughed. In another minute, she'd knock me over the head and steal the place. "Does that include utilities?"

"Yes, dear, but not cable. And if you use too much hot water, we run out," she warned.

"Parking on the street?" I asked, ignoring Jane breathing down my neck.

"We don't get many cars here," Mrs. Bodine said apologetically. "There's an alley behind the fence in back that leads to the drive. I don't know if the gate works."

The Miata might be toast within a week, but at this point, I was beyond caring. I kept telling myself the house was *outside* the Zone as I knew it—albeit by a few blocks. "Would it be all right if you keep your last tenant's deposit and I pay him back should he ever show up?"

She looked at me shrewdly. "Do you have the first month's rent?"

"I do. And references from my current landlord. I've never missed a payment." That wasn't a lie. I was very responsible. In that one area.

I wrote her a check to impress her.

She gave me the keys and nodded approvingly. "Andre says you're a good girl. I think you'll do."

Oh, double crap. Was there anywhere the man *wasn't?*

15

Okay, I'd moved a thousand times before, but they'd always been "have to" moves. This one—this one was for me. I *wanted* that gorgeous old Victorian. I was quite willing to forget surveillance vehicles and hot-air corpses in my excitement. Being closer to Max-in-a-mirror was actually a *plus* in my new mood.

Jane dropped me off behind the tenement and promised to locate her guy with a truck. I think she was a little jealous of my good fortune, but she really didn't grasp the price I'd already paid for working in the Zone.

Well, it wasn't exactly a price. I hesitantly glanced at myself in the dresser mirror before heading off to work. I was still short, still had a hawk beak and crooked teeth. But the swingy curls and great legs . . . Even partially concealed by a skirt, the legs looked good. I needed to go shoe shopping.

The mirror thumped as if a fist had struck it, and Max appeared. He was blurrier here outside the Zone, and I shivered at what appeared to be smoke swirling around him. He looked both furious and worried.

"*You need help, Justy,*" he pleaded inside my head. "*Get out!*"

But he was gone before I could rebut. "You're not telling me anything I don't know," I told him, keeping my hands on the glass, just in case he was listening. "But my choices are kind of limited right now."

A final week of school, and then I could land a real job, pay someone to clear my record, take the bar exam, and get on with my life. Hopefully.

While untangling my life, I had mostly done just enough to survive, to skate by. Except now I seemed to have taken on a few additional causes—which I wasn't handling very successfully, I reminded myself before I got too cocky. I still didn't have the funds to hire the Geek to hack the bank. I was pretty clueless with this detection business—both literally and figuratively.

Afraid the bugging devices could suck information out of my neighbor's cable lines—which was where I stole my Wi-Fi—I didn't even dare Google the names Cora had given me for the diplomatic plates. I dragged out my backpack of textbooks, added my netbook and some cleaning supplies. I stuck some instant coffee, a pot, a few other kitchen necessities, and a change of clothes into a shopping bag. I wasn't hanging around to be spied on any longer.

The turds in the Escalade knew where I went every day, so I just gave them the finger as I sallied out the front door to my Miata. Let them think what they would of my excess baggage.

After taking the interstate and ascertaining that I wasn't being followed, I veered off before the bridge and circled back to the Victorian to drop off my stuff. Then I drove straight to Chesty's and parked in the alley. The guy in the suit leaning against a telephone pole on the corner spoke into his phone. I still couldn't believe anyone was actually bothering to stalk me, but if they were, I was giving them no reason to suspect I was anything other than a student and an underpaid flunky. I was still hoping they would go away when they got a taste of just how boring I was.

I should have asked Schwartz if there was some way of bugging telephone poles and Escalades, but I really needed to know whose side he was on. I'd taken him for the straight-and-narrow sort. Lying— or fudging the truth—on a police report pushed him closer to my territory. Or maybe he'd been corrupted by the Zone.

I didn't anticipate being ambushed the moment I walked in the back door of Chesty's. I nearly dropped my deposit bag as one of the cooks emerged from the kitchen, grabbed me, and lifted me from the floor in a bear hug. He chattered in what could have been French or Hindi for all I knew.

The rest of the cooking staff poured into the hall to pat me on the back or head or wherever seemed reachable. At least some of these spoke English, and I gathered I was being awarded a hero's welcome.

No one seemed to think it was unusual that I was three inches taller and not limping. Apparently, keeping my head down and my mouth shut meant no one had known I existed, until now.

I noticed Sarah wasn't anywhere about, and I wondered if she'd fled our fair bar for safer territory.

"I didn't do anything, folks," I protested. "I was just there. How's Diane? Has anyone heard from her?"

"She's all right," one of the English-speakers said. "Andre told her to take the week off. Ernesto is pissed, because she's one of our best workers."

"Did Ernesto actually *do* anything about the lighting in the alley?" I asked, more comfortable with these practicalities than with being lauded as some kind of hero.

Still, I was fine with the big bowl of spicy chili and the plate of tacos they set in front of me once they'd led me into the kitchen. My breakfast donuts had worn off.

"New lights installed first thing this morning," the cook said proudly. Tall, skinny, and younger than me, if I could judge by the acne hidden by beard scruff, he held out his hand. "Jimmy Jones. I'm the soup and bread chef."

I had a notion there were fancier terms in fancier restaurants, but this was the Zone. For all I knew, Jimmy stole tires for a living before he landed here. Chances were pretty good he never graduated cooking school.

"Pleased to meet you, Jimmy. This chili is delicious." I had to wonder where people in the Zone bought ingredients, but I wasn't insulting my newest best friend by asking. I might as well get used to chemical poisoning if I wanted to eat anyway.

The others introduced themselves, and I tried to keep a running list in my head, but the brain cells were limited. At least I knew I had pals in the kitchen who wouldn't be trying to lop off my head in their knife fights. Not soon, anyway.

I noticed the gray-haired weirdo carefully bagging a plastic chili bowl on the other side of the kitchen. "Who is that?" I whispered to Jimmy, tilting my head in the guy's direction. Surely, if the kitchen was feeding him, he wasn't one of the spies.

"Crazy guy, used to work at the plant," Jimmy whispered back. "May still work there for all I know. Andre said to feed him, so we do. Sometimes he brings us what he calls his latest invention, but we're all afraid to test them after one blew up the pantry."

"He gives me the willies," I murmured back. "He keeps staring at me, and he looks kind of familiar somehow."

Jimmy shrugged. "We just call him Paddy. Don't know more."

At least he'd not attacked me with a tire iron. He'd simply warned me away from his family, so I guessed I'd label him harmless.

Paddy ambled off without giving me a second look. I scraped up the last of the yummy chili and carried my glass of Sprite out of the kitchen as the head chef yelled at everyone to get back to work. The waitresses wouldn't be in for a few more hours, but preparation was already under way for the evening crowd. I got out of their way.

I nearly dropped my glass in astonishment when I entered the bar and found Max's pals Gonzo and Lance sitting there.

"Tina, looking good!" Lance bellowed as I juggled the glass to the counter and ran around to give the big lug a hug. "Cool place to work. How can I get me one of these jobs?"

I laughed. He was eyeing the nude murals on the wall and the stage, which seemed to have mutated to babes with whips and leather just for these boys here. Who needed artists when we had the Zone?

Max's biker buddies were about as reliable as six-year-olds. They did what they wanted, when they wanted, and no more.

"You're the wrong sex for bussing tables here, buddy. And they already have a bouncer."

"And I bet he's a fairy. Can't let the studs in with the mares." Lance nodded wisely. He wore his dirty brown hair in a ragged ponytail at his nape. A scar from a knife fight marred his otherwise nice jaw. He never said, but I had a feeling he was one of Max's college friends who'd gone off to war and come back a little warped.

I punched his bulging bicep, but the leather jacket could take the blow. "Macho turd. Now put me down and tell me what's brought you down here. And why do I think Max wouldn't approve?"

"He hated the Zone," Gonzo rumbled, dropping some oily mechanical parts on Ernesto's clean bar. Gonzo resembled a Mack truck more than anything human: big, square-built, shiny roof, with a few teeth missing from his grill. But he was a mechanic par none, including Max.

Yeah, mirror-Max clearly had no fondness for my workplace, but he'd never said anything in the months we'd been shacking up. I really hadn't known the man, I was realizing.

"Why?" I asked. "And why didn't he tell me?"

They looked uncomfortable. Even with my new five-five height, I was only half their size, and there were two of them. They still looked as if I was about to whip them.

"I killed a man last night," I told them casually and watched their eyes widen with question marks.

I didn't feel casual. I still wasn't entirely certain what I'd done, but a man was dead, and even if he was a demon—or worse yet, a government spy—I'd sent him to hell.

I'd sent him to hell. Like Max.

Not ready to go there yet—especially after that

last fiendishly smoky image. So I got in their faces.

"He was hurting someone and I had to stop him. See, I'm a big girl now. If there's something I need to know, spit it out."

Gonzo redirected my question by holding up a greasy cable. "The brakes were cut."

That stopped me in my tracks. Gonzo wouldn't have hauled just any old brake line down here. I went behind the bar and poured whiskey for them and topped off my Sprite with vodka.

Gonzo shoved another mechanical piece at me. "Steering mechanism tampered with."

"My Escort?" I whispered, staring in disbelief. I couldn't tell a cut brake from a fishing line, but the cable he was showing me had been neatly severed at least partway.

"Max didn't like the Zone. The Zone didn't like him," Lance said enigmatically. "Babe, I think you better get out of here."

That was what Max kept telling me. From hell. Or purgatory. Or my imagination. I took a stiff drink of my Sprite. The boys did the same with their whiskey.

"He never said anything when he was alive," I said angrily, newly fortified with alcohol. "Why didn't he make me leave then?"

"You were his best spy. A few of us helped him out a time or two, but we get too busy and you're steady. His old man is some bigwig at Acme and Max didn't like him knowing he was watching." Lance took another swallow and wiped his mouth. "Max should have told you, but he didn't know this was all going down so fast."

Crap. I was mourning the bastard, when all I was to him was a spy? I contemplated taking out my compact and stomping up and down on it. "Who was I spying on? I never told him anything that everyone down here doesn't know. And what does his dad have to do with anything?"

Lance shrugged. "He didn't talk about it much," he admitted under my glare. "He just wanted his dad hanged from the highest tree and you were one of his ways of gathering evidence. His dad has something to do with the chemical companies that make nerve gas weapons. It's all hush-hush."

"You think his *dad killed him*?" I asked in horror, finally connecting the dots.

"Someone was sure hoping to get you or him or both." Gonzo pensively examined his oily parts. "We kinda thought you ought to know as soon as we found out. Max liked you a lot. He'd want us to help you get out of here."

I couldn't take it all in. I was just a lowly law student and underpaid bookkeeper. I didn't know anything anyone would want to kill for. But I couldn't think of any good reason the guys would lie to me. That they thought Max liked me didn't ease my anger or guilt. I was just one terrified, roiling stew of emotion.

"I can't quit school now," I murmured. That this occurred to me first showed my twisted mind. Earning my law degree was more important than my life. I'd spent a lifetime searching for justice, and the paper to put me on that path was nearly at my fingertips. If I couldn't right wrongs, what was I?

I could answer that one—*nothing*.

Milo had climbed out of my bag when I dropped it to greet Lance. Now that I held my head in my hands, with my elbows propped on the bar, not paying attention to him, he rubbed against my jaw and purred.

I stroked him, reminded that I had friends here. Those kids to avenge. A job to do. A new apartment I wanted very badly.

And good legs. I would never be normal again, so maybe I should just go shoe shopping. I had all those clunky boots to replace.

"And you guys think I should run and hide and not try to find out *who killed Max*?" were the first astonishing, angry words out of my mouth.

They looked at me as if I were crazed, and rightly so. It wasn't as if I had brawn or wealth or sources of power—I wasn't even making any progress in tracking those diplomats whose names Cora had given me. And if I didn't get to work, I wouldn't have the money for the new apartment, much less to pay Geek Boy for tracing the guy who'd hit the kids. Finding Max's killer was an even bigger task.

I was losing it, but if someone had killed Max . . . they would suffer. The anger sank deep into my bones much as the pain in my leg once had.

"How you going to do that?" Lance asked.

"Did you tell the police about the Escort?" I

demanded, thinking official resources were better than mine.

"They had the car hauled to a junkyard. They'd say the evidence had been tampered with," Lance said scornfully. "They're not going to believe us."

"Max would want us to get you out," Gonzo repeated.

"If Max had wanted me out, he should have told me so," I said stubbornly. "It's too late now. I'm staying. And I intend to find out what's going down. Will you help me dig into his father, or do you want no part of it?"

The guys looked alarmed. They were tough war vets. I couldn't believe I'd scared them. A heavy hand fell on my shoulder, and I sighed, just before ramming my elbow backward into a taut, hard abdomen. Chest. My aim was off because of my new height. "My party, Legrande. You're not invited."

He didn't bother backing off even after I put all my strength into the blow. "Your guests endanger you as well as my property," he said as if I hadn't registered an objection. "It would be wisest for them and their loved ones if they departed and didn't return."

Lance got a mean look in his eyes. "You and who else gonna make us?"

I rubbed my temples and watched Milo crouch as if deciding which man to leap on for his supper. I *so* wasn't up for Testosterone Wars.

"Did I say anyone would make you?" Andre asked with that amused undertone that made me want to jab him again. "You are free to come and go at will. But just as we don't allow smoking because it's hazardous to the health—especially if the building blows when you light up—I like to advise Clancy's friends of the dangers to their health if they linger in the Zone."

He damned well should have warned *me*. But I heard the ominous undertone of admonition that the boys probably didn't. Andre's next step would be to throw them out on their asses, while smiling and telling them farewell.

"He's not shitting you," I muttered. "I guess that's why Max hated the Zone. It's a chemical explosion waiting to happen. And if his dad is involved in not cleaning it up, or placing his factories over the safety of people, then he's sitting on an atomic lawsuit. He would be my very first suspect. Andre, remove your hand from my neck before I cut it off."

"Your wish is my command, princess." He backed off, leaning against the sink counter and crossing his arms. Amusement still flickered around his mouth, but the tension in his muscles spoke differently.

Lance and Gonzo never looked amused on a good day. They glared at Andre, then looked at me. Lance was apparently appointed spokesman by some unseen communication. "Another good reason to take you out of here," he said with a growl, scrawling his phone number on a napkin. "You don't think we're letting Max go down without a fight, do you?"

"No, I didn't expect you to let this go," I agreed. "But right now, I have no idea how to follow your lead. You let me know if I can help you, and I'll do the same. How's that?"

"You want us to rearrange that guy's face?" Gonzo asked with a trace of eagerness.

"Nah, I can do that all by my little lonesome, but he's pretty, and I like looking at him. So we'll let him think he owns the place for now." I was tired of serious business. I bit back a smirk at Andre's grunt.

Then, just to tick him more, I traveled back around the bar to hug my boys. They were lugs, but they were *my* lugs. I smooched them both on the cheek. "Max will be real happy to hear that you're looking out for him. Don't keep me out of the loop, okay?"

Fortunately for me, the dunces didn't question my foolishness about Max being happy. Or maybe they'd lived so close to hell that they understood the fine line between life and death.

"Don't like this, babe," Lance said, hugging me. "Maybe we'll go over to visit Max's folks and bust a few heads and see what leaks out."

"Just as long as it's not your brains, I'm okay with that. I need you guys to stay alive."

I got teary-eyed as they stomped out. Hands on hips, I swung around to let Andre have a piece of my mind.

His gaze dropped to my new legs and sandals and he swore, in French.

16

Fortunately, the deposits began arriving as Lance and Gonzo walked out, so I didn't have to do more than glare at Andre, don my reading glasses, and return to work, after tucking Lance's number in my bag. If Andre had said anything in English about my new enhancements, I'd have had to punch him out, and broken knuckles would have slowed me down. I'd much rather hit someone than try to rationalize what was happening to me.

Damn Andre for noticing what no one else seemed to.

With the boys gone, Sarah came out to mop and Andre found better things to do than nag me. I wondered if Frank had traced the license plates he'd been taking pictures of the other day, but I was pretty certain Andre wouldn't tell me in any event.

Knowing someone had killed Max—and that that someone was very definitely not me—I could barely concentrate on what I was doing. Just as he'd been telling me from my mirrors, *Max hadn't been trying to kill me.* He'd felt the brakes go out and had been trying to steer the car away from me. Max had died for me, and I might have sent him to hell.

I had to clench my teeth to keep them from chattering, and tears kept filling my eyes so I couldn't see what I was writing. By the time Cora arrived with her deposit, I was practically snarling with frustration, fear, and grief. She took one look and poured me another Sprite.

"Frank says the van on the corner belongs to a corporate spy agency," she offered without my asking.

"Those same 'corporate spies' probably killed Max," I said without preamble. "His brake line was cut and his steering tampered with. And they've bugged my apartment." I didn't know that last for certain, but it made sense. Bugging places was what spies did.

Cora released a string of truly creative epithets that would have made Shakespeare blush, and I could have sworn I saw a snake's head slither across and disappear from her arm like a demented tattoo. She pulled out one of her many phones and apparently called Frank to relay the information.

When she hung up, she covered the tally sheet I was working on with her hand, forcing me to look up. "We gotta get you somewhere safe, hon." She gave my legs a knowing look. "Before you whack anyone else."

I'd been afraid killing people and my new perks might be related, and now Cora seemed to be verifying it. I had no idea how this worked, and was too afraid to ask.

"I'm on it," I declared, not letting my sinking stomach intimidate me. "Next time I whack someone, I'm going to ask to be invisible."

She snorted. "You're not taking this seriously. Those big guys don't play fair, and they have the funds to make problems disappear."

I smiled perkily. I'd gone far beyond proactive paranoia to clearly insane. "Oh, do they get prettification rewards for killing people, too? Maybe I should go looking for a guy with great hair and big pecs so I know who cut the brakes. Only it would be nice to know *why*."

She pounded my skull with the heel of her hand. "This is serious shit, girl. We're all at risk here. I'm paying to keep my mama in a real nice nursing home. I lose my job and she goes into the street. We get corporate assholes down here investigating this cesspool, they'll shut the whole damned place down. Where else are we gonna go?"

I smacked my palms against the bar and glared back at her. "Max wasn't an asshole, but he was the one trying to shut down the Zone, and all that got him was dead. I don't think the 'assholes' are shutting anything down. Suits who hire corporate spies *exploit* people like us. Read your history. We're expendable waste, cannon fodder, no more than animals to be used for experimentation. They're far more likely to be using us than shutting us down—because that's how the money is made."

I had not consciously been thinking any such thing, but my tongue flapped faster than my brain. And I thought I might actually be onto something, so I let it keep flapping. "As far as those guys out there are concerned"—I jabbed my finger in the direction of the front door, where the suits in the Escalade hung out— "we're a mutant breeding ground, and they're either trying to figure out how to breed more of us, or exploit what we've got, or both. Our best bet is to keep a low profile and let the air out of their tires."

"I take it that's a metaphor," Cora said carefully.

"For all I know, they've bugged this place like they've bugged mine." I shrugged. "Maybe we all ought to talk in metaphors."

Her gorgeous eyebrows raised to her hairline. "I'll get Frank on that. You have the deposit ready for me?"

I shoved the bag over with the final tally. "All yours. I'm off to study."

In truth, I was operating on overload, so jittery that I could barely stand still. The injustice of it all was juicing me like some freak meth high. I needed my law books. I needed focus. I needed . . . organization. I wanted to take all the irrelevant weirdnesses, gather them into a ball, and give them direction, preferably a cannonball trajectory straight toward Max's killer.

I couldn't do that, of course, so I settled for law books. Then I ate supper in the kitchen. I scrubbed pots like a heroine. And I took Schwartz outside with me when I was ready to leave.

The new security lights reduced the blue glow to near-invisible and eliminated shadows. The good detective frowned when I checked under the chassis for tampering, but he caught on quickly and helped me look.

Once I eased my fears, I climbed into my car with relief and waved good-bye to the unsmiling Schwartz. If he approved of my new legs, he didn't show it. I hoped Cora told him about Max, because I could handle only one problem at a time right now, and I was focused on my living space.

I avoided a tail by leaving the Miata at the old place and hitching a ride to the new, so it was after eleven by the time I tested the front door of the old Victorian. Mrs. Bodine had very properly locked her foyer. I used my new key in the lock. The same one worked on the door to my place. I figured I'd change that first chance I had. I didn't want anyone snooping while I was out.

A bedraggled sheet of notebook paper had been pinned to my door with a safety pin. I grimaced at the damage it had probably caused to the old wood. I'd thought Mrs. Bodine couldn't climb the stairs. No one else besides Jane knew I was here—unless the note was for a former tenant.

Once inside my gorgeous new palace, Milo scampered around the hardwood floor, hunting for kitty entertainment while I opened the pencil-scrawled paper.

> *the universe is one and you need me to help*
> *you understand. yr mother refused to accept*
> *her calling and is unfulfilled as a result. you*
> *were born to this, justine. but violence is not the*
> *answer—themis*

Themis? The writer of the creepy messages about Saturn being in conjunction with Mars or whatever *knew where I lived*?

Freak-out. Clenching my teeth to prevent them from chattering, I collapsed cross-legged on the floor, no longer surprised that I could do so without pain. How could this invisible personage know so damned much about me? *Invisible.* Was this related to the thief? Or did the devil watch me from Hades?

Someone or something obviously noticed my actions. My skin crawled at the idea of all these unknown forces intruding on my privacy.

How did my tree-hugging hippie mother fit into this? If roaming the globe and never having a relationship left a person "unfulfilled," whoever had written this had nailed Dee Clancy all right. My mother was still looking for love in all the wrong places. Or maybe just acceptance. Because she wasn't happy with herself?

Point to ponder, but still not helpful.

Who the effing crap knew my mother? Scrambling for sanity, I'd have dismissed the note as door spam—except they knew my name and apparently knew what I'd done. That shot another shiver of fear down my spine. Fear that then turned to anger.

I didn't like being chastised for defending someone against a rapist. If violence wasn't the answer, what should I have done, polished his nails?

Maybe the Zone or the Universe was trying to communicate with me. I was flipping nuts enough by this time to have expected answers in cereal boxes. I could sure use a few answers. In the spirit of insanity, I dug paper and pen from my pack and wrote back:

> *Fulfillment for me would be finding out who killed Max. Do you have a phone number?*

Okay, that was brave. But now what did I do—set it on fire and let the smoke blow up the chimney like a message to Santa Claus? *What the hell . . .* I stuck a wad of gum on the back and attached it to my door. I had officially taken a flying leap into the loony bin.

After flinging my impossible question to the Universe, I needed to ground myself in something more practical, like who had run over the kids. I had no idea where to start hunting down corporate spies, but I had names to go with license plate numbers that I could research. It wasn't as if I had a bed to sleep in.

I turned on my netbook and looked for an open wireless connection. It's amazing how many schmoes leave their networks without password protection. I found three and chose the strongest. I was uncertain how reliable the Internet would be this close to the Zone, but my choices were limited.

I Googled all four names associated with the partial plate the kids had given me—two representatives and two senators were using cars with those plates. One senator was old and had been around since time began. The second senator was from a filthy rich local family who'd bought his way into power. The representatives were fairly new to D.C. and had probably never been to Baltimore. I doubted that they would know the Zone existed. I checked their websites but they were meaningless unless one lived in Kansas or Nebraska.

So I focused on the senators: the old one, Senator Ted Towson from Tennessee—you could write a country song about that name—and the younger one, Senator Dane Vanderventer from Maryland. Rhetorical question—if you were me, which one of those two would you pick as the bad guy? The local one, of course, the rich, young power broker who'd probably grown up knowing about the Zone.

But just in case I was wrong, I checked out the old Tennessee guy. Teddy Boy had a head of glistening white hair and a big toothy smile of expensive dental work. His website showed a good ol' boy wearing jeans and a cowboy hat, shaking hands with farmers in front of golden haystacks. He had a mouse of a wife, two daughters, and three grandchildren. The wife was an orthodontist, which explained the good dental work on the entire family.

I didn't want the hit-and-run driver to be a family man, no matter how unctuous. So I looked up the local boy with total prejudice. If cowboys can judge villains by the color of their hats, I could judge by the color of their websites.

Sure enough, Dane wore a tailored suit and his page featured him standing with the president and several world leaders. Unfortunately, he wasn't the fat cat I was expecting. Widowed and childless, this guy was looking *goo-ood*. He had to have a personal trainer to look that toned dining on the rich food they served up in D.C. Styled, chestnut hair framed a warm smile and cleft chin, better than James Garner and Clint Eastwood rolled in one. He kind of favored Max, actually, without the long curly hair. But the eyes looked flat and soulless, I decided, based on nothing.

If I could have picked perps by picture, I'd have been all set. But even I knew that wasn't rational. So I put Dane on the top of my bad-guy list, opened the window overlooking the harbor, and curled up on the floor to sleep.

For a pleasant change, come Saturday morning, no one knocked on my door at some unearthly hour, and my phone didn't ring to wake me up.

I did, however, wake to the sound of my window sliding open wider and turned over in time to catch a glimpse of blue-jeaned leg climbing out. I lurched from sleeping to awake in two seconds flat and lunged to grab a grubby athletic shoe, but the owner had already disappeared.

Literally.

I blinked, got up on my knees to look over the low sill, and saw no one. This window was to one side of the porch, not over it, so I'd felt safe in leaving it open. But it might have been possible to sit on the porch rail and swing over the sill if one was long-legged and limber enough.

I turned around and hunted for Milo. He was watching me with interest but not making any noises like he'd seen anything suspicious. I hastily checked my bags and found nothing disturbed, not even my netbook. Weird. Maybe I'd been dreaming.

Well, so much for leaving open windows to pleasant breezes if they invited nightmares.

Still marveling that my hip was giving me no grief even after sleeping on a floor, I dragged toiletries and a change of clothes out of my shopping bag and took my first shower in my new apartment. I probably should have cleaned the tub and tile first, but given what I'd been living with lately, mold and mildew weren't of terrible concern.

The bathroom mirror was old and gray and the light over it was dead. I hung a shirt from the light to cover the mirror. I didn't know if my Max fixation would show up here, and I wasn't ready to find out.

I hadn't gone shopping for new shoes yet, so I wore the wedge-heeled walking sandals again. Because of my uneven legs, I'd never really been able to walk far in them. Now I could roll up the elastic waistband of my skirt and see unblemished calves and ankles. I could wear miniskirts, if I wanted. That was some kind of scary.

The apartment was less than half a mile to the businesses on Edgewater, so I jogged down to see if anything was open. The minimart on the corner had coffee and donuts. The guy behind the counter had green teeth and directed me to a market three blocks north of the Zone.

Dragging my fascinated stare away from his chompers, I sipped my coffee and wandered outside and up the street to see what kind of market dared to nestle so close to the Zone.

I was pleasantly surprised to discover one with fresh produce on stands outside, just like in New York City. We'd lived in Jersey my junior year in high school, and walking all over the city had been my escape. I had a fondness for the Big Apple. I gathered up some fruit and lettuce, found a basket inside, and loaded up with cereal and milk and the basics of life. The guy behind the counter looked perfectly normal, balding, and probably of Indian or Pakistani descent. He even scratched Milo under his jaw when my nosy cat peered out to see what was happening. Milo purred, and I took that as a token of acceptance from my perceptive kitty.

I could easily get into urban living.

A dark-haired teenager hobbled from the back on crutches, and I recognized her from the limo mishap. Despite my part-time attempts to bring her some real-time justice, part of me wanted to duck and run, but I took a deep breath and stood my ground. This was my new neighborhood. If I was settling down here, I wanted to learn to do it right.

"Glad to see you up and about," I said. My arms were full of bags or I'd have held out my hand. "My name is Tina Clancy. I was there the day the limo hit you."

She nodded. "I remember you. You looked like you could call down lightning, you were so mad. I'm Jennifer Barr."

"Nice to see you again, Jennifer. And, so you know, I'm still mad. I'm looking for that limo, but with so little information, it will take time."

The man behind the counter looked worried. "We shouldn't make trouble with men like that. My daughter is all right now. I don't want people asking questions."

I understood his attitude better than I should have. I was starting not to like it. I merely smiled. "If I get my hands on him, he won't have any teeth left to ask questions through. But I'll not drag you into it, okay?"

The man didn't look happy, but Jennifer gave me a thumbs-up.

Except for the dying-young part, I really *wanted* to be Saturn's daughter, dispenser of justice. On my way back to the house, I designed a Supergirl suit and Batmobile in my head.

Now if only I could figure out how to scare away suits in Escalades, I could almost convince myself that I had superabilities.

I could have sworn an abandoned department store dummy winked at me as I traversed an alley shortcut through the Zone. I put my head back on straight and practically ran the rest of the way home.

17

❧❦❧

I left Milo to guard my new place while I traveled with Jane back to the old one, slipping inside from the rear. I stayed inside packing up clothes and dishes while the truck guys hauled out my bed and couch. They reported looky-loos in the parking lot, but that happens with any moving activity. I still had to assume my spies were suspicious and keeping an eye on the movers.

Before Jane's friends finished packing up the trucks, I merrily went out the front, faking a limp, waved at the Escalade, and climbed into my Miata, praying no one had had time to tamper with it overnight. Since the SUV seemed to stay in the lot, I didn't know who they had tailing me. Whoever it was, I intended to keep them very occupied while the guys moved my stuff to the new apartment. Anything Jane might have thought she owed me was completely wiped out by the convenience of having friends with trucks.

I stopped at Goodwill and happily picked up some new ankle-breaking shoes and a few other necessities at a penny-per-pound price, then moseyed on to the library to do some research for one of my finals and to poke around a little more on Senator Vanderventer. Not unexpectedly, his name and that of Max's wealthy family, the MacNeills, turned up regularly together. I didn't run a genealogy, but from the stories it looked like there might even be a family connection.

It seemed beyond odd that a rich senator would be driving himself, much less banking near the Zone. So I could have been looking for someone who had permission to use his vehicle. Damn. I didn't want a chauffeur to be guilty. My trailer trash prejudices were definitely showing.

I drove to Chesty's and put in a few hours cleaning up during the lunch hour, though on Saturday the big business came later and Ernesto wouldn't need me again until the dinner crowd.

Jane called to say the truck with my stuff was on the way. Leaving the Miata parked at the restaurant, I slipped down back alleys toward my new place. Now that I could walk without pain, I was kind of liking the proximity to my jobs, although I didn't like leaving my new car in the Zone, even if it distracted spies.

I could have sworn the Zone had added two new Dumpsters and a new angle in the alley since I'd been out here last. I skirted as far around the tin bins as I could and jogged faster, glad that it was broad daylight. Dipping statues had been amusing. Moving behemoths were not, especially if evil lurked inside them.

I had no way of sneaking inside the apartment without being seen, but I'd worked out that problem. In the alley behind the Victorian, I pulled on a bright yellow Indian tunic spangled in funky little mirrors that I'd bought in my bargain bag. I knew I couldn't hope to fool the spies forever, but pretending to be someone else just for a while would be fun. I pinned up my hair, wrapped it in a hijab, and sauntered back to the street. With my swarthy complexion and prominent nose, the Middle Eastern look worked, even though I was pretty certain my mother was born in this country. My bet was that spies wouldn't connect button-down me with someone in Muslim disguise.

I grabbed a box from the truck and followed the guys up to my place. I'd hoped to get more cleaning done before everyone arrived, but dodging spies sucks up time.

My silly message was still stuck to the door. I didn't see any sign of my landlady or the other tenants as the guys efficiently arranged my meager furniture in the big rooms. I bought pizzas for everyone. While the men ate, I hung my clothes in the closet so they could take the boxes back to Jane. When the truck was empty, I gave them passes for free drinks at Chesty's and Bill's bar so they could wet their whistles. Jane wouldn't be moving until tomorrow, so I figured it wouldn't hurt if they got a buzz on tonight. They'd earned it.

Milo prowled around the boxes of dishes and examined his favorite couch. I gave him fish for supper and debated leaving him to guard my stuff while I returned to work. I couldn't change the locks until Monday.

"Want to stay here or go with me?" I asked him, as if he could answer.

He tilted his head as if considering, then climbed to a stack of clothes on my dresser that I hadn't put away yet and kneaded a nest. Guess that answered that. I set up his litter box in the mostly empty pantry.

Feeling just a little lonely in my spiffy new apartment, I finally braved the newly moved cracked dresser mirror. I'd long since removed the shiny tunic and hijab. I was back to my preppy button-down shirts, even though I'd worn jeans for mop-slopping. I might not have been a lawyer yet, but I did my best to dress like one on my limited budget. On Monday, I'd be able to wear my kicky new sling-backs, which I was strangely looking forward to.

Max appeared almost instantly, his long, dark curls looking as if he'd run his nonexistent hands through them. "*Babe,*" he said warily.

"You make me think I'm losing my mind," I warned, speaking hastily before he disappeared again. "But it's not guilt worrying me anymore. Someone cut our brakes."

His eyes widened in shock. How could I possibly be imagining this?

"*I don't know precisely where I am, but I'm learning to navigate,*" he said with surprising clearness. He looked startled that he'd managed to say that much. I doubted that I was looking stoic in return. "*Your mirrors are like windows in the darkness. I thought I was attached to your place, but maybe it's just you and your mirrors and not the place. Weird. Your grandmother found me.*"

"My *grandmother*, Max? You really want me to believe an elaborate hoax like Themis? You ought to remember I don't have one." I was almost disappointed—I'd *told* Max I had no family. This couldn't really be Max. Or even my imagination, now that I thought about it. A grandmother had never been one of my fantasies.

"*Themis says your mother didn't grow up under a cabbage leaf.*"

I dropped down on my bed and stared. That was what my mother had always claimed when I'd asked. I was in too much shock to know how I felt.

"Themis is my grandmother?" Did I want to believe that? Why would Max lie? If this was Max— and I realized I truly wanted it to be him—I had to try to accept what he was telling me. "You can talk to her? Is she with you and where in heck are you?"

"*Feels like purgatory, but don't worry, she's not here. She's living on a different plane than reality, I suspect.*" He looked pleased that he was able to carry on a conversation. "*Her messages are bizarre.*"

"Being Saturn's daughter isn't precisely explanatory, if that's what she's telling you," I said dryly. This had to be the most *bizarre* conversation I'd ever carried on. "She seems displeased about my dispensing justice by bopping a few heads."

He looked vaguely alarmed. "*Don't go killing anyone else!*" he shouted. "*I'm pretty sure it's bad as well as dangerous. You don't want to end up here with me. You just finish your exams and stay as far from the Zone as you can.*"

"Not happening, babe," I said. "Not until I find out who hit those kids and what happened to you. And I *like* this place."

I could have sworn fire flared up around him before he disappeared. Max was usually pretty laid-back, but I had a habit of arousing his temper, among other things. My mother liked to rely on men. I'd never found them reliable. So I didn't waste much time trying to feed their egos—even when they were in hell, or purgatory. Same difference, as far as I could see.

I left through the sliding glass door to the porch. I wanted to see if my new superlegs would let me be the tomboy I used to be when I was little. I triumphantly shimmied down the post without breaking anything, and took the back alleys to Chesty's. On the way, I kicked a Dumpster that seemed to purposefully block my path. It thudded hollowly, just like it should have.

When I arrived, Ernesto took a good gander at the new swing in my hips and remarked that I could fill in for Diane. I considered smacking him for sexism, but I wasn't particularly surprised or displeased. Waitressing was part of my résumé, and I needed the money.

Tiny costumes that screamed for male attention were the real problem. I'd come prepared for mopping, wearing jeans and athletic shoes. The other girls helped me to find a skirt that covered my ass and a leather halter top that actually fit, if exposing half my breasts counted as coverage. With the judicious use of a few pins and a pair of borrowed heels, I was in business.

Finally, I might make enough money to pay Geek Boris. I hoped he'd found a way into the bank's computers or cameras. Those kids deserved a little justice.

I passed Schwartz in the hall, and he literally spun around and stared as I sashayed past. I was out of practice wearing heels, but I managed a hip sway for his benefit. Sue me: I was horny, and I'd never looked sexier in my life.

I served drinks and pasta and dodged pinches while hiding my crooked pearly whites, flaunting my long legs, and keeping an eye out for suits. The Saturday night crowd was rowdier than the weekday patrons, and I had to memorize orders because my eyes weren't good enough to see to write them down. Wearing reading glasses didn't inspire tips.

I noticed a guy in black sipping a martini in the booth Andre and I had occupied the other night. He'd even doused the light as I had. I didn't know if his choice of seat was supposed to send a message or if he was practicing back-to-the-wall defense. I just knew he looked as out of place as the pope in a roomful of drunken sailors.

Briefly wishing Andre were here to lean on the stranger, I quickly dismissed that idiocy. I didn't need a man to do my work. After a hasty conference with the waitress assigned to that booth, I exchanged it for one of my livelier tables.

Swinging my hips in time to the music the dancers were writhing to, I approached the back table when the man in black's drink got low. He had a bad view of the stage and he was all alone—sure signs of a stakeout if I'd ever seen one . . . from my knowledge of them on TV.

"Another martini?" I inquired, leaning over to give him a good view and a fresh napkin.

"Just tonic." He did a fine job of pulling back into the shadows so I couldn't look at him.

"Here on business?" I made a show of mopping up the moisture from the old napkin. "Waiting for someone? We have a great ravioli tonight."

"Just tonic," he repeated.

Man, I was really lousy at this spy business. "Got any special requests for the girls? They owe me a few favors."

I noted that with that offer, he drained his glass. Customers who occupy space and don't spend money are a profit-killer. I knew how to make them nervous enough to either order or get off my turf. I was getting under his skin.

"No requests."

"This is how the dancers put food on their kids' table," I said with a hint of disapproval, adding his glass to my tray. "I hope you're not one of those hypocrites who think hardworking mothers are better off starving in the street."

He glared at me. I flashed him another smile and wiggled off.

I'd rather have hit him upside the head with a law book, but he wasn't doing anything except looking out of place. I just had this yucky feeling that he was waiting for me to do something weird—like blow off the roof or cut someone in two. Hey, maybe whoever was spying on me knew I could talk to Max!

That hit close to home, too. With my apartment bugged, they could have heard me talking to him. Maybe they thought he wasn't really dead, and that I was hiding him. Since someone had already killed him once, that gave me a shivery feeling. Were *murderers* watching me?

The Man in Black stayed there all evening while I tucked cash into my bra. I couldn't figure out a good way to pin my usual safety pocket inside a skirt that barely clung to my hips, so I figured my exposed cleavage ought to have a better purpose than titillation.

At midnight, I decided to turn into a pumpkin. No one was eating. The kitchen had gone home. The rest of the staff could handle drunks. I needed study time. And I wanted to see what the suit would do when I left. I changed back to my jeans, secured my wad of cash in my safety pocket, and ran into Schwartz at the back door.

"Andre says I'm to see you home," he said blandly.

I snorted. "Tina says Andre can stuff it up his nose.

I have a better plan. Let's see where the suit in the back corner goes once he realizes I've left."

"I need this job," Schwartz warned.

"Yeah, and you've got an old mother in a nursing home you don't want turned into the street?" I asked sarcastically, repeating Cora's plaint as we stepped into the bright glow of the security lamps. I couldn't see anyone watching the door. That didn't mean they weren't there. I stuck close to the wall, totally grateful that I was still walking straight after being on my feet for hours.

"My mother is fine and living in Florida," Schwartz said with an air of bewilderment. "But thanks for asking."

"Okay, I apologize. I've been hanging around so many bad guys I forgot there were still honest ones. Are you with me on the suit?"

"I don't mind spying on the suit, but I'm still seeing you home," he said stubbornly, edging along the wall where the security light wasn't as bright. He was too big to hide, but he didn't look out of place patrolling.

"I have a new home now, and I'm not inviting anyone in," I told him. "So let's just play turn-the-tables-on-the-spy and pretend I levitate home, okay?" I clung to the wall behind him.

He didn't argue but led the way around to the parking lot. "I traced the plate on the Escalade at the apartment," he said conversationally as we took an alley toward the street. "It belongs to the agency Frank already told you about."

I'd kind of figured that. So now I needed to hack

a corporate spy company to see who had hired them. Piece of cake. I'd earn enough with tips in maybe a year, if I wiggled and jiggled enough.

It would have been cheaper to move to Seattle.

I peered around the corner to the parking lot. As I said, not too many people liked to drive their cars down here if they could avoid it—for many good reasons. Emerging from the alley, we scared off a bum stripping tires from an old Chevy, and Schwartz swiped the keys from a customer too drunk to unlock his door. While he called a taxi and babysat the drunk, making a very public spectacle of himself, I found a nice hiding place between buildings where I could watch the street. A shiny black Lincoln on the corner looked like my best bet. I was wagering corporate spies fit in better in D.C. than they did the Zone. The taxi drove off with the drunk just as the suit emerged from the club, catching Schwartz in the middle of the parking lot. Schwartz coolly nodded and strolled on as if he'd been patrolling. The suit didn't even acknowledge him as he spoke into his phone and headed for the street.

I'd already jotted down the license plate of the Lincoln. I wanted a bug of my own to plant on the man or the car, but the Zone messed with technology, which was probably why we were seeing actual spooks here instead of bugs.

I was about to shrug off the bunch of them, when the suit made his big mistake of the evening.

A half-starved hound loped up to him, hoping for a scrap of some sort. And the big lout in his polished

Italian loafers kicked the poor mutt out of his way as if the creature were no more than an empty beer can.

No one kicked dogs while I was around.

I was off that building and flying toward the street before Schwartz caught me mid-stride and bodily lifted me from the ground. His arm was strong, and he held me a bit closer than necessary. I was liking the sensation of hard male crushed against my breasts, except he was in my way. Rather than battering one of the good guys, I furiously visualized the Lincoln's tires exploding.

And they did.

While Schwartz and I watched in stupefaction, the suit's tires exploded one by one. The dog ran off in terror. Schwartz flung me back to my hiding place. And the corporate spook stood there, immobilized, phone in hand.

I did a victory dance and scored one for the Zone, but it was probably better for all concerned that I stayed out of sight. I slid deeper into lurking shadows just before the suit turned in my direction. Yep, the suspicion in his eyes meant he believed I'd done it. Max's fireball and the wind thing and the rapist's swamp monster death had given me a real bad rep.

I'm not swearing I had anything to do with previous oddities, but even I couldn't prove I'd just blown up four tires because I'd thought about it. This was the Zone after all. Maybe it read minds. I *wanted* to try blowing up the spook to see what happened, but with Themis and Max both warning me against my propensity for violence, I gallantly refrained. Who was

I to question the denizens of hell or heaven, or maybe even the Zone.

Intelligently, Schwartz intercepted the suit before he could make a move toward the building where I was hiding. I kind of had the notion that the cop wasn't helping me so much as protecting the spook. My victory dance had probably been a little off-putting.

"Problem, sir?" Schwartz asked politely. "These things happen down here. It's usually not safe to leave a fancy car for very long. Chemical reactions, you know. I'll call the tow service. Would you like a taxi?"

I almost cackled. He was smooth, was the good detective. After frying Max and cutting a rapist in two, blowing up tires seemed pretty tame, and I didn't dwell on it for long.

When Schwartz ambled up after the tow truck left with our suit, I held out my hand. "You're good," I told him, "and I give credit where credit is due."

He didn't take my hand but gave me the Look, the one cops do so well. "Do I dare walk you home, or will you blow up my ears for asking?"

"It's the Zone, Schwartz, not me. I wasn't anywhere near that car. You were there." I was developing an unhealthy ability to lie blithely. Not knowing what was truth, I could brush off anything. "Wouldn't it be better if you stayed here, looking after the more defenseless females?"

"It's the defenseless males who cross your path that I'm worried about. Your car's in back. How are you getting home?"

"Not by car. Really, I'm fine, Schwartz. And if

Andre asks you where I'm living now, you won't have to lie." Pearl might have told him by now, but he didn't have to know for certain.

"Andre bothering you?" he asked, eyes narrowing.

"Andre ought to bother everybody. Beware of men with power over you. That's my maxim." I shoved my fingers in my jeans pockets and stared him down.

"You may be officially nuts." He backed off, just a little.

"I have finals this week. My future is on the line. I'm allowed to be crazed. Thanks, Schwartz." And just as I'd turned to go, I realized that keeping his mind occupied with something besides me might ensure that he wouldn't be on my tail all night. And speaking of tails . . .

"Oh, Schwartz, if you're not married, I can hook you up with Cora. Just give the word."

I'd seen the way he'd looked at her. I figured he was just as horny as me. We were as totally incompatible as I was with Andre. Of course, I'd thought Max was my kind, and look how well that had worked out.

"I'm not married and I'm not hooking up with Cora, but thanks for the thought." The good detective gave a salute and marched back to the club.

Pity I didn't do lawmen. They couldn't be trusted to turn a blind eye when it was needed. But as long as we each knew where the other stood, Schwartz and I would get along.

18

It had been an excruciatingly long day. I was ready for my own bed in my lovely new home. I pulled the hijab out of my purse and wrapped it around my hair as I slipped from the alley toward the front of the Victorians, skipping the sidewalk and clinging to the shrubbery. Shimmying *up* the post was not a task I wanted to tackle in my exhaustion.

I stopped short and swore at the sight of a glossy black Escalade sitting across the street. I'd left my car at the club to make them think I was still there.

I'd never driven it to my new place. How could the rat finks have found me so fast? I hadn't had time to change my locks. If spies had bugged my new place, I was taking somebody down.

I was working up to a righteous fury, debating raining bricks on their windshields or ripping the roof off the SUV, when a muscled arm seized my waist for the second time that night. I only had to smell his musky aftershave to recognize my attacker, and that didn't stop me.

I hated people who take advantage of my size, even if I was no longer a shrimp. I swung my elbow back as hard as I could and slammed into a familiar hard diaphragm. I simultaneously aimed my sneaker heels at his kneecaps and bounced my head backward to take out Andre's too-perfect nose.

Prepared, he dropped me before I could do any damage. "You're going to have to trust me, Clancy," he whispered harshly. "You can't take on the world by yourself."

"Trust you?" I asked in incredulity, hating that he knew where to find me but knowing it was inevitable. "Why don't I just start carrying asps in my pockets?"

"Not a bad idea. If we can't get rid of these assholes, I'll have to call in Cora. Give me the keys to your car."

Standing in the shadows between overgrown shrubs, Andre held out his hand to me while keeping an eye on the street. He so obviously expected me to do as told that I was insulted.

"What has Cora got to do with anything?" I asked, ignoring his outstretched hand and inching forward, debating dashing for the door, except I knew it was locked.

I wasn't afraid of Andre. I just didn't want him hanging around, *helping* me all the time. I didn't like being obligated personally to someone who was my boss. It was bad mojo. Worse yet, I liked his bad-boy sexiness even better than Schwartz's hard-body good looks, and that was a really bad sign. My hormones were jumping like grasshoppers.

"Ask me another time. Just give me the keys, Clancy. Let's see what happens if I drive your car past these bastards."

Andre was too slick, too polished, too deceptive, too everything for me to trust him, but he was there, and the spies were really starting to tick me off. I actually liked the idea of seeing what would happen when he drove past in my Miata. I didn't particularly like leaving it at Chesty's if it could be taken some-where safe—away from my new place.

He waited patiently for me to do as told, and my stupid hormones must have responded to his manliness, because it sure wasn't my brains at work. I dug out the keys and smacked them into his palm.

"Are you going to wear a wig?" I asked spitefully.

He didn't bother to smile as he shoved the keys into his pocket and checked the street again. "You let Max drive your car. They'll just figure you've got a new boyfriend. I'll lead them back to your old apartment. Wait until they're gone before going in."

"What if they've already bugged the place?" I demanded.

He finally gave me an amused look. "Pearl would sooner let in bats than anything smacking of official-dom. It should be interesting now that you're here."

He didn't give me time to question any of his assumptions. He took off at a lope toward the alley, leaving me to contemplate blowing up the Escalade's tires. But if I did, Andre couldn't lead them away. I'd really have liked to know if I could blow them up now that I wasn't in the Zone, though. The temptation to experiment was powerful.

Andre had been right to ask *what* I was. I didn't know myself. In a few short weeks I'd gone from passive, mousy student to angry avenger capable of blowing up tires, not to mention winds and cars. My old Escort was someone else's fault, admittedly, but had my fear and anger somehow condemned Max to a purgatory between heaven and hell?

I didn't know and I was afraid to find out.

I pulled out my compact and aimed it at the street.

"Friends of yours?" I asked.

Not hearing an answer, fearing Max had left me for good, I turned the mirror back toward me. From what I could tell in the dim light, Max was scowling.

"*Friends of my family's,*" he said. "*Couldn't swear to it, though. Where are you and how long have they been out there?*"

"They've been camped at my apartment all week. When I got the new place, I thought I'd lost them." If anyone had seen me talking to a compact, they'd have had me locked away, but the streets weren't crawling with people. I probably should have asked Max questions, but I was afraid of breaking down in tears. I don't suffer emotion gladly, and I was having a hard time accepting that I might actually be talking to my dead boyfriend. Insanity seemed safer.

Instead, I leaned against the porch where I could keep an eye out for Andre driving by. None of the houses along here had security lamps, or bothered turning on their porch lights, so the shadows and overgrown shrubbery were nicely concealing.

"His family owns most of the chemical companies in the Zone," Max warned. *"I told you to stay the hell out of there."*

The way he said *his family* sounded familiar. Wasn't that what the gray-haired guy, Paddy, had said—*Stay away from his family?* That was just stupid. Not the same. I shook off the memory.

"If you'd left me your fortune," I said mockingly, "I wouldn't have to work and I'd be long gone to the Pacific Northwest, now, wouldn't I?"

"I didn't know I was going to die!"

"Maybe you're the one who should have stayed the hell out of the Zone." I was having mixed feelings about this whole situation and taking them out on someone who couldn't fight back. Uncool. "I'm sorry. You have no idea what it's like being me right now. And I don't want to know what it's like being you. If I can find some way of sending you to the light or whatever, I'll do it," I promised.

"I'm damned well not going anywhere until I nail whoever did this to us. Let me learn more. And get

away from those goons!" Max shouted in that macho way of his I used to ridicule.

The Miata knocked up the street. Probably had a piston going . . . if Miatas had pistons?

"Gotta go," I whispered, closing up the compact.

I watched with interest as the car rolled past the Escalade. A Honda bike put-putted from a street at the top of the hill, falling in behind the Miata at a distance. Punks.

The SUV stayed where it was, so I did, too. Fortunately, the May evening was warm. I really needed sleep, but I was too tired to shinny up to my balcony. My muscular new calves ached from the badly fitting shoes and from standing up for so long. Running probably wasn't in the equation, either. I'd overdone it showing off today.

My phone buzzed about fifteen minutes later. My eyes were too weary to check ID. "Yeah?"

"I'm at the apartment. Where's the SUV?" Andre.

"Still here. A Honda bike followed you out. You'll have to go in. Take a look around and see who else is there," I advised.

Cursing, he cut me off. Let him know how it felt to be followed. But I was too exhausted for fury. If the SUV didn't move soon, I was going over there and knocking in a window. Maybe I'd leave on the hijab and pretend I was a Muslim terrorist. That seemed like the kind of thing that might put the fear of God into Max's uptight family. Why on earth would they be spying on me? Did they think I'd run off with the family millions?

Or did they really think I was hiding Max? If so, who did they think they'd crisped?

I didn't want to think about his family, but I'd had enough time to work through the spy's thought process. I had to assume the suit at Chesty's had communicated with the spooks in the Escalade, so they knew I'd left the Miata at the club and that Andre had just driven it to the old apartment. They couldn't have known where I'd gone, but they probably knew it had to be on foot. They'd somehow guessed the Victorian, possibly by following the truck. They still didn't know for sure that I lived in any of these houses—except I hadn't been with Andre when he'd driven the Miata to the apartment. That had been a mistake.

So I was correcting it now.

I still had my deposit security gear in my messenger bag. I pulled out the shackles and, still wearing the hijab, crossed the street. I don't know whether the driver even saw me coming. He was on his phone, discussing deviltry with his evil associates. I yanked open the door, Maced him, snapped cuffs on his wrists, and hauled him to the street before he knew what hit him. I ground my heel into his phone and hopped up to the driver's seat. They were going to seriously regret thinking one lone spook could keep up with me.

The seat and wheel were unfortunately set for a six-foot-plus goon, but the extra length in my legs kept me from having to stand on the gas to get it going. I might have run over the guy's foot as I pulled away. I didn't bother checking the rearview mirror to find out. Mad wasn't even beginning to cover how I felt at that point.

I drove the $75k piece of equipment to Max's favorite biker club, the one where Lance and Gonzo usually hung out. I didn't know anything about the high-tech spy gear in back, but I was betting a few of our war vets did, or they'd know someone who could find out.

My phone buzzed again as I parked the monster truck. This time, I checked caller ID in the overhead light as I opened the door.

"I took care of it," I answered and told Andre, before turning off the phone entirely. I really didn't want to hear his shouts of fury, not any more than I meant to take out the compact and have Max yell at me, too. Men didn't get to be the only vengeful mavericks.

Leather-clad hulks were already strolling out of the bar, surrounding the vehicle. When I jumped down, they eyed me with suspicion. Most of them hadn't seen the new, improved me, so it took a moment before bells began to ding in their thick, pot-smoked heads.

"Tina?" one asked, coming up to study me closer. "What have you been doing with yourself, babe?"

"Hiding from Max's killers." I threw that out there just to stir the hornets. Nothing they liked better than a little outrage. "The jackasses have been following me around in this, and I got a little tired of it, so I thought I'd hand it over to you. Take it apart, find out anything you can, then sell it for parts."

I wanted to add that Max had said the SUV probably belonged to his family, but I refrained. Max was theoretically dead after all, and tolerance for craziness only went so far. "Lance and Gonzo are on the case, so give them what you find out."

"Babe," one of the guys drawled in awe, surveying the equipment inside, "we're going to party on this one. We'll throw Max a real Irish wake."

"Make sure you invite me. Can someone give me a ride?"

"We've got Max's bike, babe. Take it. He'd want you to have it."

One of the more scarred vets wheeled out the old Harley. I knew him as Crazy, because he literally was crazy. PTSD did no one any favors. But I wasn't turning down his offer.

"Fair trade," I agreed. I hugged a few necks, they copped a few feels, and then I hopped on the bike, roared the engine, and howled off. The Harley was solid metal, better than the plastic Miata any day.

Gloating all the way back to the Victorian, I coasted down the alley so as not to wake the neighbors, found the gate, and rolled the bike inside. I leaned it against a shed that looked as if it needed the Harley to hold it up more than the bike needed support.

I slipped through the shrubbery and checked the street to see if my victim was still around, but there were no black vehicles and no men in chains visible. The spy had been rescued. Now that I was safe and sound, I turned on my phone and called Andre. I got his voice mail, of course. He was mad and probably not speaking to me.

"Leave the Miata at the apartment," I told him. "The bums will need another SUV and Lincoln after this evening. I'm going to bed. Good night."

I unlocked the front door and slipped upstairs to the apartment without seeing or hearing a soul. The note to invisible Themis was gone from my door, although the gum still stuck. Since only tenants had keys to the front door, now I had to worry about my neighbors. And their guests. But not tonight.

Milo leaped happily to greet me, or to beg for more food. It's hard to tell with cats.

I did a quick survey of electric outlets. There weren't many, and none of them seemed to be bugged. Milo wasn't growling. I was hoping I was clear. If I stayed home all day Sunday and ordered a locksmith on Monday, maybe this place would be safe.

I didn't have curtains on the windows, so after taking a shower, I pulled on one of Max's old T-shirts that I'd found when packing and used it as a nightdress to make my way back to the bedroom.

And that's when I saw that the bedroom window was open—and I was damned sure I hadn't opened it.

19

Had the invisible thief decided to visit my apartment? That was one way of making me want to kill him, for sure. I didn't have much worth stealing, so did that make him a pervert or a spy? I really hadn't focused too hard on a problem I couldn't see, but given the mood I was in, I was prepared to change my mind.

Scouring the room for some way of blocking the jamb, I spotted a fluttering paper that looked out of place. I'm not a neatnik by any means, but I owned so little that I was cautious with my possessions. I liked everything properly stowed so I couldn't lose it. Paper did not go on my dresser.

Was Max passing me messages from beyond the veil now? Creeped out, I didn't want to investigate . . . which meant that was precisely what I did. Always face a challenge or you lose, that's my motto. So I was probably born crazy.

The paper was no more than a clipping showing Senator Dane Vanderventer and his hoity-toity society grandmother at some society event. *WTF?* Was Max or the Zone trying to tell me something? I studied the paper closer and finally caught the date—*the day Max had died and the kids had been run over*.

My hand shook a little—the society tea had been at the Vanderventer estate, which was apparently on the rich side of Baltimore. Senator Vanderventer had been in town that day!

If this was the work of the invisible thief, I wanted him on my side.

I didn't, however, want him in my bedroom.

Hoping the open window meant he'd escaped and not just entered, I closed my window and broke a broomstick to fit between the upper and lower casements. I didn't want anyone letting Milo out in the middle of the night, and I was too damned tired to even think about this latest development.

I missed having Max in bed beside me, but it felt too weird to open my compact. Besides, we had way too many issues, especially if his family was spying on me. Just before I closed my eyes, I had to accept that a cool guy like Max had picked up a cripple like me not because he saw my shining personality, but because he knew I worked in the Zone. Or maybe because I wore biker boots. Who knew? I dropped off to sleep without wasting more time.

I woke to daylight and Milo walking on my face, demanding food. When had the damned cat grown large enough to leap to the bed?

I realized an unopened packing box sat close enough for him to jump onto, and I shoved it toward the closet as I sat up. "You may be male, but you're not human, Catboy. I don't mind sharing my bed, but I don't even allow real men to boss me around."

I filled Milo's bowls, fixed cereal, dug out my reading glasses, and sat down at my shabby table to study. I was older and more experienced now. I didn't have a need to party every night to hide my panic over finals. My grades were solid as a consequence. If I hadn't gotten into the fight with the provost and had to lose credits with the transfer, I would have graduated two years ago. I was determined not to blow my chances again, not for invisible thieves or corporate spies.

I was pretty sure the spies wouldn't have me arrested for car theft. Even if they could have identified me, crooks usually didn't squeal on crooks—not good business to have the cops asking questions. But I thought I'd let them cool off before I showed my face in public again. The guy I'd Maced might be feeling vindictive. I probably ought to burn the hijab and tunic.

Declaring war on the Establishment was never smart, I knew, but I was down to my last damned week of school and couldn't contain my natural tendencies much longer. I could just hope that whatever the spies were up to meant they didn't actually want me out of the picture, or I'd be in big trouble. I'd learned the hard way—by spending long months in a hospital while exhausting every recourse to unsuccessfully sue the college and the cop who'd shoved me—that authority held all the power. I intended to be that authority one day so I could make things better for people like me, but for now, I shivered and focused on case law.

Andre called first, followed by Cora, then Schwartz. I wasn't interested in talking. I turned off the cell. If they just wanted to nag, then to hell with them. I'd been taking care of myself for a very long time, and I liked it that way.

On a study break, I idly checked to see if there were any more notes from the Universe on my front door. More dirty trash had been stuck to the gum. Unfolding the paper, I recognized the same pencil scrawl as earlier. My skin ought to have crawled at the idea that an unknown entity had been outside my door, but after the invisible-thief invasion, this was nothing.

Themis or the Universe had responded to the notebook message I'd stuck on the door about fulfillment being finding Max's killer.

Justice will be served with time and thought.
Use your head, not your anger.

I noticed they didn't provide the requested phone number. *Very useful, Grandma or whomever.* I was thinking I wouldn't give them mine. Instead, maybe I'd give myself a graduation present and track down Themis and fly to never-never land for a visit. First, I had to graduate.

While I studied, Milo explored. When I did nothing interesting, he got bored and took up a lookout position in the bay window. I gave him a pillow and checked the street—no surveillance vehicles in sight. After a while, my little kitty gave up his vigilance and took a nap.

At noon, someone rapped at the door. I was ready to eat, so I checked the peephole. Sarah. Shit, Andre was sending minions to let the whole world know where I was. So much for my anonymity. But I couldn't take my rage out on Sarah, so I tucked away my glasses and opened the door.

She still wore low-cut tanks that emphasized her outlandish breasts, but she wasn't looking as bruised and gaunt as she had the first time we'd met. Maybe chimp life agreed with her.

"If Andre sent you to check on me, make him pay you for the favor," I said, gesturing for her to come in.

"Why do you talk about him like that?" she asked in curiosity, gazing with awe at my gorgeous front room. "He's been nothing but nice to me, and he found you this great place. What do I have to do to get him to look at me like he looks at you?"

"You're not paying attention. Andre looks at *all* women like that, and he has nothing to do with this apartment. It's all mine—I found it." Realizing I'd sounded a bit harsh, I backed off a little and noted, "I was just about to have lunch. Want anything?"

Following me back to the kitchen, she saw the fruit bowl I'd created after yesterday's shopping spree, and she perked up noticeably. "Banana?" she suggested.

I shot her a look but she didn't seem to be joking. "Help yourself," I told her, rummaging in the fridge for sandwich makings.

"Your long legs are prettier than the breasts I got," she said, peeling her banana. "Was that for killing the rapist?"

I nearly conked my head on the refrigerator doorframe as I swung around to stare at my unexpected visitor. I was still holding the bread bag in my hand. Trying to be cool, I tossed it to the counter, but Sarah wasn't even looking at me. She was watching Milo prowl at her feet.

"Why do you ask that?" I asked cautiously. I'd learned a thing or two in trial law class, after all.

"You're a daughter of Saturn, too, aren't you?" She left Milo alone when he growled and stalked off, stub tail raised in indignation.

"Supposedly, but I don't even know what that means."

She looked at me strangely. "Your mother didn't tell you we were born under a rare stellium of planets and asteroids that only occurs once every twenty-eight years?"

"Um, my grandmother said something about a Saturn transit, but she's pretty ditzy," I said, trying to sound nonchalant while a chimpanzee told me more about me than I knew myself.

"Yeah, sometimes getting the story straight ain't happening," she agreed. "I didn't believe my mother when she said I'd find out what it was like to send people to hell, but she was right."

"You send people to hell?" I asked a little too casually as I dug out peanut butter and wished I'd had the banana she'd just consumed.

"I figure I sent Danny there, and that's why I got breasts. I looked it up, and Saturn has almost reached its apex again, so my time's, like, almost here. I'm carrying a knife now so I can off any creep who comes at me, just like you. Maybe my breasts will turn out prettier if I kill someone I'm not married to."

This conversation was getting pretty scary. "Did your mother say you're *supposed* to kill people? Isn't that a little drastic?" I smeared peanut butter on bread as if we were discussing the weather.

She shrugged and poked through the fruit bowl for an apple. "She said we only get gifts if we send people to hell. We don't get anything for making them behave. I'd love to have hair like yours."

Despite the fact that I was totally freaking out, I did my best to stay cool. "I'm not sure doing the devil's work for him sounds like a good idea. I really don't think that's what justice is about."

She crunched the apple. "Well, you have to be smart about it. My mother was stupid and just shot the evil drug dealers she owed money to. She looks good, but who's to notice if you're in jail?"

This was not a healthy conversation. I kind of wished Andre were here to listen to this. He would never believe me. Shy, sweet Sarah had a murderous felon for a mother and was contemplating sending people to perdition as if hell were a cruise ship and her reward plastic surgery.

I wondered if I should open my compact and let Max have a gander. Digging in my bag might make her suspicious, though, and I sure didn't want her calling me evil and turning her murderous inclinations my way.

I didn't think telling her she needed counseling was going to work.

"If you believe bad guys only deserve capital punishment, then shouldn't your mother be dead, too? Wouldn't it be better to reform her?" I asked conversationally, as if we were merely discussing the disposal of banana peels.

I always argued in favor of reform in class, but mostly, I just wanted the bullies off the street and out of my face. But listening to Insane Sarah, I had to wonder what I expected to happen should I find the limo driver who'd run over the kids. He deserved to fry in hell, and I could use better eyes, but was sending a jerkwad to hell in exchange for benefits really justice?

She seemed to perk up at my question. "I'd not thought about that. Mom killed a bunch of people, but the cops couldn't pin anything on her. She declared self-defense on the one that got her locked up. But she probably belongs in hell. You're right!"

She slid off my kitchen stool anxiously. "So I can tell Andre you're fine and just studying?"

She seemed eager to leave. I was eager for her to go and more than a little disturbed by her visit and the new look in her eyes. I'd kind of thought family loyalty would lead her toward that whole "as a daughter of Saturn, my mother was administering justice," argument. The cop who had shoved me had used that "injured while upholding the law" crap. Apparently, the appeal of fixing her breasts was more pressing, and I wasn't holding out good odds on her mother living the month out.

"You can tell Andre anything you like," I said curtly.

Sarah's smile was more sly than pretty. "So, you don't have a thing for him or anything? He's up for grabs?"

I was thinking I'd better warn Andre that a ghoul was after his soul, but I shrugged in answer to her question. "I've known Andre for years. There's nothing happening between us."

And with that reassurance, she made a beeline for the door, saying, "I think I'm liking the Zone now! See you later," and sailed off on her own little ship to hell, closing the door after her.

Milo sniffed the crack to make certain she was gone, then leaped to the bay window to verify her departure.

I wasn't so hungry anymore. Daughter of Saturn? Such things existed? Themis *wasn't* a crackpot?

After fighting a need to spew my lunch, I knew I'd

have to track down that website I'd read earlier and find out more. I needed way more information if I was going to die young. If my mother knew about this shit, why hadn't she told me?

Probably because in her vague world, ignorance was bliss.

The prison system ought to be warned not to let little Sarah visit her mother, but I had no idea where her mother was incarcerated, or if interfering with the hands of the devil would get me slapped. I'd never given the devil and hell a moment's thought until these last weeks, but they were pressing ugly on me now. If they existed, I didn't want any part of them.

Andre would say I was nuts if I told him about Sarah. I needed someone who understood. I took my sandwich into the bedroom and leaned my hands on the dresser.

Max appeared instantly in the broken shards. "*You don't look happy, babe.*"

"Did you hear any of what I just heard?" I was probably talking to a figment of my imagination, so it wasn't an unreasonable question.

"*Didn't hear anything. I think you maybe have to be near it for me to see and hear you directly,*" Max said with what might have been a shrug. "*I'm making connections, learning how things work. There are different dimensions. Maybe Dante was right about levels of hell. All I know is there's a veil between here and there. I haven't worked out how to get past it.*"

Oh shit and crap. As long as I continued to think I was losing my marbles from stress, I could hope I was clinging to sanity. But I was in over my head and going down fast when I started *believing* Max was facing hell because of me. Did I have to believe Sarah? Could both of us be batshit nutzoid?

"Max, I'm thinking you were sent there wrongly, and that's why you're not frying in eternal flames," I said bluntly, not knowing any other way of handling this if Max truly was on the other side. "Things are happening too weird for me to grasp. So far, the only clue I'm getting is from a chimpanzee."

I told him about the conversation with Sarah, and he frowned. I wanted his burly arms around me when he did that. It was disconcerting to have nothing but hard, cracked glass for comfort. I was perfectly aware that a shrink would say my imaginary Max was my way of coping with his traumatic death, but I was learning that the real world didn't know a lot about this alternate universe I seemed to be occupying. Which ought to have worried me but didn't.

"*Daughters of Saturn are real, babe,*" Max warned. "*Maybe it's why I dug your vibes from the first. Your mother copped out by not telling you what you are.*"

"And because of that, I sent you to hell!" I wailed, facing up to my guilt.

"*Or maybe you gave me an opportunity to get even,*" he corrected. "*If it hadn't been for you, maybe I'd just be dust in a coffin right now.*"

That perspective left me cogitating instead of shouting, and Max took advantage of my silence by lecturing.

"*Like I said, I've been asking questions. Word*

is, with Saturn coming back around in a couple of years, all the Daughters born twenty-six years ago are gaining their powers. You have a little time to learn to deal with them as they grow. Your kind got a bad rep because no one has believed in Saturn in centuries, so his daughters are mostly loose cannons. Maybe you better listen to Themis. Killing people isn't helping your karma."

"Planets can't have kids, and neither can dead gods! I'm already damned, aren't I?" I asked with a sigh. "What difference does it make if I off a few more no-goods? Maybe I'll join you."

He shook his head vigorously. *"Don't go there, babe! I don't know the alternative, but you deserve better. Maybe you have the power to dispense justice through law."*

I snorted. "Yeah, that's happening with your rich family breathing fire down my neck and an arrest record blotting my escutcheon. Even if I pass the bar exam, the ethics and character committee has to examine my application for a law license. Explaining away riots ought to be a joy after they learn about the rest of my questionable behavior. Make room for me down there, Maxie, I'll be joining you eventually."

He swore and tried to pound the glass but vanished. I was thinking maybe he should clean up his act if he ever wanted to get out of wherever he was. Temper probably wasn't a virtue. Maybe I should ask what other questionable tactics he might have been indulging in besides using me for a spy.

I had way too many questions and never enough time to ask them.

The Zone warping me made more sense than believing any rot about planets or dead gods. Andre had said people changed, sometimes for the better, when they lived down here. Chemical imbalances could be cured maybe. Science had logical foundations. Woo-woo, not so much. If I wanted to deal in the superstitious, I could say that I got Milo as a prize after I generously went hunting for Andre's deposit bag and that I found my apartment after saving Diane. Not buying it.

I called Cora.

"Hey, hon, what did you do to Andre? He's fuming at the ears, and it's not pretty," she sang into the phone. "Amusing, but not pretty."

"He tried to save me from the bad guys last night, but I took them for a ride instead. But because he cares, I've got one for him: Sarah is a full-fledged maniac and will probably try to off her mother soon. Oh, also, she's got the hots for our fearless leader. He might want to try not taking this one to bed."

"Why don't you tell him yourself?" she asked in amusement.

"And be accused of jealousy? Not happening. The man's ego is too large for his pretty shirts. But Sarah is a bunch of bananas shy of a boatload. You should take a look into her background, starting with the mother she claims killed drug dealers and was thrown behind bars."

"Will do, because you're making me curious.

Frank is hacking into the corporate spy company at Andre's request. It's looking like they're on the payroll of Acme Chemical, among others," she warned. "Any luck so far with our diplomatic hit-and-run driver?"

"I'm thinking Vanderventer," I responded in answer to her question, wondering if the invisible guy was listening in. "And the really curious part—his family and Max's are seriously in bed together, and I'm thinking they own at least part of Acme Chemical." I couldn't very well tell her Max had told me about his family. "It all has to wait until finals are out of the way, but it stinks worse than a chemical spill."

"Nothing stinks worse than a spill, I'm here to tell ya. Maybe I'll have Frank dabble a little in this. Acme is huge enough to keep the authorities off their backs even after their little 'accidents.' They're dangerous. Back off, get your studying done, and let us do the snooping."

"No choice right now, but I'll be back on the job shortly. The Geek's on it, too, if you want to exchange news."

After I hung up, I realized I was really looking forward to going after Dane Vanderventer and Max's family. It was a pity I had to finish school before I could even begin to look legal.

And before I could even think of taking the bar, I had to find someone respectable who could clean up and explain my arrest record. I was pretty sure my apologizing for egging the provost and staging a protest that caused the administration building's roof to catch on fire would not pacify any ethics committee, especially if they found out about me starting fights in funeral homes, working at Chesty's, and offing rapists. Maryland is kind of picky about who can become a lawyer.

Maybe I'd better start playing nice to Andre. I needed to find a good lawyer to give me a reference, and Andre was the only person I knew with enough money to pay a decent salary so I could hire one.

Did that mean I was planning on staying in the Zone instead of getting the heck out of Dodge?

20

On Monday I called a locksmith to change the front door lock and rig up window locks, and I asked Pearl to let him in. The locksmith would cost me my tip money from Saturday night, but I needed my sleep.

I wheeled into school on Max's Harley, handed in a final paper in one class, and got off for good behavior in another. I took the extra hours at the library to wrap my head around confusing case law that I feared would be on the next exam, then motored back toward the Zone. Milo had opted to stay home, and

I needed to check on him and park the bike before going to work.

Milo was growling when I arrived. I picked him up and carried him to the bedroom, where the locksmith was working on the sliding glass door.

"Not a lot you can do with glass doors," he complained. "A key isn't a good idea in case of fire. Just locking it and putting a stick in the bottom is your best bet. Same with the window. The broomstick is good. You could call a security company, but breaking glass will wake you up as fast as alarms."

"Maybe I can stretch electric wire across and just fry intruders," I said grimly.

"As long as you don't forget and fry yourself," he agreed, handing me an invoice and new keys for my front door. "You need a big dog."

"I have an attack cat." Milo stood on my shoulder, still growling.

"Looks like a baby bobcat with those whisker tufts, but he won't deter thieves. Get a good handgun." Whistling, he took my cash and let himself out.

"I'm darned well not shooting anyone," I declared aloud, in case the Universe was listening. I'd had time to get real nervous about hell. An extra few inches of height and good hair weren't worth eternal damnation, even if the outer rings allowed me to look through mirrors.

Realizing I'd never given hell a thought until Max showed up in my mirror, I seriously considered finding a shrink, but I didn't want to end up in solitary confinement, either. A prison is a prison, even when it's called a loony bin.

"C'mon, guard cat, let's see if the food isn't better at Chesty's."

Forgetting evil locksmiths and forgoing his sunny spot in the bay window, Milo took his place in my messenger bag. I'd have wished for a cat's easy life, but given my weird experience of the past week, I held off actually vocalizing wishes, or even thinking them.

Since I'd been riding the bike, I was wearing cutoffs instead of jeans that hit above my ankles. I needed a new wardrobe if I meant to continue biking. I hated to give up my lawyerly preppy skirts, but practicality won out. I'd either end up mopping floors or wearing a ho costume by evening, so I donned a pair of leather capris that Max had bought me and added a black spandex halter top. Maybe Ernesto would let me wear this outfit instead of a skirt.

On the off chance that I might fit in some studying, I picked up my backpack of books and strolled down the back alley to Chesty's, wearing my new heels. Learning to strut after years spent wearing corrective shoes was a bit of a challenge, especially when dodging mobile gargoyles. The creepy feeling of being followed by gutter ornaments worked my nerves badly, but it's not smart to punch out concrete.

The Miata was parked behind the club when I walked up. I'd have to find a safer place to park it—maybe some fancy condo complex. That ought to keep the spies busy and guessing for a day or two. They couldn't know for a fact where I lived unless the gargoyles told them.

Sarah wasn't around when Milo and I bummed our lunch in the kitchen. I wondered if Cora had passed on my message to Andre and if he'd taken action. Or if he'd promoted Sarah to head honcho over me. Since I hadn't been told differently, I took up my usual position at the bar, donned my reading glasses, and began counting the club's weekend revenue while waiting for the other deposits to show up. I'd much rather have been out in the great spring day.

Sarah arrived sporting hair the color of an orangutan and *lots* of it, stacked high and frizzy on top of her head. She looked like some kind of unpleasant throwback to a prior century. I'm not talking about Madonna with her missile-breasted body armor—because *that* worked—but serious beehive hairdo. She grabbed a broom and looked equal parts defiant and self-conscious as she began her routine.

I was glad I didn't read newspapers. I didn't want to know if a serial drug-dealer killer had died in her prison cell. I didn't like justice being dispensed for perks, but could I honestly make that argument after killing a rapist? No judge or jury had been involved in the rapist's death. At least Sarah's mother had been convicted honestly. Judgment calls are hell.

"Has Andre come in?" Sarah asked when she got close enough to where I was working to talk without shouting.

"Not that I know of. Word to the wise . . ." I

glanced over the top of my glasses to her hair. "He likes to do the chasing."

Which was the truth, the whole truth, and nothing but the truth, and Andre owed me for putting her off like that. She grimaced a little and returned to sweeping.

She preened a little when Andre strolled in wearing one of his fitted silk shirts, a tie, and a sexy fedora that belonged in the 1940s. He threw Bill's deposit bag and the Miata keys on the counter, took one look at Sarah, winked at me, and strolled on out the back without saying a word.

Damn, that man was hot. And annoying. I pocketed the keys. Sarah went back to drooping. I guessed even killers could have self-esteem issues.

To my surprise, Boris the Geek stopped by to inform me he had the information I wanted.

"I've had extra expenses this week," I told him. "It may be next week before I can pay you." I was hoping really hard he'd go ahead and give me the names anyway.

He took a stool at the bar and covertly watched Sarah work. She was apparently growing used to people coming and going and didn't perform her startled-chimp act. After watching Andre stroll through, she didn't notice poor nerdy Boris, but the Geek was better off staying off her radar. I poured him a glass of water and threw in a lemon to soften him up.

"The camera only shows a hand, no faces through the tinted windows. I'll discount that one. I backed up the transaction list to a USB drive," he said cluelessly.

"It will keep. Interesting the amount of money that goes through that little branch bank."

"I don't advise taking up bank robbery," I warned dryly. "I suppose there's no chance you'll give me the information in advance," I proposed, since he didn't seem to be focusing on me and my problems. "It's in the interest of justice for those kids who got run over."

Boris was just registering my suggestion when Milo leaped, growling, to a chair, then onto one of the tables, and glared at the door.

"What's wrong with your cat?" Boris asked.

"Don't know, but maybe you and Sarah want to go in back—now." I started gathering up the money and tucking it into my bag as the other two scarpered. I didn't have my handcuffs anymore, and the memory of why had the hackles on the back of my neck rising.

Goons, being goons, probably didn't take lightly to having their expensive Escalades and surveillance equipment stolen, if they'd guessed I'd done the job.

The front door slammed open before I had time to lock the bag and grab Milo. Holding up nasty-looking guns with long barrels, two hulking suits in black entered, swinging their weapons back and forth to intimidate an audience of me and cat.

Bullies endangering friends, pets, and my place of employment guaranteed the Red Haze of Fury wiping out logic cells and casting me into motion. I had time to hurl a bottle of vodka and duck before Milo performed his Mighty Cat act and leaped for the Asian guy, who had the ugliest mug.

The vodka bottle clipped the crew-cut skull of the blond goon, and he swore as it broke and filled the air with alcohol fumes. I tamped down thoughts of fire as quickly as they occurred, as a precaution. I really didn't want to burn down my workplace. I tucked my reading glasses safely on a shelf and tensed, waiting for their next move.

Ugly Mug screamed as cat claws gouged his jaw and Milo took a bite of something tender.

A shot hit the row of tumblers hanging above my head and glass shattered around me.

"Mary Justine Clancy, you're under arrest—come out now and no one will get hurt!" shouted the one *not* screaming like a little girl.

Like I was handing myself over to just anyone who shot at me! "Badges, gentlemen," I called saccharinely. "Lay them on the counter."

Okay, mocking them was asking for trouble, but what choice did I have? I couldn't make a run for it without Milo. Heck, I couldn't leave at all without risking being shot. It wasn't as if Chesty's had any walls to hide behind. The bar formed a low, open island in the middle of the room. I might have vaulted over the back counter and dashed across the stage, except I figured these guns were big enough to hit a target across half the state.

I couldn't see Milo from beneath the bar, but I could hear him growling and Ugly Mug cursing, probably trying to pry cat claws out of skin. Cats don't come when called, so there wasn't any reason to reveal my anxiety for him. The thugs would just use

Milo against me. I'd learned a lot about bullies in my growing-up years.

Two more shots rang out and more glass rained down. As if that was a signal, the door from the kitchen hall slammed open, and a parade of people straggled out, hands over their heads. Boris was first, wearing a terrified chimp around his neck. The kitchen staff followed. I glanced in incredulity at the horde of black-suited men holding vicious-looking weapons shooing them forward.

"For me, boys?" I cried in incredulity. "Gee, you shouldn't have."

If this was Max's family at work, then I seriously believed they'd killed him. These goons looked like mafia. They'd had plenty of opportunity to take me out, but I was beginning to suspect they wanted me for other reasons and needed me alive. I didn't want to find out why.

I checked, but Andre wasn't among their captives. Just the meek, mild, and terrified. Jerkwads, threatening the innocent. Justice juice rampaged through my veins, obliterating any last semblance of logic.

"They haven't shown any badges!" I shouted, just to make everything clear. I wanted witnesses that I really wasn't under arrest.

The red rage was escalating, but I was beginning to recognize that anger was a trigger for weirdness, and I was determined to keep it in check. I didn't want any more people dying on my watch, so I rose from behind the bar, hands on top of my head.

Visualizing tornadoes and exploding tires wouldn't help me this time. I located Milo, who I swear had grown to twice his size and was trying to rip off Ugly's ear. The moron was batting around his gun, unable to maintain a good grip on both cat and weapon. He'd kill us all if he had the safety off.

"Milo!" I shouted. "You'll get us killed. Jump down from there."

He howled a mighty howl and instead of doing as told, leaped to the head of Blondie. The cat's newly gained bulk nearly knocked the thug over. Startled, Blondie shot off a round that took out a dangling ceiling light.

Fine, if no one was coming out of this alive, I could channel Dean Martin in *Rio Bravo*. I liked a good joke as well as anyone.

"Duck, everybody," I yelled, vaulting over the bar and swinging my spike heels high and wide at the same time. Damned good thing I was wearing leather and spandex. My shoe connected with the wrist of the blond brute, the one wearing vodka perfume and a cat hat. He lost his grip on his weapon and it spun across tables and underneath a booth. Milo leaped back to Ugly Mug, tackling his gun arm this time—my cat learned quickly.

I was counting on the thugs in back not daring to aim at me for fear of taking out their partners. Stupid, maybe, but what did I know about gangsters?

Instead of intelligently grabbing my ankle when I lunged, my victim grabbed his bruised arm in insulting disbelief. Obviously, he hadn't paid attention in tae kwon do. That mistake gave me time to regain my footing and practice a little kickboxing.

While he was whining, I swung and nailed his balls with the spike of my shoe. He crumpled in half while the kitchen staff squealed and more shots whizzed over my head, nearly giving me heart failure. Milo had Ugly's arm ripped to the bone and wasn't letting go no matter how much the guy jiggled and screamed. I *know* my cute kitty had reached bobcat size to perform this miracle.

With gunfire ringing in my ears, I wasn't precisely calm or thinking clearly. I just wanted to keep anyone from getting killed. Insanely, while rolling under a booth table so I'd have my back to the wall, I envisioned a downpour sweeping the shooters off their feet.

To my utter astonishment, the sprinkler system not only kicked in but burst pipes in its eagerness to flood the place. *Freaking awesome! Saturn, be my daddy if this is what you can do.*

Figuring I had only this one chance at seizing the moment, I rolled out from behind my table shield, grabbed a chair, and ran like a berserker at the perps holding my friends hostage. At the same time, the front door slammed open again, and I heard an official-sounding shout—something about halting in the name of the law.

Schwartz. Three cheers for the marshal, but I wasn't placing any bets on the cavalry arriving.

I didn't hesitate but swiped the lemon knife from

the counter as I raced past the bar. Against guns, it wasn't much, but I could hope the flood would dampen their weapons. Not that I know anything about guns except what I'd seen in cowboy movies. I had a notion these were slightly different from old-fashioned Colts.

White-coated cooks knew to fear knife-wielding crazies. They scrambled out of my way, hats flying. The chimp squealed and leaped to the head of one of the jerkwads with guns. He swung his weapon high in shock when Sarah's foot-paw-toes-whatever wrenched his necktie, and she plastered her belly on his face. His high-pitched scream of terror was nerve-wracking.

"*Don't kill him, Sarah!*" I shouted senselessly.

She wrapped her paws around the goon's neck and started shaking his head loose. So much for obedience, but I didn't have time to bring her down. I went after a black dude with a gun at Boris's temple. The Geek had lost his Coke-bottle glasses and twitched nervously while the guy holding him debated a course of action. With Milo eating one of the goon's pals, Blondie rolling on the floor with spiked balls, a third being smothered by a chimp, and Schwartz coming at them in uniform, gun upraised, through a drenching downpour, Boris's captor had cause to worry about his health. I doubt my paring knife figured into the equation, but unlike murderous Sarah, I made it a point to halt short of decapitating anyone.

Into the deluge roared Andre, bursting out of the kitchen carrying what appeared to be an assault weapon very much like the ones the troops carried in Iraq. His roar alone was sufficient to cause Boris to drop in a dead faint, dragging his captor halfway down with him.

After that, life got a little confusing. Andre rattled off a round to prove he meant business. Boris's goon dodged, dropped the Geek's deadweight, and leaped behind me, out of the way of my paring knife and assault chair. Grabbing me by the neck, he jerked my head back and no doubt thought he'd use me as a shield to make his escape.

Andre laughed. With good reason, I suppose.

My captor wasn't tall and I was wearing five-inch heels. I stood on my toes and slammed my head back, breaking cartilage. Blood spurted. Not caring that the hold on my neck was already loosened, I jammed my iron-spiked heel down on his arch, missing leather and connecting directly with all those sweet little bones that hurt like hell when crushed.

Action was happening elsewhere but I could only be in one place at a time. Milo screeched his earsplitting howl. Sarah's victim slumped to the floor with her paws around his throat. Andre shouted something about me halting the water as he whacked a spare thug with the length of his barrel. By not using bullets, he presumably protected his building from further collateral damage. His weapon had practically taken out walls once already.

I liked my image of black suits washing away in a flood, but sprinkler systems had limitations, and most of the villains were either on the run or ready for an ambulance. I'd have to work out the logic of my visionary processes some other time. Swinging around, I let off steaming anger juice by grabbing the dude who had tried to hold me hostage and kneeing him while envisioning dryness. By damn, it worked, too. The pipes stopped raining water down on us.

I think it took a moment or two before the adrenaline-high crowd realized we were winning. Jimmy Jones grabbed a butcher knife and chased one of the suits out the back door. Schwartz collared Blondie and Ugly Mug. Sarah's victim looked kind of blue and wasn't going anywhere. If she'd spoken the truth earlier, she might be up for another infernal award.

Andre had his automatic pointed in the face of the guy who'd dared to grab me. The rest had split.

With the sprinklers off, we wiped our faces and looked around at the damage in awe.

Ernesto stepped out of his office, white-faced, phone to his ear. "I called the cops."

Andre reached out and dragged me back to earth before I could fly through the air and rip off the cowardly bastard's face.

21

⬦⬦⬦

While Schwartz and the walrus-mustached Officer Leibowitz handcuffed two hulking, silent, and injured suits, medics bandaged the arm of a third and carried off a fourth on a stretcher with a sheet across his face. None of us had a good idea how many had escaped. More men in blue warily entered, and Ernesto set his kitchen staff to cleaning up. Sarah in either form had disappeared. And so had my cash deposit.

Swearing, I hunted all around the bar, but my bag and all its contents were gone. *Again*. Should I find this dipshit thief, I'd personally wring his wretched neck. Maybe I'd ask for better eyesight as my reward for sending him to hell. That seemed fitting. X-ray vision, maybe.

"Clancy! Into my office," Andre shouted above the uproar.

"You don't have an office," I said sourly, gathering Milo into my arms and hugging him. He was kitty-size again, but I knew what I'd seen. He was a mutant, just like me.

I was a mutant. I could drench villains with sprinkler systems and blow up their tires—in the Zone, anyway. I wondered if I could only assault bad guys or if anyone could suffer from my temper. I shivered in my wet shirt and wanted to crawl in a hole. Andre's summons did not register in my new misery. He was looking unusually faded, anyway. I figured he wouldn't kill me anytime soon.

The cops were looking for bullet holes in the ceiling to explain the sprinkler system failure. I didn't disillusion them, although I could have pointed out that bullet-shot sprinklers didn't usually turn themselves off. Water was mysteriously dissipating, but the Zone could have been thirsty for all I knew.

Boris the Geek sat up, looking sheepish. One of the crew had found his glasses, and I handed him a bar towel to dry them off. He tested them, then dug into his pocket to produce a thumb drive. "Maybe you better keep this. I'll take payment whenever you have it. What's with the chimp girl?"

"I think she's hiding. Best to steer clear of her

anyway. I'll find you a nice pole dancer. Or a cook. Wouldn't you prefer a cook?" I wasn't really paying attention to what I was saying. I was too dazed to be coherent. I held up the thumb drive and gazed at it blankly.

Oh, right, bank transactions. My hit-and-run creep. Another lifetime. I was still reeling from recognizing the power of my suggestions—and that corporate spooks had decided to take me out. I don't know which had me most off-balance.

"Nah, that's okay." Boris intelligently waved off my offer to find him a girlfriend. "Tell Andre he'll have to come up my way from now on." He staggered up, clinging to his glasses and looking for escape as the police started taking notes. I had a feeling he liked to fly low, under the radar of officialdom.

I nodded toward the kitchen hall where the cooks were coming and going with mops and pails. "Try that way. I won't mention you."

He nodded in gratitude and slinked off.

"Clancy, get your ass in this office now!"

I looked at Detective Schwartz, who looked back at me, face blank. I shrugged, donned my reading glasses again, and moseyed in the direction of Ernesto's and *my* office, burying my face in Milo's tufted neck. He purred. He actually purred.

I'd been attacked—shot at—had my deposit bag swiped, watched a chimp kill a man, and visualized a flood into existence. Really, what could make my day worse?

The instant I walked into the office, Andre took

one look at me and flung Ernesto's coat in my direction. I let it hit the floor before I worked out what he wanted.

My halter was soaked. Anticipating my waitress costume, I was wearing one of my sexiest bras under it, and it was soaked, too. I was pretty visible. My hair dripped down my face and neck. I wouldn't be dry soon. Murmuring sweet nothings in a kitty ear, I set Milo on the floor, slipped the coat on, and wrapped it around me. I finally realized I couldn't stop shivering.

"Nice machine gun, Legrande," I said, trying to sound like my usual smart-mouthed self.

But I wasn't myself. I didn't know who I was.

Andre obviously didn't either. The Brits have a term for it—gobsmacked. He looked gobsmacked as well as unusually insubstantial, but my brain wasn't fully functioning, so I could have been imagining his looking gray around the edges.

He shoved a hand through his wet hair and apparently fought an internal struggle. Wet silk clung to muscled pecs and plastered to six-pack abs. Andre liked to stay in shape. The image of him wielding an assault rifle like Robert Conrad in *Wild, Wild West* filled my head like a movie poster. Steampunk television kind of fit the day's events.

"The invisible thief stole the deposit again," I said conversationally.

"So do what you do and make him visible," he said crossly. "What in heck *do* you do?"

I shrugged and slumped into a hard plastic, retro-round chair Ernesto apparently thought looked cool.

Or maybe he just didn't want people to get comfortable. "Want me to experiment and find out?"

That set him back a bit. Damned good thing he had the smarts to work out just how dangerous that could be. Who knew what would happen if I visualized invisible thieves turning visible? Ink pots could rain from the heavens. My bet was that this Saturn business relied on items at hand and wasn't too literal, especially since I didn't think too logically when juiced. Which led to me wondering how mad I had to be before I could do anything.

"You'll have to press charges against those jackasses out there," he said conversationally. "I can file trespassing and maybe even hit them with theft of the deposit. The staff can probably have them charged with terrorizing. But you're the one they threatened with false arrest and shot at."

"I need a lawyer," I decided. "I have to face an ethics committee before I can get my license. I already have enough black marks against me that I'll be lucky to survive the interview. Publicizing what looks like a drug deal gone bad or a mob hit won't help me."

"Working at Chesty's probably won't win you any favors, either," he said with casual cruelty. "We need to remove you from sight until we figure out who's at the bottom of this."

Remembering the thumb drive clutched in my fist, I must have developed a stony expression as I pondered revenge. Andre leaned his palms on the desk and glared.

"What?" he demanded.

"I need to hole up in my room to study. I'll just

leave the house for finals. When that's done, I'll find your thief. We can renegotiate job terms after that."

"Dammit, Clancy! Your rooms aren't a safe house! You'll endanger everyone in the place if these morons can't get at you on the street."

"I can move into the law school's library," I said with a touch of sarcasm. "Think corporate thugs will dare the hallowed halls of the Baltimore judges' alma mater?"

Except for that gray around the edges bit, Andre looked good when furious. I thought he might start pulling his hair or mine, but Schwartz rapped on the partially open door and let himself in.

"I need to ask questions for the report," he said tonelessly, circumspectly not engaging in eye contact with either of us.

"The guy with bruised balls shot the sprinkler system when I kicked him," I told him, feeding him lines as he had me earlier. "The ones who got away stole the weekend deposit."

"How many thugs are needed to steal a bar deposit?" he asked skeptically.

"The weekend deposit for the entire street. The tally is probably a soggy mess on the bar somewhere. Substantial sums are involved." Well, they were substantial to me, but probably weren't worth the price of a cadre of mercenaries.

I must have really ticked off someone with lots of pocket change.

"What about the dead guy?" Schwartz deadpanned. He was digging this alternate history.

"Big dude went apeshit and throttled him for trying to run with the money," I said solemnly.

"Apeshit?" He was having a hard time keeping a straight face with Andre snickering.

He asked a few more cursory questions and departed. Raising a mocking eyebrow at Andre, I grabbed my backpack from my cubicle and followed Schwartz out. Let the honcho steam in his own juices for a while. Fury obviously didn't suit Andre. He needed to get his cool back.

I grabbed Milo and told Ernesto I'd be back next week if he needed me. I had one of the busboys run the Miata keys over to Cora's office with a message asking her to drive it to my old apartment.

By next week I probably wouldn't have any job at all, but I knew my priorities. I wasn't going to blow years of hard work by failing finals.

Instead of going into my apartment after walking there, I simply jumped on the Harley and went to school. Maybe I could find a cubicle to sleep in for the night.

By the time I noticed the strange looks I was attracting as I marched through the library's marbled halls, I realized I was still wearing a man's ugly suit coat over my soaked halter and capris. The ride had partially dried them, but I undoubtedly looked like a homeless hooker.

Shock has strange effects on the mind. Mercenaries had tried to kill me. I had good reason to be half out of my mind with fear.

I found an open computer and inserted the thumb

drive in the slot. The information Boris had collected opened in Excel with each bank teller neatly labeled across the top, the name of the depositor down the side, and the amount deposited filled in at the appropriate cross section. Very neat job. Boris had earned his pay.

I scanned the list of bank account names down the side. No Vanderventer jumped out at me, of course. The Acme Chemical Company had made a very large deposit. I went back to the thumb drive and looked for a file on the times of deposit. I had to trace the depositor to the teller to the time of deposit. The chemical company had been there nearly an hour before the hit-and-run. Nothing was ever easy.

I started working from the times of deposit. I couldn't tell which teller number belonged to the outside drive-through, so I had to look at them all. With a little more study, I had the names of five possibilities, companies that had made deposits in and around five o'clock, just before the bus arrived. One deposit was to Ace Associates. Boris hadn't provided detail, but my bet was that a jerkwad like Vanderventer, driving a government limo after taking his grandmother to a society promo op—as per the invisible intruder's newspaper clipping—had stopped to make a payoff to his goons at Ace.

Swearing, I debated how much my life was worth if I was shot, compared to what it was worth if I failed the exams. I printed out the information, stuck it into my contract law book, and then hid the thumb drive in the stacks under Bank Law.

Okay, I was now officially paranoid.

I went to the restroom to attempt to make myself look less crazy. Milo leaped out and availed himself of the facilities. My cat knew how to use a toilet. Maybe I should have thought twice about bringing him into a ladies' lounge.

I glared into the mirror at my curly locks as I combed them into their newfound perfection. Having great hair was not worth my soul. I just didn't have that much vanity.

And then I realized what I was doing—looking for Max in the mirror. He wasn't there. I wanted to weep. Of course he wasn't there. I rummaged in my bag until I found my compact.

Max appeared wavering and faint in front of my reflection. "*Vanderventer*," he confirmed in my head. "*Use me*."

Apparently without the Zone, he didn't have the strength to linger, and he faded away. He'd said he couldn't see what I was doing unless I stood in front of my mirror. Did the bar mirror at Chesty's count? Did he know what had just happened? If not, what had he meant by *use* him? How?

I'd heard of students who suffered nervous breakdowns under the stress of finals. Maybe that was me. In any event, I didn't want to run into those goons again.

Use Max. I shrugged. I could use Max's buddies.

It was well past happy hour. I knew where to find them. Carrying my hope for a future in the books on my back, I hopped on the Harley and headed out to a real biker bar where the guys weren't too fond of suits and Escalades.

22

Even though this was only Monday and not a weekend party night, the boys at the bar greeted me with upraised beer bottles. I was too mentally and emotionally wiped to celebrate. I located Lance and strode straight back to his booth.

"Babe." He raised his glass in salute. "That was some awesome prize you brought us. Gonzo cleaned out the mechanicals, and we've got Tech Head drooling in cyber heaven over the gear. Max would be proud."

"Doubt it." I threw my backpack on the bench and slid into the booth. Milo hopped out as soon as I sat down. I watched him worriedly as he set out to explore, but he'd tackled gangsters. My guys shouldn't hurt him. "They came gunning for me at the club. I need a hideaway until I can finish finals. Know anyplace I can squirrel away?"

"Max's place is paid through the end of the month, but his family cleaned out the personal stuff. It's still furnished. We could find you an air mattress," he suggested.

I didn't know how I felt about that, but it did belatedly trigger a question that had been at the back of my mind. "What happened to all Max's books and papers? Did the family take them, too?"

Now even I was referring to them as "the family." I had to keep visions of mafia mobs out of my head.

Lance grinned smugly through his three-day-old beard. "We got there first. Knew he wouldn't want his papers pawed through by that family of his. Haven't burned them yet. You want a look-see?"

I really needed to study, but the guys loved bonfires and would take any excuse to start one. Those papers weren't long for this world, and I had a feeling I'd regret not looking into them. "Yeah, can you just store me with the papers for a while?"

He looked a little confused until the skinny guy in camouflage they called Tech Head wandered over and threw down a disc.

"They heard everything you ever said after Max died," he said without preamble. "The equipment is registered to Ace Associates. Their network is picked up by a feed at Acme Chemical. No imagination. These punks think we're stupid."

He took a seat beside Lance and stretched his boots under the table. "Acme was Max's hot button, so I played with the equipment and picked up recordings to and from the Escalade. It's all on there." He nodded at the disc. "They're so paranoid, they're recording each other and anyone who blinks in their vicinity."

My stomach rumbled, and I wasn't certain if it was because I hadn't eaten in hours or because I wanted to vomit. "Any clue who they are or what they want?" I asked with trepidation.

"The snoops don't know nothing," Tech Head asserted. "They kept calling Acme, asking what they should do next. They had guys tailing you every which way but not a one knows why. They filmed the funeral home and got you walking to your car but not any of the fighting. Some bigwig screamed at them about that. They photoed your movers and they were following their truck all over town. If anyone is putting two and two together, it ain't the snoops. I particularly liked the frame of your little bug driving by with the top down and the dark-haired guy at the wheel. They cursed up a storm over that one. They were running out of ideas, sounded like."

I rubbed my aching temples. "But no reason why they're following me? This is crazy."

Tech Head shrugged. "Got to be related to Max since that's when it started. Did he give you anything or say anything about Acme?"

I just barely kept from saying that Max would have told me if Acme had anything to do with the spies. Not only would I have had a hard time explaining dead Max talking, but Max *had* warned me—about his family. If I traced Acme's ownership, I knew it would lead back to the MacNeills, probably the Vanderventers as well. None of this told me anything.

"Take me to Max's papers," I said wearily. "And to a burger."

The gloom of a cloudy evening was settling in, but I could see well enough to judge that the rusted-out, leaning tin shed behind the bar, where they'd stored Max's boxes, was no place for sleeping. No wonder Lance had been confused when I'd asked to be stored with the papers. I'd obviously been living too long in civilization to think they would actually store papers somewhere safe, or dry. It started to rain, and the shed leaked. Crap.

I trudged back into the bar, ate my burger, fed Milo tidbits, and contemplated my next step.

I was still hoping, optimistically, that my hijab disguise and missing Miata had confused my followers about my whereabouts, so I didn't want to call Jane's movers if Acme was onto them. Of course, now that they were a few goons short, they might have given up, but I couldn't count on it. Maybe I should have gone with the suits just to see what in heck they wanted, but they hadn't appeared to be reasonable people.

I debated calling Schwartz, but he was a nice

guy with two jobs. Plus he was a cop, and not to be
trusted. He didn't need to know about the shady side
of town, and I could have gotten high just breathing
in here. And we'd best not get into where the Escalade
had gone. Apparently, my moral sensibility wasn't
offended by car theft or drugs, but Schwartz was nicer
than me.

Cora couldn't fit all those boxes in a Mini Cooper.
That left me one choice. I glared at my phone awhile
before I punched in Andre's number.

An anonymous white utility van pulled up at the bar an
hour later. I was standing under the overhang, waiting
out of the drizzle, Max's boxes lined up along the wall,
and Milo in my bag. The boys hadn't thought it a wise
idea to let strangers into their shed, which contained
other cartons and crates besides Max's. If these were
the boxes the rapist had wanted, they might be hotter
than stolen parts.

Andre climbed out of the driver's seat, looking
cool and substantial again. He gave me a once-over to
make certain I wasn't freaking out or holding a gun
on him and silently began lugging boxes to the back
of the van. I grabbed what I could, and those of the
guys still capable of walking straight helped. In a
matter of minutes, Max's life was inside Andre's van. I
was pretty certain Max would not be pleased.

Really, though, it's just not right for your boyfriend
to be dead and still inside your head. It's hard to move
on like that, so we could both have been displeased, I
supposed.

There was just enough room in the van to roll the
Harley into the back with the help of my guys. Andre
watched silently. I had no idea if he was ready to blow
up or just had nothing to say. At that point, I really
didn't care. My alternatives were shrinking with each
passing hour. I was still thoroughly frustrated that I
was wasting study time.

I had goons gunning for me, a van load of
potentially explosive material for which a man had
died, a boyfriend in hell, and a life that was falling
apart. I needed someone to talk with. Woo-woo Themis
and Max weren't helpful, and Max's biker friends were
limited in their understanding.

Andre probably wouldn't believe me, but he was
the only other person who knew about the boxes.
Who else could I turn to?

I climbed into the passenger seat while he got
behind the wheel. I checked on Milo, and he'd fallen
asleep, looking all cute and kitteny and not in the least
bobcat-like. Even my pet was weird.

"Where to?" Andre asked without inflection.

"Know an empty warehouse?" I slumped in the
seat, as much from exhaustion as for concealment.

He turned the ignition and backed out without
answering.

I got it. If I wouldn't talk to him, he wouldn't talk
to me.

I didn't know why I was resisting Andre. He'd
offered me a job, given me the Miata as a reward,
come to my rescue with an AK-47 or the equivalent.
He'd even mentioned the apartments and would have

taken me to see one if I had asked. And he was here now, the only semi-sane person I could count on.

Instinct continued to rebel against offering this man with so much power any part of me, but I just wasn't seeing any choices here.

"Max's family owns part of Acme Chemical," I said conversationally. "He was investigating his family business when he died. Those boxes contain his papers."

"Says who?" Andre demanded gruffly. "A bunch of stoned bikers?"

Well, there was another reason I'd been stalling. I rolled my eyes and considered opening my compact, but having Max and Andre yelling at each other wasn't conducive to my limited sanity.

"Max trusted his friends," I said calmly enough, trying to keep my weirdness to a minimum for the sake of rational communication. "Acme apparently hired corporate spies to record everything I've done since the funeral."

He snorted. "Hope you didn't do anything too personal."

"My boyfriend is *dead*," I reminded him. "Let's not get too perverted. I'm trying to be careful here. If Acme was spying on me, then they were also spying on the Zone."

"Yeah, I gathered that. What I want to know is *why*."

Finally, he sounded as if he might be coming to life.

"Because we're weird?" I suggested. "Maybe we're their own personal zoo or monkey experiment."

"Not until you blasted Max," he reminded me.

"I didn't blast him!" I said, summoning righteous indignation. "His brakes were cut and his steering mechanism tampered with."

"Like tires go flat and sprinkler systems flood when you're around?"

Not going there. I'd been mad that day. Had my powers somehow cut Max's brakes? I hadn't asked for him to die, but if my powers were metaphorical and not literal, then damning him to hell pretty well included death. It was my turn to sit in silence, refusing to talk. Andre didn't need to know that, did he?

"All right, I apologize," he finally said. "Sarah might intentionally kill someone, but you wouldn't."

I sneaked a peek at his profile, but we were driving down dark roads and all I could see were his wide shoulders and his too-perfect nose. I wondered if Saturn had sons and if so, who Andre had killed to get that profile.

"Sarah intentionally killed that guy today, and probably her husband and her mother, not that any of them were a great loss to the world," I informed him. I hadn't spent a lot of time philosophizing over vigilantism but I *was* a wannabe lawyer. I was pretty much on the side of judges and jury. Reluctantly, I concluded that Andre needed to know I was a loose cannon, for his own safety. "I just damned Max to hell, and he stupidly went."

Andre hit the brakes, but whether it was because he was nearing a stop sign or because of me, I couldn't tell. I just waited stoically for his response. I had to feel my way through this one inch at a time.

"You know for certain he went to *hell*?" he asked with interest.

"I know he's dead and his ghost is talking to me in mirrors. Don't know if that qualifies as hell. I never sent anyone there before."

He pondered that for a moment. "You think you're talking to Max in mirrors?"

"Yeah."

Or going insane, but Andre was pretty astute. He'd have caught that, too.

"Is he saying anything useful?"

"He said to stay away from you and the Zone. That's probably useful but not practical, especially since the asshole was using me to spy on the Zone before he died."

He glanced in my direction before asking, "You were mad at Max before his car crashed? That's why you damned him?"

"I thought he was going to kill me! You'd have done the same."

"And after you found out his brakes were cut, did you grieve?"

I stared at him, trying to figure out where this was going. "Of course. I'm not made of stone. We had six good months together."

"So now you think he's still alive and in a mirror?"

I looked at him suspiciously. "I don't know about alive."

"Denial," he said flatly. "This is the stage of grief called denial. You'll start bargaining with the mirror before long, promising to do better if he'll just come back. And when he doesn't, you're going to really sink low."

"Not buying it," I said firmly, although I knew I was skirting the truth. Was promising to track the guy who had almost killed the kids my way of bargaining with God? My way of promising to do better if only God would send Max back to me?

I flipped open my compact. Max wasn't coming in clearly, but I thought he looked wary. "I have your boxes in a truck. Where would you like me to take them?"

"*Dangerous,*" he said inside my head. "*Burn them.*"

"Nope, not burning them. Saturn's daughter demands justice, remember? I'll probably join you in purgatory if I don't do my job."

"*Justy, you're a pain in the butt,*" he said wearily. "*Find the file on Vanderventer.*"

"And do what with it?" I asked, but he was gone again.

Merely acknowledging my one-sided argument with a piece of glass with his usual snarky look of disbelief, Andre steered the van into an industrial storage area surrounded by chain-link fences. He punched a code into the gate, and it swung open to let him in. The man had more resources at his disposal than I wanted to consider.

"Saturn's daughter?" he finally asked as he drove between corrugated tin buildings.

"Long story. Max says there's a file called Vanderventer in the boxes. Is that useful information?"

"You already knew Vanderventer owns part of the chemical plant, didn't you? No, that's not proving anything except your overactive imagination."

"Then there's not a lot more I can say. I don't have time for investigating Vanderventer, Acme, or the Zone. My goal is to stay alive long enough to take finals. Everything else is optional."

"All right, I'll accept that. Want me to go through those papers? Or put Frank on them?"

I was torn. I really wanted to do it myself. But lives could be at stake if we didn't know what was going down. I'd just wasted an entire evening hiding when I needed to be studying.

"I'll look at the Vanderventer file first," I decided. "We'll know better how to proceed after we find that."

23

I was still wearing Ernesto's jacket against the chill of a spring night. At least the cheap polyester had finally dried. Sitting on the floor, grateful for my healthy legs, I leaned against the wall and flipped through the files in my lap while Milo fell asleep on top of my bag. If I really believed my legs had grown because I'd sent a rapist to hell, I'd have squirmed in discomfort, so I refused to believe it.

I'd had no idea Max had been hiding all this crap. Why the hell hadn't he kept computer files? Or at least a sane organizing system? All this time, I'd just assumed he didn't use computers because he liked doing cash business to avoid taxes. Instead, he'd been spying on me and his whole family and, with a true paranoid flair, kept his files off the radar with *paper*. Paper that he could burn without leaving a trace. Paper that couldn't be sorted without knowing his system.

Andre was still unloading boxes, working up a sweat. I was feeling guilty about pressing my boss into hard labor. Now I would owe Andre, big-time, and I hated being obligated to anyone, especially to anyone in authority. I'd spent too many years as a loner to fully comprehend how payback worked, but I was pretty certain Andre wasn't helping out of the goodness of his heart—although hard work looked good on him. I liked his sweaty, dusty forehead better than the smirk.

The storage unit had fluorescents overhead, not exactly great for my weak vision. Finished with the first stack of files, I put my new legs to work and crawled among the boxes. I was wearing my geeky glasses and an overlarge coat—not exactly a sexy look. But Andre's gaze was on my ass when he dropped a box nearby. I was still ticked that he didn't believe I talked to Max.

"Finals," I said conversationally, distracting his attention while pawing through another box. "I have another exam at noon tomorrow. I'm reserving energy for that."

"No, you're not. You're releasing it by frying tires and drenching my damned club." He flung down the last box and kicked it next to the wall.

"You'd rather I'd gone quietly with the spooks?" I asked in incredulity, looking up from the box I'd just opened. Max's handwriting and bad spelling were giving me a headache.

"No, I'd rather you waited until Schwartz and I had time to gather forces before you started attacking them! They had guns. You didn't!" Pretty Boy wasn't looking so pretty in the green glare of overheads. He looked Hulk furious. Was it my imagination, or was he starting to fade around the edges again? Definitely my imagination. I preferred his Jim Garner cool to the irrational Hulk.

"Okay, next time I'll sit around and twiddle my thumbs in hopes someone better at beating up people will come along and save me. That totally works." I kicked a box toward him. "Here, that one is labeled Acme. Take a look."

"If you shake a nut tree, nuts will fall out," he said enigmatically, flipping through the files without much interest. "You should have let me take care of the Escalade."

"Andre, you so know that isn't happening," I retorted in a pitying tone. "I've never had anyone take care of me, even when I was a kid, and it ain't happening now. I'm grateful for your help, don't get me wrong. But if I can do it myself, I will. And just how can you be so damned certain I was responsible for your weak sprinkler system?" I asked, just to irritate him.

"Because that's what I do," he replied. "I put two and two together and figure out where the threes are coming from. I've had years to perfect that talent, and I haven't wasted it flooding bars. I've been watching you, waiting to see what you'll become. Don't underestimate me or any other Zone inhabitant. We have our uses."

"Should I ever pass the bar exam, I'll remember that," I said, not wanting to learn more for fear it would set my hair on fire. I was just happy to know he didn't know what I was any more than I did. Digging through another box, I triumphantly removed a fat file labeled Vanderventer. "Got it. Let's go home. I have a friend I'd like to look through the rest of these."

I didn't know if Jane could afford the time, but at some point, someone had to follow Max's lead.

I was flipping through the file and didn't hear Andre walk up behind me. He hauled me off the floor, swung me around, and hugged me so tight, I could feel the press of his shirt buttons against my boobs, although the damned file kind of got in the way. His hand crushed my head into his shoulder so I couldn't read his expression.

"Until we know what you are and what you can do," his voice rumbled against my ear, "you have to start thinking of yourself as a rare treasure needing constant protection. Got that?"

His breath was warm in my hair, and I really enjoyed the masculine hardness pressed against my soft bits. I wanted to wriggle and test his arousal, but triumph only went so far. I didn't want to be rare or protected.

"You make me sound like a loggerhead turtle. I am not a protected species, or if I am, I want it to be a wolf or a tiger." I shoved at his shoulders. He didn't completely release me, but wary of my dangerous knees and feet, he let me keep a distance.

"Talk to me after next week." I relented when his breath against my ear gave me warm shivers. "I'll be your golden lamb. Right now, I just want to study and finish school and keep out of sight. How am I supposed to do that?"

He growled in a way that made my insides all weak and watery. He might not have been bulky-big like Max, but Andre had testosterone out the ears. And I responded to his embrace. I didn't have to like it—especially if he was as warped as me. I wriggled some more, until he let me go.

"If it takes bodyguards and Humvees, that's what we'll do," he said. "You won't like what you find in that Vanderventer file, so I want people with you twenty-four-seven. You have a hair trigger."

"Do not," I argued, jerking away from him and marching for the door. "I just think faster than most people."

"You don't think at all or you wouldn't have stolen the Escalade! You really didn't think those bums would take that lying down, did you?"

"I got rid of them, didn't I? And their nasty equipment as well. If they mean to follow me around, they might as well learn it will be a damned expensive operation." I was *proud* of my accomplishment. The spies were the douche nozzles, not me.

"Your damned expensive operation has practically put *me* out of business." Andre pried open the warehouse door, checked outside, then pulled it back enough for me to slip out. "You're a walking loaded weapon and someone needs to put a safety lock on you."

"That someone being you?" I asked scornfully. "Why don't you waste your time trying to 'figure out what I am' while I go somewhere quiet and study?"

In the ugly security lighting, I could see him debating his reply. His eyes burned like coals when he suppressed his fury. "You endanger anyone you're around," he concluded. "You've not only threatened the macho of dangerous men, but humiliated them badly in front of people they consider scum, and in the eyes of their bosses. They won't be polite next time."

He opened the van door and practically heaved me in. I hunkered down, scowling, knowing he was right. Over the years, I'd learned the psyches of bullies. That didn't mean I paid attention to their messed-up heads or used what I knew to avoid them—hence the martial arts lessons—but I understood them. Their minds were fairly simple, after all; they wanted control and domination because, without it, they were terrified.

Which meant the goons had to take me out to feel superior again. Would I ever get a break? Have a normal life sitting quietly behind a desk?

I'd tried that these last few years. Hadn't liked it much. I scowled some more.

Andre slid into the driver's seat and started the

ignition. I thought about asking where we were going, but I wasn't sure I wanted to know. I was still chewing on the very little information he'd fed me earlier. He put two and two together and figured out where the threes came from? So he observed and figured out the oddities in the Zone. And then he used them. Oddities like me. I could easily become another tool in his arsenal. That notion bothered me.

The van pulled up at the flower shop Andre owned on Edgewater. Silently, we locked up the van and got into the convertible parked there. He put the hood up. Tinted glass concealed us. I didn't see any Lincolns or Escalades around, but the feeling of being watched never left me these days.

"I'm trusting you, Clancy," Andre said, almost angrily. "I don't trust anyone, but you," he muttered, and drove down a back street I didn't recognize. "Something is happening with you that we haven't seen in the Zone. Around here, good comes with bad, but mostly it's shades of gray. I want to believe that you're the good break we need. Which probably means I've finally gone over the edge like everyone else."

"Yeah, thanks for the vote of confidence," I responded without enthusiasm. "If it helps, I don't trust you any further than I can see you, either."

He shot me a look I assumed was one of scorn, since I couldn't really see him in the dark. Because I'd gone this far in baring my innards, I asked casually, "Have you ever heard of the Daughters of Saturn?"

"Sounds like a female band. Should I have heard of

them?" The Mercedes purred like Milo, sliding up to a gate with a key card lock. Andre pushed in a card and the gate slid open.

No information there. I didn't really want to explain. "Probably not. Just something I heard."

I watched with interest as we drove behind what appeared to be an abandoned brick edifice with a loading dock. The blue neon lighting didn't mar the buildings, so we weren't in the Zone as I knew it, but the early-1900s industrial architecture was similar. Attached buildings without signs or lights or any indication of habitation occupied at least a city block. In the beam of his headlights I could see not grassy backyards, but lots paved with crumbling blacktop and gravel sprouting weeds.

Only this one building had a gate around the parking lot. Three stories tall, with boarded windows on the first floor and gaping emptiness above, the place didn't scream security.

Andre drove the Mercedes up the loading ramp, opened a rusty, automatic overhead door, and pulled inside. After he turned off his headlights, a dim bulb illuminated the interior of what appeared to be a typical garage decorated with trash cans, snow shovels, and the kind of things garages stored. If this had once been a store, it had been out of business for a while. There was no inventory on the wooden shelves lining the walls. He'd found the perfect location to protect his pricey car.

"Why couldn't we leave the boxes here?" I asked, wondering where "here" was.

"If Acme's goons really are after them, I don't want them anywhere around this place," he said curtly, without explaining why.

He climbed out and I followed suit, gathering up Milo, my backpack, and the Vanderventer file while the garage door closed behind us. Andre took the heavy backpack and slung it over one shoulder as if it were a jacket. He opened a door at the far end, and we strolled into another storeroom. Boxes and barrels were scattered in disorganization around the walls and on metal shelving.

He continued to a door on an interior wall, guided by a pale night-light. Or at least, I assumed it was a night-light. It was hard to imagine electricity in a building that smelled as old and musty as this one. Maybe the light ran on battery power.

I almost turned around and refused to follow, when he disappeared down cellar stairs so dark I couldn't see my fingers in front of my nose. Milo was peering out of my messenger bag with interest and not growling, so I sucked it up and set my heels on the first step. No spiderwebs tangled in my hair. No rodents squealed and ran. I found a rail and dared to touch it as I edged my way down in the dark.

"Are you a vampire who sees without light?" I asked, just to make certain Andre was still ahead somewhere.

"Sorry." He flicked on another dim light that glowed softly along the stair treads. "I'm so used to the path, I don't even notice."

I still couldn't find the source of the light, but at least I could see the stairs had an end ahead, and I could follow Andre's graceful male stride downward. I was feeling way more dependent than I liked, but I desperately wanted to stay alive and graduate, and I didn't want my beautiful new home contaminated by Cadillac gangsters.

We followed what appeared to be a dimly lit tunnel long enough to traverse a city block before we took more stairs going up.

"Does the Zone breed paranoia?" I asked, realizing that this tunnel was meant to conceal Andre's movements, just as I'd used back alleys.

"We have security issues. You've thrown us into turmoil. We'll need to develop a better plan once we settle your problem."

There it was again, the ubiquitous *we*. "You're running an underground organization? To do what?"

"Not underground. Right out in the open. And survival is our main agenda."

At the top of the stairs, he used several keys to unlock a metal door. It swung open noiselessly, and he held it, waiting for me to precede him inside.

"Said the spider to the fly," I muttered, clomping into what appeared to be a perfectly normal kitchen, one with granite countertops and shiny stainless steel appliances. The kind of kitchen I'd never had and never thought to have. "This your place?"

"I own it, if that's what you're asking." Without more explanation, he led the way to more stairs.

Ah, so he was protecting his lair by not bringing the boxes here. I had to wonder if I wasn't more dangerous than the boxes.

I don't know a whole lot about architecture, but I was pretty sure the narrow back stairs we were taking were meant for servants and that only old buildings had them. And the layout reminded me of the Victorian boardinghouse I was supposed to be living in. I'd never seen Mrs. Bodine's kitchen, but the placement seemed right.

My glimpse of the second floor didn't look exactly like the floor I lived on. The wood was clean and polished, for instance. But the similarity was strong enough that I realized we were probably in a row house neighboring the one where I lived.

"Is this where you had the vacancy?" I asked. "In your house?"

"One of the second-story apartments is available," he acknowledged. "I hadn't realized Pearl's tenant had permanently disappeared. Good detective work on your part," he said grudgingly.

"Why are we continuing up if you have a vacant apartment?" I asked, starting to balk.

"There are beds upstairs. Desk, computer, kitchen stocked with food. How many more days of finals?"

This was almost Tuesday. My last final was Thursday. "Three." I glanced longingly at the lovely wood glimpsed from the second-story landing, and wrinkled my nose in dismay at climbing to the third floor— where Andre lived? Or was that his place on the first floor? "I still have to leave the building to go to school. You can't really hide me here."

"We can play mind games with the bastards for three days. C'mon. I haven't got all night."

His impatience spurred me on. He wasn't acting like a would-be lover, despite our earlier embrace. He opened a door at the top of the stairs and startled a gray-haired man who looked remarkably like Andre.

24

"Tina, my father, Julius. Dad, this is the Tina Clancy I've been telling you about."

I shuffled files and bags until I could hold out a hand to shake. If this was what Andre would look like in thirty years, I approved. His father was slighter in stature, but he had a full head of salt-and-pepper hair and just enough wrinkles around his eyes to look experienced and amused.

He bowed over my hand in a courtly manner while studying me as if I might be the secret to locked doors. Milo didn't growl, so I trusted his instincts.

I still didn't trust Andre. He hadn't mentioned his father's last name, and I was betting it wasn't Legrande. He knew I'd snoop, and he didn't want his past revealed.

"I apologize for the late intrusion, sir," I said politely. "Andre thinks I need dragons to guard me."

"I'm not a very good dragon," Julius claimed, "but not too many people bother me here. No one will know I have a guest unless you tell them."

Andre allowed a few more pleasantries, then, with his usual impatience, ushered me down the hall to my hideaway. Or prison, depending on how I decided to look at it. The accommodations were pleasant, but they weren't home. I didn't even have Milo's litter box, although now that I'd learned my kitty was toilet-trained, I didn't worry too much.

At that point, I was too tired to care much where I lay my head. Andre left with promises to have Cora bring some stuff from my apartment that I required. I showered and conked out.

I staggered out of bed in the first gray light of Tuesday dawn and hit the books for my noon exam, but I needed caffeine. Wearing last night's leather capris and halter, I slipped down the hall to the kitchen and found the pot already cooking. I filled a mug, and almost jumped out of my shoes when I turned around to find Julius in the doorway.

"I would fix you some breakfast, but I fear my

cooking skills only extend to bowls of cereal," he apologized.

Breakfast would be excellent. The greasy burger I'd consumed at the biker bar last night hadn't helped my metabolism. My current situation was uncomfortable, but my peripatetic childhood had taught me how to make myself at home anywhere. "I can cook, if you have the groceries. What would you like?"

"I don't suppose you can make omelets?" he asked wistfully.

"Easy." I shrugged and checked his refrigerator—as Andre had promised, it was fully stocked.

Everything was too damned normal. I kept waiting for the sky to fall as we consumed a ham-and-cheese omelet and English muffins. I could probably count on the fingers of one hand the times I'd had a normal breakfast in a real home. I had been working toward that reality for a long time, but after recent events, I was pretty certain this was as close as I would ever come.

I returned to my books while Julius cleaned up the kitchen. He promised to look after Milo while I was busy. I almost felt sane buried in the mysteries of contracts and torts. Law made *sense*. I loved the balance and justice of it. I was determined to ace my tests and see what life looked like from the other side of school.

Before long, Cora arrived with clean clothing and the rest of my books. She came via the front door like a normal person, although she glanced around with curiosity. "Andre's place?" she whispered as she handed over the bags.

"His father's." I'd already ascertained that Andre

wasn't anywhere around, and there didn't appear to be a room for him.

She filed that information in her encyclopedic mind and nodded. "I thought I ought to tell you that Frank hacked the corporate spy logs yesterday. Ace's main client is Acme Chemical, but they apparently do a good side business running investigations for some of the owners."

I narrowed my eyes. "I don't suppose that includes names like MacNeill and Vanderventer?"

"It does." She didn't look surprised that I knew. "Your name appears in both files."

I didn't let the dangerous red rage build this time. I simply wished Senator Dane Vanderventer a pleasant dip in hell—fry his toes a little so he knew what torment felt like.

I hadn't looked up the MacNeills because they hadn't run over any kids lately, and I'd already damned poor Max, so I didn't wish more trouble on them. Yet. They could be innocent parties for all I knew.

But it was a good bet that a car linked to Dane Vanderventer had run over those teenagers, and if he was prowling the Zone, then it was an even better bet that he'd sicced his thugs on me for reasons unknown. Did he know I was trying to track his limo?

Still, that didn't explain the rapist who had wanted the *boxes*. Max's boxes, presumably?

"There's not a damned thing I can do about Ace or Acme at this point," I admitted. "We have no proof that they've done anything wrong except hire thugs. I can't confront Vanderventer about the kids if I want to take the bar exam. Beating up a senator will not get me through the ethics committee."

Cora looked surprised that I'd even consider confronting him. "We just need to know who we're dealing with so we can stay out of their way. You don't have to do nothing, girl."

Yeah, I did. I didn't know why, but I fully intended to get in the faces of my nemeses one of these days. Just not today.

I thanked Cora and showed her out. I shoved my fury and Vanderventer out of my mind and got down to the nitty-gritty of law.

When it came time to head out for school, Andre reappeared up the back stairs. I could almost have gotten into this skull-and-crossbones stuff if I hadn't been so nervous about graduating. In expectation of his arrival, I'd changed into a prim, straight sundress that now hit above my knees. My feet ached from wearing the spike heels all day yesterday, and Cora hadn't brought over my sandals, so I lowered myself to a stodgy pair of kitten heels she'd chosen to go with the dress. I was hoping to maintain my lawyer cred for just a little while longer.

This time, I didn't shiver so much when we crossed under the street—I'd finally worked out locations—to the Mercedes. No wonder he kept the car intact. No one would look for it inside an abandoned warehouse.

I kept my head firmly buried in the law test the rest of the day. I didn't hear the news about Senator Dane Vanderventer being hospitalized for third-degree burns from a charcoal fire, until Andre hit me with his smart phone when I left the law building. He didn't even wait until we were in the car.

"Two and two," he said with a smirk, jogging toward the administrative parking lot where he'd parked illegally. "Cora told you about Vanderventer and Ace, didn't she?"

I couldn't read while running after him. Not until we were in the car and racing down the highway could I don my glasses and scan the screen.

Vanderventer had been cooking on his balcony when he'd apparently knocked over the portable grill, at nine o'clock in the morning.

No one grills in the morning.

I'd talked to Cora around nine.

I'd wished Vanderventer a cozy dip in hell.

I choked and flung the phone back at him.

"See something familiar?" Andre asked dryly, returning the phone to his pocket. "Not water pipes this time?"

"That's ridiculous," I asserted. "He was miles away. I cannot hurt someone miles away, far outside of the Zone. I will not take the blame for this, unless you just want to dump all the world's problems on my shoulders."

"Denial," he taunted. "You're excellent at denial. Go talk to your dead boyfriend and see what he says."

I hadn't even thought about Max while I was focusing on the test. I'd come out of the testing center feeling pretty damned good, and Andre was raining on my parade.

"Did you read the Vanderventer file?" I demanded,

turning the tables. "What did you find? Anything to get angry about?"

"I used to *work* for Acme. So did my father. I already know who owns the plant and who's responsible for the chemical spills and worse. I don't need a damned bunch of paper to tell me who at Acme cuts cost corners, lies, cheats, and steals to cover their asses when accidents happen. Unless you're rich and powerful enough to take down a senator and his cronies, there's nothing you can do about it. And we don't *want* to do anything about it, if they just leave us alone. So, no, I didn't read the file, and no, I wasn't angry enough to dump hot coals on Dane, although there have been times I've considered it."

"You're on a first-name basis with a senator?" I asked.

"We went to school together, and that's all you need to know." Andre swung the Mercedes off the interstate onto the exit leading to the harbor.

I could have done a whole lot with just that one statement if I'd had time, which I didn't. I knew rich boys like Dane Vanderventer didn't go to public school, for instance. Which meant Andre had either once been rich or had been a scholarship student at a ritzy school, making him fabulously intelligent. I was wagering on the latter.

"So you're mad at me because you think I fried an old friend of yours?" I asked, sounding nonchalant. "*Now* who has weird ideas?"

"I'm missing yesterday's deposit," he said curtly, avoiding my question. "Since I know you didn't have time to steal it, and I'm pretty certain the thugs didn't manage it, being busy destroying Chesty's, I'm guessing we have the invisible thief to blame, right?"

My happy mood was fading rapidly. I eyed him warily. "That's my guess."

"Do that funky thing you do and find the thief," he ordered.

"You want him dead or alive?" I asked sarcastically.

"I don't care how you find him. The insurance company refuses to cover another loss. I'm tired of being ripped off. Just picture him caught."

"You're serious?" I stared at him, and he wasn't laughing.

"There are a lot of people depending on me for their income. I'm dead serious. I take back what I was thinking yesterday. Let's experiment."

"Oh, well, sure, as long as I have the grand Andre's permission." I waved my hand airily. "Let's visualize our grabby thief appearing with his hand stuck in a cash drawer." Privately, I visualized Andre giving everyone raises, but the hand-in-a-cash-drawer idea appealed to me, so I invoked that thought, too. I didn't like thieves who jeopardized my job.

Five minutes later, just as we turned down the back alley behind the abandoned storefronts, across from the Victorians, Andre's phone rang. He halted the car, read the text, handed it to me, then began backing out.

Cght thef read the message from Bill. I hated text messages. They reminded me of Max's bad spelling.

Andre obviously had no such problem. He gunned

the car back to the Zone and parked in front of the bar and grill. It was after four, so the cash drawer should have been counted and the deposit prepared, but I hadn't been there to do them.

I still wasn't seriously believing my visualization had caught a thief at work until I walked into the bar—and saw a skinny, tattooed teenager with his hand stuck in the huge brass till of the oversize mechanical cash register.

He flickered out when he saw me. *Flickered*. He disappeared. I could see all the bottles and the shelf that he'd been standing in front of. He reappeared again when Bill shook him by the scruff of his collar. This was the little freak who'd been sneaking into my apartment, leaving clippings?

"I just walked away for a minute," Bill said with disgust. "Do I call the cops?"

Andre shot me a glare of victory. "Not yet. Let's get his story."

I was suffering the nauseating sensation that this was all about me.

"Clancy, you have to let him go if we want to question him," Andre said conversationally.

"What?" Bill and I both asked at once.

Andre stared directly at me with an expectant look. "*You*. You're wanting to slam his face into that register, aren't you? Don't. Open the drawer. Dispense justice. Do whatever it is you do."

"Me?" I think I actually squeaked. Andre was looking at me with an expectation and respect that not only aroused my frustrated hormones, but made me think he was actually seeing me as some kind of freakily violent Lady Justice.

I sent the tin statue above Bill's door a quick glance. She winked at me from beneath the blindfold again.

Uneasily, I edged closer to the teenager. "Who are you?"

It was only when I got closer that I could see he was wearing my good Clark wedge-soled sandals. *My shoes!* He'd been in my apartment again. I would have to crush him.

He looked too terrified for me to fear. Or to crush. Was that my skull earring in his ear?

"Nobody. I'm nobody," he said, shaking in his— *my*—shoes.

"Oh, you're somebody, all right," I said in as threatening a tone as a five-five female in kitten heels could carry off. "You're the somebody who stole my deposit twice, aren't you? You're a somebody who saw that limo fly out of the bank and run over kids and you used their grief to steal my bag and run. You're a low-down somebody scum who would sneak into my apartment and steal my damned shoes while I was sleeping!"

He was weeping and cringing, and I visualized the drawer opening and letting him go. Bill kept his hand on his collar as he collapsed on the floor, rocking back and forth in tears.

"He *made* me do it," he sobbed, over and over. "He made me. . . ."

25

I didn't have another test until Thursday. This was Tuesday. I had time to torture a teenager. I was just feeling too disoriented to put much effort into it.

The question *What am I?* burned a sick sensation through my skull.

Bill gave me a hamburger, but in my head, I was still seeing visuals of a senator being fried by flaming charcoal and me laughing about catching a thief in a cash drawer. I was not only a freak, but a damned dangerous one, especially since I had no way of knowing if the Forces of the Universe would take my suggestions literally.

I would surely be joining Max in hell. I desperately needed to talk to Max, but I wasn't revealing that peculiarity to an audience currently staring at me as if I'd developed horns. Or maybe a halo.

My spaghetti-strap dress couldn't protect me from the chill. I didn't have a sweater. Andre noticed me shaking and poured coffee. Bill had tied up our thief, but even the ropes vanished when the kid intermittently flickered out, so Bill had to wrap the rope around a hook in the ceiling so he couldn't run. I didn't ask what the quite-industrial-looking hook was doing up there. It was hard to imagine anyone hanging macramé plant holders in a bar, but it would have been a good place for a plant, if plants actually grew down here. I couldn't remember seeing any.

Maybe they were invisible, like the kid.

"It's Leibowitz, man," the kid kept saying. "He told me if I didn't pay him, he'd turn me in to the station for theft. Look at me, man!" the kid cried. "You know what they do to people like me in prison?"

"You mean people who steal shoes?" I asked, not wanting my Clarks back now that his grimy feet had been in them. But I did remember the day I'd seen Leibowitz berating a skinny teen, taking advantage of a Zonie because the cop knew invisibility was no defense in the real world? "What did you do, steal Leibowitz's pretty badge?"

I rubbed my brow, trying not to think of the patrol cop with anger or I might melt him like Frosty the

Snowman. This was just a kid, probably gay if the shoes and his comment were any evidence, a misfit living on the streets, and Leibowitz had demanded bribes. Where was the justice here?

"I was hungry, man!" the kid cried, looking at me with pleading red eyes. I was guessing it was from weeping and not his natural color. "I just took his hamburger when he wasn't looking. He doesn't need to be eating that much anyway! I was doing the dude a *favor*."

I was in such a state that I almost choked on laughter. I was actually starting to like the little twerp, in a totally condescending, Clint Eastwood sort of way. I knew what Clint would do.

If the real world couldn't deal with an invisible thief, he would dispense justice on his own. I'd rather have dispensed of Leibowitz, but that was owing to personal dislike and wouldn't have hinged on an objective trial. "Wild west, vigilante justice," I muttered. "Doesn't work. I *know* that."

Bill looked at me with skepticism, but Andre followed my thinking. "You have to admit that we don't have courts that can deal with invisible thieves. And invisible thieves don't make good witnesses against lousy cops. The Zone needs its own form of justice."

I shot him an angry look. "Are you a damned mind reader?" I didn't wait for him to answer, probably because I was already creeped out and didn't want to know. "What makes me the purveyor of justice? That's what you want, isn't it? Why me?"

He held out his hand. "Give me your compact."

I must have looked incredulous as I rummaged in my bag. Andre didn't respond, just waited. I slapped the cheap plastic powder case in his hand, wondering if Max would appear for Andre. That would serve both of them right.

Andre turned me around so my back was to the bar and held open the hand mirror in front of my nose. Since he was holding it, I didn't see Max, more's the pity. I really wanted to shake Andre as badly as this day was shaking me. I looked blankly at my fancy hair in the tiny compact. No horns protruded yet. "And?"

"Look at the mirror behind you. What do you see?"

Curiosity getting the better of fear, I squinted into the little mirror and tried to focus on the big mirror behind the bar. I could see the back of my head. My hair was mussed from the convertible ride. I reached out to adjust Andre's hand so I could see to comb out the mess.

On my left shoulder blade I was wearing a small tattoo of balance scales just like Sarah's.

Shit. Shit. Shit. Shit.

"Where did *that* come from?" I whispered in horror. Law firms weren't big on tattoos. And while this one was reasonably discreet, it didn't convey sunshine and roses. I'd have to quit wearing tank tops and sundresses. And here I'd wasted all this time trying to be invisible. How long had the damned thing been there?

"I don't drink. I don't get tattoos while drunk!" I protested.

I reached over my shoulder and tried to rub or smudge the image; then I licked my finger and worked on it some more. From what little I could tell in the compact mirror, I had no effect.

"Two and two," Andre said, returning the mirror to me.

Now that I was holding the compact, Max instantly appeared, looking alarmed. I shut him up and shoved him in my bag. I hadn't come to terms with the MacNeill family just yet. I hadn't come to terms with myself. I gave Andre the evil eye.

He shrugged. "Sarah has one just like it. She showed up the same day you tried to set fire to the bank. She killed her husband. You killed your boyfriend. Her husband was abusive, so she probably had right on her side more than you did, but you thought you were defending yourself. You were defending yourself every other time, too. Try doing something for someone else now."

"I was saving Diane and the kitchen staff!" I protested. "It isn't all about me. What are you getting at?"

Andre looked at me thoughtfully. "I'm not sure yet. Still doing the peculiar math . . ." He looked back at the young thief as if suddenly remembering what had begun this conversation. "Now, it's about *him*." He nodded in the kid's direction. The boy was still flickering in and out, but now that he was watching us with curiosity, he was mostly in. "You caught him. What do you want to do with him?"

"Tina caught him?" Bill asked. "She wasn't even here."

"Does your cash drawer usually freeze when someone's hand is in it?" Andre asked, not even bothering to look away from me. "She did it. She told me she was doing it."

I had. And laughed. I was one sick puppy.

"What's the tattoo got to do with it?" I whispered, looking away from Andre because I couldn't bear the accusation in his eyes.

"Not certain yet, but coincidences don't happen down here. Things happen because they're meant to. Show us you're on our side." His voice was cold. I wondered what he'd do if I told him to jump off a cliff.

Probably jump off a cliff.

Which made him a fool or a damned courageous bastard to say such a thing to me, the dispenser of bad justice.

Saturn's daughter, dispenser of justice. Sarah and I were daughters of a farmer god, or from a planet with rings. Whatever. Better than Satan, I guessed, but maybe not by much.

I spun the stool around and studied the kid hanging from a hook in front of the plate-glass window. "What's your name?"

"Tim," he said sullenly. "And you're sleeping in *my* place. You changed the locks! Where was I supposed to go? It was bad enough when the old lady threw out all my stuff. I needed new digs. That takes cash."

Suddenly things were starting to make some sense. I wasn't happy with the invasion of my privacy, but this kid had obviously suffered a shock or two.

"What happened to turn you invisible?" I asked.

He shrugged. "Don't know. I was just coming home from the movies one night, and some rat bastard started chasing me. I tripped, and I knew I was going to get creamed, and then I just disappeared." He looked weary, as if he'd repeated this story to himself too often.

I wasn't a scientist. I couldn't analyze what chemicals had done to the Zone. Or even to Andre or Sarah. But I was willing to gather evidence.

Had that been what Max was doing—gathering evidence of Zone anomalies? It still made me furious to think he'd hooked up with me because of where I worked and not because of me. I was glad all I'd been able to tell him about was moving statues, not invisible people.

"It took me a long time to come back," the kid continued. "I was there, but no one could see me. You know how hard it is to get food when no one sees you?"

"So you stole it. You grew up down here?" I tried to apply case law but I was pretty certain there was nothing relevant.

"Yeah. My mom had a place above the florist. But she got busted for dealing weed a few months back, and I couldn't pay the rent. Mrs. Bodine let me do odd jobs, and I did some dishwashing and then I found a job over at a goth shop so I could make rent, and Mrs. Bodine let me have a place cheap if I did the repairs."

"And then you got chased by a bully, disappeared, and tried to steal a sandwich from a *cop*." I prodded him rudely, not liking the position Andre was throwing me into. Prosecution had never been my goal.

"I was *hungry*," he protested. "I couldn't go to work when no one could see me!"

"Make a good ghost," Bill said stoically, polishing his bar glasses.

"I don't think ghosts get paid," I replied, trying to figure out what in heck I was supposed to do here. There was nothing fair about being both judge and prosecution. But Andre and Bill were just listening, while I was doing all the work. Interesting. Usually men do all the pushing around.

The kid was starting to flicker again.

"Have you been eating since you started stealing our cash?" I asked.

"I can sort of stay visible sometimes now. I can go to fast-food places," he said, staring at his toes.

Toes. Ugly male toes in my Clark sandals. I shoved the anger back in place again. *It's not about me.*

"So you pay for food now and don't steal it? But it's okay to steal money?"

His hands were tied, so he couldn't do more than glare at me. "I never stole nothing until Leibowitz came along and wanted a handout every time he saw me. He said I'd disappear in jail and never get fed. I *like* working. But I can't work like this."

"You pay for your food?" I pressed, trying to determine the level of his crime. "Or do you just steal everything, now that it's so easy?"

I was pretty certain there was a lesson for me in that question, but my head was too close to exploding for me to investigate ethics and morals and anger management and philosophy all at once.

"I pay for it when I'm visible," he agreed sullenly. "And I would have got my apartment back but you got it first."

Oh, right, lay on the guilt. "Those your plants?" I asked, putting florist and kid and dead plants together in a big leap of faith.

"Yeah, they were my mother's. Mrs. Bodine said it was okay to move them in there, but she never goes outside and can't take care of them. I didn't want to scare her too much by creeping around."

For caring about an old lady, I wanted to forgive him right then and there, but the shoes and the earring were eating at me. I didn't have much, and I liked to keep what I owned. Okay, so now it was about me again.

"The shoes?" I asked sarcastically. "Did they belong to your mother, too?"

He looked at the monstrous big roses on his toes and wiggled them. "You never wear them. I thought if nobody could see me, I could see how they looked, but you came home and I had to run."

Bill and Andre snorted. I wanted to bang my head on the bar. The kid was really getting to me.

"Is that my earring, too?" I asked, just to present all the evidence to the court of one.

He looked embarrassed. "It's cooler than mine. You had two, and I never saw you wearing them. You wear preppy stuff. I figured you didn't like skulls. I didn't have time to take it out."

I rolled my eyes and turned back to Bill. "He stole from your cash drawer," I reminded him, then looked at Andre. "And your deposits, which I'm sure you'll continue nagging the insurance companies to pay back. I'm not holding him because of a pair of shoes and an earring. What's your verdict?"

I wasn't doing this all myself. Justice demanded better.

"You're not going to fry him?" Andre asked with interest.

"Why the devil would I fry him?" I asked. "Yeah, he made me mad." I had another thought and whirled around to the kid again. "Is the tabby Manx your cat?"

He nodded slowly. "Sort of. I found him in the garbage and took him in. But then I disappeared. He knew where I was and followed me, so it wasn't good for him to hang around."

Which explained why Milo didn't growl at my invisible intruder. Milo trusted him. Milo had good instincts.

I turned back to my jury of two. "A kid who takes care of plants and cats and has good taste in shoes can't be all bad. He needs a home and a job."

"I can tell you who the guys are who busted in Chesty's," Tim said eagerly, now that it looked like I was a pushover. "I sneaked around and listened. I could spy for you."

I don't like spies and I think kids ought to be in school, but I could see this was a special situation. I waited on Andre.

"I can find you a room and put you to work," he said with deceptive disinterest, leaning back against the bar with his arms crossed. "Who are the goons?"

"You gotta let me down from here," the kid intelligently insisted. "I can give you their names."

At Andre's nod, Bill let him down. A minute later, I had six names scribbled on a bar napkin.

I was seriously in the Zone. If I really could dispense justice by visualizing, I wanted vengeance on the shits who had taken my friends hostage, shot up Chesty's, and given me gray hairs by following me and bugging my apartment. I wanted to turn them into gorillas in the zoo so people could watch them poop and fornicate all day.

But much to my distress, I realized they might have families who would miss them. I didn't want innocents to suffer. And the owner of one of these names was already dead from chimpanzee suffocation. Schwartz had hauled two more down to the station for formal justice, and the other might not have an arm left.

Could I really dispense informal justice? And if I did, would it cause unanticipated harm elsewhere? I was itching for revenge, but I didn't want to be a vigilante.

"Do you know which of these jerks are still on the loose?" I asked, not really expecting an answer.

Tim nodded eagerly and checked off two names.

"Very useful, man," I commended him, tucking the information away for future pondering.

"The tattoo turns gold when you do whatever it is you just did," Andre said nonchalantly.

I glared at him. I hadn't done anything except ponder justice. "I need food and study time before I can employ more traditional means of hunting jackals. What are you doing with him?"

The kid was eagerly slurping down a Coke that Bill had given him.

"Let him rent the empty apartment and keep him out of trouble," Andre said with a shrug.

Decision made, justice administered. Scary, but not the bad kind of scary. More like the *Man, I really hit that hoop* kind of power-proud scary. I couldn't let it go to my head, though.

Which meant I couldn't visualize two goons into a zoo. I needed to be alone so I could pull myself together. Maybe I could talk to Max a little. I needed to be reassured that I was still just me, although me branded with the scales of justice. I wondered when that had happened. I wasn't prone to checking myself out in mirrors and I didn't have a man in my life to see me naked anymore—which meant it had probably happened after Max died.

If I really had caught a thief and set fire to a senator, I was no longer in a position to keep my head down and my mouth shut. Although it might be wise if I practiced doing so before power went to my head. To be or not to be—that was always the question.

My phone rang. I didn't recognize the number. That could just mean the Zone was hungry for meatballs.

What the heck . . . I answered because it was simpler than making a decision.

"The administration at your former school just forwarded your records, along with the criminal charges filed against you," Schwartz said. "The top brass are breathing down my neck. Someone wants you gone. Lie low, will you?"

Oh, crap. Just when I'd thought I was finding my way, the cops had my number again. I was pretty sure daughters of Saturn weren't invulnerable. My leg could still break if I was pushed down stairs.

26

Andre's Mercedes sidled up to me before I even made it out of the Zone. He gestured for me to get in. Rather than be hauled around like a gunnysack again, I complied silently, slamming the door.

"Cora conjures snakes when she's mad," he said conversationally. "Started a few years back when one of Frank's clients came after her with a shotgun. Put the fear of God in the bastard when a python swung down and stared him in the eye."

"I wasn't mad when I imagined catching the invisible thief." I leaned my head against the window and did my very best not to think, because I really wanted to make those goons walk naked through the park and I knew I didn't dare.

"No, you do insane things when you're mad, like stealing Escalades from thugs. But it's probably all connected somehow. Tim doesn't disappear when he's mad. Sarah turns to a chimp when she's frightened. Some of us eventually learn control."

I glared at him for that *us*. "You're putting two and two together? Cora conjures snakes and you just get math?" I asked, just to keep from answering the question in his voice. "If you're included in that 'us,' what else do you have going for you? That's hardly enough for a guy who's lived here all his life."

"I was Special Ops, trained for war and accustomed to harsh situations, stewed in chemicals on the battlefield and since birth. My father worked for Acme at one time. I may be immune to the worst of it, but I'm not entirely immune. I just try not to do anything dramatic. But you and Sarah are the only ones who receive rewards for your actions."

"Cora always looked like that?" I asked jealously, focusing on the shallow rather than his limited revelations.

"Not when she was a kid, but she grew into it. And that's another thing—most of us grew up here or lived here a long time. Even Sarah has lived nearby since before the flood. We have chemicals in our blood. You're the only newcomer. I think you're an entirely new development. I want to believe the

Zone has claimed you for its own purposes. For *our* purposes."

He pulled the car into the garage and closed the door. I slammed out and started for the stairs.

As we took the steps beneath the street, I finally got a handle on the discrepancy in his story line. "You *want* to believe in a magical dispenser of justice, but you *don't* want to believe Max is still around. Your two and twos are all about what you want, not what is."

"They *buried* Max," he said curtly. "He's gone. Let him go."

"He won't go until he gets whoever killed him. He was investigating the Zone. I'm thinking you're the one who wants to keep Zone secrets."

"I did not kill Max! Cripes, Clancy, you're a head case. But I don't believe you're talking to a dead man in your mirror. Weird in this life, yes. In the next? Hardly."

Not arguing with nonbelievers. "Whose kitchen is this?" I asked, changing the subject by admiring the fancy kitchen.

"Mine. And thank you for cooking for my dad. He won't leave the house anymore, and home-cooked meals aren't my specialty."

Damn, I wanted to like him. But I'd watched Andre at work for too long and knew he wasn't to be trusted. He lied without blinking. Maybe they taught that in Special Ops school. There was far more to him than he was letting on. I'd let the comment about his *trying* not to do anything dramatic pass by because I wasn't ready to deal with it. If attacking with AK-47s wasn't dramatic, I'd hate to imagine what was.

Upstairs, Milo greeted us at the door, wrapping himself around my ankles in welcome—or a blatant plea for kitty treats. I calculated that Andre was just like Milo, playing nice to get what he wanted. I simply wasn't sucker enough to buy what he was selling. I opened his father's refrigerator door as if I were in my own home, found apples and cheese, and sat down at the table while Andre talked with his dad in the front room.

Frustrated that the painful disaster at my former school was coming back to haunt me, leaving me vaguely nauseated and feeling hunted, I pulled Max's Vanderventer file out of my backpack. I knew I needed to be studying, but I was hiding in someone else's house for a reason. I wanted to know the name of the nasty player out to get me.

I handed Milo a piece of cheese and began reading Max's atrocious handwriting. I earned scholarships because I'm not dumb and because I can read fast— once I learn to translate gibberish. I was halfway through the file with a muscle in my jaw jumping when I pulled out my compact and opened it.

"You're Dane Vanderventer's *cousin?*" I asked Max when he appeared.

He scowled. "*Second cousins. Took you this long to find out? What have you been doing, sleeping with Andre?*"

I snapped the compact closed. Men are a pain in the ass.

I snapped it back open a few pages later. "Your butter-wouldn't-melt-in-her-mouth *grandmother* owns half of Acme?"

He rolled his eyes. "*That's old news, Justy. Not relevant. Her husband and Dane's grandfather were brothers. They died and left their fortunes to the grannies. They're old witches more concerned about their wealth than chemicals. Don't get sidetracked.*"

"Then tell me what the hell I'm looking for!" I shouted . . . just as Andre entered with a peculiar expression on his face.

He glanced from the mirror to me. "Magic mirror?"

"Unless you have something useful to say, Andre, go back to work." I defiantly left the compact open. Max watched me warily.

I could tell Andre was looking over my shoulder at the mirror. I didn't know what he could see, but Max's eyes narrowed, so I knew he was looking back.

"You should have killed her, man," Andre said sardonically, speaking to the mirror. "She's mean, she's secretive, and she doesn't play well with others."

Guess that answered one question—I wasn't the only one who could see Max, at least while I was holding the mirror.

Max snorted. "*That's what I love about her.*"

Andre didn't seem to hear Max's voice, since it was inside my head. I quickly dismissed the fake male camaraderie and went straight to the big stuff.

"You *love* me?" I asked in incredulity. "That's a load of crap, Maxim MacNeill. My questionable charms are why you *used* me—because you knew I was tough."

"*So, I had other things on my mind,*" Max admitted. "*But that's changing. You're changing, Justy. Get me out of here so we can work together. There's weird shit going down at the plant that's being covered up, and Dane's part of it. I don't think even the grannies know.*"

"Give me something, *anything,* to nail Vanderventer, Max," I pleaded. "I don't know how to get you out of there, but Vanderventer is here and I can reach him."

Andre snorted and straightened. "If all he's telling you about is Dane, then he's useless. You'd learn more from Paddy, if he was coherent."

"*Leave Paddy alone!*" Max shouted. "*He wouldn't hurt a flea.*"

"Paddy?" I asked, before remembering the senile old guy wandering around Ernesto's kitchen. He'd warned me to stay away from his "family." "Is Paddy related, too?"

"*Dane's father. He's harmless,*" Max asserted. "*He tried to prevent the chemical spill and got cooked. Brains on chemicals, not pretty. He lives in his office these days.*"

"Acme cooked Paddy's brains and that's why you want to bring them down?" I asked in incredulity. Now I knew why Paddy looked familiar—he had Max's eyes.

Andre squeezed my shoulders. "Max, if you're in there, you better understand that your girlfriend can wish your family to hell if they make her mad. Acme makes chemical weapons for the government. You should be teaching her some common sense instead of inciting her to breaches of national security."

Andre's touch woke me up to the dangerous rage building inside me. I glowered, closed the compact, and put my head in my hands.

I'd actually visualized catching a thief and caught one. Maybe I ought to visualize Max free from wherever he was. He had been a bad boyfriend, but he didn't deserve hell. I concentrated on visualizing Max by my side, but it just didn't happen.

"It's not funny, Andre," I muttered, twitching away from his grasp. "I could have turned the kid into a gorilla. I have no idea if I could have turned him back."

"Setting a gorilla loose down here might attract attention," he agreed solemnly, but he backed off at my reminder that I was a loose cannon. "I'm thinking you'd better limit your imagination to immediate punishment like hand-slapping and not get into anything long-term like gorillas."

"Thanks, that's real useful, Legrande. Just drop me on another planet without a guidebook, why don't you?"

"That's what I'm saying, Clancy. Study. Stick to school. Leave the bad guys alone. Let me take care of business until you get the hang of whatever in heck you're doing."

"If Dane Vanderventer was driving the limo that knocked over those kids, he's going to pay," I warned. "And now that I know who he is, it's doubly suspicious if he was down here the day Max died."

"Dane Vanderventer is a conscienceless bastard who is guilty of so much worse, you'd have to send him to hell to make him pay," Andre warned. "While he might deserve it, *you* deserve better than acting as a minion for the devil." ˙

Yeah, that was kind of my thought—or would have been, if I believed in the devil. Jury was still out on that one. I scooped up my books and Milo and headed down the hall to lock the door of my assigned room behind me. I needed my privacy back.

My damned phone rang again. I hadn't been this popular in school. But in case Schwartz wanted to give more bad news, I opened it. A vaguely alarmed text message with Max's phone number scrolled past: *there are challenging aspects in your chart. what are you doing?*

Oh, I don't know, messing with the Universe? Wasn't that what I was supposed to do? I was pretty certain Max didn't mess with charts and that I must be dealing with freaky Themis. I was annoyed enough to type back, *Toying with bullies,* and left it at that.

I opened my netbook to my Facebook page and raised my eyebrows at a message from my mother: *Your grandmother is worried about you. How on earth did you find her?*

Themis was really *my grandmother*? And sending me idiot messages? That was just about par for my course. Had catching the thief really disturbed the Universe? Well, that, on top of showering thugs and exploding tires and . . . Cosmic shake, rattle, and roll, I guess.

There were so many ways I could answer that. For the sake of family harmony, I simply responded: *She found me. Your mother, I presume?*

That was all the socializing I could tolerate for a while. We were obviously not a chatty family. I collapsed on the bed with a law book and let Milo sleep on my middle.

But I couldn't concentrate. I needed to prove I hadn't killed Max. I needed to find out who had. That should take the pressure off me, keep the cops off my back by diverting their interests elsewhere.

I probably shouldn't have stolen the Escalade.

I really truly did not want to be tortured with the arrest scenario again. I didn't take rough handling with a smile. If I'd had the ability to create tornadoes back in my college days, an entire precinct would have been gone with the wind. Along with a crooked provost or two.

So—who would cut my brakes and why? I really would have to work that out, wouldn't I? Damn. Nothing was ever simple.

I ran my hands into my newly thick hair and tugged. It hurt. The hair was real. My legs were real. Tim, the invisible kid, was real. I was pretty sure it was too late to move to Seattle and a normal life— especially if my boyfriend would visit me from hell wherever I went.

It would have been nice to believe Max really did love me, but wishful thinking didn't do anyone any good, and it certainly wasn't going to bring Max back or change my newly weird life.

I could wield *justice*. I could get even with bullies.

The question remained, what price did I pay to do so?

27

❖⟨⟩⟨⟩❖

I cooked up a pot of Spanish chicken for supper—
enjoying the luxury of having a sliver of time to spare
and someone to cook for. Julius was appreciative, and
he made relaxing company, unlike his annoying son.

I fell asleep early over my books.

I woke up at 3:00 A.M. thinking about Vanderventer
being hospitalized for burns. And remembering that
the Invisible Kid should now have a place in the
apartment right below me. Why lie awake and fret
when I might be able to do something for a change?

I craved the freedom of actually having the power to act. Was that how people in authority felt every day when they got up?

I'd always despised authority figures, and now I might be one. Sort of. Freaking weird.

I crawled out of bed and donned jeans and a Henley and my new athletic shoes. Dropping Milo into my bag—he was outgrowing it already—I sneaked down the stairs to the second story. I didn't know which apartment had been vacant, but I heard a TV in one. Would the kid have a TV already? Maybe that was how he spent his stolen cash.

But he'd given me the info on Dane and his granny, so I was willing to offer him a chance to redeem himself.

I knocked softly. Remembering that Tim was terrified of bullies and most of the world, I slipped a note under his door rather than shout and risk waking Andre on the floor below.

He opened it a moment later and watched me warily.

"It's time the Zone acquired a posse," I informed him. "You want in?"

He blinked several times, flickered a bit, then opened the door wider. "I don't want to get in trouble."

"Yeah, I know that feeling. It passes." I glanced around. The apartment had apparently come furnished. Well, shoot. Most of the stuff was better than mine. Too late to take up Andre's offer now. "Can you turn the invisibility on and off with any accuracy?"

"Sometimes. It's harder when I'm nervous."

I nodded. "That makes sense. Harder to think

when nervous. I don't want to make you nervous, but I have a tough job and think you might be the guy I need."

He glanced uneasily at my shoes in the corner. "I'll give back your shoes, but Mrs. Bodine gave all my stuff to Goodwill."

"If I had money, I'd take you shopping and help you buy it back, but we'll just have to make do for now. Keep the shoes. Did you leave me the note about the limo running over the kids at the bank?"

He twitched. "Yeah. The bastard hit Jennifer. She's one of the nice ones who don't think I'm a freak. I'm sorry about the deposit, but I'd just copped the bolt cutters and had to turn them back before the florist missed them. I had to take the bag then or starve."

"You picked the wrong damned days to rob us, but I understand the necessity of using chaos as cover. Maybe we can make that work for us. I want to nail the guy I think ran over Jennifer. Are you with me?"

"Nail him? Crucify him?" He looked interested and horrified.

"Mostly I want to make him pay, but first, I need to know for sure if he's guilty. I don't like picking on innocent people." I'd studied my printout of the bank deposits but had no proof except that the senator was one slippery bastard. "Everyone ought to have their day in court, right?"

"That's why you're here at three in the morning?" he asked in confusion. Not the brightest lightbulb in the lamp.

"Well, you're not actually sleeping," I pointed out.

"Neither was I. Most people aren't at their best at this hour, but I'm betting we are. I want to make a hospital visit."

"You're nuts, aren't you?" he asked without inflection.

"Probably. But I caught you, didn't I? Let's catch someone really bad this time." Before they got me first. I was damned tired of hiding. I was thinking *acting* instead of *reacting* to threats was a better move.

To hell with cops and threats. I wasn't going down without a fight this time.

"What's the plan?" He eyed the shoes with longing, probably figuring sandals were safe and I wasn't. He was right.

"I want a demon to think I'm a witch," I said with satisfaction.

Going out the front door, holding our breaths in hopes Andre didn't hear us, I checked to see which Victorian we occupied now that I was actually *using* the front door. The one with brown and yellow trim. I'd known it wouldn't be the pink one.

At my behest, Tim took my keys, slipped over to my apartment, and grabbed Max's jacket and mine. Andre had had my Harley delivered to the backyard, so Tim met me there. No point in alerting any lingering spies that I was still around.

Tim was skinny enough to wear my leather jacket. I wore Max's. Milo rode in my well-protected messenger bag. I trusted the cat's instincts more than I did mine. Or maybe he was just my talisman.

I'd already Googled the news stories and knew where Vanderventer had been hospitalized. At this time of night, we could get there in an hour, but high-security D.C. hospitals wouldn't let just anyone in. I called Tech Head, and he agreed to meet us there. After I'd given him the Escalade's equipment, he would have walked on hot coals for me. Fortunately, it was Vanderventer I wanted walking on coals. I just needed wireless gear from the techie.

We met in the shadows of the hospital parking garage a little after 4:00 A.M.

Tech Head nodded at Tim. "This the guy you want wired? He'll never get past security."

We both looked at Tim's tattoos and rings. I hoped the doors didn't have metal detectors. He shifted from foot to foot, but if he flickered, it was hard to tell in the dim light.

"We're about to experiment," I told him. "Show us how it works."

Tech wired him up and explained the system. I could tell the kid was wound tight. I plugged in my earpiece and we tested the distance from the top to the bottom of the garage. I could hear everything Tim and Techie said. While on the roof, I also located the hospital service entrance.

"We're good," I told my biker friend. "Let the boys know where I am if all hell breaks loose."

"Roger, wilco." He saluted and jogged off, quite willing to leave the troublemaking to me. He'd picked the nice safe alternative of working *behind* the scenes of action. If I'd been smart, I'd have done the same, but no, I had to sign up to be a lawyer on the front lines, in the public's face. And now I was doing it supernaturally, and less lawyerly.

I couldn't believe I was doing what I was doing right before my last final exam. I was a day and a half away from finishing law school and about to blow ethics out the window. But this might be the only time Vanderventer would be where I could find him. They'd probably let him loose tomorrow.

"We'll get you a set of pretty scrubs," I promised Tim. "What color do you like?"

"Salmon," he said grudgingly, following me out of the garage and around to the black hole of the hospital's service entrance.

Behind the hospital, engines steamed, Dumpsters reeked, and mysterious boxes of hazardous waste were locked and waiting for pickup. A linen truck was being unloaded. I waited until the driver went inside, then hauled myself into the interior of the van. I found a couple of sets of scrubs and threw one out to Nervous Nellie. I tugged the other on over my clothes. The jacket and Milo were problematic.

I carried both as if just arriving for work. Tim imitated me. We strolled through the door the van driver had left open, found a couple of open lockers, and stored the jackets. I kept my bag slung over my shoulder and pushed Milo's head inside. "Hide, fellow," I told him.

We made awkward partners. Tim could disappear if he heard anyone coming. I couldn't. I knew how to use the computers on the information desks to locate patients. Tim didn't.

I posted him as guard once I found a desk in an empty corner and told him to speak into the mic if he saw anyone approaching. Information desks are usually run by senior citizen volunteers. Their computers have to be simple. This one had the login and password taped to the bottom of the keyboard.

Once I knew what room Vanderventer was in, I steered Tim toward the elevator. "If anyone questions me, just stay invisible and cause a disturbance," I told him. "We'll keep this simple."

I was out of my friggin' mind and taking this justice business too far. I didn't even know for certain that I could visualize punishment. What if the guy was innocent and I pictured something bad just because I got mad? I'd have worried my new superpower only worked in the Zone, but I'd battered the reporters at the funeral home, and even caught Tim while I was cruising down the highway.

But I *hadn't* imagined Max slamming into a bank.

That really wasn't my fault. It hadn't been until Max's funeral that I started doing totally weird things. Maybe I could blame my insanity on my ex's family.

I could only hope Tim was with me when I strolled past the night desk, pushing a linen cart. I'd thrown a sheet over my messenger bag, just in case hospital flunkies didn't carry around purses containing cats. I guessed they'd be considered unsanitary. Oh well.

Vanderventer's room was quiet and dark. I left

the linen cart in the hall, slipped inside, and closed the door, hoping that was Tim's frightened breathing I heard next to me. I'd spent a year in a hospital nowhere as elegant as this one. I still knew the routines. I moved the emergency button away from the bed while glaring down at the sleeping patient.

The senator was even better looking with his cleft jaw in stubble and his dark hair mussed. I ought to have pulled out my compact and let Max have a gander, but that would have been indulging too far. Milo peered out and growled threateningly, even though the patient was sound asleep and not menacing anyone. Kitty intuition worked for me, but I still needed proof that, at a minimum, he'd been the one who hired the goons who'd shot up Chesty's and endangered my friends. If he'd been driving the limo that hit the kids, I didn't know if I could keep him from roasting in hell through and through.

They'd tented the covers over his burns, so the charcoal must have landed on his feet. I'd wanted him to take a pleasant dip in hell and fry his toes a little so he'd know what torment felt like. Interesting metaphorical interpretation. Good thing I'd restrained myself from damning him as I had Max. Looked like I'd have to experiment with my justice powers. Did I have to be angry or terrified to actually send someone to hell, or was there a magic phrase? Since I was on a fact-finding mission, I probably shouldn't experiment now.

One of the senator's hands sported a small bandage but the other was unharmed. Tim stationed himself on the injured side and flickered out. I stayed close to the door, ready to flee at the first sign of danger. I'd had Tim wired, mostly for his safety and in hopes of taping a confession, but no amount of wire would save me.

"Hey, Dane," I said softly. I'd told Tim to tug the patient's nose to wake him, but I couldn't see if he was following my instructions. "Max sends you greetings from hell."

Vanderventer stirred restlessly. I watched a handful of the senator's hair rise up from its scalp as Tim yanked it. *That's my boy.* Dane woke instantly, to full alert.

"Remember me?" I asked sweetly.

His head swiveled until he located me in the dark. My scrubs were a bright enough green that I wasn't totally invisible. I didn't know if he could make out my face.

"Who are you?" he demanded, hunting for the call button I'd intelligently relocated.

"Your worst nightmare. No one can enter, and the devil is on your shoulder, waiting to send you to join Max in hell if you lie."

Bless Tim's little heart, he picked up my cue beautifully. He must have jabbed Dane's shoulder. When the patient yelped in surprise and brought his hand up to the place he'd been poked, Tim apparently pinched his injured hand. That brought a much louder curse.

"I'd be very quiet, if I were you, Senator. That way, we can keep this just between ourselves. Should the media arrive, it would become a three-ring circus in here. I can attest to that. I might clear a path through the reporters for myself, but you're kind of stuck, aren't you?"

"Justine Clancy," he muttered angrily. "I warned them you were trouble."

I smiled. "Really, I wasn't. All I ever wanted to do was mind my own business. And then someone cut my brakes, killed Max, ran over a bunch of nice kids, and then made the mistake of bugging my apartment and following my every move before coming after me with guns. Since I find it hard to believe Max's family would take him out, no matter how annoying he is, I have to assume you're the shadowy figure behind all this."

"Don't be ridiculous!" he sputtered. "What would I have to do with a low-life bum like Max? And why should I care what you do?"

None of this would be useful on Tim's recording. Getting confessions sounded so much simpler in books. I prodded harder. "You don't lie well, Senator. I thought you were supposed to be better at this— you know I exist or you wouldn't have warned anyone about me. You wouldn't happen to be the one pressuring the cops to lean on me, would you? Really bad move, if so." I popped open my compact, but we were out of the Zone, and Max was kind of hazy. "Anything you want to say to your cuz, Max?"

Vanderventer almost came out of the bed. Tim apparently shoved him back down. The patient did a fine job of biting back a shriek. "What the devil are you doing to me?" Vanderventer cried in a low voice.

"I'm not doing anything except standing here talking to Max in hell." Trial law was my favorite class. I'm quick with responses, even if I'm not always so clever with the quality. "Guess the devil thought you might be worth checking out, too. Think Max would send him?"

Max was making noises and faces but I really couldn't see or hear him well. I just figured he was unhappy with me. Story of my life.

"You have one of those Zone freaks here with you," Dane grumbled, punching his pillow and attempting to sit up.

"'Zone freaks,' that's nice," I said nastily. "And who made us freaks?"

"What do you want?" he demanded, not taking up that chemically laden question.

"A confession would be good," I said. "I copied the plates off your limo when you ran over those kids just before Max died. Maybe you'd like to make restitution? You could keep it anonymous. Most of them don't have insurance, or the ability to replace the stuff of theirs you ruined."

"I didn't run over any kids. I don't know what you're talking about."

His hair stood on end again as Tim yanked it. The senator swatted at empty air and reached for the light with his bad hand. Tim apparently swatted him in return, because Dane jerked his injured hand back and cradled it against his chest.

"A little warning, Senator. Your chemical goo didn't

just affect my hair. I've learned that when I wish for something—say, seeing you dip your toes in hell—odd things happen. What exactly were you doing playing with charcoal this morning?"

"You're crazy," he spluttered, but I could tell he was worried. "Maybe my chauffeur was driving my car, but I wasn't anywhere near where Max died."

Milo growled and tried to climb out of my bag. I pushed him down, while wanting to believe I had my very own lie detector. I grew bolder. If Dane had been around when Max hit the wall . . .

The light in my brain flicked on. Vanderventer had hightailed it out of the bank like a bat from hell because someone had warned him Max was likely to hit the wall in the bank's vicinity. They'd been tailing Max, waiting to see where he'd hit. The bastard. For all I knew, Vanderventer had been hanging around, waiting for it to happen. Any way I looked at it, the senator had to have known Max was going down.

And proving it in a court of law would be next to impossible. The police weren't going to search a senator's phone records. For all I knew, he'd been using a throwaway phone. I could have tortured his spooks into snitching, but I wanted to go for the boss man.

"A nice fat check to Barr's Groceries will work wonders." I returned to my sweet voice, trying to keep my rage down. "They'll see the money is distributed. That doesn't mean I believe you about your chauffeur, but I'll be good and look for proof. Unless you want to confess, of course," I added. "Confessing would be safer than waiting for me to find evidence, because once that happens, I just hand you over to the police and a proper court."

"This is blackmail," he grumbled. "I'm calling the cops as soon as I can reach the phone, Clancy," he retorted, not unexpectedly. "You're the one who'd better run and hide."

"Oh, I think not, Senator. This is all a dream. I'm safely home in bed. I have witnesses. But if that check isn't special-delivered in two days, I really will be your worst nightmare. Good night."

I heard a smack and saw the senator wince and turn his cheek. I slipped back to the linen cart and left Tim to catch up with me at the elevator.

The screams that followed us warned I didn't want to ask what had slowed him down. Jennifer had been nice to the kid, after all.

28

I treated Tim to hot chocolate and donuts before we crept back into Andre's house just past dawn. If Andre heard us enter, he didn't drag himself out of bed to complain. I just had to hope there weren't any spies watching, because I'd pretty much blown my cover if they were.

I was pretty disappointed that we hadn't terrified the senator into a confession of any sort. He was a tough bastard. I let Tim keep the wire gear, in case we had better opportunities. I hadn't expected a lot out of my midnight foray, but I had hoped for at least a hint of a direction to follow. I wasn't sure where to turn next. I still had no real evidence that Dane Vanderventer was our villain.

I showered, then prepared French toast for an appreciative Julius, before returning to my quarters to study for the last final. After tomorrow, that law degree would be mine.

Except my thoughts kept wandering, as I tried to find ways of applying my new visualization skill to job hunting. Nothing was coming to me, though. I was having a hard time believing in superpowers, and after Max's death, I had a very real fear of even pretending to use my deadly gift. From everything I've read, with power comes corruption. I knew I'd end up in hell if I used mine for purely selfish reasons. Heck, I might end up there for using them period.

I had to find a normal means of earning money that paid enough so I could hire a lawyer to clear my name so I could find a real job. It would have been nice if I could have done all that in time to take the bar exam in July, but I doubted I could make that. Not that I knew how to do it, but I had a notion that using superpowers for money didn't reflect high moral standards. Maybe I should ask Themis. Or Sarah. Ugh.

I studied without interruption. No one banged on the door with angry accusations about news reports of the devil haunting a D.C. hospital. I probably needed to minimize exposure of my new gift so that weird activities couldn't be traced back to me. With a little practice, maybe I could make people think what

I want them to think, instead of instigating the action.

Actually, that would be scary.

I would have preferred a gift that provided automatic proof of wrongdoing, instead of making me work for it—I really wanted to know what was happening at Acme that might have gotten Max's brakes cut.

Damn superpowers. Not all they were cracked up to be.

My thoughts traveled to that storage unit with Max's papers. After the encounter with Vanderventer, my thirst for justice was running high. I had a lot of pent-up frustration needing release. I had meant to call Jane and send her over there if she had time. We could look at the papers together. I couldn't hide forever.

By noon, I'd given up on books. I needed out of the house. The windows told me it was a gorgeous May day meant for enjoying. I was done playing at good little hermit.

I wore the mirror tunic, spike heels, and short shorts to distract from my face, and pinned and covered my remarkable hair with a fedora I borrowed from Julius. Maybe Cora would have a sun hat. I had this idiot idea that the goons would only look for preppy me, and I could walk right past them dressed like an idiot. If they were there at all. Or if they even knew I didn't limp any longer. Thinking they might have noticed I'd grown gave me the creeps. So I hoped the spies were still explaining themselves to the police.

I headed down the street, enjoying birdsong and

sunshine, at least until I hit the edge of the Zone. I felt as if I'd been asleep these last years and all of a sudden, my eyes were open.

No pretty pansies adorned colorful planters along the edges of a hazardous waste zone. No trees grew. If there had ever been awnings, they had vanished. The only soft surfaces in sight were the people jostling each other on the sidewalks. The neon buildings lost their glow in daylight, simply looking stark and forlorn against the backdrop of the rusted chimneys of the abandoned plant. At least fast-food wrappers and cigarette butts didn't line the gutters—Mickey D's wouldn't open their doors anywhere near here, and cigarettes caused explosions. I really ought to check out the inside of the florist. It might be a little shop of horrors.

I took the main street instead of the alley. I was in a humor for confrontation with goons, not Dumpsters. A gargoyle bent down from the florist's roof and gave me the evil eye, and while that didn't bother me as much as slithering garbage cans, it did keep me from exploring the shop.

Milo hung out of my bag, occasionally growling at an abandoned cur slinking from one alley to the next. I hadn't spent many weekday lunch hours down here. I hadn't realized how many employees escaped the chemical and steel plants to hit the Zone at noon, or maybe it was just the lovely day that drew them out.

I had to wonder how safe it was for them to eat here. Or were they all gaining some strange superpower with their cheeseburgers?

Actually, I kind of liked the idea of factory workers gaining psychic abilities to keep the powerful Vanderventers of the world in check. But it was probably a dangerous idea for me to imagine it, so I filled my head with white light and entered Chesty's, whistling.

Diane was back, looking better than ever. If Vanderventer was responsible for sending a rapist to spy on us, he needed to be sent to hell twice. But without proof, I could do no more than follow Diane back to the kitchen, where I was regaled with tales of the miraculous flood mop-up and repeats of the gunman story.

When the staff started crowing over raises in their pay, I got a little uneasy. I hadn't picked up my pay from Andre yet. Had I really visualized him into giving us money? Superpowers could really provide money? Dangerous temptation and probably hazardous to my afterlife. I bit my tongue until I knew more, but it only seemed fair that Andre pay a reasonable wage to decent people who worked hard.

I tested Jimmy's tortellini soup and agreed it was to die for. I was testing appetizers when Paddy walked in, and Max's warning reared its ugly head.

Paddy was Dane Vanderventer's *father*. He possibly lived at Acme. If anyone knew the family secrets, he did.

"Why does Ernesto allow Paddy back here?" I asked Diane, who had stopped by to grab an anchovy cracker while filling her tray.

She glanced at the gray-haired man looking like a bum in shabby khakis and torn sweater and shrugged. "Because Andre says so. We've fed him for as long as

I can remember, even before Ernesto. He's a harmless old guy."

"You don't know who he is?" I thought it might be wise to verify Max's claims, just in case I really was imagining Max.

"He's just Paddy. He brings us little inventions in return for food. As far as I know, they all end up in the trash. Gotta get this soup up front." She trotted off, tray in hand.

I took my plate of appetizer samples over to the shabby old man and set it down in front of him. "We met at my place on Westside, Mr. Vanderventer. How is your family?"

He'd been entering Lily's apartment. I'd moved before I could question her. Had she been another spy? Or part of the family he kept warning me away from? I hadn't known her well. Neither of us was at home much.

Paddy was more interested in the food than in me. He studied the construction of a fancy bruschetta topped with a pyramid of olives and cheese, pinned together with toothpicks. The appetizer chef should have been an architect.

"Doing fine," he said absently, plucking off a cheese cube without bringing the structure tumbling down.

He hadn't disputed the name I'd called him by. "Is your son out of the hospital yet?" I asked innocently. "I hope he wasn't too seriously burned."

That caught his attention. Gray eyes eerily like Max's narrowed as he studied me and discarded a toothpick holding an olive captive. "We don't speak," he said flatly. "Stay away from them."

"Why? Because they'll harm me or because I can hurt them?"

He looked confused and returned to studying the tray. Apparently the bruschetta didn't appeal. He chose a ham wrap concoction.

"I'm crazy," he said carefully.

"Yeah, aren't we all?" I ate the remains of the bruschetta he'd rejected. "Whoever killed Max was crazier than both of us, though."

He nodded as if in agreement, or approval of the appetizer. His thick gray hair brushed his collar and covered his ears, but the distinguished man he'd once been was reflected in the still-sharp angles of his face. He exhibited none of the puffy, red-eyed weakness of an alcoholic or addict or even a schizoid. He knew good food and how to get it. Except for his clothes and hair, he'd been taking care of himself.

"Power makes men mad," he said enigmatically.

"So we should go back to the Greek system of democracy and all draw stones and the ones who draw the wrong color are stuck governing for the next year?" I asked, testing his history.

He snorted. "The wealthy would be in Spain when the stones were drawn. They'd just buy whoever was in power that year."

"Wow, that makes you more cynical than me." And just as sane, relatively speaking. "So if I want to find out who cut Max's brakes, where would I start?"

"My mother," he said as if it were an epithet. "Eve is the root of all evil." He popped a sausage blanket into his mouth and shambled off.

Max had said the grannies were more interested in money than Acme. Max had been known to be wrong, though. Crazy men had been known to be crazy, too.

Citing Eve as the root of all evil was not only lunacy but implied that women were to blame for the bad choices of men. Religious fanatics around the world latched onto that fallacy, pointing the finger of shame at the oppressed sex for the failures of the sex in power. Stupid bullies, all of them.

It wouldn't do to grow angry, or I could be burning down mosques and temples and cathedrals around the world. I was curious enough to wonder if I could, and still sane enough not to try. How long could I maintain that sanity? I needed to look at the website claiming Saturn's daughters died young. They probably flamed out from the sheer exhaustion of restraining themselves.

I debated between returning to my safe room to study, finding Andre and demanding access to Max's papers, or hunting down Dane's grandmother. Hunting a granny seemed simple enough.

First, I called Lance to learn if they'd made any progress in uncovering the perpetrator of the Escort's damage. Gonzo would know, but Lance talked more.

"Hey, babe," Lance greeted me groggily. Noon was kind of early for him. "Heard you had a little trouble. You okay?"

"I'm fine for now, thanks. Max's papers are ugly reading. Have you found out anything about who would try to kill him?"

"Half his family, a few cops, and a biker or two," he

said with a chuckle. "That direction goes nowhere. But we did find out he was visiting the Vanderventer estate that afternoon. Gonzo says it's possible the brake lines were cut only enough to leak out over time, and the accelerator line can be fixed to give out under stress, so Max may have driven away without noticing. His great-aunt lives north of the harbor from you."

The Vanderventer estate? Where Dane's grandmother had been serving tea?

"Aunt?" I asked warily. I still didn't know the whole family tree. Was Paddy's wife—Dane's mother—still in the picture? Were there more aunts and uncles?

"Old lady Vanderventer," Lance explained. "Seventies. Senator's grandma."

Bingo. The granny Dane was sharing tea with that afternoon. One of the grannies who owned half of Acme, and who Max had said liked to shop. Stupid men, always underestimating the power of women. Granny had the motive to keep Acme operating and the money to hire thugs, and the opportunity to have said thugs cut the Escort's brakes.

"And did you know all the time that Max was from a rich family?" I asked, just so I'd know if I was the only clueless idiot.

"We don't ask questions, babe. He didn't bust us, so we didn't bust him."

I rolled my eyes at this simple platitude, but it was probably the best Lance's foggy brain cells could produce. "Thanks, buddy," I told him. "I don't think granny would crawl under a car, but someone there must have."

"Yeah, that's what we're thinking, but we can't muscle around an old lady to find out."

"That's what you have me for. Let's see what I can do."

I hung up before he could argue. I was amazed Andre hadn't already appeared to heave me over his shoulder, but he probably believed I'd actually study when I said I would. Foolish man. I'd like to have believed he was lining up AK-47s in my defense, but he had no way of knowing what I meant to do next.

I didn't see Sarah until she sidled up to me after I tucked away my phone. She still looked like a fuzzy-headed orangutan, but I think she was a few inches taller than I'd seen her last—in torso, not legs, I guessed, glancing down at her stubby appendages. Had she been wishing she was taller while she was strangling a goon?

I was doubting her sanity as well as my own, but she thought we were buddies, and I didn't disillusion her.

"Hey, I was thinking . . . if you don't want to off the bad guys, I could be your bodyguard and do it for you," she suggested, keeping her voice low. "I want to be one of the dancers, but Ernesto says my legs are too short."

Yup, she'd wished for longer legs like mine. Chimpanzees and poles, a real natural, but probably not a crowd pleaser. I didn't say that aloud.

Generously refraining from lecturing about the dangers of *offing* anyone to a serial killer's daughter, I simply said, "You know, I hadn't really been thinking about bodyguards, but if I do, I'll think of you first. Thanks for offering."

Before Sarah could make any more homicidal suggestions or someone told Andre I was out and about, I gathered up Milo and traipsed over to visit Cora at the detective agency.

29

Cora had the front door open to let in sunshine and fresh air. She beamed at me when I entered.

"I don't believe in astrology, hon," she said in greeting, "but I sure could change my mind if Saturn's daughter can waltz a few naked dudes through here."

"And that would be justice for whom?" I asked, taking one of Frank's swivel chairs and making myself at home. I'd spent too many years biting my tongue not to enjoy saying what I thought. Cora was plugged in and smart enough to know as much as I did, given that astrology crack. She'd been talking to Andre and doing her research.

"Did you get your paycheck yet?" I inquired innocently.

She removed it from the drawer and waved it happily. "Buck-an-hour raise! Nordstrom's shoe sale, here I come. I haven't bought shoes since I moved my mom into that home."

I didn't know whether to cringe or glory in Andre's undoing. I hadn't really meant to empty his pockets, but people needed a basic living wage, and those working in the Zone deserved hazardous-duty pay.

"I need to check over at Bill's to see if he has mine," I said, covering up my nervousness by changing the subject. "Got time for a quick look-see for me?"

"Can't leave the office," she warned. "Frank's out and I'm holding down the fort. How's our invisible thief doing?"

"Haven't seen him today."

I actually said it with a straight face.

She threw a paper clip at me. "We need to find something to dump over his head so he can't duck out like that. We'll never know where he is."

"He makes his clothes vanish. Don't think paint will work." Milo crawled out to sniff around the office. I pushed a foil package of apple cake I'd liberated from Chesty's across the desk. "An official bribe. Will you look up Dane Vanderventer's grandmother? I don't even know her name."

Cora's eyes widened, but after examining the goody

package, she popped the top of a diet Coke, offered me some, and roused her sleeping computer.

"Public figures are easy," she said, typing lists into Google. "Charity balls, divorce courts, obits, in big letters on front pages." She began calling up websites and printing.

"How do you get a computer to work down here?" I asked, skimming printouts to be certain they weren't menus from China.

"Snake charming," she replied ambiguously. "And Frank ran the cable. I'm betting it connects with Schwartz's precinct and nothing down here."

The cable might have been out of the Zone, but the hardware wasn't. Either the Zone was afraid of Cora's snakes or I'd better be careful how much of her info I believed.

Not wishing to really analyze atomic and/or chemical effects on underground wiring, I examined the paper as it came out of the machine. First one was a photo with Gloria Vanderventer next to two ex-presidents. In this light, with printer ink, she looked blond, toned, and nowhere near . . . whatever her age was. She looked younger than her son Paddy. Good plastic surgeons, excellent hairdressers, and physical trainers would do that for you, I guessed.

I skimmed through reports of donations to alma maters, chairmanships of foundations, and dinners hosted for her grandson. There was even one photo with Max's grandmother, the woman in the hat at his funeral. Both women were grimacing as if it were a strain to be in the same room together. Nice to know other families were as dysfunctional as mine.

I pored over stories of the Vanderventer dynasty. Max's grandfather and great-uncle had inherited a fortune from their parents, and both had built a legacy of Baltimore industries. Paddy was the only surviving son of either of the two brothers. Max's mom was one of their daughters. Paddy had a degree in chemistry. Max's mom had her MRS degree, marrying Senator MacNeill while he was still a junior congressman. He had power, she had wealth—the perfect couple.

Dane Vanderventer had walked into MacNeill's Senate seat when the older gent resigned after the lobby-bribe scandal. Gloria Vanderventer had campaigned—lobbied—her grandson into the seat. At that point, she'd already outlived Dane's granddad. I wondered why Paddy hadn't been an option, but apparently Dane was a chip off the grandmaternal block.

None of this was really news, just confirmation of politics as usual. I took out the rap sheet with address and vital statistics and stuck it in my bag. I probably could have asked Max for this information, but he'd only have yelled and then probably not given it to me. So I skipped a step.

Thanking Cora and returning to the spring sunshine, I knew I should go home and study and save the Vanderventers for the weekend. I even called Jane, pretending I should gather more evidence before taking any drastic steps.

"How well did you do in chemistry?" I inquired.

"Is this a trick question?" Jane replied, suspicious.

"Am I supposed to crack your code or just hang on while you bluff whoever's there with you?"

"I have Max's research on Acme," I told her, appreciating how quickly she'd figured me out. "There's a lot of chemistry jargon. I was hoping to find someone who could translate." Given Max's handwriting, we probably needed a *team* of translators.

"Not me," she said decisively. "I'm taking a second job at Starbucks and it's all I can do to count cash. Hey, in case you don't know, the higher-ups at the precinct are foaming at the mouth to bring you in. And you're now officially 'Max's bitch' at the courthouse. Whose tail did you pull?"

"Max's bitch," how sweet.

Anger began to pool in my gut, not a good sign. I let Jane off the hook with some meaningless nonchalance and actually turned my churning fury toward home, trying to force myself to think of books.

A black Lincoln cruised by and slowed down. My paranoia escalated.

As far as I knew, the latest spies hadn't kicked any dogs or done more than drive down the street. I could explode their tires for that, but I wouldn't. I was still trying caution, especially if the cops intended to breathe down my back. Been there, done that, had the shattered bones to prove it.

But I didn't believe I was going home to study any longer, either. My mind had skipped straight past reason to I *despise bullies* mode.

Tim as my one-man posse had worked last night. I wasn't sure how effective he would be for long periods of time. I needed Schwartz and Andre and Bill, maybe even spooky Frank. But with no evidence, I couldn't persuade them to my cause any better than I could convince the police that something was rotten in Denmark. I was starting to sympathize with Hamlet.

I was tired of waiting passively, taking whatever shit the Universe threw. I didn't want guns catching me by surprise again. And I wanted to know who had killed Max. If all I'd done was terrify the senator into siccing the cops on me, maybe I needed to skip the law and go where the money was.

Cora had already said she couldn't go with me. I didn't think Tim had a phone. And anyway, there was only one person left crazy enough to join me without question. I was more nervous about taking on Sarah than a senator, but maybe she and I could form our own goon squad. Or gorilla band. I snickered nervously at the bad pun.

I slipped on down the alley, taking the back street to Chesty's. Just for fun, I called Andre and left a message. Lance already knew my next step and hadn't volunteered to ride shotgun, so I didn't bother him again.

Sarah was totally thrilled that I included her in my quest for justice.

I should have forgotten the whole idiot plan the instant she nodded and tucked a kitchen knife in her beehive. "This is only an evidence-gathering mission," I warned her. "No killing."

"Only in self-defense," she said eagerly.

Crap, I'd seen that scenario countless times. But

beggars couldn't be choosers and all that. "I'll be back in a few minutes to pick you up," I said in resignation.

It would be a little more than a few minutes. I had to run back up to Julius's and pull on jeans and change out of the mirrored shirt into a henley. Still inappropriate for visiting, but my hideout wardrobe was limited.

Then I had to take the Harley to my old apartment on Westside to pick up the Miata. I didn't want Sarah turning chimp on me if she took fright at the Harley's speed. It was after two by then, so I ran up to check on Jane. She greeted me at the door with a whiny blond toddler over her shoulder.

"Tina! I hope you're not rethinking your move because I can't help you with chemistry," she said worriedly. "Come in and let me put Bobby down for a nap."

Jane's furniture was as worn as mine, but she had an eye for design. She'd stuck dried wildflowers in a mayonnaise jar and hung old photos with frames rescued from trash bins and spray-painted in glossy red. Clever.

She'd hung bright red plastic plates on the walls in the kitchen. Maybe I should hire her to do my place should I survive long enough to ever have money.

Jane returned and filled a couple of red plastic glasses with iced tea. I complimented her on her décor, and she cheered up.

"It's a pity people who live on nothing can't afford interior designers or I'd have my niche," she happily agreed.

"Write a blog about designing on the cheap and

ask for donations. When you get readers, sell ads," I suggested. "Anyhow, I just stopped in to give you a heads-up; I didn't dare speak on the phone. I don't know what's going down at Acme Chemical, but I think Max was killed to keep it quiet. And I think Dane Vanderventer knew about it."

I didn't mention the connection with the kids, not wanting to stretch credulity too far. The kids were my own personal vendetta, a wrong maybe I could right, even if I couldn't bring Max back.

"Warn your boss," I continued. "And when it turns out you're right, maybe you'll get credit for being in the know."

She shrugged. "Unless I give him proven facts, he won't listen, but I'll see what I can do."

Facts and evidence were damned difficult to locate. I couldn't off a senator on suspicion of rottenness. I grimaced at the reminder. "I'm just keeping you current. Andre has the keys to those files I told you about. If I get blown sky-high like Max, you can tell Schwartz what I was doing. He's one of the good guys."

She nodded uncertainly. "You're not planning on getting blown up, are you?"

I grinned and bounced the Miata keys in my palm. I'd finally turned a corner, picked up my chin, and seen the light. Or gone around the bend. Whatever. I was tired of being intimidated. To hell with cops and administrative control freaks. A brand-new Clancy was emerging from my self-imposed chrysalis. *Max's bitch, indeed.*

"I turned the tables and may have made a few

people mad. Now I have to up the ante or run. I'm not running."

Jane grimaced at my challenging grin. "I'd run."

Fair warning. But it felt soooo good not to keep my head down any longer. I'd been repressing a lot of steam.

Out in the parking lot where Andre had left my car, I noticed my little Miata had a new windshield and the convertible roof was up and working. I was pretty sure Papa Saturn hadn't fixed my vehicle, so I figured I owed Andre again, drat the man. He still hadn't returned my call.

I wondered if I should worry about him but decided he could take care of himself. Besides, if he'd figured out what had caused his sudden urge to enrich his employees, he was probably plotting ways to kill me. Or sobbing in his beer. His fault, entirely. He'd dared me to experiment with my visionary powers. He'd been warned.

Looked like I couldn't delay any longer. It was time for a showdown at the OK Corral. Even though I knew the real history of the famous shoot-out was messy and no one came out a hero, the movie version worked for me. I put the top down and breezed over to pick up Sarah. She was ready and waiting. She hopped in, and we headed for the highway.

Milo rode with his fur blowing in the wind, admiring the scenery.

"What will we do when we get there?" Sarah asked excitedly.

She'd brushed her wiry hair into a knot at the back of her head, but the wind was whipping it loose already, revealing the blade. I wondered for a minute if hairdresser Sam could fashion hair sheaths for knives.

The north side of the harbor was another world, one with yacht clubs, glass-walled, high-rise condos, designer boutiques, and beautiful people sipping ten-dollar coffee in open-air cafés. They had no problem growing trees. Planters spilled over with colorful flowers tended by an army of landscapers.

Sarah read my Google directions while I maneuvered narrow, hilly, unfamiliar terrain. My jeans and shirt looked out of place among nannies strolling down the middle of quiet lanes in designer sundresses, pushing SUV strollers that cost more than the Miata. Oh well.

We located the Vanderventer mansion in a cul-de-sac on a hill overlooking all the nouveau riche below. Nothing screams old money more than a fenced park of a yard in the middle of real estate that sells for a thousand per square foot. The Vanderventers had probably made half their fortune by selling off strategic parcels as the city moved in this direction.

The drive was blocked by a guarded gate, of course. I cruised past without stopping. The only ID in my possession had *mud* written on it as far as the Vanderventers were concerned.

30

❖

I hadn't thought the back gate would go un-monitored, but I'd hoped Gloria Vanderventer knew nothing about me or my pretty red Miata and that her security guards would have no reason for concern when we drove up behind the FedEx delivery truck.

I was wrong.

The black suits emerged from the shrubbery as soon as I turned off the ignition behind the pool house. I'd hoped to do a little exploration first. So much for that theory. I reached for the keys to back out, but I had the top down. One thug leaned over and snatched them from my hand.

I eyed their big black automatics with skepticism. "Look, fellas, I've tried to be polite," I told them, doing my best John Wayne drawl. Beside me, Sarah was shaking in her high heels, and Milo was growling like a wildcat in the backseat. I figured I didn't look much like John Wayne, but I had the attitude. I wasn't mad yet, and I wanted to give them fair warning.

"At Chesty's," I continued explaining with deliberate patience, "I let the cops handle it so you could bail out. But if you keep pointing those things at me, I'll get really pissed and do something drastic."

The tallest thug was talking into a headset and not paying attention. The other two sported grim expressions that said they'd like to use me for target practice. All black suits looked alike to me, especially the Caucasians. Looked like Lady Vanderventer wasn't so much into color. They weren't the suits from Chesty's, so maybe they weren't smart enough to be afraid. How many damned bodyguards did these people employ?

I slipped my cell from my bag, punched speed dial for Andre's number, and hit speaker so they wouldn't see the phone. I got voice mail. Maybe I should have let Techie put a tracking device on me. "Hey, the goons have me cornered at Gloria's," I said. "You might want to bring in the cavalry."

At least Andre would have a good idea where to find my remains.

The guy with the headset reached over, found my

cell, and crushed it in one fist. Damn, I'd have to dip into the grocery funds to buy a new one.

I swung the door open hard enough to take out his midsection, but I wasn't wishing any more deaths just yet. Sarah was still looking terrified enough to turn into a chimp, which would set the goons back a step or two.

Headset Guy grunted at the impact of my plastic door, but he'd jumped back enough that I only bruised his thighs.

"He says to take her over to Max's place," he said, signaling the armed two not to shoot. "Wrap her up and haul her out."

As one of the suits came around the car to grab Sarah, she squealed like a pig, and, as I'd feared, shifted.

"*Watch out!* That thing killed Ralph!" Headset yelled.

A gun went off, and chimp Sarah crumpled in the driveway.

I screamed bloody blue rage, with a curse on my tongue, but before I could spit it out, a fourth goon stepped out of the shrubbery and jabbed a needle in my arm. I went down wishing them to hell, but I had a fuzzy feeling I wasn't connecting.

I thought I heard a man scream and another shot ring, but I was beyond reacting. My last thought was of my cat. Where was Milo?

I couldn't say what my first thought was as I started to wake. I smelled kimchi cooking and groggily gagged until I recognized the stench. It took a bit longer before

I correlated the cooking with Max's apartment and his Korean neighbors, then another bit before I deduced I was on the broken-down couch that came with the apartment. By that time, I had enough marbles to realize I wasn't alone. I kept my head down and my mouth shut—and listened.

"Just find out where she hid Max's papers and get rid of her," said an authoritative voice I'd heard last from a hospital bed. "Do I have to lead you by the hand?"

Huh, they wanted the papers, not me. How humiliating. And here I'd thought I was special. Guess my new superpowers weren't as scary as I'd thought if Senator Vanderventer had put in a personal appearance to say farewell, even after I'd tried to put the fear of God in him. Maybe I should have called on Satan after all. Damn, now I'd never learn how to use my gift for good. Evil triumphed again.

My brain obviously wasn't in full gear.

"There was a shitload of boxes, boss," a male voice protested. "She ain't gone anywhere that can hold those boxes. The trucks at her place only had furniture. Something is fishy."

"The damned boxes didn't disappear on their own," Dane shouted. "Max wasn't a magician! What good does it do to get rid of the witness if you leave the evidence?"

"He wasn't supposed to wait until rush hour to leave," one of the goons whined. "We didn't have time to make it to his place. You should have hired more men."

Nice to know that Max's chronic lateness had a purpose. Okay, did that count as evidence that the senator had killed Max? Well, had Max killed, since I couldn't envision a Vanderventer crawling under an Escort.

Could I whack him now?

Probably not. *Focus, Tina.* I'd developed a resistance to drugs in my year of hospitals, so I was probably awake faster than they expected, but I was still pretty woozy. Just forcing myself to lie still took all the concentration I possessed.

"Hire more men, so I could have an *entire army* of complaining morons?" Dane thundered in irritation. "Make her talk. She knows."

Hmm, yeah, I recalled the boys had taken the boxes and probably anything alcohol-based before Dane and family cleaned out all but the ratty furniture. This crappy couch smelled like beer.

Focus, Tina. Papers?

Andre had hidden the papers. Hadn't a clue where, though, I thought woozily. One storage shed looked the same as another to me, kind of like these black-suited goons. I kept my eyes shut rather than get dizzy watching their shiny leather shoes pace the shag carpet.

"She'll be out for a while," one sounding like Headset Thug said. "Maybe we ought to send someone to search her computer like I said last time. Check her contacts."

"Ralph said she didn't have a computer! And if you hadn't played ape man and crushed her phone, we'd have her contacts," Dane said caustically.

Huh, they'd searched my place as well as bugged it. Good thing I usually carried my little netbook with me. I fuzzily tried to remember if it was still in my bag. Well, before they'd had a chance to look—*damn them all to hell.*

And nobody went anywhere.

Apparently I hadn't put enough force behind my wish, I started to think, but then it occurred to me that the first time I'd done that, I'd blown up a car and a bank. So maybe not a good time to damn anyone if I didn't want to blow up myself. Wow, that was one nasty drug they'd used on me.

"Just call Legrande and you'll have all her contacts here in minutes, if that's what you want," Dane continued. "Just get me the damned boxes and get rid of her!"

Ouch. Not good. I didn't want thugs hurting my friends. Maybe I should wake up. But I couldn't tell them what they wanted, so things would turn nasty if they knew I was awake. Where was the red rage when I needed it? Probably drugged, like me.

I suddenly remembered Sarah, and my gut lurched. My blood started to heat. They'd killed a harmless chimp! Well, not so harmless, but certainly an animal.

"Maybe Max didn't have the boxes," Headset suggested. "Or he gave them to his biker friends for one of their bonfires. We can just get rid of Clancy and be done."

A familiar growling from a distance caused the hair on my nape to rise. Milo! Had they brought Milo here to kill him, too? That fed the fires of rage nicely, but my head wasn't quite on straight yet. I knew I didn't have evidence for a court of law, but I was going to have to act to protect my friends and the Zone.

"We can't take that risk," Vanderventer said dismissively. "The media would have a field day if they got their hands on my father's lab reports. Wake her up."

Someone kicked the couch and shoved my shoulder. I rocked my head groggily but kept it down. These goons had killed Max and shot Sarah. Vanderventer was paying them. They'd kidnapped me and threatened murder. I was fully justified in sending them all to hell—which would certainly be the easiest thing to do.

But I wasn't a fan of the death penalty even when it had the full force of the court behind it. I was pretty certain condemning people to death similarly came under the heading of one wrong not correcting another, and probably worked in the devil's favor. I didn't want to end up like Max. Max hadn't deserved to end up in limbo like that.

So I needed to find an alternative. If I sent them to some war-torn country in Africa, would that be enough? *Could* I do it? I wished I'd had more training before being dumped with this much responsibility.

Someone smacked my face, and I almost sent him up in flames right then and there. Smoke should have been pouring out my ears, except I bit back my fury, lifted my chin, and glared. I wasn't certain I could sit up yet. Given how quickly the rage was building, I figured they'd keep smacking me until I killed someone.

Insanity Is Me.

"Where are Max's papers?" Dane asked, not even bothering to pretend he was a nice guy, which told me he didn't intend me to leave here alive.

Nastily, I noticed he was wearing a special boot on one burned foot and wasn't walking so well on the other. He'd ripped the bandage off his hand, and it looked red and painful. *I'd done that.* I could do it again. I just needed to concentrate.

"Storage unit on Westside," I lied from my prone position. I was getting damned good at lying. "But we've made copies of the important stuff." We hadn't had time to read it to know there was important stuff. Oh well.

"What unit, and where are the keys?" Headset demanded, looking as if he'd like to smack me again.

Lying there trying to look limp and brain-dead, I took my time answering, I studied their weapons while straightening out my buzzed brain. "You won't find the keys unless I show them to you," I stalled. "Let me go, and I'll take you there."

"Dump out her bag," Vanderventer said in disgust, waving his good hand to indicate the bag on the floor. So much for hiding the netbook if it was in there.

Max had said, *Use me.* Could I call on him for help? I needed my compact.

One of them emptied my messenger bag. No computer. Nice. Headset began to sneeze as cat hairs sprayed the room. The compact landed in the middle of the room, out of my reach unless I wanted to stagger up in front of all those guns. "This is a stupid place to kill me," I said conversationally, looking for a way to take out three automatics and a senator.

"True. That's why we'll just blow out your brains, leave the gun in your hand, and the police will call it love-struck suicide," Goon Number Two said cruelly.

I snorted. "Yeah, right. You just keep on believing that. And you won't find my keys."

I struggled to sit up, desperately wanting my compact. It was really hard to focus with so much happening at once. I was plenty mad enough to kill, but practicing restraint required more thought than I currently possessed.

Goon Number Three used his big foot to scatter the contents of my bag around the floor. The compact landed near my feet, begging to be picked up. It was the only weapon I had. Even if Max couldn't help, I'd practiced throwing ninja stars. I wasn't good, but my choices were limited.

"Why won't we find the keys?" Goon Number Two asked, picking up my beloved messenger bag and trying to tear it apart. The steel reinforcement caused some consternation.

"Hidden pocket," I said nonchalantly, trying not to accidentally activate a wish to blow off his head, and not sure I could, given my hazy state.

Headset Guy stood over me with his ugly weapon. "Tell us, or I can make you suffer before you die."

I was running out of delaying tactics—and restraint. Pain was not my friend, and the inside of my skull was pounding like a timpani now that I was sitting up. My head might not have been working, but hundreds of hours of training had honed my kicking reflexes just fine. I'd kicked his popgun from his hand before either of us knew what I was doing.

Goon Number Two dropped my bag and fired, but I was already on the floor, grabbing my precious compact to my chest. Showed my brain wasn't functioning. I needed to go after the gun.

Headset Guy tried to stomp me, but I got his kneecap with my next kick, and he went down hard, screaming in agony. *Old knee injury,* I thought smugly, rolling across the nasty carpet.

Shots rang out over my head, but this wasn't a large room and I was a moving target. They were as likely to hit each other as me. The good senator was screaming curses. I tried using them inside my fuzzy head, cursing the thugs, but apparently trying to dodge bullets limited my rage. I needed an instruction manual for my useless talents.

I hooked my heel behind Goon Number Three's knee and tugged him off-balance. His shot rang wildly, and I heard a scream from Number Two. Score two for the babe.

A bullet scorched my ear before digging into the floor, and I shouted *"Dammit!"* to the Universe. Apparently I wasn't clear enough. The Universe didn't provide. Headset Guy returned to stomp my wrist, and my compact skittered away.

Goon Number Three yanked me upright, giving me time to look around.

Shithead, otherwise known as Number Two, was

nursing a bloody shoulder. Headset could barely stand. The senator was so red with fury, I thought the top of his head might blow off. Three held a gun to my already wounded head. Not good.

The compact was surrounded by big, heavy shoes. It called to me. Maybe Max wanted me to join him in hell.

"All this firepower for little ol' me ?" I taunted. If I was going to die, it was going to be with my head up and my mouth flapping.

"Oh, for Christ's sake, let her loose, and maybe she'll pull the keys out of her magic bag of tricks." Limping awkwardly, Dane paced the small floor while he waited for his henchmen to produce the magic key.

"You'd better find those keys or we'll whack off your hands at the elbows," Headset growled, nursing his damaged knee as he retrieved the bag.

I was too focused on the compact to be intimidated. The mirror was right there, at my feet. I could practically feel Max's energy bursting at the seams. *Ninja star, here I come.*

I hadn't given up on blasting them to hell yet. I had a plan now.

I dived for the compact the instant they let my hands loose.

That's when all hell really broke loose—and I didn't even conjure it up.

31

The front door slammed open. Dane's goons reacted by spraying the entrance with bullets.

I dropped and hit the floor on my shoulder, clinging to my compact and Max while thinking as fast as my dead brain allowed. Maybe the floor position got my neurons jumping, because the wheels were back to spinning.

Apparently smart enough to stay out of bullet spray, Andre waited before appearing in the doorway, wielding his AK-47 and looking invincible. After he saw I was down, he unloaded his lethal weapon on the bullies diving for cover.

Once the bullets stopped, hulking Bill the bartender climbed in the window and began swinging a bludgeon at Goon Number Two, who was plunging in his direction. Schwartz kicked in another window, police automatic drawn. My heart beat a little faster knowing I had friends willing to risk their lives for me, but this wasn't over yet.

Just like at the OK Corral, there would be no winners if I didn't do something soon. I'd never had many friends, and I kind of wanted to keep these.

"Hold your guns, or I'll shoot her!" Dane shouted, pulling a pistol from his pocket and aiming it at my head. I froze. So did everyone else.

I had no idea if a little thing like a derringer could kill, but my rage had reached its limits.

Besides, Andre had turned his wicked weapon at the senator. I'd owe him into eternity for killing for my sake. Not happening.

Deciding that if I was going out, I might as well go with malice aforethought, I brushed a kiss across my compact. "Assholes like you, Senator, belong in hell, not good men like Max!" I cried, then flung the compact straight at Dane's pretty head just as Andre pulled the trigger.

To my utter startlement, the compact flamed on like a meteor. Or maybe that was just what it looked like to me.

The plastic case hit Dane square between the eyes, causing him to stumble sideways. Andre's bullet merely grazed his shoulder, but the derringer went off at an awkward angle. The senator grabbed his forehead as if my little missile had blinded him, then stared incredulously at blood blooming on his immaculate white shirt. Off-balance, he slipped and fell on his protective bootie and went down.

What, exactly, had I done, if anything? The riot erupting around me didn't give me time to think. Headset had regained his popgun and was fighting his way toward the door.

Andre wore the expressionless visage of an automaton bent on murder, like the Terminator. He'd shot at a U.S. senator—and instead of being horrified, he retained his Special Ops face. That he wasn't spraying the room with cover fire, but instead stood over me, willing to shoot again without a thought for himself, was inhuman.

I still wouldn't let him go to prison for me.

Not knowing if we'd killed the senator, I pulled together my fried brain cells and visualized the remaining goons in a distant African prison. They needed to be taught a lesson. Did I have to say it aloud? How? "Let the big bad bullies be bullied by real animals," I shouted. If coherence counted, I'd lost the battle.

A siren followed my insane declaration. The goons looked at each other, then dived through the window. Bill was so startled, he barely had time to smash his bludgeon against their muscled rears as they fled.

Well, that had been anticlimactic after imagining African prisons. Had I expected them to vanish like genies into bottles? Got that wrong, if so.

Only the bad senator remained, sprawled across the floor with blood pumping from his chest and a stunned, vacant look on his handsome face.

I looked at Andre and his gun, ready to take down a squadron of goons, and not a target in sight.

"Not dramatic, are we?" I asked, but I sounded awestruck instead of sarcastic as I pressed a hand to my bleeding ear. I'd come *that* close to dying.

Still looking grim, Andre lowered his weapon. Schwartz was on his phone and racing out the door after the fleeing baddies. Bill kind of looked blankly at the crumpled senator on the floor before taking out a handkerchief and attempting to apply it to Vanderventer's chest wound.

Milo appeared from nowhere to lick my face. I was crying. And shaking. Rather than fight my fear, I curled him in my arms and wept into his fur. I think I might always associate the stench of kimchi with gore and death. I was trying hard not to hurl up my guts. I couldn't look at Vanderventer.

We had killed a *senator*. I needed to visualize us somewhere safe but I was too stunned to think of consequences. Maybe I could take full responsibility. After all, I'd thrown a fireball. Like the police would believe that. Even I didn't know what I'd done. Story of my life.

Finally shifting out of Terminator stance, Andre knelt down to help me up. He didn't complain when I collapsed into his arms and wept incoherently instead, blabbering about Sarah and Milo and Max and African prisons until he probably thought me insane—not at all my lawyerly self.

"It's okay, Clancy," he kept saying, rocking me back and forth as Milo escaped to prowl the room. "It's okay. Everything's going to be okay. I may wring your neck, but thanks to your cat, everyone is fine."

His threats calmed me more than any other re-assurance could. I could feel the hard muscle beneath his silk shirt, trusted his strength, but didn't trust myself. I had no business being attracted to a man who made his own laws. But he'd been here when I needed him, and that was so precious that I couldn't let him go just yet. He sounded strangely distant, as if trying to separate himself from the scene, but he didn't shove me away. For that, I was grateful.

"Milo?" I questioned through my sobs, trying not to wipe my nose on his pretty shirt, but I'd already smeared it with blood.

"Yeah, when I found your weird cat wandering around the storage unit without you, I knew there was trouble."

Remembering his voice mail, I punched his arm and struggled to break away. He wouldn't let me.

"I told you where I was going!" I probably hiccupped more than shouted. "I tried to reach you. Don't go blaming me because you weren't answering your phone."

"There's no signal at the storage place," he protested. "I had to go out to the street to get your message. I thought you were studying, damn you! I wouldn't have known you'd gone anywhere if it hadn't been for Milo raising such a racket. He took us to Sarah first."

Schwartz returned, and men in blue filled the room. The ubiquitous medics were swarming. I wasn't leaving Andre's arms anytime soon, so I ignored them while they worked over the senator. Tomorrow's papers would be gloriously gory.

"Sarah," I wept. "I didn't know they'd kill a chimpanzee!"

"They didn't. She's alive. Don't ask. Just play nice for Schwartz's pals, okay? Or should we have you sedated so you don't have to talk at all?" Andre still held me, scowling protectively anytime anyone official hovered. Since the cops thought he was calming a hysteric, they left us alone.

"I may have sent the spooks to Africa," I whispered. "Is Vanderventer dead?"

He cast a glance toward the corner. "They're working on him. That ninja compact trick was pretty good. If I'd known you could do that, I wouldn't have tried to take him down. We'd better put our stories together. This could turn ugly."

If they really looked, they'd find Andre's bullets in the wall. I was pretty certain it was likewise a derringer bullet in Dane. Maybe he would live. Ugly wasn't even close if he did. I shivered.

"He paid those goons to cut Max's brakes," I murmured, trying to keep it together. Milo climbed on top of me, fighting with Andre's arm to crawl closer. I shifted position so he could curl up against my chest. His rumble of satisfaction was almost as good as Andre's strength. "He was going to kill me for those boxes. Did you find anything useful?"

"Lab experiments. Accident reports. Test rats doing the conga for all I know. Paddy would have to interpret, and I don't think we can trust his competency. I don't want anyone not from the Zone looking at them."

I nodded. "Don't tell anyone where they are. That's Zone business." I'd have to tell Jane they were gone, just in case she asked. Whatever was in them had caused too many deaths to risk innocents.

Andre looked startled, then grim. "Got it. If anyone mentions them, we just figure the bikers probably burned them."

I wanted my compact back, but when a cop carefully sealed it into a Baggie, I could see it was no more than a molten lump. I didn't think they'd be taking fingerprints off that anytime soon. I needed to go home and talk to Max in the mirror. I hoped he was still in my mirror, because I was feeling pretty bereft right now. I needed more reassurance than Andre could give me that I'd done the right thing, even though I wasn't entirely certain what I'd actually done.

"You came to my rescue," I whispered. "It was self-defense. We can all swear to that."

He nodded, but he continued to look grim as he surrendered me to the medics.

There wasn't much they could do except take a blood sample for drugs and plaster my ear. I winced, and not just because I'd been an inch away from death. I wondered what they'd find in my blood besides whatever the spooks had used to silence me. Surely medics wouldn't test DNA, right?

Even though all Baltimore officialdom had arrived to cover the scandal of a senator in a shoot-out, Schwartz had been the first on the scene, and he took charge. In his best officious Nazi stance, Leo pulled out his notebook and droned on about receiving a report of screams emanating from a vacant apartment. He'd been in the area hunting for a missing person and intervened when unauthorized personnel attempted to break in the door.

I was really starting to like Schwartz's creative writing talents. Under his presentation, Andre's weapon of mass destruction belonged to the men holding me hostage. Andre had merely grabbed it to defend his missing employee, who'd yet again been mugged for his cash deposit.

The insurance company was so going to kick Andre's ass if they had to cover one more fraudulent deposit. I struggled to protest, but Andre pinched me into silence. After all he'd done, I couldn't argue over invisible money. It at least lent some credibility to my kidnapping, however infinitesimal.

"And the senator?" an officer with lots of pretty badges adorning his chest asked suspiciously.

Schwartz looked at me. His talent for lying only went so far.

I don't know what made me do it. The same instinct that had told me to fling my compact was the only excuse I had for what I said next. I still didn't have evidence a court would accept that Dane had ordered Max killed.

It didn't matter. If Dane wasn't dead, I wanted his

punishment to be private, painful, and long-term, and I wanted to be the one to choose the sentence. I didn't want him buying his way off with expensive lawyers. So again, with malicious forethought, I lied.

"The senator is my boyfriend's cousin. We were on the phone when I was mugged. He tried to rescue me, and those goons that got away *shot* him, with his own gun!" I started weeping again. Flimsy story needed more work, but tears were always a good cover-up. "Then they told him to bring money and not call the police! It could have been an assassination attempt," I cried, ingeniously, adding, "Detective Schwartz saved us both!"

Call me anyone's bitch, would they? I'd make putty of the boys in blue.

A cop saving a senator made a lovely promo op. The bigwig officer nodded in approval, jotting notes of his own. Schwartz looked a trifle startled but didn't correct me. I was learning to manipulate cops as well as the media. If I didn't go to hell for twisting the Universe to my whims, I would go for prevarication of the highest degree.

I was seriously starting to believe in fiery depths. That compact thing had scared the wits out of me. Yeah, I'd used the compact as a ninja star and startled a senator into shooting himself, but the hellish flame-on? Never once occurred to me. I wanted to believe that Max had grown so furious, he'd turned into some kind of flaming superpower to take his cousin down.

I would start believing in witches and zombies soon.

"I want to take her home," Andre said with that air of authority he commanded too well when he wanted. "Detective Schwartz knows where to find us. We'd rather keep this out of the media, if at all possible. The senator's family doesn't need any more grief right now."

The police captain hummed thoughtfully.

I hugged Andre and let him help me up while I still snuggled Milo in my arms. The family of senators could keep lots of things hushed up, and that was just the way we liked it.

The Zone's secrets would remain in the Zone.

32

Andre was looking pretty gray around the edges by the time we got to my glorious Victorian apartment. He had that transparent look he'd had after the bar incident, but he still wanted to come in with me. I simply couldn't invite him in while Max lingered. Dropping Milo inside the apartment, I kissed Andre at the door.

And almost instantly regretted my decision to keep him out. The man held me as if he really meant it, as if my almost dying had shaken him. Or turned him on, which would be perversely like him. Damn, his kiss was sweet and fervent, and I wanted so much more that I stomped on his foot and shoved him into the hall.

His pained look had little to do with my running shoes stomping his Italian loafers. "You shouldn't be alone, Clancy," he warned. "You shouldn't even be here. Come back to my dad's place."

"Finals. Tomorrow." I ached in a thousand places and simply wanted sleep, but I'd blown my study time. I needed to satisfy my driving urge to see Max; then I could hit the books. Hours, mere hours from finishing school. Focus, I could do—now that the drugs were out of my system. No man was going to stand in my way. "Tell me again Sarah is okay."

"Sarah has a hole in her upper arm and a terrified vet bandaging her. She shifted on him. I sent Ernesto to bring her home. I'm posting the invisible kid at your door if you won't come home with me."

"Give Tim a bed," I said curtly. "Don't go getting ideas, Andre. I'm taking that test tomorrow, then we'll talk."

He nodded acceptance, although even through his gray weariness, the gleam in his eye said he had schemes of his own. Andre would always have schemes of his own. Whether they matched mine remained to be seen.

I rushed back to the bedroom the instant Andre left. I waited in front of the cracked mirror, rubbing its shattered glass, desperately needing to talk to Max.

He didn't show. That was the reason I'd damned

him to hell in the first place—he was never there when I needed him.

I cried, I shouted, I smacked the glass, splintering more pieces to the dresser. No Max.

It was almost like losing him all over again. I fell on the bed, weeping, and didn't hear Tim arrive until he pounded frantically on my front door, which had Mrs. Bodine shouting worriedly from her window below. Her frantic cries caused me to struggle out of the covers, wipe my eyes, and end my pity party. I opened the door for Tim, and he let in movers with a two-cushion foldout sofa from Andre. Tim watched me warily, but even while wearing my sandals, he was my pal. I wasn't going to bite off his head for helping.

"We'll go shopping after I take my test tomorrow and collect my pay," I promised. "Help yourself to the food."

I had no interest in eating. I let Tim settle into his sofa in the front room, with a TV he'd retrieved from Julius's house. I hadn't realized I had cable. Leaving him to his reality shows, I locked myself into my bedroom with my books.

I fell asleep before dark and didn't wake until dawn. I tried to call Max again, but my mirror reflected only my shadowed eyes and sallow complexion.

Max had told me that he wasn't going anywhere until he'd nailed his killer.

Did that mean bringing down Dane had given him enough satisfaction to move on to a better place? Trying to believe that made me feel a tiny bit better, but not much, not yet. The wound was still raw, and my emotions were pretty out of control. I was going to blow my afternoon exam if my eyes kept leaking.

I showered, checked my bust, biceps, and behind to make certain I hadn't developed any new assets that might mean Vanderventer had died, and dressed for school in my usual skirt and button-down and my new kitten heels. You'd have thought at least one of my fellow students would have noticed by now that I didn't wear boots anymore, but nooooo, they'd all been too centered on their books. Law students.

I fixed eggs for Tim and still had time to put in an hour or two on my studies before someone pounded on my door.

I glanced over my shoulder and contemplated running for the balcony and sliding down a pole to make a break for it. Tim actually flickered out. Some bodyguard he made.

But I'd turned a page yesterday. I was no longer hiding. I stuck my chin out and yanked open the door.

More black suits stood outside. Before I could scream and start kicking, one held up a shiny badge. "Secret Service, ma'am. If you'll come with us, we have a few questions."

"No can do, gentlemen." I stood firm against these intimidating figures of authority. I'd had quite enough of being bullied. If they tried to shove me down any stairs, I'd take them down with me. After what I'd seen and done, I wasn't that terrified little girl any longer, thank you, Saturn.

"I have my final law exam this afternoon. I need to finish studying. I would be delighted to accommodate you this evening, after the exam."

I couldn't believe I was actually rejecting the Secret Service.

"This is a matter of national security," the polite speaker insisted. "The senator has questions."

Oh, hell. He was alive. Now I really would have to kill Vanderventer. I mean, *really* kill him. I was so not going to miss my final because he wanted Max's damned boxes. "Planning on hauling me out at gunpoint?" I asked.

"He told us you'd give us trouble," the first one said without concern. "He said to tell you that Max needs to talk to you."

That shut me right up.

"Tim, tell Andre I'm leaving with these nice men," I called to the empty room, grabbing my purse. Milo peered from his pillow at the window but didn't attack, so I had to assume these guys were legit. "And then they'll be dropping me at the school. I may need a ride home."

The suits didn't say anything about my plans for them or even my talking to an empty room. They merely escorted me down the stairs. Mrs. Bodine peered from her parlor, waving warily.

"Shall I tell that nice newspaper reporter friend of yours that you're a hero?" she called sweetly.

Mrs. Bodine had a devious and evil mind, and I wasn't entirely certain she'd be working in my favor if she called Jane and blasted my predicament all over the media. I waved back at her. "This isn't about me, Mrs. Bodine. Detective Schwartz is my hero."

The suits didn't shove me impatiently or do any of those things Dane's goons had done. I wasn't even certain they were carrying weapons, and their black Lincoln Navigator wasn't as badass as the Escalade.

"Nice wheels, guys," I told them as they assisted me in with a helpful hand to my elbow.

We rode in tense silence to Bethesda and not to the D.C. hospital I'd sneaked into a few nights ago. Why would Dane Vanderventer say Max wanted to talk to me? If I found Max in Dane's mirror, I was going to spew. I might move to Africa with the goons, providing they'd actually gone. I'd no idea what I'd accomplished in my drugged state.

Did I have time to kill a senator before taking my final?

I couldn't help checking my watch. Traffic had been bad driving to the outskirts of town. I needed to be at the school in downtown Baltimore in a little less than two hours. I needed my Harley to zip between lanes. Damn. I glanced longingly at the doors, but the hand on my elbow was firm. We took the elevators up to another private suite, one less impressive than the one I'd visited earlier.

I gulped and hoped Andre wasn't too far behind. I'd damned the senator to hell less than twenty-four hours ago. I didn't know if I feared my anger or arrest more.

The man in the bed had a burn shaped like a sideways V above his nose where the open compact had hit him. Despite the huge bandages padding his chest and shoulder and straining at the tailored linen nightshirt some underling must have brought for him, he'd managed to shave. He would have looked almost distinguished if it hadn't been for that dab of shaving soap left by his right ear.

An icicle replaced my backbone.

Max had always left soap in that same spot on his face. He claimed it was because he was right-brained and his left brain didn't see his right ear.

The expensively styled dark hair was Dane's. The cleft chin, square jaw, and slim basketball-player build were the senator's.

The lively, knowing eyes were not.

And the laughing smile on his lips—*way* not Vanderventer's.

I didn't know whether to upchuck or throw myself in his arms.

"Lookin' good, Justy," the patient said in a polished voice that was sooo not Max's gravelly drawl.

I may have shrieked. I may have fainted. I'm not entirely certain. I woke up with my head shoved between my knees while I sat on the edge of a hospital recliner.

"Give us some peace, guys," Dane's voice said when I struggled against the hand holding me down. "We've been through a lot."

The men in suits looked dubious, but they backed out at an imperious wave from the man in the bed. I was pretty certain Dane Vanderventer had never called the Secret Service "guys," just like he would never have known Max's private name for me. I gulped air and pushed upright again. I didn't know what to call him.

Maybe the drugs I'd taken yesterday had permanently altered my brain, and I was hallucinating. Maybe Vanderventer had control over my mind. Maybe he was the devil.

Once the door closed, Max/Dane gestured for me to come closer. I shook my head and kept my rear planted in the chair.

"I'm not believing this any more than the mirror," I informed him. If this really was Dane, I wanted him to think I was crazy.

"You did it, Justy," he said proudly. "You brought me back. And since my damned cousin was responsible for me dying, seems it's only justice that I come back as him."

Okay. Overload. I was certain my brain was about to fritz out. Lights flashed, bells rang; it was like Vegas in there.

"That defies the law of physics and certainly logic," I managed to say through the chaos. "Dane *died*?"

"He killed himself with his own gun, may my cousin's soul rot in hell," the man in the bed agreed. "But I was right there to take his place, thanks to you, Justy. You have a mean throw for a girl."

"Oh, damn," I whispered. "I was trying so hard not to kill again." I touched my head to be certain my hair was still the same and glanced down at my feet, but I wasn't seeing any differences.

"It's all right, babe," he said soothingly. "You did good. You did just what you were supposed to do. You just gave the devil his due, and he let me go in return." He patted the bed again. "Come over here and let me touch you. Do you know how frustrating it is to see you looking gorgeous and not be able to touch you?"

I reached behind me for a pillow and flung it at him. "You lied to me, Max, you filthy turd! You told me you had no family, and you've got a freaking bunch of rich bigots and crazy people who want to kill me!"

With his arm swathed in bandages, he couldn't easily swat the pillow away, but he was laughing as he let it fall to the floor. "You nailed the rich bastards better than I ever did. I was afraid if I took you to see them, I'd frighten *you* off, not them. Now that I've seen you in action, I figure you'll terrify the snots when I introduce you."

"I'm not going home with you, you rat fink, soul-stealing, mirror lurker!" I shouted. "I'm taking my final, and I'm damned well getting on with my life, and you can take your lying, sneaking ways into government, where you'll fit right in."

"Justy!" he called after me as I stalked out, but I wasn't listening.

Not going to listen. *Not listening, la la, la.* I needed my sanity back.

I all but covered my ears to wipe out the sound of his voice while one of the Secret Service guys turned on the sirens and flew me past traffic and over to the school. The other stayed to guard a ranting senator who had obviously lost his mind.

I ran into the classroom just before they locked the doors. I grabbed a test and sat down.

I realized I could read it without my glasses.

33

With my brain popping and fizzing like cold water in hot oil, and my thoughts on anything but law cases, I turned in the worst exam of my life. I barely made it through the interminable afternoon.

Max, alive? In *Vanderventer's* body? No freaking way.

I could see without glasses. I'd sent *someone* to hell. Bodies apparently didn't matter. It was the soul that counted, and Dane's was gone. Now that Max was back, did that mean my hair would fall out?

I was damned. Why bother with mundane things like finals and hair?

Behind the wheel of an unmarked cop car, Schwartz waited for me in the circle drive of the law building, where only official cars were allowed. I couldn't say a sedan made me feel any safer than the SUV, but after yesterday, Schwartz practically wore a halo in my book. I climbed in without mouthing off.

In fact, I didn't say anything. I'd just blown my final. I wouldn't be graduating. There probably wasn't any point in graduating. I'd somehow doomed myself, and I had yet to understand why or even how.

"The chief is recommending me for a lieutenancy," Schwartz said somewhat diffidently when it became apparent I didn't mean to say anything. "Did you arrange that?"

"I can't even arrange my life, much less yours," I said grumpily, slumping in the seat and watching the world go by outside the window.

And then I had a thought and rolled my eyes heavenward. *Max.* Troublemaker Max in a senator's body—that was a biggie. That was *huge.* Maybe the devil had big plans because all hell was likely to break loose once Max walked the hallowed halls of Congress. Dane's grandmother would be a screaming wreck should he dare cross her threshold as Dane and act like Max. Maybe I really ought to move to Seattle. Or join my mother in Bolivia. I was starting to see the appeal and wondering if running from the punishment she'd inadvertently inflicted had been the reason for our roving life. "You kept Senator Vanderventer out of the news. He's showing his appreciation."

He nodded, frowning. "We weren't even in the Zone, and I could have sworn I saw you throw a flaming weapon of some sort. Did you knock some sense into him?"

I snorted. "Yeah, that's one way of looking at it." I'd helped the devil knock out Dane's soul and import another. No biggie.

"Cora predicted I'd get a promotion," Schwartz said warily. "Do you think she really can see the future?"

No, I thought she'd been messing with his head, but I didn't want to rain on his parade. "At this point, I'm willing to believe in space aliens and vampires. Did you ever catch the thugs who ran off?"

"They took flights to Uganda before we could catch them," he said with puzzlement. "If they had passports and money, why would they choose an area in the middle of civil war?"

"Oh, I don't know," I said airily, my heart thumping oddly. "Like attracts like? Thugs attract thugs?"

"African armies hire foreign mercenaries?" he asked dubiously.

Heck if I knew. They'd killed Max, shot Sarah, and meant to kill me. If there was any justice in the world, Dane's bullies would learn what real machete-wielding, bloodthirsty villains could do. They'd either side with the forces of good or the forces of evil and decide their own fates. I washed my hands of them.

Actually, the knowledge that I'd imparted a little justice—real justice, not the rot-in-jail-and-do-nothing kind—perked me up a little. I was going to hell, so why not do a little good while I was still on earth?

Maybe, just maybe, I could right some of the wrongs for Zone inhabitants, who couldn't take their complaints to court. Instead of running from my Saturn-given talents, I might as well take advantage of them, now that I knew what was possible. *Uganda!* Very impressive, daddy-o.

"Whatever," I said with an airy wave of my hand. "I didn't have time to thank you for coming to my rescue yesterday. That was way above and beyond the call of duty, and I'm glad you're getting a promotion out of it."

"I'm not glad," Schwartz said grimly. "I'd rather have been commended for real heroism, and not lying to cover up a dangerous shit. Why did you do that?"

"Because we now own that dangerous shit," I said, without thinking. Sometimes, my brain works in mysterious ways, like I have a layer with a mind of its own. "Like it or not, Vanderventer is now part of the Zone."

"Andre is in way over his head this time if he thinks he can control a man as powerful as that," Schwartz warned.

Hell, no, not Andre. I was the one holding the reins on a fire-breathing dragon. I was still too bewildered to know if this was a good or bad thing. Vanderventer wasn't *Max*, my Harley-riding, barrel-chested, busted-nosed Max. I didn't know what the hell Vanderventer was, but the wealthy, smooth-talking, slick-looking politician was not from the world I knew.

Of course, neither was Max. He'd lied to me all along.

"Where are you taking me?" I asked, to escape the rut I was digging and because he'd driven right by my house.

"Chesty's. Andre has pulled another of his disappearing acts and everyone is tired of doing their own deposits. Or they haven't done them at all, would be my guess." He swung the sedan down the alley and into the parking lot, blocking Ernesto's Hummer.

"Disappearing acts?" I recalled Andre looking a little gray after his Terminator act yesterday. But his kiss had been plenty hot later. "Does he do that often?"

Schwartz shrugged. "He always comes back, slicker than ever."

Another mystery to ponder. First, I had to accept that Max was walking around inside Vanderventer. Wondering about Andre morphing into the Terminator was well beyond me.

It was after five, but if Andre's people needed me to make the deposit for him, I could probably do that. Feeling back in the groove again, I entered the back door of Chesty's and waved at Jimmy, who was stirring a pot over the stove. It seemed kind of empty back here. The waitresses and dancers would usually be gathering for the rush hour crowd.

Schwartz escorted me to the front, and I wondered if Andre had assigned him as my bodyguard. I would have to get nasty about that, but I was too brain-dead at this point.

I was even stupidly reaching for my now-unnecessary reading glasses when we walked into a scene clearly out of the orgy books.

The nude murals on the walls had been decorated with balloons dangling from their boobs. I could have sworn the painted figures were gyrating in glee. Streamers were taped from the dangling ceiling lights down to the bar, where a crowd was jostling for free drinks. They had to be free, because Andre's employees couldn't afford to indulge here, and the crowd consisted completely of people I knew, and that was every troll in the Zone—from the florist to the Geek, and Boris had sworn never to visit the Zone again.

Shouts and applause filled the air as we entered. Someone turned on a loudspeaker blaring, *"We are the champions!"*

I nearly turned around and fled. I chose to believe the party was for Schwartz's benefit and it wasn't all about me. I shoved him forward.

One of the dancers swung around her pole wearing little more than streaming ribbons. Swinging and wriggling to the music, another dancer caught Schwartz's tie and dragged him toward the stage, where she shimmied all over his front, leaving him dazed and glassy-eyed.

Ernesto shoved a beer mug into my hand. "Good to have you back, kiddo."

Cora dropped a lei over my head. Or I thought it

was a lei until I realized there was a snake amid the flowers. It flickered its tongue in friendly greeting and writhed to the tune of the song before slithering down my arm and back to Cora.

By that time, I was too shell-shocked to do more than pat the flowers in wonder with one hand and guzzle the beer in the mug in the other. Snakes, chimpanzees—what was the difference, after all?

Even nerdy, four-eyed Boris raised a beer in salute without taking his eyes off Diane's breasts as they danced. Or she rocked and he squirmed.

Wearing a bandage around her shoulder, Sarah sulked in a booth with Officer Leibowitz—I remembered I owed him some Saturnian justice time for blackmailing Tim. They eyed the revelry with resentment. I wasn't going there. I knew Sarah had wanted to kill someone for longer legs, and she'd missed her chance. She'd have to get over it.

I was amazed Leibowitz was here until I located Andre and forgot the beat cop. I was relieved to see my boss was back to his normal self, looking slick and talking to a distinguished silver-haired gentleman in an exquisitely tailored suit. I recognized the impossibly thick, silver hair, but it was Andre who held my attention.

He wasn't wearing anything so civilized as a tailored suit or tie, but my Special Ops guy stood out like a shining planet in a sunset sky. The damned man was wearing all white, with the exception of his red silk shirt. The combination was striking against his dark coloring, drawing me like nails to lodestone, even though I wanted no part of the man he was with.

The movie with Jim Garner and the smarmy mayor came back to mind as I crossed the room at Andre's gesture of welcome. I would have hoped Andre would fling his drink in the man's face, except he wasn't holding one. I had to remember this wasn't a spaghetti western or even a comedy, no matter how my escapist fantasies took it.

"My partner, Senator, and, with your help, a budding new lawyer!" Andre hugged my shoulders.

Or held me up to keep me from falling or coming out fighting, whichever struck me first as I shook hands with Max's father and pondered the *partner* comment.

"Not a senator any longer, my boy," the older man said affably, studying me with more interest than I deserved. "Just Michael MacNeill these days. I leave the governing to my nephew. Heard you know him?"

"We've met," I said guardedly. I wanted to know what Andre had meant when he called me his partner and a budding lawyer, but I was learning there was a tricky dividing line between keeping my mouth shut and letting the world know what I was thinking.

"Dane sings your praises for helping out in that difficult . . . contretemps . . . yesterday. You and your friends have done a fine job of holding back the media, and the family appreciates it."

There was that *family* reference again. Apparently MacNeill spoke for the Vanderventers. Jane ought to be hearing this. I swiftly scanned the partying crowd, but Jane wasn't anywhere in sight. She wasn't part of the

Zone, and she was better off out of it, even though I regretted hiding the truth from her.

"The world has enough ugliness," I said pleasantly, with enough ambiguity that Andre pinched me.

For Special Ops, he smelled good, woodsy and sophisticated at the same time. He felt good, too, pressed against my side. The mindless hum of hormones helped me past the protests shouting in my head. Andre was a fine way of stirring the adrenaline now that Max wasn't Max anymore.

I regretted that, too. I was prepared to shoot down anything Michael MacNeill said, figuring he did it at Max's—Dane's—behest. I was pretty damned certain that Max had no intention of letting his father know his soul was alive and occupying his cousin's body.

I was pretty amazed that I now believed souls existed. Quite an education I was receiving lately.

"Dane said you have a good head on your shoulders," the ex-senator said appreciatively. "That's why he wants me to assure you that you'll have no problem with the ethics committee when you apply for your license. We need more smart, mature lawyers like you around here, looking after our hardworking citizens."

I tried not to snort beer out of my nose. "Thank you, sir," I said dryly. "Glad you don't mind if I represent the people of the Zone."

"Just remember, they need to vote!" he said jovially, pounding me on the back. "Well, must be going. Just wanted to reassure you that all will be well. My commendation will go a long way."

Thinking about the poor test I'd just taken, I wondered, *Even if I flunked?*

I watched him stroll toward the front, shaking hands as if he were still a politician.

And then I noticed Paddy sitting in a corner, violently shaking his head as if he had a nervous disorder. The cousins-in-law didn't look at each other as Michael strode out. I was pretty certain I hadn't seen the end of Acme Chemical or their goons. I hadn't cured the Zone of its weirdnesses. I'd killed three people and sent Dane to the dark side. My heavenly balance sheet was showing a serious deficit, and I didn't know how to correct it.

"MacNeill delivered the check to help the kids run over by the limo," Andre whispered in my ear, preventing me from doing anything rash.

And what could I do, anyway? Reject MacNeill's commendation when it meant I had a chance of someday passing the bar and being in a position to help people? If I could believe I was rewarded for sending people to hell, could I believe this was a reward for *not* sending the goons to hell?

Ugh. Enough philosophizing. It was party time.

"We should let Tim tell the kids about the windfall," I replied, keeping my eyes on the front door until I was certain MacNeill had gone. Why did I have the feeling I'd just shaken hands with the devil? Did my new superpower condemn me to keeping company with hell's minions?

"You're learning, Clancy," Andre said with approval. "It's really not all about you. Or me. It's all about us."

And his nod indicated the reveling crowd of Zone trolls.

I thought I understood. Getting angry wasn't good. Staying cool and helping others had given me a posse and a home. Getting laid might clear my head.

I slanted Andre a seductive smile, shook off his arm, and joined the dancers on the stage, wrapping my new leg around a pole, letting my swingy hair fly, and exuberantly twirling with one arm in the air just as if I'd done this every day of my life.

We are the champions, indeed.

Maybe I'd teach Andre a lesson or two before I took him home.

ACKNOWLEDGMENTS

This book would never have happened if not for the Cauldron understanding my warped fantasies of unmasked avengers and sending boyfriends to hell. Bless you for being willing to play outside the lines.

My immense gratitude goes next to my agent, Robin Rue, who unquestioningly accepted my diversion from Normal and intrepidly sent my madness to all the right people.

And for the final product, I give credit to my editor, Adam Wilson, for taking on someone else's project and making it even better than I had imagined. That takes vision as well as intelligence. Thank you!

Last, but never least, my hugs and kisses go to my husband, who never once flinches when I tell him what I'm doing—or when people ask him where I get my ideas. That's forbearance well beyond the line of duty! I love you.

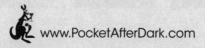

More bestselling
URBAN FANTASY
from Pocket Books!

More Bestselling Urban Fantasy
from Pocket Books!